Spirits of Grand Lake

D.P. Benjamin

Spirits of Grand Lake

Book Three
in *The Four Corners Mysteries Series*

D.P. Benjamin

ELEVATION PRESS

Spirits of Grand Lake
By D.P. Benjamin

For more information, please see *About the Author* at the close of this book and visit benjaminauthor.com

Cover photo by John F. Williams.
For more information, visit his website: johnfwilliamsphotography.com.
Phone: 303-501-2745

Cover design and interior design and formatting by Donna Marie Benjamin.

Elevation Press
P.O. Box 603
Cedaredge, CO 81413

Ordering information: Quantity sales. Special discounts are available on quantity purchases by book clubs, corporations, associations, and others. For details, contact the publisher at the address above.

ISBN 978-0-932624-12-3

1. Main category— [Mystery-Cozy] 2. Other categories— [Colorado]—[Detective]

© 2022
Elevation Press
Cedaredge, Colorado
www.elevation-press-books.com

*For information on services offered by Elevation Press,
please see the final page of this book.*

A Note Regarding *The Four Corners Mystery Series*

Readers have wisely requested an explanation which ties together novels included in this series. For those who've read the introductory books, the following will serve as a refresher. For those new to the series, this information provides essential background. To supply further context, the final pages of this book list the upcoming titles and plot summaries of each novel in the series.

Set in Arizona, Colorado, New Mexico, and Utah, *The Four Corners Mystery Series* explores diverse regions which share a common border. Featuring breathtaking vistas of lofty mountains, high plains, and desert panoramas, the series chronicles the exploits of two fearless investigators.

Raised in a hardscrabble Arizona mining town, twenty-something **Anne Scriptor** has survived a troubled childhood to become a skilled archaeologist. She has no interest in solving crimes until she meets **Trinidad Sands**, a thirty-something Colorado native. He's a law school dropout and recovering alcoholic who channels his keen powers of observation into detective work while also managing a productive lavender farm.

Their paths first cross in *The Road to Lavender*, then merge in *A Lavender Wedding*. Book three is a prequel entitled *Spirits of Grand Lake* in which Trinidad relates the story of how he became a detective. More adventures follow as the couple continues to unravel mysteries which haunt the beautiful, often rugged, and sometimes deadly landscape of Western America.

Acknowledgments

The past is like the future, only later.
Dallas "Fingers" Heckleson, Texas Ranger Emeritus

Creating a fictional character is much like adopting a shelter pet. The small dog that barks the loudest will definitely attract your attention, but so will the largest pooch in the pound who cringes in a corner and trembles like an autumn aspen.

An editor once informed me that *all characters are fictional.* Therefore, he noted, my use of the phrase "fictional character" was criminally redundant. I beg to differ since most of the actual people I know serve as definitive proof that *not all characters are fictional.* In fact, I know several characters who are not only real, but abundantly so.

My copyright page declares that "all characters and events in this novel are fictitious and any resemblance to real persons, living or dead, is purely coincidental." However, some of my characters possess the mannerisms and personalities of genuine folks.

For example, Dallas Heckleson, my irascible Texas Ranger, is a composite of three larger-than-life individuals: my loving father, Leonard W. Benjamin, whose fanciful yarns inspired my writing; the late Wayne Hamrick, a decorated Marine Corps veteran; and Hoot Harlan, a tall-talking retired lawman and dedicated member of the Cedaredge Rotary Club.

Trinidad Sands, my hero detective, is likewise an amalgamation of real characters. Trinidad's daredevil spirit and his fierce loyalty to friends are traits modeled after two classmates from my Greeley (Colorado) High School class of 1963: Butch Butler, our class president who drowned the summer following graduation, and Laverne Walker, a U.S. Army medic killed in Vietnam on April 16, 1967, two days shy of his 23rd birthday. Both young men were accomplished athletes and stalwart classmates who are greatly missed.

Furthermore, those who follow my novels know that Trinidad's partner, the incomparable Anne Scriptor, is a fictional character who reflects my affection for three very real women: my dearly departed friend, Tina Elisabeth

Kjolhede; my late mother, Carol Ruth Benjamin; and her stillborn daughter, Ann. In the near future, I'll honor my late sister, who never experienced life and whom I never knew, by marking her lonely grave with a new monument bearing the inscription: "Ann Benjamin, Heaven's Girl Detective."

Ann Benjamin's mortal remains reside in the Baby Land section of Greeley's historic Linn Grove Cemetery. Because the single date October 3, 1942, describes both her birthday and final day on Earth, my proposed revision of her headstone is sure to raise eyebrows. Which seems appropriate since I think of my late sister as a mischievous tomboy and I've written Anne Scriptor that way too. So, it pleases me to believe that both my fictional and my real character would enjoy perplexing cemetery visitors.

In addition to acknowledging the influences of five memorable men and a trio of influential women, I have a host of others to thank for their invaluable contributions to the current novel. Mark Petterson reviewed my German translations. Sharon Grotrian polished my law enforcement chatter. My dear wife, Donna Marie Benjamin, formatted my cover and interior text, not to mention providing invaluable moral support, processing countless revisions, and blessing me with the gift of time to write. Skip Bethurum and Dave Ferry provided sailing tips. Alma Evans guided my thoughts on journaling. Cover photography is by Grand Lake's own John F. Williams.

Jack Casey, Bob Scott, Dr. David Noe, and Dave Ferry provided background on Rocky Mountain National Park, Grand Lake, and Grand Lake Lodge. Messieurs Casey, Scott, and Ferry also served as Beta readers. Beta readers navigated through early versions of *Spirits* and enriched the story with their questions and suggestions. Other Beta readers include Stacy Malmgren, Ardon Barnes, Karen Grant, Jerry Tegtman, Jane Everett, Ginny Warner, and Kim Taylor.

Spirits of Grand Lake is, of course, a fiction. While the historical dates included in this book are more-or-less accurate, I've taken liberties with certain elements of the topography in and around Grand Lake, Colorado. My ghost town, Lark City, bears a general resemblance to the actual boomtown of Lulu City which lies inside the borders of Rocky Mountain National Park. Some elements of my alpine settings are fictional though most of my descriptions of topography are reasonably accurate.

Spirits is the third book in my newly imagined *Four Corners Mystery Series*. The first book, *The Road to Lavender*, earned a third-place finish in the 2019 Rocky Mountain Fiction Writers' Colorado Gold Contest. *The Road* also received the 2020 Southwest Book Design Production Award from the New Mexico Book Association. My second book, *A Lavender Wedding*, has proven to be a perennial book club selection and popular e-book. There are seven books in the mystery series. For a comprehensive list of past and upcoming titles, please see the closing pages of this book. You'll also find a list of seven titles included in my *Great Land Fantasy Series* as well as information about Elevation Press, a service for independent authors.

Donald Paul Benjamin/October 2022

Dedicated to the memory of my dearly departed parents,
Leonard William and Carol Ruth Benjamin—
loving people who made me laugh and
taught me to follow my dreams.

Traversing this Novel

A typical novel proceeds in chronological order. The reader encounters an exceptional challenge when a story moves back and forth between the present and the past—which this novel does.

Action in this novel takes place in 2019 with flashbacks to the past. To aid the reader, I have included a discrete timeline at the start of each chapter. In addition, chapters which take place in 2019 are formatted in a typeface which is quite different from the lettering used in chapters describing events prior to 2019.

At the close of this novel, the reader will find a chronology of events which contribute to the history and mystique of Grand Lake, Colorado. Readers are welcome to refer to this chronology as needed.

Also, prior to the mid-point of this novel, I've inserted a brief outline of the life and times of a major character which, I trust, the reader will consult—not now—but later upon arriving at that crucial juncture.

Happy reading!

Photo of Grand County mining community c.1885
Grand Lake Area Historical Society

Prologue

2019/June 7

Ranger Dallas Heckleson reloaded, steadied his aim, and fired again. Striving to make each shot count, he banged away in a solitary effort to subdue a mismatched array of lifeless targets: empty beer bottles, aluminum cans, and an old cottonwood stump. While reducing the stump to toothpicks, he couldn't shake the feeling that something was missing.

"By dog," he told himself. "What we need 'round here is a healthy dose of friendly competition."

That evening, hoping for a positive response, the old ranger telephoned Lavender Hill Farm. With luck, Detective Trinidad Sands would welcome the idea of a shooting match.

"Sounds great," the detective agreed. "When are we talking about?"

"How about tomorrow?"

"Well—" Trinidad hesitated.

"Busy?"

"Sort of," the detective admitted. "Day after tomorrow's the date of our Lavender wedding."

"Double-dang it," the old ranger lamented. "I plum dis-remembered the thing. I had that-there invite tacked up on my 'fridge big as brass—if it'd been a snake in grass, it would have bit me—but it got misplaced when I done the spring clean-up. So, tomorrow's off, I guess."

"Not necessarily," Trinidad suggested. "Let me ask the little woman. Hold on a minute."

The little woman thought it was a great idea.

"Let me talk to him," she suggested. "Bride-to-be, Anne Scriptor speaking," she told the old ranger.

"Yes, miss."

"I think you two boys should definitely spend tomorrow together," Anne said. "My stick-in-the-mud future husband poo-pooed the idea of a bachelor party. But that means he's underfoot here at the farm while I've got a bridal shower to attend and a million other details to manage. If you could see your way clear to taking him off my hands for the day, I'd greatly appreciate it."

"Bless your heart, I'll do it," said Heckleson. "Certain as it crows and the sun is up, I'll do it! Tell y'all what, little missy, you folks come on out fer breakfast first thing in the mornin' and bring two cars. Y'all can head on back to the farm after breakfast to do them bride things and I'll keep our favorite detective busy with target shootin' and fine victuals. It's most-wise the least one bachelor can do for the other."

"It's a date," said Anne. "We'll get up early and be there at the crack of dawn. Chores all done and appetites raging."

"Can't ask fer more," Heckleson agreed.

Chapter 1

Into the 'Dobies
2019/Dawn on June 8

The following day broke bright and clear at Lavender Hill Farm. Trinidad Sands was justifiably proud of his high-altitude acreage, a working spread which, each year, yielded a high-quality crop of lavender. Resplendent with fertile fields of compact bluish-purple shrubs which please the eye and dazzle the remaining senses, the farm was a regional landmark and namesake for the nearby village.

Situated at the foot of the lofty Grand Mesa, Lavender Village and its famous farm were separated from the higher ground by a band of low desolate hills which locals call the 'Dobies. The slang is a variation of the word adobe and it adequately describes the muted brown pallor of the desolate topography. Composed of ancient shale deposited millions of years ago by a retreating and now-vanished primordial ocean, the succession of undulating mounds forms a striking contrast to the soaring, tree-covered mesa.

As dissimilar to the featureless 'Dobies as the Moon's alien landscape is to the panoramas of Paradise, Grand Mesa is a sprawling wonderland of forests and lakes. Encompassing a vast region, it stretches for 500 square miles. Some claim it's the largest flat-topped mountain in the world. Certainly, it dominated the Western Colorado skyline which greeted the early-rising couple. The working farm was Trinidad's pride and joy and Anne shared his enthusiasm for the land. Standing in the farmyard, the two held hands and watched the first hints of dawn.

"Love that sunrise," Anne said. "Almost as much as I love you."

"Certain you can stand to be parted from me for a whole day?" Trinidad asked.

"I'll manage," she teased. "Certain you can survive in the wild clutches of the 'Dobies?"

"I'll manage," he responded. "Race you there?"

From the verdant fields of Lavender Hill Farm, it was a ten-mile drive over rough asphalt to reach the stark lowlands of the 'Dobies. Leaving the pavement with Trinidad in the lead, the playful couple steered into an undulating expanse of dirt hills following an improvised racetrack of hairpin turns which meandered more-or-less northward. Gathering speed on a straight stretch, they raced through a moonscape of mounds—a topography of smooth, rounded contours interrupted here and there by the occasional knuckle of a dark volcanic outcropping. Plumes of dust marked their progress as the detective and his bride-to-be guided their disparate vehicles through a brown wasteland—an unadorned vastness which spreads out from the base of Grand Mesa like a lumpy expanse of hardened chocolate.

Maintaining a head start in his sturdy Honda Ridgeline, Trinidad grinned as he glanced in his rearview mirror. Anne was well behind, tooling along in her Nissan truck and eating dust as he careened along the soft dirt road leading to Ranger Heckleson's isolated domicile. Anne's funky pickup was no match for his dependable vehicle, but she loved her little truck and he almost regretted the need to beat her in this innocent contest of speed.

Almost.

A mile from their mutual destination, he checked his mirror again. The Nissan was nowhere in sight. The detective hit the brakes and was preparing to make a U-turn to rescue his future bride when the little pickup suddenly appeared on the road ahead. Somehow Anne had discovered a shortcut, taken an ambitious angle, and slipped into the lead. Choking in her dust, Trinidad hastily rolled up his window and soldiered-on, knowing he'd never overtake her.

The old ranger's brown two-story stone house was perched on a rise overlooking a brown landscape. Everything was brown—the porch, the house, the surrounding hills, the butte where the ranger made his isolated home. Even the matching all-terrain-vehicles which he and the detective planned to drive cross-country to reach the even more isolated shooting site—even these utilitarian vehicles were brown.

Anne arrived first. Ranger Heckleson greeted her with a friendly wave from his elevated porch. As she parked and started up the wooden stairs, Trinidad appeared and prepared to take his loss in stride.

After a congenial breakfast on the side porch of the rambling structure, Anne didn't linger.

"Don't aim to be the third wheel at your bachelor party," Anne said as she favored the men with her winning smile. Bidding goodbye, she started her old yellow pickup and left to wind her way down Heckleson's precipitous driveway, a sharply descending exit which corkscrewed off the steep hillside.

"That gal's a pistol," Heckleson noted. "So, it's just us chickens now and I've got the day all planned up. I know y'all won't want to be drinkin' hard today. And I don't offer no cake with no damsel poppin' out," Heckleson apologized. "But I can offer-up jugs of lip-smackin' apple cider and some fine home-cookin' and guarantee a day of sympathetic companionship. Plus, also, how often does you get a chance to kill a hillside of tin and glass?"

How often, for sure? Trinidad thought. Standing in the old ranger's yard and watching the dust tail of his future bride's truck fade from sight, the detective reminded himself that it'd been years since he'd chosen to fire a weapon, or had to.

Left alone, the two men mounted their ATVs and headed farther into the 'Dobies.

Twenty minutes later, they reached the old ranger's makeshift shooting range. The range was a bare-bones site with high-banked walls and a backstop of mud and rock. Heckleson hadn't created it. He'd merely discovered it while exploring his surroundings. If the discarded pull-tab beer cans which littered the site were any indication, decades had passed since some enterprising weekend shooter had first burrowed into the terrain to carve out the place. While shaping the site, a mini-dozer had scarred the ground with a crazy-quilt pattern of tread marks, leaving behind a distinctive trail which hardened to memorialize its passage. It was a modern-day fossil record which Trinidad imagined his future wife, a trained archaeologist, would appreciate.

The inquisitive Miss Scriptor might want to know what inspired the maker. What, she might wonder, would motivate a person to gouge this primitive alcove into the southern face of one of Western Colorado's rolling dirt hills? Why build a rifle range in this particular corner of the 'Dobies?

The spot was isolated, of course. You wouldn't want a shooting range in a populated area. But this particular alcove was no more isolated than the spot next door. Was there something about the place which appealed to the maker? Why this place? Was it the southern exposure? Did the maker have a vision? Or did it just end up here because the day was ending and the dozer low on gas?

"Why here?" Anne, the enterprising scientist, might speculate.

Trinidad's shooting partner had asked himself a similar question a month ago when he'd taken up residence in the 'Dobies and discovered the makeshift spot, although he phrased it differently.

"Why not?" the old ranger had wondered aloud when he first saw the place.

The two friends took turns shooting—warming up to get a feel for the rifle. Then the competition began. The men shot for an hour—plinking cans and bottles while they sipped apple cider and passed a lazy morning in sociable competition. At the close of the first round, Ranger Heckleson took another drink of cider, positioned his noise-dampening earmuffs, and centered his ample frame on the old school desk which he'd renovated to form a passable shooting bench. Drawing a breath, he exhaled expansively, aimed his rifle downrange, and squeezed the trigger.

"Dang," he sputtered as his third and final shot also went wide. "Bright was in my eyes."

With his own ears protected, Trinidad couldn't hear the precise nature of his opponent's excuse, but the geyser of dirt kicked up by Heckleson's miss was unmistakable.

"That's five bucks you owe me," the detective reminded the portly lawman. Trinidad had positioned himself behind the firing-line and folded his lean frame into a ramshackle lawn chair. The summer sun was persistent and he was content to sit back and take advantage of a shading umbrella. He removed his muffs, but showed no inclination to rise.

"Double or nothin'?" the ranger suggested as he cleared the chamber, lovingly placed his Winchester 94 on the benchrest with the barrel pointed downrange, and knelt to pick up his spent brass.

"Shoot again in this heat?" the detective voiced a mock protest. It was certainly hot—pushing 90—but, in truth, Trinidad welcomed another opportunity to fire the ranger's vintage lever-action weapon.

"How's about one more round," Heckleson proposed as he counted out a new set of cartridges. "Twenty bucks to the winner?"

"I'll take that bet," the detective said aloud as he extracted himself from the low-slung folding chair.

A final round of shots and Trinidad watched with amusement as the old ranger counted out nineteen one-dollar bills and a single Eisenhower silver dollar.

"That makes your twenty," Heckleson grinned. "And before y'all go celebratin', this-here Ike dollar ain't no priceless heirloom. I got a coffee-can-full of these, but I ain't about to surrender my 1972-Denver-minted Eisenhower. That's my one special rare-type coin which, this week, is bein' auctioned off on that-there eBay. My nephew is in charge of that particular in-line auction since computers and me ain't on speakin' terms. And young Bud has got some collector yahoos up to $10,000—or so he tells me. That'll be a tidy sum if he pulls it off, I reckon."

"Let's give somebody a cheap thrill," said Trinidad as he pocketed the folding money, picked up a flat stone, and knelt to carve a shallow trench in the dirt. "I'd like to see the face on the metal detectorist who waves an electronic wand over this patch of ground," the detective chuckled as he dropped the Eisenhower in and refilled the hole.

"You little devil," Heckleson declared and his hearty laugh echoed in the morning air. "And here I thought y'all was such a straight-arrow. I reckon that pretty young gal of yours is what brings out the imp in you."

"I reckon you're correct," Trinidad agreed. "Race you back?"

The two men were still three miles from Heckleson's hilltop home when they spotted it. Charged with balancing the folding chair and collapsed umbrella on his ATV while also steering the scuttling vehicle, Trinidad had fallen behind. It was beginning to look like this was a day destined for losing races. The detective was following the ranger's tracks when he topped a rise and saw the apparition.

Heckleson had already pulled to a stop and dismounted. Standing in a tiny patch of scrub grass, the old ranger held the Winchester in one hand and scratched his head with the other. Trinidad was smiling as he parked his ATV and walked over the hard-packed terrain, telling himself that his cautious companion had probably pulled the rifle from his vehicle scabbard on pure instinct.

"Here's a puzzle," said Heckleson.

"Yeah-boy," agreed Trinidad as he joined his baffled friend.

The two stood there a moment in silence, staring alternately at the stifling sun, the bone-dry landscape, and the hull and towering mast of a shiny blue and silver sailboat—a decidedly out-of-place anomaly sitting miles from water, beached and abandoned on the dusty ground.

Chapter 2

The Land Was Cheap
2019/9 a.m. on June 8

The detective and his host were sitting on the porch of *Heckleson Headquarters,* as the old ranger liked to call his citadel home. Situated like a castle on a pound cake, high in a sprawling land of mud and rocks, the stone house was visible for miles. A continuous porch ran along two edges of the house, creating both a long side porch and a broad back one. Both porches offered memorable views, but the back porch faced Grand Mesa and was the more spectacular.

"I see Rose is bringin' down some of her cows a bit early this year," said Heckleson as he drew the detective's attention to a distant point where the 'Dobies met the shoulders of Grand Mesa. The two men peered that direction to watch the motion of miniature cowhands on miniature horses riding herd on what looked like a slowly roiling dust cloud. "More cider?"

"Please," said Trinidad as he surrendered his empty mason jar. "Watching dry-hole range-work makes me thirsty."

"Speaking of which," observed Heckleson from inside the house. "How's your lavender crop irrigation holdin' up?" Though Trinidad remained on the porch and his host stood in the kitchen, an open pass-through allowed the two men to carry on a conversation.

"My shares are still producing," said the detective who, in response to his host's whistle, reached behind his head and up to the level of the pass-through to grasp his refilled jar.

"Enough ditch water then?" Heckleson asked as he returned to the porch and settled into a padded chair. He descended cautiously, balancing his own brimming jar and a sizeable cider jug. Pinning his elbows at his sides, he wriggled into his seat like an eel—an awkward maneuver designed to avoid the hazard of hooking his broad-boned forearms on the chair's protruding headrest.

"Dang," said the ranger. "Mountin' Texas longhorns on these-here chairs seemed like a good idea at the time. Now I find myself dancin' around them. It makes a body wonder if interior decoratin' may not be my long-suit."

"I think they add character to the place," said Trinidad. "Here's to your artistic temperament."

"Here's to whatever that means," agreed Heckleson. "And here's to your health and prosperity."

They drank the toasts and sat in silence, watching a hawk ride a thermal breeze high in the Western Colorado sky.

"Quite a view you've got here," said Trinidad.

"Can't beat it fer overlookin,' agreed his host.

"Tell me again how you happened to settle on this particular roost," Trinidad said.

"The land was cheap," said Heckleson.

"Glad I was absent the day you hauled all these building rocks up that chutes-and-ladders bear-trap you call a driveway," Trinidad said and the two men shared a laugh.

"Day's gettin' on," said the ranger. "I wonder should I feed us and get y'all back home?"

"Does that mean we ain't gonna talk about the sailboat?"

"What sailboat would that be, I wonder?" Heckleson asked—his face sporting an expression which was both whimsical and inscrutable.

"The one out yonder on your side lawn," said Trinidad as he pointed in the general direction of a tall naked mast just visible among the domes of the ubiquitous 'Dobie hills.

"Oh," said the ranger in mock surprise, "that sailboat? Well, why don't y'all either dazzle me with brilliance or baffle me with bullshit, and tell me, Mr. Hotshot Detective, what to make of the scene of that-there crime."

"Is it a crime scene?"

"Y'all tell me, Slick," the ranger said and he was pleased to see Trinidad grin at his use of the nickname which the local sheriff had bestowed on the detective years ago.

"Well, we've got a dry-docked sailboat," Trinidad said as he enumerated his observations. "All the brass fittings missing—no cleats, no winches. Compass gone. Trailer missing. Lines missing. Outboard motor missing. Helm and rudder gone. Mainsail and headsail gone. No jib. No shroud. No telltale. I'd say somebody stole a boat and trailer, stripped off everything valuable which they could carry, dumped the craft and took the trailer."

"Mainsail? Jib? Telltale?" Heckleson chortled. "Where'd y'all learn such sailor talk?"

"Did I ever tell you about my early days and how it was I became a detective?" Trinidad asked.

"Never thought to ask," the ranger admitted. "I seem to recall that y'all was het up as a kid to look fer your twin sister who'd gone missin' and, as we both know, that very sister is due to be at the weddin' tomorrow—so seems like that worked out all right. So, I just figured that was what got y'all goin' in the detectin' business."

"My search for my sister was part of it, for sure," Trinidad admitted. "But that's another story which I'm saving for the wedding."

"Sounds to me like, how-some ever it worked out, y'all was born with a magnifyin' glass in your tiny little fist and a Sherlock Holmes hat on your curly locks."

"Well," said Trinidad with a glance at his watch. "If you put the coffee on, then serve up lunch and supper, and don't keep me out too late so's I can get back home and get my beauty rest before tomorrow's wedding— if you do all that—I've got a whale of a tale to tell you."

"Done and done," the enthusiastic ranger shouted as he jumped to his feet. "I love a good story. So, just go on ahead and begin talkin' whilst

I rustle up some coffee, think up what to serve fer lunch, and fire up the old slow cooker to get supper started!"

As his host busied himself in his clean but chaotic kitchen, the detective remained on the porch, collecting his thoughts and trying to recall when he'd last been obliged to recount the distant past. His bride-to-be knew the entire tale, of course, just like he knew about the skeletons—figurative and literal—in Annie's past. But the intimate couple hadn't been in a rush to reveal what amounted to ancient history. Instead, they'd parsed out anecdotes a few at a time—a drop here, a drop there—like a sporadic spring rain. Given the limitations of time and the old ranger's apparent appetite for a full accounting, a gentle shower wouldn't do. Only a steady downpour would suffice and Trinidad wondered if he was up to the task.

No sense starting, he told himself, *unless I'm willing to tell all.*

"Need me in there?" Trinidad asked aloud.

"This here's a one-man roundup," Heckleson assured him. "Y'all just move a bit closer and lean yourself onto the lip of my pass-through and commence your tale. Some say I'm about as coordinated as a one-legged hombre in a butt-kicking contest, but I'm sure able to listen and work at the self-same time. And, since the pass-through frame makes it look like you're on a TV show, I'll just pretend you're one of them common-taters bringin' me up to speed on the news of the world."

Chapter 3

Dropping Out
2019/9:30 a.m. on June 8

"You know, of course, that I'm named after my birthplace. Early on, the town of Trinidad was a sleepy little settlement, still is in some ways," the detective said. "I was born down there in southeastern Colorado in the shadow of Raton Pass—a stone's throw from New Mexico. I grew up miles from the ocean, but longing to be a sailor. That was on account of my mother's brother, my Uncle Paul—I'm middle named for him, you know? Uncle Paul came home on leave in 1942, left his watch cap behind, and sailed off to World War II, never to return. I never knew him, but folks, especially my grandma, say I'm the spitting image of the fallen hero. He served on a minesweeper, on the forward deck gun crew, and was killed in 1943 during the Invasion of Sicily. They gave me his old cap. I still have it."

"Y'all was dressed in that cap the day I met your plane at the airport in Colorado Springs," Heckleson recalled. "It was rainin' cats and cradles that day when y'all flew in to meet up with your long-lost sister."

"And, need I say again that it was you, my favorite Ranger Emeritus, who made that sweet and long-delayed reunion possible?"

"Just basic law-work," the old ranger blushed. "And y'all already thanked me fer that more times than I deserve. So, get on with your story and leave me out."

"You're way too tangled up in my story to leave out," Trinidad suggested. "But I'll move on for now. As a young boy with a cozy watch cap and a head filled with stories of my heroic Uncle Paul, I naturally grew up longing to go to sea. I drew pictures and wrote stories about the adventures I'd have. So, when I was in junior high and another uncle, this time on my father's side, opened up a boat refitting business in Denver, you can bet I begged to go work there in the summer. Which is how Mr. and Mrs. Sands' only son, a noodle-armed kid, ended up working for his irascible Uncle Lawrence at the Chatfield Reservoir Marina and boat rental concession. For six glorious years, from seventh grade to high school graduation, I spent every summer there, working on motors, mending lines, rescuing stranded boaters, and learning to sail."

"If that's your story, I'm impressed," the old ranger said. "A story about a shave-tail youngster who makes good warms the cocktails of my heart."

"Thanks, but that's all background," Trinidad explained. "The main thread of this story begins in 2006 when I was a footloose and disenchanted college student. Are you following this so far?"

"Clear as a dinner bell," said Heckleson.

"Good," said the detective. "So, 2006 rolls around and our would-be sailor has put away his dreams of the ocean. I found myself at the University of Colorado, in Boulder, majoring in pre-law, drinking too much, and miserable. Long-story-short, I dropped out. Didn't tell my folks. Just picked up my bedroll and pack, fired up my old Nash Rambler, and left town. Got lost. Ended up in Estes Park. Slept in the cargo bay of my old station wagon. Got up the next morning, hung over. Started the Rambler and rolled along up there above timberline, traversing Trail Ridge Road. I was feeling free and even whistling a tune until the car died before I got to Grand Lake."

"Go on," the old ranger encouraged his guest. "And, fer the love of Ike, hurry up and get to the part where there's a woman—there's always a woman."

"Yeah-boy," Trinidad said and he shifted his weight as his loins stirred involuntarily. "There was a woman all right—"

"Details," Heckleson demanded. "Boy-oh-boy, how I wish I could get y'all to drop that Western Slope twang just once, so this story would move along. Remember, I'm 65 and I'd sure love to hear the end of this before I die completely."

"Well," Trinidad began. Then he paused to exhale a genuine sigh. "Her name was Meg. Five-foot-nothing in her stocking feet. She rescued me off of Trail Ridge, gave me a ride into town. One thing led to another. I moved in and watched her in the Grand Lake 4th of July parade. She was sitting on the prettiest little bay mare you ever saw."

"Forget the bay! Let's hear about the dang romance!" Heckleson demanded and when Trinidad gave him a quizzical look, the old ranger blushed. "Hell—don't look at me like I'm a gossipin' old woman," he pleaded. "I ain't got no television here. But I've got an active imagination. So, let's have some damn details. Don't leave a fella wonderin'."

"Details?" the detective asked.

"Details," Heckleson repeated and Trinidad wondered if the grin on the old ranger's face might cement itself in place, never to be erased.

"If I didn't have a strict policy of kissing and not telling, I could report enough particulars to make your hair curl. But I'll say this much, her skills as a spectacular lover were exceeded only by her remarkable ability to cook a vast array of satisfying meals including succulent spareribs, glorious heaps of pan-fried chicken, and tantalizing desserts."

"I gotta sit down a minute," said the old ranger and it took some time for him to regain his composure. "So, I'm gonna have to believe that y'all decided to spend some time in Grand Lake and not just fer the spectacular scenery, I'll wager."

"And you would be correct," Trinidad agreed. "Now that I have your attention, would you like to hear the rest of the story—my rambling tale about how I came to choose detective work as my life's mission?"

"Son," said Heckleson, "y'all go right ahead—I'm all ears."

Chapter 4

Autumn Arrives
2006/September 1

The charms of Meg Del Monte could only satisfy Trinidad for so long. Relishing his freedom as an unattached college dropout, he was a young man looking to expand, not limit, his options. Throughout July, their affair flamed, then it fizzled when August signaled the end of her seasonal job at Grand Lake Lodge and the amorous young woman went back home to Oregon.

"I'll write," she lied.

"Me too," he lied.

With Meg gone and the final days of summer fading, Trinidad transferred his affection to the vibrant, tempestuous hues of an emerging alpine autumn.

Getting colder, he told himself. *Time for me to move on or get a j-o-b.*

He'd hung around Meg at work enough to watch her managing the concierge's desk at Grand Lake Lodge and decided to give that a try.

"Can you spell it?" asked the staff manager.

"Con-see-air?" asked Trinidad.

"Yes."

"Can I write it out?"

"If you can," said the manager whose stifled reply suggested he was struggling to suppress a grin.

Trinidad sat on the lodge's main porch in a broad suspended swing. He was hunched over, teetering back and forth, as he labored with pencil and paper to imagine how such a foreign-sounding word might be constructed.

"Close enough," the manager announced when he reviewed Trinidad's work. "You begin tomorrow. Show up in a clean shirt and tie or I'll know the reason why."

Trinidad's career as a hosteler seemed bright with promise. Helpful and upbeat by nature, he soon gained a reputation as the go-to guy for dinner reservations, automobile rentals, recommended hikes, secret fishing holes, live music venues, under-the-radar beer joints, and sundry other duties which fall to a young man charged with making each guest's stay a pleasant one.

And he learned to spell "concierge" and "sundry" and "venue" too.

All of which serves as an introduction to how a young college dropout with unfocused prospects and a blossoming drinking problem happened to become a detective.

Chapter 5

Pause
2019/9:45 a.m. on June 8

Trinidad paused in his narration. He could see that Ranger Heckleson was frowning.

"Is this a happy story," the old ranger asked, "or what my nephew would call *a bummer?*"

"Some happy. Some sad. Some mysterious," Trinidad assured his audience of one.

"Okay then," said Heckleson as his enthusiasm returned. "Take a second to tell me how y'all like your beef done so's I kin set the slow cooker perkin! Then forge ahead."

"Medium-rare is my cup of tea," the detective said.

"Done and done," said his host.

Chapter 6

Restart
2006/September 1

Continuing his story, Trinidad recalled that two other young people shared his 2006 concierge duties—one male and one female and both over 21. The man insisted on being addressed by his last name, which was Casey, and the woman went by the lyrical name of Bambi. His co-workers wanted nothing to do with the job's late evening hours which interfered with what they characterized as their own personal night work.

As a result, Trinidad's daylight counterparts coveted the lodge's morning and afternoon shifts, respectively. Their work completed, every day, at sundown, the couple made the rounds of local pubs, drinking and dancing. This carousing was predictably followed by a cruise of Grand Lake. After spooning in a canoe, if the rumors were true, the amorous twosome kept each other's particular company until sunrise.

Their affair, Trinidad decided, was just that: *their own affair.* As for night work, Trinidad was happy to oblige. He wasn't jealous or even envious of Casey and Bambi. When it came to seeking companionship, there was no shortage of sweet young things and women of a certain age buzzing around the lodge, so he saw no need to cultivate a steady girlfriend. Besides, he did his drinking alone. So, he worked evenings without complaint.

Which was just as well because, if he hadn't been working nights, he might never have met Buster Bishop. Might never have rescued the old-timer and marched confidently out of Grand Lake to pursue his associate degree in criminal justice. Might never have become a detective or a lavender farmer. Might never have encountered his future wife, fallen in love, and proposed marriage. Might never have spent his bachelor party at Ranger Heckleson's and might never have regaled his host with the story of his past-life in seventy-seven chapters.

Chapter 7

Cruise
2006/Morning of September 15

Surrounded by water and watercraft, Trinidad celebrated his birthday by surrendering to temptation. Spending off hours at Grand Lake Marina, he made himself useful in hopes that somebody with a boat would offer him a ride. For five hours straight, he helped sailors and powerboaters load and unload cargo. With unbridled enthusiasm, he patrolled the wharf, trying to look official without getting in the way. He caught and secured the lines of docking vessels and un-cleated lines for those casting off. He offered a steady hand to arriving and departing passengers and crew, serving all comers whether those individuals were embarking or disembarking. He toted and carried, ran errands, fetched drinks, and even rescued a hapless puppy that took a header off the heaving deck of a sailboat.

In short, he rekindled all the go-fer duties he'd performed for his uncle at Chatfield Reservoir. He began his cavalcade of service at seven in the morning. By lunchtime, he was on a first name basis with a score of mariners, some of whom—quite naturally—recognized him as a concierge and presumed—somewhat correctly—that his dock-side labors were an extension of his lodge duties.

"Young man," a matronly woman inquired after he'd helped her load a pair of bulky ice chests, "does one tip?"

"All part of the service, ma'am," he assured her.

This exchange was overheard by one of the marina's paid employees, an older man wearing coveralls and sporting a pained expression.

"Look here," the man complained. "What do you want to go about discouraging tips for? What's your game?"

Trinidad had anticipated resistance from the dock's regular workers.

"I'm from the lodge," he explained. "I'm here to help out our visitors."

"Well," the man sounded doubtful. "Just don't cut into my action."

"Wouldn't dream of it," Trinidad assured him. "Let me give you a hand."

After fifteen minutes invested in helping his would-be challenger gather up and stow away a gaggle of errant lines, the enterprising youth had gained a ready convert. The two shared a warm handshake and the man introduced himself as Jake Angstrom.

"Thanks, buddy," Jake said. "And tell the lodge thanks too. Many hands make light work."

"Glad to help," Trinidad said and flashed his patented grin.

"Hey, kid!" came a shout from the wharf.

Trinidad and Jake turned to witness the arrival of a sleek powerboat.

"You want this one?" Trinidad asked Jake.

"All yours, sport," the dockhand assured his younger counterpart. "That's Bob Ferryman, our local celebrity and notorious non-tipper."

"Got it," said Trinidad as he hurried to catch a line tossed by Ferryman.

"New here?" asked Ferryman as he nudged his powerboat into the dock.

"Just started today," Trinidad said.

"Knew I hadn't seen you around. Give me a hand?" Ferryman motioned him aboard.

"Catch anything?" Trinidad asked as he helped the friendly man gather up a disorganized jumble of fishing tackle.

"Wasn't really expecting or trying to fish," laughed Ferryman. "I snagged all this gear at the islands when I pulled up my anchor. You'd be surprised what people chuck overboard when their amateur fishing trips don't go as planned."

"Some of this stuff is brand new," said Trinidad as he noted a price sticker still clinging to a spinning rod."

"Don't I know it," Ferryman observed. "Takes all kinds, I guess. Me, I still use my granddad's old outfit. The fish don't seem to be all that impressed with the latest and greatest angling gimmicks. Have you seen the bobbers with a built-in fish finder? Crazy stuff. Me, I just use an old-fashioned bobber and watch to see if it's floating or being pulled under."

"Can I help you gas up?" Trinidad asked.

"Does it show?" Ferryman chuckled. "You heard my inboard buzzing, I reckon. You know your boats, it seems. Truth be told, she's thirsty as all-get-out. I was all the way down to the islands and back again—so—yes, I'm in need of fuel. Drop that salvaged gear on the wharf. I've got a feeling old Sourpuss Angstrom will find a use for it. Probably sell it back to the same as tossed it in the drink in the first place. Anyhow, hop on board and ride around to the pump and I won't say no to having a hand over there."

"Grand Lake has islands?" Trinidad asked when they were underway.

"Not on Grand," said Ferryman as he cruised toward the lakeside gas pumps. "Over on the farthest arm of Shadow Mountain Reservoir. Just this side of Green Ridge?"

Trinidad shrugged.

"Well, you know where Highway 66 crosses over the Granby Canal. It's— Ah hell, why don't I just show you the spot?"

And, just like that, Trinidad got his ride.

After a brief visit to the service dock which served as a lakeside gas station, Ferryman proposed a detour.

"Gotta swing by my boathouse for a minute to pick up my spare spark plugs," he said. "But, don't worry, the engine's fine—just a precaution."

A sweeping turn took the two travelers back along the town waterfront and past a three-storied wooden monument to pioneer handiwork which housed the Grand Lake Yacht Club.

"The Tea House," Ferryman called it. "Highest altitude yacht club in the world, so they say. Anyway, for my money, it's the world's highest registered yacht anchorage. Inspired by Sir Thomas Lipton himself—the guy with the vintage moustache whose portrait used to be featured on his Lipton Tea packages. Don't know that he ever set foot in these parts. But the British gent did journey as far as Denver where, around 1912, he agreed to sponsor a trophy to encourage a yearly sailing contest here at Grand Lake. Who knows what tall tale the Grand Lake boosters told Sir Lipton? But the guy was Scottish and I think one of the boosters was a Scot—so that might have been the connection. The inconvenient reality that the contest itself had yet to materialize didn't faze the tea merchant and died-in-the-wool yachtsman who returned to England and shipped a lavish loving cup to Colorado. Have you seen the thing? It's a beauty. Sterling silver, about three-feet high with seahorses on the wings and an angel—maybe Gabriel—on top blowing a silver horn. Anyway, mind your head."

Ferryman steered the lively boat toward the constricted maw of a lakeside boathouse. To Trinidad, the weathered structure looked as ancient as the yacht club building—maybe older. Gliding inside, the boat and its occupants entered a dark and humid world. The sun was shining brightly, but only a few rays penetrated the dusky interior.

"Just be a sec," Ferryman assured his guest as he cut the engine and climbed out of the gently bobbing craft. "You a beer man?"

"I am," said Trinidad.

"Great," Ferryman answered, his voice muted as he reached the boathouse's wooden door. "Gotta have this damn thing fixed someday," he added as he pried the door open.

Watching his host, Trinidad was temporarily blinded as a shaft of midday sun shot into the dim boathouse.

"Right back," the man's departing words were truncated as the door slammed shut behind him.

Left alone, Trinidad stood, stretched, and changed seats. As he maneuvered the boat, Ferryman was providing a running narration and, sitting in the stern, his passenger found it difficult to hear. The sounds of the engine, the chopping water, and passing wind conspired to swallow conversation. His host was a fount of information and Trinidad wanted to absorb this local man's knowledge of the lake and the boat.

The boat. Trinidad thought. Then he asked himself. *What's her name?*

Leaning over the gunwale, he looked along the beam to examine the calligraphy which spelled out the boat's name.

Osprey, he read. "Osprey," he said aloud as Ferryman returned balancing pasteboard containers on top of a red and white ice chest.

"That's her alright," Ferryman agreed then he stood still for a moment staring at the boathouse's dark ceiling.

Trinidad followed his gaze and saw that the overhead woodwork was thick with willowy strands of vintage spiderwebs.

"Been slacking on my housekeeping," Ferryman explained. "I keep meaning to clean up that ceiling. On the other hand, why don't I just trot out the universal bachelor excuse that it's the maid's day off?"

"I hear you," said Trinidad.

"Toe the line?" asked Ferryman and he punctuated his question with a nod.

Taking his cue, Trinidad stood to attention and took possession of the ice chest.

"Well remembered," said Ferryman. "You're a sailor it seems."

"A veteran of Chatfield Reservoir," said Trinidad. "Ever hear of it?"

"A pocket-lake out Littleton way on the Front Range," Ferryman recalled as he cast off bow and stern lines, engaged the blower, and ignited *Osprey's* engine. "Watch your head again. All astern."

Reaching open water, Ferryman urged the boat toward the middle of the 500-acre lake, leaving the shore far behind. Habitations rimmed Grand Lake, but these soon grew muted and distant. Beneath a cloudless sky, the watery surface resembled a broad canvas—an expanse of cobalt blue, framed by a boundary of turquoise mountains and golden aspens. Looking in all directions, Trinidad saw no other boats. The travelers were alone, an isolated speck on a glistening inland sea.

The broad lake was tranquil. Even the momentary swirl of *Osprey's* wake did little to disturb the surface. The boat etched a trail of silvery foam which swiftly vanished as blue water rolled beneath her keel, removing all evidence of their passage. The undulating lake spawned elongated waves which melted into shallow ruffles, giving the lake a corrugated appearance, like the uniform furrows of a plowed field.

The temperature was mild. Sampling the seasons, mid-September seemed content to occupy an intermediate niche which fell between the glow of warmer months and the chill of the coming equinox. It was an ambivalent day—one which hinted at autumn while stirring memories of summer. The air was crisp, but not cold, and mitigated by earnest sunshine which added luster to the Osprey's wake and highlighted the leading edge of each gently passing wave.

"Heaven," the word escaped from Trinidad.

"Close as I'm likely to get," Ferryman shouted as *Osprey* surged onward.

Trinidad pressed his feet to the deck, searching for vibration, testing himself to see if he could feel the engines and guess the nature of Osprey's drive system.

Inboard, of course, he thought. *Even an uninitiated landlubber can comprehend the difference between a conspicuous outboard motor protruding from the stern and a more-or-less invisible inboard engine. Which leaves something in the inboard family: pod-drive, stern-drive, v-drive, and direct-drive. Now, what does the evidence suggest I can eliminate? My host isn't steering with a joy-stick, so scratch pod-drive. Plenty of leg and seat room in the stern with no bulging engine housing taking up space, so scratch direct-drive. Ferryman is pushing the boat hard, but not much of a wake, plus I should be sitting directly above the drive and I don't feel anything, so scratch v-drive.*

"How do you like your stern-drive?" Trinidad ventured.

Ferryman looked at his passenger and grinned.

"I like it fine," he said. "Inboard engine, out-drive steering—what's not to like about the I/O system? Ah, I'm a poor tour guide. We've already passed· a local landmark and I missed pointing out the site of *The Shootin'*. Do you know about *The Shootin'*?"

"Some," Trinidad admitted. In fact, he knew more than he cared to know about the 1883 ambush on the shore of Grand Lake. Nell Pauly's little paperback *Ghosts of the Shootin'* was required reading for the young folks staffing the concierge desk.

"Glad I read that little book," Trinidad had informed his co-worker at the start of September. "Every fifth visitor asks about it."

"Lucky you missed the rush of summer tourists," she'd quipped. "In the summer it's every other visitor doing the asking. Lots of folks are curious when it comes to gunplay and murder."

Moments later, Ferryman powered down and pointed to starboard. Following his gesture, Trinidad looked over the side and seemed to see a ghostly shape glistening below the surface of the crystalline water.

"Is that what I think it is?" asked Trinidad.

"Rowboat," said Ferryman. "Or what's left of it."

"How did it happen to end up underwater?" his passenger asked.

"Tends to happen when curious kids throw rocks in until the thing sinks," Ferryman smiled.

"Anybody we know?"

"Could be," Ferryman admitted. "Things happen when you grow-up on the water."

"You're a native, I take it."

"Close enough. Been coming here with my folks since the early '60s. Moving on—"

Ferryman made a wide turn and increased speed for a time until he once again slowed down.

Looking toward the bow, Trinidad saw they were headed for a slim opening dead-ahead. As the boat drew nearer, the opening revealed itself to be a squared metal portal rising out of the water with a stairway on either side. He'd seen this pedestrian bridge on the maps he handed out at the concierge desk. Those same maps disclosed that this particular overarching footbridge marked one end of a narrow waterway linking Grand Lake to Shadow Mountain Reservoir.

As they glided under the footbridge and into a no-wake zone, Trinidad recalled pictures he'd seen of the cramped canals of Venice. The only thing missing was a gaggle of yodeling gondoliers—and the gondolas, of course. He glanced over his shoulder to catch a parting glimpse of Grand Lake, then turned his attention to the narrow passageway. He knew from his well-learned map, what was coming next. Farther on, near the edge of Shadow Mountain Reservoir, would be another overhead obstruction, a wider and taller vehicle bridge which carried Jericho Road above the channel.

Can a pair of boats pass here? He asked himself. *Or is this a one-way channel?*

With houses pressing in on both sides, there might be just room in the constricted waterway, and barely, for one inbound and one outbound boat to pass one another. As if in answer to Trinidad's unspoken thought, Ferryman drew his passenger's attention to another vessel ahead. As the new arrival maneuvered to make a proper pass on their port side, Trinidad could see it was a sleek sailboat, mast down, moving under power from the Shadow Mountain side.

"There goes an ambitious guy," said Ferryman as he nodded in the direction of the passing sailboat. "Don't recognize him, but he's gotta be a local."

"Why a local?" Trinidad asked.

"No weekend warrior who comes up here from Denver or some other Front Range locale with limited time on the water and a long drive home is gonna take the time to take his mast up and down and up again. Can't get through this channel with a mast, so I'm certain this guy is a local with time to burn."

"You'd make a good detective," Trinidad ventured.

"Too late to start a second career," Ferryman laughed.

"So, I have to ask, what is it that you do exactly?"

"This," said Ferryman and he let go of the wheel to gesture broadly at the vastness of their picturesque surroundings. "I do this."

The pair rode in silence for a time until they neared the Jericho bridge.

"Feel the current?" Ferryman asked. "We're fighting it. That's the sensation of water flowing the wrong way. Being forced into the Adams Tunnel and pumped under the Continental Divide to Lake Estes, then shoved farther east to water prairie farmers and Denver and the general Front Range population. Don't get me started on that."

This business of the water transfer was another popular inquiry on the part of visitors who wanted to see the west portal of the Alva B. Adams Tunnel. Once they understood the scope of the undertaking, the average visitor marveled at the audacity and ingenuity of the Colorado-Big Thompson Project which, years ago, Senator Adams had shepherded through Congress. Spanning just a hair over thirteen miles, the tunnel dives nearly three-quarters of a mile beneath the Continental Divide—the backbone of the Rocky Mountain range.

Trinidad had resisted memorizing the plethora of details associated with the CBT Project, but he had the general concept down and some of the more dramatic numbers stuck in his head. Left to Nature, water originating west of the Continental Divide flows west and water originating east of the divide journeys eastward. But a collection of vigorous, gravity-defying pumping stations which feed the Adams Tunnel invert Nature to send western water east.

Trust a politician, Trinidad thought, *to find a way to make water run uphill.*

Destined to make a 150-mile-long, 65-mile-wide journey, impounded western water is forced beneath the Rocky Mountains to reach the other side. Along the way it touches thirty-five miles of additional tunnels, a dozen reservoirs, and more than ninety miles of canals, all of which comprise the Colorado-Big Thompson Project. Conceived in 1938 and fully activated in 1957, the project spanned the turbulent 1940s and gained patriotic traction as a vehicle to achieve the mission of feeding the nation during World War II. Ultimately, the project has supplied auxiliary water to thirty municipalities in northeastern Colorado and irrigated over 600 acres of Front Range farmland.

As a boy, Trinidad had witnessed for himself the dust-dry landscape of Eastern Colorado. He'd spent two summers there helping his elderly uncle on the old timer's sprawling ranch. So, even as a boy, he understood what a boon the project was to prairie farmers and ranchers. Mostly he recalled his irascible old Uncle Golba Dolph cussing and steering the ranch's ancient truck around watermelon-sized dirt clods as the two bounced overland to check the fences on his spread.

"Some folks think we grow cattle and stub hay out here," said Uncle G.D., his ubiquitous pipe wobbling in his mouth as he spoke, "but snakes and cactus is what we grow, son. You see them windmills? Back in the day the water don't just show up; we had to drag every inch of it out of the ground. Without the Adams' flow, we'd be in a pickle."

Despite the project's accomplishments and the benefits delivered to his uncle and others, Trinidad was well-aware that the water scheme continued to rankle denizens of the Western Slope.

"Don't get me started," Ferryman repeated as *Osprey* passed under the Jericho bridge and entered the margins of Shadow Mountain Reservoir. Freed from the no-wake zone, the boat sped onward.

Knowing the tunnel and the project were sore points with his host, Trinidad decided to change the subject.

"Are we likely to encounter shallow water where we're headed?" he asked. "Around the islands, I mean."

"Some," said Ferryman. "To give you a proper tour when we reach our target, I'll need to lift the out-drive to avoid colliding with snags and such. And, just so you know, I plum forgot to mention the lookout tower which we also passed. But, not to worry, I'll point out all my omitted landmarks on our return trip. As for the islands, you can see the trees in the distance now. I want to get there pronto in order so you can understand the reason I named my boat."

Moments later, they drew abreast of the first island—which looked to Trinidad like a floating collection of pine trees balancing on an onyx dinner plate. This initial enclave was small, about a dozen trees square, but they soon encountered other, larger islands. Threading his way between the islands, Ferry reacted to a low water buoy by cutting the engine and raising the out-drive. It was then, with the engine silenced and the boat drifting, that Trinidad heard the sounds. Plaintive and high-pitched, a series of half-chirping, half-whistling echoes resonated among the island trees—the unmistakable cry of a familiar raptor.

"Osprey," Trinidad said aloud.

"Bingo," Ferryman confirmed. "Let's take a break and see if our feathered friends favor us with a concert."

The two men invested nearly an hour, drifting among the islands, listening to the birds and watching them kite among the floating forests. They might have stayed longer, but the afternoon was waning and responsibilities imposed by the real world could no longer be deferred. The reality beyond the mystical islands was clamoring for attention. The pair had obligations. Trinidad needed to get ready for his night shift at the lodge and Ferryman had a dinner date. Besides, time was needed to conduct the promised tour.

Firing up the engine, Ferryman guided *Osprey* along the shore of a heavily wooded forest which formed the eastern coast of Shadow Mountain Reservoir. As they traveled onward, Trinidad's guide drew his passenger's attention to the lookout tower visible on a high ridge. Having pointed out that landmark, Ferryman turned toward the center of the reservoir, intending—Trinidad surmised—on racing full throttle across the broad water to reach the passageway and return to Grand Lake.

They were making progress in that direction when the wind freshened. The breeze gained strength and Ferryman looked skyward. Seconds later, he abruptly turned the boat to steer back toward the shore. Pursuing a deliberate course and battling the force of a steadily rising off-shore breeze, he appeared to aim at a point on the shoreline which lay directly below the lofty lookout tower. Seemingly intent on increasing his speed to match the ever-growing wind, he didn't slow down and it seemed to Trinidad that the boat must surely run aground. But, at the last minute, an opening appeared and Osprey glided into an isolated cove. Dead-ahead in the sheltered spot Trinidad spied a small floating dock where a handsome sailboat was tethered.

A Catalina, he told himself. *I'm guessing the rising wind has inspired my intrepid host to switch vessels.*

As Ferryman slowed *Osprey* to docking speed, Trinidad studied the site. On the landward side, a natural screen formed by tightly-packed trunks of towering pine trees hid the small harbor from view. A dogleg of land made the place similarly invisible to anyone plying the reservoir.

"Just parked *Ambler* here at dawn this morning," Ferryman explained. "Just for the day. My amigo, Scott, is hiking in another quadrant of the Arapahoe Forest. He's due to arrive here after dark. This is our shared sailboat and, tonight, it was supposed to be his ride home."

"Won't he be pissed to find you've switched boats?"

"I imagine he'll arrive here tired from his hike and be thrilled to be able to reach in his backpack, grab his duplicate key, and fire up *Osprey*," said Ferryman. "Better than having to sail to the passage, lay off, strike the mast, motor through to Grand Lake, and then rig the mast again if you want to sail home. Even if he ran the engine all the way, he'd still have to strike the mast on this side to get under the road bridge and the passenger crossing. Enough talk, we're losing the wind."

"Sounds like you want to go sailing today," said Trinidad. "Won't you have to follow the same cumbersome routine?"

"You got that right," agreed Ferryman. "Difference is I got you to help. Come on, sailor, let's get this sail unfurled."

"Aye, aye," said Trinidad.

As they readied the sailboat, Trinidad took a peek over the side and learned the Catalina's full name. She was called *The Dawn Ambler* with her hailing port listed, naturally, as Grand Lake, Colorado. While they worked, the two maintained a friendly dialogue.

"This is a sweet boat," he told Ferryman. "I wonder that you risk leaving it out here in the wilderness."

"As you may have noticed," said his nominal captain, "our floating dock ain't exactly lakefront property. The gangway's in place now, in anticipation of Scott's arrival. Ordinarily, we tuck it in. Easy enough to do by cranking our handy-dandy winch until our dock and watercraft are separated from the shore by ten horizontal feet, not to mention an offshore depth of thirty feet. Short of stocking our natural moat with alligators, we're pretty well protected from shore pirates. As for an assault by water, you saw for yourself how inconspicuous this spot is from the reservoir side."

"What about somebody in a canoe or kayak?" Trinidad protested. "A small vessel plying this coastline at eye-level is sure to spot the entrance."

"That's why we only park the dock here before and after tourist season. Fewer prying eyes when visitors are scarce. Come summer, we tow the whole shebang back home and anchor it beside my boathouse. By the same token, we usually retrieve the dock before the freeze sets in, though we've miscalculated a time or two and ended up with our little way station immobilized in ice. By the way, we've nicknamed our floating contraption 'What's up, dock?' Get it? Anyhow—even though the dock stays put here for a month or two during the off-season, we never tether a boat here more than 48 hours. In order to pull off a theft, somebody'd have to keep a constant eye on us or this spot. We don't give the tourists a chance to surveil us that closely and the locals could care less about keeping track of me and Scott."

"Sounds like you've thought of everything," Trinidad smiled.

"Just about," Ferryman agreed. "We've been at this for years without a hitch—not counting the ice now and then. We ain't supposed to dock here, of course. The Forest folks keep threatening to pull the rug out, but I notice the patrol boat makes use of our little berth from time to time. They find it handy because, if you look hard, and know where to look, there's an in-shore pathway over yonder, between that knot of trees. If you're up for a hike it'll take you to the intersection of the South Mountain and Continental Divide Trails. It's the route Scott will take tonight. Meanwhile, the rangers and other official folks tolerate our dock. So, I reckon this arrangement will stay as it is for the foreseeable future. Anyhow, we're burning daylight. What say we catch that wind?"

Chapter 8

Night Shift
2006/Midnight on September 15

Trinidad Sands had been working as night concierge at Grand Lake Lodge for two weeks when he found himself once again sitting alone and reviewing his life. Having graduated from high school at the nontraditional age of seventeen and entered the University of Colorado that summer, it'd taken the young student two dozen months to washout of his pre-law major. Citing his attitude and his low marks, he'd been invited to take a semester off. He did them one better. He set fire to his CU Buffalo t-shirt and vowed never to return.

Traditions and emblems were important to him. Named for the southern Colorado town where he was born, he was proud of his Trinidad heritage. That night in mid-September 2006, the college dropout was wearing his Trinidad High School Mighty Miners cross-country team sweatshirt. It was midnight. The lodge's lobby was deserted.

Swiveling in his raised desk chair, he surveyed the broad empty room, then tilted back to stare up at his distorted reflection in the over-polished belly of the wooden canoe suspended above the concierge desk. He took a deep breath and puffed out his cheeks. Pretending he was underwater, he saw himself submerged beneath the keel and about to ascend like a dolphin, grab the gunwale, and tip the canoe over. He imagined too, that the occupants of the canoe—Casey and Bambi, the daylight concierges—would howl and scream, respectively, when the amorous couple tumbled into the water.

It wasn't that he was feuding with his daytime counterparts, but it wouldn't hurt to take Casey's smug arrogance down a peg and he had to admit he wouldn't mind seeing Bambi wet. Trinidad's invented scenario wasn't completely far-fetched because the pair had often been spotted canoeing on the lake after sunset and in every weather. It was, he figured, a symptom of their ongoing romance.

He closed his eyes to facilitate his imaginary ambush and might have kept them closed indefinitely had he not heard the chains squeak. Tearing himself from his fantasy, Trinidad opened his eyes.

Years ago, some enterprising decorator had moved one of the lodge's famous porch-swings off the broad outdoor viewing porch. Having trundled the thing inside, that genius had used chains to suspend the broad swing from one of the thick beams which framed the lodge's open pit fireplace. An engineer must have calculated the swinging radius of the wooden contraption because, so far, no one had managed to propel themselves forward far enough to plummet into the unforgiving fire. But Trinidad figured it was just a matter of time.

Meanwhile, the chains continued to squeak and the porch-swing was in motion, but no one was sitting there. Nor was anyone warming hands at the fireplace where the afternoon's inferno had been reduced to a healthy pyramid of glowing coals. A chill ran down Trinidad's spine as he stood up and reached for the baseball bat which—contrary to the wishes of the management—he'd concealed below the rim of the concierge desk.

Better safe than sorry, he told himself as he pulled the bat from its hiding place just in time to hear a voice sounding inches from his left ear.

"Yah, baseball," the voice said.

Unlike his vision of his canoe-paddling co-workers, Trinidad didn't howl or scream. But he did utter a yelp and had just enough presence of mind to raise his improvised weapon into position and take up a batting stance.

"Strike one, sonny," the voice pronounced, followed by a strangled laugh.

"Mr. Bishop?" Trinidad ventured.

"Yah," said the man as he stepped out of the shadows to place a wrinkled hand on the desk. "And you'd be the new boy, *Ist das so?*"

"That's me," Trinidad admitted as he lowered his bat and apologized. "Sorry."

"No worries, son," said his visitor. "I might well have been a bear—a real one that is—not a wooden character like this cartoon critter." The old man patted the smiling head of the carved totem bear which stood beside the concierge's desk holding a "Welcome to Grand Lake Lodge" sign. It was then Trinidad noticed that ravages of age had reduced Buster Bishop—who was rumored to have once been a giant—to a stooped gnome no larger than the lodge's wooden bear.

The old timer interpreted the younger man's gaze and sighed, "I imagine you were expecting someone taller, *Nein?*"

"I—" Trinidad began.

"No need to apologize," the old man assured him. "I once wore a high-crowned ten-gallon sheriff's Stetson in days gone by and that made all the difference in my altitude."

Rough laughter followed this self-deprecating remark and Trinidad thought the old lawman might choke before the quick-thinking concierge uncorked his hip flask and offered Bishop a drink.

"*Mein Gott,*" Bishop sputtered. "That liquor will fill out the minister's trousers! Begging your pardon," he said as he cast an upward glance. "God be praised," he added, confirming Trinidad's suspicion that the old man was begging Heavenly forgiveness for his mildly irreverent remark about the clergy. "I was just thinking today," Bishop continued as though picking up the thread of a conversation, "some folks wake up happy and say 'Good morning, Lord' and some wake up cranky and say 'Good Lord, it's morning!' Me? I say my prayers and sleep-in."

The old man paused and Trinidad took it as his cue.

"Me too," he said.

"So, you're also a night creature—same as me—uh—no thanks," the old man held up both hands to deflect Trinidad's proffered flask. "That one swig was plenty. Strong drink and me parted ways long since. Bad for the ticker,

Doc says. Don't miss it. And, I have to say, you're starting a bit young. But pay me no mind. Wise men don't need advice and fools don't take it. So, let's get down to business, my boy. I don't imagine I can interest you in a short game of cribbage?"

Trinidad had never played, but Buster was a patient teacher and, in the course of that first game, and another twenty midnight matches, the two men—one wet behind the ears, the other seasoned and worldly—became fast friends. The old timer helped Trinidad pass the long nights and Buster seemed to relish the company. Their genial games, punctuated with Buster's never-ending stories and his quirky laughter, seemed to transform both men.

Trinidad relied less and less on liquor and the old man seemed to grow younger with each encounter. It had to be the younger man's imagination, but, every now and then, when they sat down for a cribbage match, Buster seemed a little less lame, less hunched over. Already a colorful character, the former lawman, seemed to grow more animated from time to time and his features, once drawn and gray, took on a rosy glow.

The old man was an unquenchable fountain of stories and every story had a ring of truth. Early on, Trinidad decided that his visitor was incapable of deception. Buster was seldom the hero of his own tale. More often he was the goat whose vulnerabilities and foibles and near-misses made him all the more human.

Buster Bishop didn't start out to be a lawman. His dream was to be a rodeo cowboy. A Grand Lake native, he was born, he liked to say, "Not in a log cabin like old Abe, but in a lodge cabin anyway." His mother had been a live-in waitress—an exchange student from Germany who'd trod the very floor where the men played cards. A faded photo of her and her co-workers still hung in the lodge. Leading Trinidad to the photo, the old man pointed her out.

"The pretty one," he tapped the image and grinned, as his speech took on a hint of his German ancestry. "The one *stillgestanden.*"

Trinidad studied the image. One corner bore the inscription "Wait-Staff 1921." The black and white photograph showed a line of identically-dressed young waitresses, including Buster's mother, who was indeed standing at strict attention. Then he left Buster alone.

Steeped in memories, the old lawman remained behind, quietly weeping, as the younger man slipped away to sit alone on the fireplace swing. Trinidad waited there, immersed in his own thoughts and telling himself he wasn't homesick—striving to convince himself that the mist which clouded his vision only meant he needed to rest his eyes.

Chapter 9

Looking Back
2019/10:30 a.m. on June 8

"At 85," Trinidad told his host, "Buster Bishop—known to his friends as Red—was slowing down. The former rodeo rider, bulldogger, marine drill instructor, and Grand County Sheriff, had once been a strapping specimen of Colorado manhood—a six foot-four bruiser with a barrel chest, bulging biceps, and flaming red hair. He had the photos to prove it—if only he could remember where he'd stashed them."

"I know that drill," Heckleson observed. "Just this mornin' I was searchin' high and mighty fer my spectacles and you can never guess where they was."

"On your forehead?" Trinidad speculated.

"Exactly," the old ranger confessed. "Not fer nothin' are ya a detective, son. And, say, is it good with us if I call y'all Slick, or is that a pet name preserved fer your gal and your special pals, like Sheriff Jack?"

"You're my special friend too," Trinidad said. "So Slick is okay by me. And, while we're exchanging intimacies, is it okay if I call you John?"

"I'll let y'all in on a secret if we can stand it," said the old ranger, his tone turning conspiratorial.

"Confide away," Trinidad said.

"Well," Heckleson said, "there's some call me 'Fingers' on account of my missin' joints. And there's some call me "John" which is my mid-dle-most name, but—was up to me—I'd prefer my given Christian name."

"Which is..." Trinidad prompted.

"Which is Dallas."

"No fooling?"

"Straight-up, Slick."

"Okay," said Trinidad, "Dallas it is."

"Now that's settled, how about the rest of your story? Begin over again," the old ranger requested. "Start over and I'll hold my peace."

Chapter 10

The Phantom
2006/September 25

At 85, Buster Bishop was slowing down. He'd once been a rodeo rider and bulldogger. He'd served as marine drill instructor and Grand County Sheriff, but time had reduced the six foot-four Adonis with a barrel chest and bulging biceps to a shadow of his former self.

The Buster Trinidad knew was bent and lame. The only vestige of his vanished youth was his shock of unruly hair, though where it had once been a fiery red, it was now a luminous white.

"From fire to ice," was how the man himself put it as he sported a wide grin which featured a prominent gold tooth. "Not much chance someone will call me "Red" no more."

And yet his old friends—those still living—continued to call him by that honorific. The mostly young and irrepressibly frank men and women who worked at the Grand Lake Lodge had another nickname for Buster Bishop, one which smacked of sarcasm, but which also encompassed a hint of awe.

They called him *the phantom.*

A long-term resident of the lodge, Bishop seemed at once to be both ubiquitous and scarce. In daylight, one seemed to catch glimpses of him, but always indirectly. His visage might appear over one's shoulder, reflected in a mirror or windowpane, flickering like lightning, only to vanish. Or a shadow might fall across one's path, only to melt away when a search was launched to locate the shadow's owner.

But, come sundown, the old man could be perceived in the flesh—or at least in the more manageable form of a full-bodied apparition. Bishop in the daylight was ephemeral; Bishop at night could be relied on to adhere more-or-less to the laws of Nature and the rules of the senses. Bishop by day might be glimpsed; Bishop at night could carry on a conversation. Bishop by day could be seen but not heard; at night the man spoke.

Or so Trinidad told the others who wondered aloud about their co-worker's mental stability. *What's up,* they wondered, *with this young buck who consistently requests, even relishes, the graveyard shift, and who's known to take a nip now and then? Might the lad be not only seeing, but also hearing things?*

Those doubts circulated among the staff and may explain why no one seemed to notice or care when Buster Bishop disappeared.

Chapter 11

The Badge and the Cross
2006/September 30

During a sequence of long autumn nights, in bits and pieces, Trinidad learned Buster's life story. Shortly after entering primary school, Buster learned from a family friend that his mother had been banished to Germany and that he supposedly had a brother, whereabouts unknown. With no visible relations to cling to, he struggled to bond with his foster family. Later, after deciding school was not for him, he left home, trailed south, and fell into work with a stock contractor. By age fifteen he was in Prescott, Arizona, wrangling a barn-full of bucking bulls for one of the West's oldest rodeos. Soon he graduated from trimming horns to serving as a day-of-rodeo roustabout.

Volunteering on a whim, he served five years in the U.S. Marine Corps, rising steadily through the ranks. His brief tour as a drill instructor ended abruptly when an incident which he didn't care to discuss obliged him to leave the service.

"It was an honorable discharge," he assured his young listener. "Just barely, that is. Let's just say I trailed back to Arizona a peg or two lower and with my miserable tail between my legs."

Sometime in the dim past, the old man couldn't recall exactly when, his foster parents died. There was no estate, so he stayed put and worked every dirty job imaginable, laboring in the trenches, until one day he ascended to the lofty position of contractor's agent—a raise in stature and pay which found him negotiating fees and living the high life.

In Trinidad, the old man had found a sympathetic and attentive audience. For the younger man, spending time with Buster was a blessing. It was like having his grandpa back again and whole.

Boyhood memories of his grandfather's funeral haunted Trinidad. Laid out in a half-open casket, Grandpa Sands' ashen face seemed unreal—like a free-floating death-mask. The features were three-dimensional, but also unfinished, as if roughly chiseled from a forlorn lump of beached driftwood. His hips and legs—so mangled by the train which had ended his life—lay hidden beneath a shroud of icy velvet. It was a bad memory. Buster was helping him make better ones.

Many of the old man's stories were comical. Some were inspiring. Others were deadly serious. Drink caught up to Buster at twenty-eight until he accepted Jesus and refocused his life. Plucking up his newfound spiritual courage, he enrolled in a peace officer standards and training program in New Mexico. Sweating and learning elbow-to-elbow with other earnest young men, including a dozen Native Americans training for roles as tribal police, he soon earned his P.O.S.T. certificate and embarked on a career which ultimately led him back to Grand County. Returning to his Grand Lake hometown, he started on the lowest rung of law enforcement and rose steadily until his election as sheriff.

"The badge and the cross," Bishop told his young cribbage opponent on the final day of the month, "those were the symbols of my career. I've had a full life with few regrets..." The old man teared up for a second, then managed a fleeting gold-toothed smile, and forged ahead. "Could'a, should'a, would'a, those are my big what-ifs. Could'a had a wife—should'a had a family —would'a had kids. You know how it is, or maybe you don't know. Anyway that's 31 and it's my game again. So, good night, kiddo."

"Good night, Red," said Trinidad and, had he known what fate had in store for the old timer, he would have rushed after him and kept him safe. But September ended that night and, before he had a chance to act, morning dawned and October rushed in.

Chapter 12

Bambi Taylor for Congress
2006/Dawn on October 1

"Happy International Raccoon Appreciation Day!" Bambi Taylor was all smiles as she relieved Trinidad at the concierge's desk. Ordinarily, his loins would have stirred at the sight of his vivacious co-worker. But this morning her flowing blonde locks, which were typically arrayed in an alluring set of cornrows and double-Dutch braids, were topped by the ridiculous appendage of a wonky coonskin cap.

And yet her lovely face, with its perfect nose, pouty lips, and elevated cheek bones, literally glowed with such a radiant smile that Trinidad hadn't the heart to discourage her.

"Happy International Rat—" he began.

"Raccoon," she teased. "October first is International Raccoon Appreciation Day...all over the entire world actually...that's the international part... started in 2002 by a girl who loves animals...I love animals...don't you...I'll leave you a cap...and one for Red...I know he'll love Raccoon Day...by the way, did I tell you Red's friend stopped by yesterday looking for him...a big dude he was and over-dressed for the weather to say the least...so, let Red know from me to you to expect company...meantime I'll leave a stack of appreciation brochures on the desk...or anyway Casey will...last year the big dope gave them all out...so he says...this year I'll make sure he saves some for you...oh don't forget your bat, dear boy...have a good sleep...dream of me."

Once again, Trinidad was impressed that Bambi talked for two minutes straight without taking a breath. *Great lungs,* he told himself as he discretely glanced at the young woman's magnificent chest before saying goodbye and starting for his room.

Following his habitual path, Trinidad detoured across the broad lobby in order to pause in front of the old upright Black & Keffer piano where—keeping with lodge employee tradition—he reached up to pat the front talon of the stuffed pheasant. The inanimate animal shared the piano top with a motley trio of other feathered creatures which even John James Audubon would be hard-pressed to classify. It was a ritual intended to foster good fortune—a pat for luck. Turning right, he left the piano and its nesting birds behind, passed through the porch door, and stopped at the top of the exterior stairs.

He never tired of this elevated view from what, since the early days, every lodge operator has touted as "America's Favorite Front Porch." From this lofty vantage point, he could see the sleepy village of Grand Lake—a modest settlement no more than a dozen blocks long. The space between lodge and town pulsated with the quaking of golden and crimson-mantled aspens, their bright leaves twirling in the autumn breeze. Beyond the town, mist was rising and the summit of Shadow Mountain cast a mirrored image which shimmered on the placid cobalt surface of Grand Lake. In the distance lay the snowy cap of Mount Adams.

By any measure, Trinidad told himself, *this early morning scene is a Grand one. No wonder this lake and a nearby river justified that label. Early explorers christened the waters. Mapmakers followed suit and—for a time—the names Grand Lake and Grand River prevailed.*

"For a time," he said aloud.

He knew, for better or worse, that the waterway formerly known as "The Grand River" had, long ago, been renamed "The Colorado River." Though the river was re-labeled, vestiges of the old name lingered. Hence, modern viewers continue to admire *Grand* Lake. They can also travel to *Grand* Junction, the sprawling metropolis far to the west where the Colorado and Gunnison Rivers merge a stone's throw from the site of his grandpa's grave. It suits the *Grand* Canyon, that capacious gorge the river's destined to carve downstream.

Standing alone, he balanced his bat on the wide banister, inhaled the crisp morning air, and stretched luxuriously. With one hand on the wooden railing and the other on his breast, Trinidad watched an early morning sailboat glide over the broad lake's glassy surface. With Bob Ferryman's blessing, he himself had sailed there—putting *The Dawn Ambler* through her paces. With the lake so near, he longed to take her out again. He remained standing, watching the boat, his fingers smoothing the high school crest embossed on his keepsake sweatshirt, until he was struck by vivid childhood memories—not from high school, but in the more distant past.

While studying Colorado history in junior high, Trinidad had taken part in a classroom debate regarding the headwaters of the Colorado River. A fiercely loyal Colorado native, he was inclined to be charitable to those who insisted that the Colorado River was born in the glacial cradle of Grand Lake. However, he and many others held a contrary belief that the mighty river began elsewhere, fed by its North Fork which originated higher in the Rocky Mountains.

Assigned to prove the North Fork proposition, he'd impressed his eighth-grade teacher by locating the river's source on his classroom's giant wall map. Standing on tiptoe, he placed a youthful finger on the tiny blue dot of La Poudre Pass Lake and traced the circuitous southern route of the North Fork of the Colorado River as it snaked its way to an estuary on the western shore of Shadow Mountain Reservoir. Following a theoretical line through the broad reservoir, he reached a southern exit point where the full-fledged Colorado River began.

Speaking in favor of Grand Lake as the river's point of origin was Alula Tellez, his best friend and smartest girl in their class. To prepare for her presentation, she'd utilized an overhead projector and a huge sheet of butcher paper to draw an enlarged copy of a vintage 1895 Rand-McNally map. Tracing a fair copy of the projected map using ink and colored pencils, Alula produced a compelling visual aid which made a convincing case for accepting Grand Lake as the quintessential source of the Colorado River. Using masking tape to position her hand-drawn map next to the classroom's contemporary image of Colorado, the beaming girl challenged her classmates to compare the two.

"What's different?" she asked.

Hands went up and it was soon agreed that Shadow Mountain Reservoir didn't exist in 1895.

"And what have we here?" she asked, using a pointer to emphasize a location at the southern end of Grand Lake. She then traced the broad flow originating there to a confluence with the more modest North Fork.

"The Colorado River!" someone shouted.

"But you made a mistake!" a critic chortled. "You called it 'Grand River!' That's wrong!"

"Is it?" said Alula—then a luminous and brainy blonde whose life's ambition, everyone knew, was to become a lawyer.

Turns out, both views of the headwaters of the Colorado River have merit and that particular adolescent debate was declared a tie.

Then and now, whichever origin scenario one accepted, Trinidad found it impossible to disconnect one of the West's most majestic rivers from the mystique of the deep glacial lake which stretched before him.

"Colorado? Grand?" he asked himself. "A tough choice, but that debate is closed."

Opinions regarding the river's origin may differ, but he knew the question of how the Grand River became the Colorado had been settled decades ago. It was what Alula—who, in keeping with her girlhood ambition, became a pre-law major at Denver University—would call "settled law." It's a story of transformation which is enshrined in no less a reliquary than *The United States Congressional Record*. Returning to thoughts of his school days, Trinidad remembered how his love of learning inspired him to take on a series of challenging assignments.

Much to the delight of his eighth-grade history teacher, Trinidad's final class project had explored the quest to officially rename the Grand River. He treasured that long-ago project as the triumph of his boyhood and he remembered its contents as if he'd authored it, not six years ago, but yesterday.

Reporting on events which took place in 1921, he'd told his classmates the story of Colorado politician E.T. Taylor, an influential policymaker who was famous for bulldozing legislation through Congress. The long-haul lawmaker served a dozen years in the Colorado Legislature followed by multiple terms in the U.S. House of Representatives until he died in office. The man was a Colorado legend whose passion for his state became a mapmaker's nightmare.

In a nutshell, Taylor fervently believed one thing with all his heart: he lamented the idea that the cherished river which flowed through his beloved Colorado did not bear the name of the state where the water was born. In fact, he labeled the notion "an abomination."

By tenaciously advocating that the precious water originating in his home state and flowing ever-onward to Old Mexico be renamed "The Colorado River," Taylor bucked the neighboring state of Wyoming and the U.S. Geological Survey. His neighbors to the north and the Survey favored leaving the river "Grand" or, if it must be renamed, calling it the Green River. The Green, they pointed out, begins high in the Wind River Mountains of Wyoming and gathers momentum as it courses through the canyonlands of Utah.

Taylor conceded that the Green—which stretches 730 miles from its source to its confluence with the mis-named river—was the longer of the two main waters which merged to form the so-called Grand. But Taylor labeled the Wyoming water the "mother" of the larger river and the waters flowing from Grand Lake, the "father." Clearly, he declared, the father's contribution should be given priority. It was a misogynistic argument which would have raised eyebrows and headlines in modern America, but it carried the day in 1921 and the Grand became the Colorado.

Reluctant to return to his room on that October morning in 2006, Trinidad remained standing at the apex of the lodge's ambling outdoor staircase. It was comforting to re-live schoolboy memories while also relishing the joy of such inspiring scenery. He indulged his memories and the view for a moment more.

At last, he pulled himself back into the present and was about to descend the stairs when he had a deliciously unhinged thought. He wondered whether the heartbreakingly lovely and certifiably crazy Bambi Taylor might be a distant descendant of the irascible congressman whose arguments, uttered more than 85 years ago, convinced America to re-brand the mighty Colorado.

If so, he thought, *what's to stop Bambi from running for Congress and passing a bill to rechristen the mighty Colorado the Raccoon River?*

With that whimsical image in his mind, Trinidad took one step onto the staircase. Which is when the roof fell in.

Chapter 13

The Roof Falls In
2006/Early Morning on October 1

At a mile and a half above sea level, surrounded by Rocky Mountain peaks which soar even higher into the Colorado sky, locals have grown used to capricious weather. A heavy autumnal snowstorm, followed by a week of unseasonably warm Indian Summer, came as no surprise to the intrepid residents of Grand Lake. But that changeable weather pattern must have occurred once too often. It must have been too much for the roof beams supporting the long-term residential cabins on the back-forty of the lodge. Because, just as the local population was sitting down to breakfast, that freeze-and-thaw sequence spawned an unsustainable strain which caused unhappy slabs of vintage wood to come crashing down with a resounding crack and cascading boom.

The sound was unexpected, like a startling clap of thunder on a clear day.

Trinidad heard the rumble and looked in that direction. The lodge roof blocked his view, but he could see the aftermath in the shape of an uncommon mist rising into the morning sky. The powdery haze looked like the leading edge of an avalanche and he guessed the cause.

After the crash, the insurance company would try to characterize it as an act of God. What God had in mind was uncertain. What Trinidad had in mind as he gripped his bat and raced down the wooden stairs was crystal clear. Bounding along timbered sidewalks and rushing in the direction of the chaos, he was running to the rescue, his heart pounding, his lungs expanding, as he launched a one-man crusade to save Buster Bishop.

Trinidad ran, slipping awkwardly when he jumped off the sidewalk and started uphill over a slick expanse of frosty scrub grass. Striving to conquer the hill, the sprinting youth could see the unmistakable signs of damage ahead. It only took a moment to recognize that Buster's cabin was the epi-center of the destruction. Set aside for long-haul residents, a matching pair of tiny co-joined cabins had been placed far away from tourist traffic. Most guests staying at Grand Lake Lodge were unaware of their existence or, if they noticed the diminutive structures at all, assumed they were potting sheds or maintenance pods. No one staying at the palatial lodge would guess they were places of human habitation.

Silhouetted against the bright morning sky, the roofline of Buster's cabin was crimped in an awful crease. The top slumped down in the middle, like the ruined spine of a swayback horse. The once-horizontal ridge cap was bent double at such a steep angle that shingles from the top had been pressed into the eaves below. The snow which blanketed the roof had followed the path of the cave-in, adding icy weight to the press of fallen timbers. The entire roof of Buster Bishop's cabin—a duplex which he shared with a retired camp cook—was crumpled into a concave dimple, a crest-fallen indentation like the lopsided top of an undercooked chocolate cake. Anyone inside when the roof failed would be at the mercy of smothering snow and ice and splintered wood.

As he drew nearer, Trinidad became aware of shouts and the sound of rushing feet following far behind. Up ahead, he could see a figure slumped on the ground. One thing Trinidad knew—his teenaged passion from his days as a cross-country track star—was how to run. He was yards ahead of the others and they would be long in catching-up. In five broad strides, he reached the fallen man. It was Berman, the old cook, his face covered in mud and barely recognizable, his forehead bleeding, his distinctive coveralls disheveled and soaking wet.

"Are you okay?" Trinidad asked the injured man who seemed to be in a daze.

"Yes...I think so...yes," came the halting reply.

"Where's Bishop?" Trinidad inquired and when the man didn't respond, he tried again. "Buster? Where's Buster? Where's Red?" he shouted. The man was cringing, as if expecting a blow. It was then that Trinidad realized he was standing over the old cook, his legs spread wide apart while he brandished his baseball bat. "Sorry," he said as he laid the bat on the wet grass, knelt at Berman's side, and continued in a softer tone. "Where's Red, old timer?"

"Gone," said Berman. "Gone," he repeated. Then the old man lost consciousness as others arrived in a gaggle of confusion.

Chapter 14

Strays
2006/Morning on October 2

Berman was out of touch with the world for twenty-four hours. Carried from the scene of the snow cave-in, the old cook was bundled into the back of Leonard William's panel truck. One option had been to drive the unresponsive man 48 miles to the Estes Park Hospital. Instead, the patient was detoured to the Shadow Mountain Veterinary Clinic where his forehead was wrapped in a broad bandage. Feeling revived, he was convinced to spend the night, sleeping beside a homeless and sedated border collie who'd barely survived a run-in with a renegade moose.

"A couple of strays in here, I reckon," said the old cook when his visitors arrived at the patient's shared recovery room.

Accompanied by Casey, Trinidad had made the journey in order to talk to Berman. He would rather have come alone, but it was Casey's morning to possess the old Ford Mustang which he and Bambi and Trinidad shared.

Trinidad's old Nash had given out months ago, on the lofty reaches of Trail Ridge Road, and his adventure of hiking ten miles that evening in the midnight rain had been responsible for his ending up more-or-less stranded in Grand Lake. Walking through that stormy night, he was within a mile of the town limits of the resort community when Meg Del Monte gave him a ride to her condo. Once inside, she stripped off his wet clothes, swathed him in one of her tiny bathrobes, and offered soup and tea to her fundamentally naked guest. Later that night, the two made passionate love on the paper-thin mattress of her ancient hide-a-bed. Meg took him in, amazed his libido, then rocketed out of his life almost as swiftly as she'd entered.

"Earth to Trini," said Casey.

Trinidad's thoughts of his old Nash and young Meg had pulled him into the past and, seeking his co-worker's wavering attention, Casey was rudely snapping his fingers inches from Trinidad's face.

Trinidad didn't respond, but instead glowered at his insolent companion. Casey had a way of needling others and, fully aware that Trinidad disliked the nickname, the officious clod insisted on calling him "Trini" or sometimes "Lopez." It's not that Trinidad objected to being tagged as Hispanic, it was a common misconception given his dark complexion. Moreover, although it made him a throw-back among his peers, he absolutely loved the music of Trini Lopez. But he doubted if Casey's use of the comparison was intended as a compliment.

"Lemon tree very pretty—" Casey attempted to croon the lyrics of the Trini Lopez standard.

"And the lemon flower is sweet—" a vet tech suddenly chimed in from the other side of an adjoining glass wall which divided healthy animals from cats and dogs in rabies quarantine.

"But the fruit of the poor lemon," the unlikely pair sang in a hideous duet, "is im-pos-si-ble to eat."

That woman has an excuse for yowling, thought Trinidad. *She's stuck in there with the town's mad dogs and crazy cats. Meanwhile, Casey's out here, frothing at the mouth, with no one handy to put him down.*

"I appreciate the visit," said the old timer when the unholy concert ended. "And I know I should recognize at least one of you youngsters but—" he hesitated. "Who exactly are you supposed to be and, for that matter, who am I?"

Having posed this troubling question, the confused patient tapped his bandaged head and cast a sequence of searching and bewildered glances at the faces of his two young visitors. His own face exhibited scars from his ordeal in the collapsed cabin. In addition to the conspicuous bandage, which wound around his skull and covered his forehead at a cockeyed angle, his features were distorted by a dusky bruise under one eye and a swollen cheek which gave him the appearance of the losing contestant in a one-sided prize fight.

Even Casey, who'd ordinarily have inserted a wisecrack at this point, seemed to feel sympathy for the apparently disoriented man, because he took a step forward and patted the patient's aged hand. The old cook seemed to be in a bad way. His breathing was labored and his face was as gray as his gnarled fingers.

"I'm Casey—Jackson Casey," Casey said with a gentleness which caused Trinidad to raise an eyebrow. "And this here is Trini—Trinidad Sands. We work at the big desk." When the old cook did not seem to understand, Casey added, "At the lodge. Next to the welcome bear? Under the canoe?"

"Ah—" the old timer held a finger aloft. "You be those bear boys who works with the Golden Goddess of Grand Lake Lodge. Is she—?" he asked with a lilt of anticipation as the color rushed back into his cheeks.

"Bambi couldn't make it," explained Casey. "She's on duty at the concierge's desk. Under the canoe," he added helpfully.

"Under the canoe—" the old man mulled this over as his eyes strayed to the fluorescent fixtures on the ceiling of the clinic's recovery room.

Trinidad followed the old cook's gaze and wondered, *Is it possible? Are Berman and I channeling the same fantasy of Bambi in a canoe, waiting to be dunked and then ogled by a bevy of admiring males when she climbs out of the lake, soaking wet, with her summer blouse clinging?*

"Can I have a moment? the old man asked.

"I know what you mean," Trinidad said.

"No, seriously," the old timer continued. "I need to pee. I really, really need to take a piss. Any idea where—?"

Both Casey and Trinidad pointed toward the far hallway. Berman nodded, slipped on his shoes, and left to do his business.

"You don't have to stay," Trinidad told Casey when the old cook was out of sight.

"Bambi made me promise to make sure the old crackpot was okay," Casey shrugged. "I guess I can report back that the old Kraut is no more crazy than usual."

"You're all heart," Trinidad suggested.

"As a guy who can ignore you so hard that you'll doubt your very existence," Casey sneered, "I accept the compliment. Ciao, kid!"

Ciao? thought Trinidad as he watched Casey wave a languid hand and amble toward the exit. *The pretentious show-off probably heard that bit of ostentatious hogwash in a movie.*

As he waited for Berman to return, Trinidad paced the room and fingered the harmonica in his shirt pocket. He wanted to extract the portable instrument and noodle a random tune to focus his thoughts. But he glanced at Berman's roommate and decided he was unwilling to risk disturbing the slumbering dog.

When the old cook returned, Trinidad planned to gently pump him for information. He had many questions and he wondered if the old timer would be up for them. Moments later, he heard Berman clomping down the hallway.

"Is shite-for-brains gone?" the old cook asked as he shuffled across the room.

"Casey? Yeah, he's gone."

"Can't stand the fella," the old man said as he sat heavily down on the seemingly flimsy gurney which, Trinidad noticed, had been reinforced with a thickly-woven scaffolding of wooden pallets. Following his visitor's gaze, the steadily recovering patient managed a grin. "This is the horse platform," he explained. "Sturdy enough to hold a bear, so they tell me. Sit a spell," he patted the thin mattress. "I doubt if you and me together will outweigh a bear."

"I hope Casey didn't upset you," said Trinidad as he sat down.

"That muscle-bound man's an arm-hole and an ass-pit," the old cook declared. "A reason God invented the middle finger. Begging your pardon," he added as he cast a glimpse skyward.

Where, I wonder, did our patient pick up that singular habit of cursing, then seeking Divine absolution? Trinidad asked himself that question even though he was certain the old cook was imitating Red Bishop, his now-missing neighbor. *Or maybe,* Trinidad thought, *it's a case of Bishop imitating Berman. The two definitely share mannerisms and—*

The curious concierge must have spent a bit too long processing his internal dialogue, because Berman reached over and nudged the younger man's hand.

"You asked me a question," the old cook said, as if picking up a recently interrupted conversation.

"Yesterday," Trinidad reminded the old timer.

"Yah," the old man agreed. "And now I'm prepared to answer."

Trinidad took a breath and settled in for a story. Though he'd gotten to know Buster Bishop well, he'd had no direct contact with Berman. He'd seen the old cook from a distance when he walked Buster home a week ago, but that was it. Meanwhile, he was aware of Berman's reputation. Other members of the lodge staff had warned him that the old cook was a talkative fellow of German extraction who had a reputation as someone who never met a bush he didn't love to beat around.

Berman may or may not have the answers Trinidad was seeking, but the inquisitive concierge was willing to hear him out. So far, what Trinidad knew was riddled with holes and he hoped the old cook could fill in the blanks. Yesterday's thorough search for Buster Bishop had come up empty. The old lawman was nowhere to be found on the lodge premises. Both sides of the duplex cabin he shared with Berman were completely devoid of humans, living or dead.

What the search of the ruined cabin did turn up was Buster's pet fish, still miraculously flopping in a puddle of melted snow. The fish's unlikely survival seemed to be the result of another uncommon discovery. When searchers entered Buster's side of the duplex, they found a healthy bank of flames still burning in the cabins' small double-sided fireplace.

Trinidad mentioned the mysteries of the fish and the fire, which drew a firm response from Berman.

"That ain't the half of it, sonny," the old cook declared before lowering his voice and launching into a passable Bette Davis impersonation. "Fasten your seatbelts," he warned, "it's going to be a bumpy ride."

Chapter 15

Pay Attention
2019/11 a.m. on June 8

"So, here comes a tale inside a tale," noted Ranger Heckleson. "Am I gonna need a scorecard to keep track of all this?"

"I'll be gentle," said Trinidad. "More coffee?" The smiling detective pushed his empty cup through the open maw of the porch-to-kitchen pass-through.

"As long as your bladder holds out, Slick," Heckleson said as he sported a Cheshire cat grin and filled the detective's outstretched cup.

"Where was I?" Trinidad asked.

"You'll be about to tell me Berman's shaggy dog story," Heckleson shouted from the pantry. "Or do I overshoot my guess? So, I'll be obliged to have y'all rein-in your talk fer a second, 'cause I can't no-wise hear your tale while I'm muckin' around in this condiment wilderness lookin' fer my nephew Rick's steak sauce. Don't need the sauce fer lunch, but it'll come in handy at supper-time."

As Trinidad waited for his host to resurface, he gathered his thoughts. Returning to that October day in 2006, the detective recalled that he was patiently listening to Berman's rambling account of the recent past and slowly recognizing the many clues he'd missed. This early incident in Trinidad's sleuthing career—so early that he didn't yet realize he *was* sleuthing—had taught him an indelible lesson and cemented in his mind a subsequent pledge to *pay attention* when others spoke.

"Got it!" yelled Heckleson from the depths of his cavernous pantry. "If the bottle'll been a snake in the grass, it would'a bit the hand that feeds me," the old ranger declared.

Trinidad suppressed a smile. Running true to his nature, Heckleson was—as usual—mangling yet another old chestnut of a catchphrase.

Once, at a dinner party, Trinidad and Anne had attempted to keep a running record of the conversational malaprops uttered by the totally sincere, but often wholly mistaken, ranger.

"Twenty-seven," Anne announced as they walked home at the close of the evening. "And that's giving him the benefit of the doubt on *ducking a June-bug.*"

"I can't imagine how he muddled the concept of jumping on an opportunity *like a duck on a June-bug* into the totally unrelated idea of standing beneath a streetlight and trying to keep flying insects from landing on your head," Trinidad said, recalling Heckleson's chagrin when their hostess corrected the old ranger's mistaken notion.

"That was sure a case of *the pot calling the kettle back,*" Anne suggested. "But, as our favorite ranger might say, *let's burn that bridge when we come to it.* And remember our pledge not to comment on his foibles. I, for one, have no intention of breaking his heart by correcting him in public."

"Soup's up, cowboy," Heckleson shouted from his post at the stove. "Come eat your lunch while the sun shines!"

The ranger's bellowed invitation pulled Trinidad back from the past, so he unfolded himself from an overstuffed patio chair and stretched luxuriously. *Gotta love these long summer days,* he thought as he glanced over the expanse of brown earth surrounding the ranger's lofty house, then looked closer. Was it his imagination, or was the mast of the beached sailboat no longer visible? He'd borrow Heckleson's spotting scope and take a closer look after lunch.

The old ranger's kitchen door was ajar and the screen door which barred the way was riddled with holes. Trinidad pushed his way through. Entering the kitchen, the detective paused as he reached the tiled floor where his boots crunched over a handful of buckshot.

"Looks like somebody's been using your door for target practice," he suggested.

"Gotta have that fixed," Heckleson said while he poured the noon meal's helping of rice into a strainer. "Y'all know what they say, *a stitch in time feeds the bulldog.*"

"Well," Trinidad said as he shouldered the big man aside to reach the sink and wash his hands, "I don't know about the bulldog, but I'm starved."

"Mind that rice water," Heckleson said. "I'm savin' it to put on my hair. Supposed to be filled with nutriments and the like," he added as he involuntarily fingered his unruly locks.

"Seems to be working," Trinidad noticed. "You're looking more like David Hasselhoff every day."

"Don't aim to resemble that Baywatch bimbo," Heckleson chortled. "Wolfgang Mozart is more my style."

"Didn't he wear a wig?" Trinidad observed as he dried his hands.

"Damned if we don't sound like a pair of gossipin' old hens or an old married couple chewin' the fat," the old ranger said and his hearty laugh blended with the savory aroma of tomato soup, steamed rice, and sauteed asparagus—a lunchtime symphony of sound and smells which permeated the cozy kitchen.

"Which brings me right back to my story," said Trinidad as he took his place at the table and unfolded his napkin. "You know how married couples of a certain vintage take on each other's habits and mannerisms? Even beginning to resemble one another in a complementary way?"

"Like Jean and Ruben, y'all mean?"

"That loving couple is a good example," Trinidad agreed as he conjured an image of their mutual friends. "Same smile. Same laugh. A product of years spent living together, sharing a life, finishing one another's sentences—"

"Gull-darn it," sniffed the old ranger, "don't make me all misty-eyed with such sweet talk while I'm pawin' through these jumbled-up drawers lookin' fer my spare soup ladle."

"Sorry," the detective apologized. "But you catch my drift. My point is that people who share intimate space over time end up with harmonized personalities."

"Like a couple of peas in a boat," Heckleson said as he plopped a man-sized helping of soup into Trinidad's bowl and added a dollop of rice and a handful of asparagus to the detective's plate. "Sorry, there's no gravy fer the rice. I ain't got the knack."

"I can do without the gravy," Trinidad said as he patted his stomach. "But you're right about those look-alike peas and—oh—pardon me."

The old ranger had taken his seat and bowed his head.

"Good friends, good meat, good God, let's eat!" Heckleson delivered the mealtime prayer.

"Amen," the detective laughed. "You want more story or should I save it for dessert?"

"Plow on ahead," the old ranger said between bites. "We ain't gettin' no younger and I've got a notion we've just scratched the topmost of your tale."

"You said a mouthful," Trinidad agreed, as he launched into the next chapter of his Grand Lake saga. "You'll recall that I didn't start out to be a detective," he reminded his host. "I just fell into it on account of Buster Bishop's disappearance."

Chapter 16

Musical Chairs
2006/Mid-Morning on October 2

Transporting his audience of one back to October 2006 and drawing the old ranger's imagination into the recovery room of the Shadow Mountain Veterinary Clinic, the detective picked up the thread of his reminiscence.

Berman stood cautiously that day, glanced at the sleeping dog on the next cot, and nearly lost his balance. Trinidad reached to steady the old cook, but the old timer pulled away and took several halting steps toward the recovery room door. Pausing there, he opened the door a crack, and listened. Then he looked toward the glass wall, presumably to make certain the vet tech who'd joined Jackson Casey in the morning's ragged duet was no longer lingering in the quarantine chamber.

"Appears we're alone," he said as he returned to sit beside Trinidad on the horse bed.

Like Buster Bishop, Berman must have once been a taller man, but age had whittled him down. Both men were getting on in years and, if Buster's tale of being born at Grand Lake Lodge was to be believed, he was likely to be as old as 85. Berman also appeared to be in his eighties. All things considered, both men were still relatively nimble on their feet and their minds seemed clear as a bell to Trinidad.

After one final look around the room and even a suspicious glance at the border collie dozing nearby, the old timer seemed to have established sufficient privacy to speak openly.

"Thank God that roof failed," he began and, when Trinidad raised an eyebrow, the agitated man doubled down on his declaration. "I mean it! If that snow hadn't broken through, I don't doubt that both me and Berman would be in a fine pickle."

Assuming he'd misunderstood the old cook, Trinidad started to ask, "You and Berman—?"

"I mean what I say," said the old man. "And, son, if you keep interrupting, how can I spin this tale proper?"

"Sorry, it's just that I—" Trinidad began.

"Patience, Grasshopper," the old man said and his grin revealed a set of perfect teeth marred only by a distinctive gold cap on the uppermost central incisor.

Trinidad stared at the grinning man.

Where? he asked himself. *Where have I seen that exceptional tooth before?*

"And don't look so dang surprised, Grasshopper," said the old man. "I watch television, you know, so I'm allowed to quote a line or two from *Kung Fu* now and then—or any other blessed program I want. Anyhow, the snow *did* fall-in and that's probably what saved me."

As Trinidad stifled his urge to butt in, his informant continued to enlarge his story.

Early yesterday morning, he and his next-door neighbor were sitting in their respective abodes talking, as they often did, through the shared fireplace. It was cold outside and had snowed hard and, at their age, the idea of bundling up to walk fifteen feet to the adjoining bungalow was unappealing. So, each man had remained in his own easy chair, hovering close to the fire, reminiscing and swapping stories like an old married couple.

"Which is when the bear broke in," the old timer declared. "Or anyhow, that's what Berman shouted when his front door was busted down and cold air rushed into that side of the cabin and made the fireplace sputter. I could hear a struggle and was on my feet reaching for my rifle when the roof caved-in and I was knocked senseless. I came to myself—how long later? I don't recall, but I called out for Berman and, hearing no answer, managed to squeeze through my own front door. Stumbling outside, I walked a step or two, then collapsed in the snow where you and your baseball bat and the others found me. You asked for 'Red' and I had just enough sense to lie and tell you he was gone. I said so because the truth was unhandy."

Trinidad's mouth was hanging open. Questions were coursing through his brain, but he could find no words to ask them.

"You're confused," the old timer suggested.

"That's one word for it," Trinidad agreed.

"That's what comes of running our little game," the old timer said. A heavy sigh followed this cryptic remark. It was a mysterious sentence which the inscrutable man might have intended as an internal thought because, spoken aloud, it only served to muddle an already cloudy situation.

Is it possible? The thought rattled around in Trinidad's head as other questions cascaded into his mind. *Is the old timer sitting beside me Buster Bishop? Is my months'-long cribbage opponent really Saul Berman? And what the hell does it mean that one of these old men, whom I have totally mixed up, shouted that a bear broke into his cabin?*

Watching the young man's befuddled confusion, the older man raised a finger.

"I know," Trinidad interrupted, "you're about to remind me, 'Patience, Grasshopper,' but, if I don't ask a boat-load of questions, my head might explode."

"Go ahead, son, only hold off just a bit whilst we shift locations. Looks like my roommate's coming around."

The collie was indeed awakening and his stirring activated a monitoring alarm which, in turn, triggered the sound of approaching feet as three ministering staff members rushed to the dog's aid. Ignoring the room's human occupants, the trio of caregivers focused their attention on their four-legged patient.

"Let's make ourselves scarce," the old timer suggested.

Outside the clinic, the late morning sun was shining brightly as Trinidad pulled out his flip phone and called for a taxi. The old man insisted he could walk back to the lodge, but his younger companion lobbied against it.

"I'll pay for the cab," Trinidad assured the stubborn man. "Which is out of town just now making a prescription run to Kremmling. They say it'll take at least an hour and a half, maybe two, to reach us. So, I told the driver to meet us at the west side coffeehouse where I'll buy you a drink while we talk this out."

"Yah," said his companion, "that's the best idea I've heard all day, only it's myself who'll pay for the coffee."

They walked a block toward town and joined a line waiting at the Walrus Coffee Barn.

"Make way for grandpa," shouted a man in overalls and the line shifted to allow the new arrivals to move to the head.

"Hope he's doing okay," the beaming barista told Trinidad when she brought their drinks to an outdoor table. The older man's bandaged head seemed to inspire her to ask after his health. That same injury, coupled with his venerable age, had earned a promotion to the front of the line and allowed them to place and receive their order in record time. "You need to take better care of your grandfather," she said.

Trinidad saw no need to correct the sweet-young-thing's misconception, so he promised, "I will."

"You two look alike," the barista suggested before hurrying back to her duties.

"I'll take that as a compliment," said the older man when they were alone. "I mean it," he raised his steaming cup in salute.

"Back at you," said Trinidad.

"Your questions?" the old timer extended the invitation.

"Is there enough coffee in the world to coax you into telling the truth?" the confused concierge wondered.

"Ask away," he said. "The caffeine will most likely keep me honest."

"Well," said Trinidad and his tone was dubious. "I'll start my questioning with a statement: I'm thinking that—whoever you are—you ain't the actual Saul Berman."

"Right so far," came the reply. "Why not simplify things. You can call me Red."

"*You're Buster Bishop,*" Trinidad speculated.

"The same," the genuine Buster Bishop replied.

"And my cribbage partner—my midnight visitor?"

"Saul Berman," Bishop confirmed. "That is, mostly Saul—sometimes it was me myself."

"Why? How?" Trinidad began, but the older man interrupted.

"Finally—" Bishop laughed. "Finally, we get to your questions. And you begin with 'why' and 'how' which are the big ones. Tell me, son, look close. Don't you see it?"

Trinidad regarded the old man until a thought struck him.

"Twins," Trinidad intoned the word as if he'd just invented it.

"*Zwilling,*" Bishop confirmed as he translated the idea into his occasional German. "Two peas in a pod—not counting my fake tooth, of course."

"But why different last names," Trinidad began, then he instantly made a leap of logic. "Adoption," he concluded.

"Right again," Bishop sniffed. "It's the old story of poor waifs separated at birth. Remember, it was the 1920s when the pair of us tumbled into the world. An unwed mother who barely spoke English? No father stepping up to take responsibility? Two little bastards? We were lucky somebody didn't suggest drowning us in the lake. Within a month, we were separated—mother and babies alike. She was sent back east. My brother went to Sulphur Springs before heading farther south. And I stayed here to be raised—more-or-less—by foster parents and a string of seasonal employees. Lived here in Grand Lake, mostly at the lodge, all my life, not counting two years when my pop got transferred to Texas for work. That's where I finished my high school and played football, junior and senior years."

The letter jacket, Trinidad thought. *Apparently, I've seen both brothers wearing the distinctive garment. Part of a costume,* he supposed, *intentionally worn to support the illusion that I've been interacting with a single nocturnal visitor. Where's the jacket now?* he wondered.

"Those were good years," Buster continued. "But I missed the mountains. When my folks decided to stay in the Lone Star State, I packed up and moved back. Been here ever since."

"So, no colorful detour to sunny Arizona and no tour of duty with the Marines?" Trinidad guessed.

"Nope," Buster confirmed. "Saul was the wanderer, not me. And my brother has got the run-away imagination, of course. So, he tells the story a bit different, but I'm giving you the gospel."

"And your birth mother?" Trinidad prompted.

"Brunhilda Schmitz—our sainted mother—disappeared. Apparently shipped back to the old country to forget and fade into oblivion. Years later, an unexpected note from her brought my brother and me back together at the lodge. I was retired here and living alone until Saul showed up on my doorstep one day, like a long-lost homing pigeon, somehow drawn here by fate, I imagined, until I realized that our mother had reached out to both of us. It was easy enough to convince the management to give him a home and they even let him work in the kitchen. And, since we were seldom, if ever, seen together, over the years people just tended to meld us into a single old man."

"But why change places?"

"For a lark," the old man admitted. "Did you never play musical chairs? When the music stops, wherever you are, you sit down. That's how my brother and I roll, as you young folks say. We traded places now and then to play cribbage—what was the harm in that? Saul thought you were good company and I wanted to see for myself. Anyway, it was mostly Saul all those evenings. He's the night owl. I'm the one who needs my beauty sleep," he added with a conspiratorial wink. "I'd rather be out-and-about early when the Golden Goddess of Grand Lake Lodge is on duty."

"But—" Trinidad protested.

"You're going to say that our Miss Taylor never mentioned seeing me in the daylight."

"Yes."

"Well, I kept to the shadows," Bishop explained. "There's more than one way to sidle onto the main floor without being seen. Comes of being born here and skittering around as a kid to find cubbyholes and secret passages. I developed a real slick ability to slip in and out of tight spots—a skill which, among other things, allowed me—as an adventurous boy—to steal soda-pop from the kitchen without being caught. I came and went like a ghost and my twin proved to be equally good at hide-and-seek, which is why I ain't concerned that Saul's missing."

"Because you figure he's hiding?" Trinidad ventured.

"Got to be," said Bishop. "He was always the one for being dramatic. 'Help a bear!' he yelled the other day when our roof busted. Good thing his shouting pulled me out of my chair. If I hadn't jumped to my feet, the busted beams and falling snow would've pulverized me. But a bear? What an imagination—*die Fantasie*—a fantasy inspired by the cave-in, no doubt."

It was a theory which Trinidad had accepted at the time.

Chapter 17

Regrets
2019/Noon on June 8

"Big mistake," the detective told his host.

"Like I've never once been mistaken," the old ranger assured his young guest.

"True enough, but, as we both know, in the suspicion business, mistakes cost lives," Trinidad said.

In the silence which followed the detective's words, each man seemed lost in his own thoughts. Which may be the reason both men jumped when someone pounded on the side of Heckleson's house.

Chapter 18

Clear-Sky Thunder
2019/12:01 p.m. on June 8

Snapped back to the present, Trinidad and Heckleson dropped to the kitchen floor.

Years of training (on the ranger's part) and raw experience (on the part of the detective) instantly compelled both men to duck. Instincts placed them on the linoleum as a shotgun blast shredded the back door, obliterating the screen and reducing the narrow wooden frame to a sleet-storm of splinters. A heartbeat later they heard the shooter pumping his weapon to chamber another round.

"Not today," the ranger growled as he rolled under the table, sprang to his feet like a gymnast, and snatched his rifle from its accustomed spot in the kitchen corner. He pumped three shots through the open pass-through.

The first shot spawned a yelp from the porch, the second dislodged the shotgun, and the third sent the shooter crashing to the redwood deck. A scrambling of feet signaled that a second assailant was fleeing down the back stairs. By the time the detective and the ranger had cautiously worked their way out onto the back porch, the other ambusher was long gone.

"Meth," said Heckleson as he kicked the fallen shotgun out of reach. The ranger kept his rifle pointed at the prostrate form even though the man was obviously dead. "Don't usually link-up methamphetamine with violence, but looks like somebody decided to act unusual. Only a meth-head would be high enough to bother knockin' before he pulled off an ambush. Even a blind pig knows enough to come in out of the rain." He lowered his weapon and knelt to study the assailant's face. "Why do they always look like unhappy rabbits?" he asked.

"One of our dry-land sailors, do you reckon?" asked Trinidad.

"Bound to be," said the ranger as he went through the motions of checking for a pulse. "Him and his partner must'a followed our tracks up here. Funny ain't it?"

"Funny?" Trinidad wondered aloud.

"Unusual is what I mean. My shootin' I mean," Heckleson explained. "Outside on the range this morning I couldn't hit the inside of a barn. Here in my kitchen, with me and my lunch guest fixed in the sights of some jackass, I put three shots tight into the chest. You never know."

"Until you know," Trinidad suggested.

"Yeah," said Heckleson as he stood up again, formed his free hand into a *hook 'em horns* gesture and posed the symbolic phone next to his face, his thumb against his ear and his pinky finger pointing toward his mouth. "Y'all want I should call Jack or do you want to?"

"I'll do it," said Trinidad as he pulled out his flip phone.

Forty minutes later, Sheriff Jack Treadway sat beside Ranger Heckle-son at the latter's weather-beaten picnic table, beneath the shade of the hilltop's single tree.

"That oughta do part one," said the sheriff. "Not quite open and shut—not 'til the paperwork's done."

"Ain't what y'all might call an officer-involved shootin', I guess," said Heckleson.

"Can't get that dog to hunt, since you're retired and all," Jack agreed. "So, we'll have to edit-out the 'officer-involved' prefix and focus on the 'shooting' part. You can shuffle over yonder and trade places with Trini-dad so's Madge can do your second field interview. Or would you rather have her and me trade places?"

"Tarnation," the old ranger sputtered. "You're over-cookin' my grits. Wish you'd quit treatin' me like a baby. I ain't the one that got shot and I ain't under the influence of no mental breakdown neither. I'm fit as a dollar and sound as a fiddle. So, naturally, I'm able to stand on my own two feet and walk across my own damn yard to talk to the lieutenant. Consarn-it, I wish I'd kept my badge. Maybe then y'all wouldn't be dead-set on coddlin' me like a gull-darn civilian!"

Heckleson scrambled to his feet and stomped through his dust-dry yard in the direction of Madge Oxford who sat on the hood of her patrol car. The summer heat was palpable and the practical deputy had wisely parked next to the house in the only other patch of shade on the hilltop. On his way, the old ranger passed Trinidad, who was walking across to interview with Jack.

"Do your worst," said the old ranger when he arrived and drew himself up to stand before the waiting officer. "Don't think I don't know the drill: split up me and Trinidad and conduct your blamed two-man interviews out of ear-shot of one another. Do y'all have to treat me like a blessed perp?"

"And good afternoon to you too," said Madge as she pulled out her notebook. "Let's start with the spelling of your name and your date of birth."

From across the yard, Jack and Trinidad stood for a moment watching the lieutenant defuse the blustering ranger. Then the sheriff did his duty.

"You know the drill, Slick" he told the detective.

"Yeah-boy," said Trinidad.

As he outwardly cooperated with the interview, the detective's internal thoughts focused on whether and when he was going to report the day's events to his fiancée.

Anne had left her husband-to-be in Ranger Heckleson's care. Trinidad guessed that her vision of his bachelor party didn't include the two of them almost getting their heads blown off by a drug-addled triggerman.

Probably this can wait, Trinidad convinced himself.

Annie might read in the paper about an ongoing investigation of the theft and dismantling of a sailboat and gunplay in the 'Dobies. But it would be sometime before, without his say-so, she connected the dots. He decided to go with the spirit of one of Ranger Heckleson's misaligned proverbs.

Let sleeping dogs make their own beds, the old ranger might recommend and Trinidad was inclined to agree.

At last, the sheriff, the lieutenant, and the coroner's crew wound their way down off Heckleson Hill and started out across the dry landscape. The old ranger and the young detective stood on the edge of the lofty acreage and watched the patrol car and ambulance caravan recede into the afternoon.

"Should'a seen it comin'," Heckleson decided. "Should'a called in Jack the first time somebody shot up my backdoor screen. Put it down as an accident since the first blast came from far-off and only-just tickled the wire. Never expected somebody to climb the stairs to finish the job."

"I'm guessing you've had a previous run-in with these characters," Trinidad suggested as the two men walked back to the house.

"Warned them off earlier," said the ranger. "Two weeks ago, they was carvin' donuts in the flats by my lower gate—sprayin' rocks on my fence. They was higher than kites that day, carryin' on bold as brass in an old pickup with a gun rack in the back window and a whole crapload of attitude. Then their truck and trailer disappeared. Then it showed up again. Then that old trailer-house exploded and dissolved one night in a hail of debris. Hoped it was alcohol—knowed it was meth—should'a seen it." he repeated.

When they reached the backstairs, Trinidad's phone vibrated with a text from Jack.

"Madge and Jack just now arrested the accomplice," he told the old ranger. "Found him wandering in the 'Dobies with no shirt or shoes. Says he was running from the clear-sky thunder and wondered could they take him someplace safe."

"Meth," the ranger and the detective said in unison.

Chapter 19

Rick O'Shay
2019/1:30 p.m. on June 8

"Reminds me of what my old daddy used to say," said Ranger Heckleson as he settled back onto the porch, ignoring the dark blood stain. "When me and him used to drive backroads lookin' to serve a warrant, he'd say to me, 'This be the kind'a road where *ricochet* might live.' As a kid, I thought he was talkin' about some fella first name of 'Rick' and last name of 'O'Shay.' And I'd peek over the top of the old Ford's dashboard expectin' to see some kind of gun-totin' Irishman. That ain't what he meant, of course. What he meant was we was out in the sticks all on our own and might likely get shot at." The old ranger laughed and might have choked had Trinidad not rushed inside and returned with a tumbler of water.

"So," Trinidad said as he waited for his host to regain his equilibrium, "despite what you told the others, you're not exactly okay."

"My mouth is dry as dust and I'm shakin' see?" Heckleson admitted. "Been a long time since I killed a man for any reason. Self-defense ain't all it's cracked up to be. Stand your ground is good as a slogan, but when y'all take a man down it ain't the cakewalk the movies and stories make it out to be. I don't," he assured Trinidad, "have to tell you what I mean. Or do I? Is it true what Jack told me once that y'all ain't never killed a man dead?"

"It's true," Trinidad confirmed.

"Not even in this-here 2006 caper that your goin' on about?"

"Not even then," the detective assured his host.

"Damn," said the old ranger. "Well, that's something to be proud of when I think of all the sidewinders you've tangled with over these years. Jack has told me some rip-snortin' stories to be sure, but not this Grand Lake tale as I recall. Why is that, I wonder, whereas y'all and him is such amigos?"

"Never came up, I guess," said Trinidad.

"Hmm," Heckleson wondered. "I don't suppose you're anyway near windin' up your story."

"Just getting started," said Trinidad. "Now, where was I?"

"Seems to me you'll be at the point where one twin is hidin'—least his brother thinks so."

"That's where I left off all right," Trinidad agreed. "I'll pick up the thread of my tale if you serve the cheesecake pie."

"Reckon that'll be our just desserts and just what the doctor ordered," Heckleson decided.

Seated again at the kitchen table, Trinidad dug into his pie and reignited his narrative. "As I said," the detective recalled, "I was willing to accept the notion that an old man with an active imagination had impersonated his brother, survived a cabin avalanche, invented a party-crashing bear, and curiously aggravated the situation by voluntarily disappearing."

"Speakin' of which," the ranger interrupted, "won't that pretty young *fancy* of yours be wonderin' whether her man has up and disappeared?"

Hearing Heckleson's mispronunciation of fiancée, Trinidad suppressed a smile before he answered, "Annie said she wasn't expecting me back home until after midnight and, just for luck, so's I don't see the bride before the nuptials, she has me sleeping in the neighbor's bunkhouse. So, I doubt I'll be missed unless I oversleep my wedding day."

"That gal is a pistol," Heckleson laughed. "The day's still young, son, and it looks to me like your Annie has gave you a free pass to forge on ahead. So, make tracks, let her rip, and let's make hay while the moonshines."

"You want me to continue my story?" Trinidad ventured.

"Didn't I just say so?"

Chapter 20

Marina
2006/Late Morning on October 2

Back in 2006, the antique station wagon which passed for a Grand Lake taxi arrived at the Walrus Coffee Barn and tooted its vintage horn. The two men bused their cups and saucers, waved goodbye to the bubbling barista, and climbed onboard.

"Traveling about once again I see," the driver said while he fiddled with his dashboard GPS. His accent suggested he wasn't a native.

"How do you mean?" Buster Bishop asked.

"Saul?" the driver queried as he turned to regard his backseat passengers. "Wasn't it only yesterday that I left you and your company at the dock?"

"Wrong brother," Buster informed the confused man. "And what company do you mean?"

"I—" the driver began. "Say, are you positive you're not Saul?"

"I ought to know who the hell I am!" Buster shot back—his tone impatient. "Where the hell did you take my brother and who's this company he was with?"

Wheeling down the hillside, the driver reported that he'd driven Saul and his unnamed companion out of town yesterday. The lengthy trip had taken them several miles beyond Grand Lake on Highway 34, then down a winding pavement to reach the Shadow Mountain boat dock.

"Took him and that curious-looking fellow so far out I had to roll the odometer over thrice," the driver said with a lilt that suggested he was a refugee from somewhere in the United Kingdom. "Expecting a cold front, says I to Saul's hulking companion—making conversation as I was curious why he was dressed as he was in that fur-bound suit.

"Eyes on the road, snarls my passenger," the driver recalled. "And not a word from you—pardon I mean to say no comment from Saul himself. Sitting close they was like peas in the proverbial pod. Like—I thought to myself—a spooning young couple, shoulder-to-shoulder, hips touching, like a bloody pair of Siamese twins—begging your pardon, no offense intended."

"None taken," said Buster. "We're identical and close, but nothing like a sideshow type of link-up. You're sure that Saul, my talkative brother, said nary a word?"

"Not a syllable," the driver began. "Wait—I tell a lie—he did say something. He said 'ouch' two or three times whenever I took a corner sharp. My old shocks are a bit dodgy. So, the sway of each corner caused my chummy passengers to collide even closer. 'Ouch' the old man said, like somebody was poking him in the ribs. It was a puzzle. The over-dressed gent, a good three heads taller than his elderly companion. And Saul sitting all stiff and silent like a wooden doll, pinned beside this giant panda of a man. Most curious it was."

Hearing this, Trinidad reached forward to tap the driver on the shoulder and said, "Shadow Mountain."

"Go there again?" the driver asked.

"Yes," Trinidad confirmed. "And step on it."

It took twelve highway minutes to reach the turn-off. Then came another quarter of an hour spent snaking along a narrow stretch of pavement stuck behind and unable to pass a lumbering Winnebago. Throughout the trip, the driver kept up a running, albeit one-sided, conversation. When at last the taxi reached the end of the ambling road which led to the marina at Shadow Mountain Reservoir, Trinidad and Buster were fully versed on the weather and the driver's native Wales.

Suspecting the worst, the two anxious passengers hurriedly disembarked and split up. While the station wagon idled in the parking lot, the meter stuck on fifteen miles but ticking off the wait minutes like a runaway train, the younger man searched the slips and Buster knocked on doors. But whatever trail Saul and his furry companion had left behind had become icy cold.

One fisherman and two merchants recalled seeing the odd couple—a big man wearing an unseasonably heavy fur coat walking briskly and holding an old-timer by the arm. The two might have boarded a boat—the unreliable witnesses suggested.

"Or they might have mounted a silver-plated ramp and climbed into a flying saucer," Buster grumbled.

"Kidnapped?" Trinidad ventured.

"Looks like," Buster admitted, his voice taut with emotion. "But why? I gotta sit down. I gotta think."

Trinidad glanced toward the waiting station wagon. "I'd better call off our cab," he said. "We'll get ourselves back some other way. There's a shuttle bus, I think. Meanwhile, I'll pay our driver off."

"Wait, son. Give me your arm," Buster requested. "I'm about tuckered out and I'm sweating like a Thanksgiving roast—I need to take this infernal bandage off and I gotta sit down."

The advancing day compelled the pair to seek shade. Locating a bench beneath a sheltering pine, Trinidad eased Buster down. Protected from the sun, the old timer removed his head bandage, then slumped in place and closed his eyes while Trinidad crossed the lot to dismiss the driver. He was relieved to discover he had just enough cash to settle the fare with no chance of leaving a tip.

"No worries," said the driver as he prepared a receipt. "Will the old timer be all right?" he asked.

"Mr. Bishop has had a shock," said Trinidad, "and so have I."

"I see," said the driver even though his pensive look suggested he *did not* see.

"Bishop and his brother were separated when their cabin caved in," Trinidad explained. "I just this morning learned they're twins. Until you drove up, Buster believed his mischievous brother was playing hide-and-seek. Now things look different. Do you remember anything else about the ride over here with the big man and the brother?"

The driver frowned in concentration.

"An absolute blank I'm afraid," he admitted. "Ordinarily I'm known as Wesley the Chatty Welshman—for my loquacious habit of keeping up both sides of the conversation even when my customers are silent—especially on long jaunts. I watch for clues, of course. I'm a master at studying faces in my rearview mirror. If I see friendly eyes, I keep up my palaver. Otherwise, I'm a clam. Take this trip just now. I could see that you two were a good audience, so I held forth. Yesterday was an entirely different story. The big man caught me glancing in my mirror and didn't have to tell me twice to keep my eyes on the road. Menacing he was."

"Could he have been holding the older man captive?" Trinidad posed the question.

"Captive?" the driver scoffed. "What an idea. Surely Saul would have—" He hesitated, mulling it over, then continued. "Now that you mention it— it was odd how they exited."

"In what way?" Trinidad asked.

"I'm tempted to say that the big man more-or-less pushed Saul out while also keeping hold of his arm—not helping really—more like controlling his movements. The big man paid with a fifty, refused the change, and told me to get lost. I shot a glance at Saul and seemed to see something in his eyes—"

"Something in his eyes?" Trinidad prompted.

"Fear," the driver decided. "Saul was definitely afraid. You see things driving a hack. I recall now that I was about to call it in—notify the police, you know—when the dispatcher summoned me back to town to pick up another fare. So, I stifled the urge and went about my business. Should I make that call for help now?"

"That," said Trinidad, "as you might say, would be a capital idea."

Chapter 21

Sirens
2006/Noon on October 2

Buster had fallen asleep on his shady bench and Trinidad was reluctant to wake him, but sirens were approaching. Undoubtedly, the authorities would have questions.

It was then that Trinidad smelled the smoke—an overwhelming sensation which pulled his attention away from the hastening emergency vehicles. Turning toward the water, he could see a distant cascade of billows rising into the sky above the reservoir.

"Budge up," shouted the driver as he left his station wagon and rushed toward the shore. "Looks as if someone's made a dog's breakfast of yonder knoll!"

With sirens and flashing lights converging on the marina, there wasn't time to request a translation, but Trinidad understood the general meaning of the Welshman's remarks.

Something was wrong, very wrong, on the far side of the reservoir.

Chapter 22

Tower
2006/Noon on October 2

Jackhammer Marsh lay face down on the damp ground, his spotty beard mingling with the soggy tundra, snatches of half-remembered pop tunes pulsating in his head. The changeable autumn weather, featuring early snow followed by unseasonable sunshine, had turned the meadow beneath the burning lookout tower into a muddy stew of dirt and alpine vegetation. His frantic flight to avoid the flames had carried him headlong down the tower's wooden stairway until he reached a coffin corner, crashed through the second-story railing, and plummeted to the ground below.

He felt lucky to be alive until he remembered what a shithole his life was. He surrendered to his anger and that raw emotion compelled him to rise. Standing unsteadily, the huge man patted his arms and torso, checking for broken bones. His chest ached and one elbow was sore, but he seemed largely unharmed. He'd fallen far enough to kill a lesser man, but not nearly far enough to wound a giant, let alone a giant swathed in the protective cocoon of a head-to-heels buffalo coat.

The coat was huge and warm, but his naked fingers were cold. So was his exposed bald head. He was seeking his fallen skull cap and biker's bandanna when he literally stumbled across the old man's body, also lying prone, a few feet away, also hatless, like himself, but not alive.

"Piss," Jackhammer growled. *Why does everything have to be such a hassle?* He asked himself.

His plan—his meticulously plotted revenge—had seemed so simple. Find the one who'd ruined his life. Make the old weasel tell where the treasure was hidden. Make him suffer like Jackhammer had suffered. Make him pay.

Finding the old man had been easier than he'd imagined. It only took one phone call to discover that his nemesis was not only still alive, but also holed-up at the lodge where it had all happened. Grand County Sheriff Bishop—Buster Bishop, known as Red to his friends—hadn't left town. The man had grown older, of course, so had Jackhammer—no thanks to the officious sheriff. Red Bishop was no longer handsome. Neither was Jackhammer, but Jackhammer's looks hadn't been eroded over time in the mellow descent that comes to all men as they gradually age. Jackhammer's looks had been snatched away in a single flash—extinguished forever—never to return.

Jackhammer reached out with his good hand to prod the crumpled body, feeling the contours of the familiar letter jacket, once worn with pride, now soiled and blood-stained. There was a slim chance the old man might have survived the fall. There was an infinitesimal possibility that his prisoner remained alive to answer one final question. But even as Jackhammer's searching fingers probed the prostrate form, the old biker knew it was hopeless. He'd missed his chance and now the world was once again on fire.

Leaning back to view the tower above, he studied the burning structure. The flareup had been brief but savage. When the dislodged kerosene lamp crashed to the floor, the combustible wood had ignited with the rush of a runaway dumpster fire. The wood had been instantly consumed and the smoldering remnants were pouring smoke aloft. The exterior railing had escaped untouched, as had the stone substructure. It was as if the topmost reaches of the flaming tower and the untouched ground below existed in two separate universes.

In a reversal of scripture, the celestial heavens seemed to burn while, here on the ground, the underworld was uncharred. But it was all the same to Jackhammer. Wherever he roamed, high or low, his world stayed the same—wherever he was, it was always hell.

The sound of sirens reached him from across the water.

Time to move, he told himself.

He found his skull cap. He'd have to leave the bandanna behind.

Time to disappear—for now.

Chapter 23

Point-of-View
2019/2 p.m. on June 8

"Hold on a piece," Ranger Heckleson interrupted the detective's story. "How-come do y'all have any notion of what this-here Jackhammer character was feelin' and thinkin' with yourself so far off from his point-of-view, as in clear over on the other side of that-there big reservoir."

"It's a fair question," Trinidad acknowledged. "Can you trust me 'til nearer the end when all will be revealed? Or would you rather I stop talking now and resume my story after the wedding. You'd have to wait until after the honeymoon too, of course, you know how things go."

"Tarnation," Heckleson sputtered. "If y'all think I'll just sit up here on pigs and needles, twiddlin' my thumbs until you and your new bride get back from your honeymoon, you're barkin' up the wrong tree house. Let's move on fer now and I'll hold my tongue."

"You want me to go on with my story?" the detective asked.

"Didn't I just say so?"

"Okay," Trinidad said. "Let me move my story back across the water to the marina and the arrival of emergency vehicles. You can, I'm sure, imagine the chaos."

"Been witness at many a crime scene, so—if I'd been back there in 2006—it surely wouldn't have been my very first rodeo," the old ranger declared. "But let's hear your version, could be I'll learn somethin' new."

Chapter 24

First Responders
2006/Afternoon on October 2

The cab-driver's 911 call had alerted authorities to an instance of elder abuse plus a possible kidnapping. That initial call was followed by a subsequent notice of smoke being spotted on the Shadow Mountain hilltop and the two messages had gotten tangled, causing lawmen and firemen to converge at the identical map coordinates. The whole armada had been obliged to negotiate the same meandering pavement which had slowed the progress of the taxi. It was a passage which was made all the more arduous when the advancing firetrucks and patrol cars encountered the same Winnebago driver who, upon reaching the cramped marina and discovering no place to park, had turned around and started back toward the highway.

By the time the emergency vehicles crept past the rolling roadblock, the fire on the far ridge had run its course. A slurry helicopter arrived, dipped its cable-tethered monsoon bucket into the reservoir, hovered over the site, and drenched the barely smoldering lookout tower with 2,000 gallons of icy water.

"Sheriff there?" the 'copter pilot's voice inquired on the shared frequency. "Affirmative," was the response.

"Copy that," the pilot replied. "Best send him over. No place to touch down and looks to be a body on the ground, over."

"Say again."

"Fire out. Body on ground at base of tower. Do you copy?"

"Copy. Fire out. Body at tower. Will respond. Out."

A Forest Service utility boat serving the marina was dispatched to ferry a crew to the burn site. Sheriff Al Crosswind, a deputy, two paramedics, a hotshot team, and a coroner technician went over on the first load.

The boat was back a half hour later.

"Sheriff says to bring the brother," the deputy informed Trinidad. "You a relation?"

"Not exact—" Trinidad began.

"My caregiver," Buster lied. "Where I go, he goes."

"Fair enough," said the deputy. "Suit up."

Trinidad helped Buster cinch-up a life jacket.

"Stay close, care-giver," Buster whispered. "If it's Saul over there, I'm for certain sure gonna need a truckload of care."

Chapter 25

Brother
2006/Mid-Afternoon on October 2

When the utility boat reached the far shore, Trinidad was not surprised to see the official watercraft making use of Ferryman's clandestine dock. He and Buster were disembarked, relieved of their life jackets, and told to wait.

Twenty minutes later, Buster Bishop leaned hard on Trinidad as they watched a coroner crew descend the steep trail which connected the shore and the lookout tower. Three burly men were struggling downhill, one on each end of a modified stretcher and the third man walking alongside, straining to keep the conveyance upright. One of the men was a deer hunter who'd welded rods and pipes together to create a collapsible carrier designed to transport an animal carcass from a lofty kill site to a distant hunting camp. The thing was an elongated device, a kind of curved metal ladder, which resembled a traditional stretcher with the exception of a descending shaft in the middle on which a pushcart wheel was mounted. The single wheel bounced along the uneven ground, bearing the weight of the cargo, but also jostling the load.

Stopping a discrete distance from those waiting on the shore, the cart-bearers paused while Buster shuffled forward to identify his brother. Then the crew gently transferred Saul's blanketed body from the teetering cart to a zippered body bag. Lifting Buster's late brother and strapping the body to a rugged rolling gurney, the trio of first responders wheeled their sad burden over the gangway to reach the waiting utility boat.

"Do you think they'll let us walk back on our own?" the old man asked.

"You sure?" Trinidad wondered. "It's a fair hike to go all the way around."

"I need to show you something," the surviving brother insisted.

"If you're up to it," Trinidad sounded skeptical.

"I've got all day," said Buster. "Nothing ahead for me now except figuring out how to get my brother into the ground and that I ain't looking forward to. A walk in the woods is what I need right now, if you're game."

Trinidad relayed Buster's request, but Sheriff Crosswind was reluctant.

"Even cutting my senile predecessor some slack," the sheriff said, "it's a stretch to delay my investigation while Red goes for a stroll in the trees."

"It's a big ask, I know," Trinidad agreed as he favored the lawman with his most charming smile. "But I'll have him back by dark, if you can see your way clear to giving him a few hours to mull things over."

"I ain't impressed by your schoolboy logic, kid," the sheriff said with a tone that suggested he was intent on needling the young man standing before him. "Too damn many loose ends to let you two go off and tramp on your own through the remote landscape of our Arapahoe National Forest," the sheriff decided. "If I wasn't so busy here, I'd wipe that grin off your face and send you home to your mama."

The sheriff stared hard at Trinidad. The impolite lawman was obviously trying to get a rise out of the inexperienced concierge, but Trinidad didn't take the bait. The overbearing officer held his gaze a moment longer before backing off.

"I'll grant Red's wish, but only if my armed deputy goes along." He summoned the junior officer to his side. "Woody, I'm sending you overland to keep an eye on Red and this young pedestrian. Are we clear? Don't screw this up. Now, move your butt. Grab some water from the boat," he told his deputy. "And hustle back."

When Trinidad revealed the sheriff's plan to assign them an escort, it was Buster Bishop's turn to express reluctance.

"I already got you for a nursemaid," he complained. "What do I need with two nannies?"

"One nanny and a bodyguard," the returning deputy corrected.

"Which is which?" Buster retorted.

The old man proved to be a strong hiker, setting a pace which left the portly deputy behind.

"What's your hurry?" Trinidad asked as they rounded a bend and reached what appeared to be a small pile of discarded lumber. The wood was weathered and nearly indistinguishable from the surrounding terrain.

"Remember this spot!" Buster shouted.

"What—?" Trinidad began, but the old man signaled for silence as the deputy emerged from the trees.

"You jackrabbits need to slow down," the deputy panted. "I'm supposed to be watching after you two, not competing for pole-position."

"Just stretching my legs," said Buster. "But I think I overdid it. Can you call for a ride on that thing?" He pointed to the deputy's lapel radio.

"You don't mean we should go all the way back to the shore?" the deputy complained.

"Shorter than going around," Buster suggested.

"Hold on," the deputy sputtered. He gave the pair a withering look and, shaking his head, walked a short distance away as he fired up his radio to seek instructions.

"I don't think we're making any friends out here," Trinidad noted.

"Ain't hiking out here to make friends," Buster whispered. "Out here trying to get one step ahead of the enemy."

"Who are we talking about?" Trinidad asked.

"Somebody's been following us since we left the shoreline," Buster whispered as he zipped open his jacket to display a soiled bandanna. "The ambulance boys gave me this thinking it was Saul's. I know these damn colors and the varmint's still on our trail—don't you feel it, son?"

Trinidad looked cautiously around and ventured a guess.

"Your brother's bear?"

"Seems likely," Buster whispered as the deputy returned. "And here comes the only reason you and I ain't dead at this moment."

Chapter 26

Rain

2006/Early Morning on October 10

Eight days passed while Buster mourned his brother. The date set for Saul Berman's last rites proved to be a stormy day. Buster's brother had invested in an out-of-town cemetery plot which meant a road trip in the rain.

"We'll need four more pallbearers," Trinidad said.

"Make it five—I'll be useless in this mud," Buster declared.

"The sun might come out," Trinidad suggested.

"And ruin a perfectly dreadful funeral?" Buster sounded skeptical. "Not likely."

The two men were on their way to the Woody Canyon Funeral Home on the outskirts of the thriving community of Estes Park. It might have been more convenient to conduct the ceremony and burial in the smaller settlement of Grand Lake, but Buster felt obliged to make arrangements to transport his brother's body along Highway 34, up and over the Continental Divide—48 miles in the rain to reach Saul's preferred final resting place in Estes.

Buster had discovered the brochure in his brother's things and, looking at the photo of the Woody Canyon "team," he had a notion that his brother was persuaded to purchase the plot by the attractive female sitting in the front row of the glossy image.

That's Saul all over, he told himself.

The two-hour journey meandered through Rocky Mountain National Park via Trail Ridge Road—America's highest stretch of continuous pavement. The hearse drove slowly, the scenery was spectacular, but the views were lost on the grieving brother.

"Crap," Buster spat out the curse as the hearse topped the 10,759-foot pass and started down toward Estes. He repeated the profane observation six more times during the descent.

"Now there's something you don't see every day," the hearse driver commented as the rooftops of Estes Park appeared on the down-bound highway. When neither of his passengers took up the conversation, the persistent man added, "A bear on a motorcycle—well he *was* there," he insisted as he reached up to adjust his rearview mirror.

"Crap," said Buster.

Despite the pouring rain, Trinidad rolled down the vehicle's rear window and looked behind.

"Nothing there now," he announced.

"I'm telling you he was—" the driver began as he swiveled his head around to evaluate Trinidad's viewpoint.

"Red light!" cautioned Trinidad as the hearse skidded to a stop.

"Watch where you're driving," Buster complained. "Or do you get paid extra for delivering three corpses?"

Chapter 27

Recruits
2006/Mid-Morning on October 10

"How do you imagine these sissified gents take a piss," Buster Bishop whispered.

"A fair question," Trinidad agreed. "But beggars can't be choosers."

"I reckon not," Buster replied. "Anyway, I guess today's edition of *Ride the Rockies* is up a creek anyhow."

"Shouldn't ride a bike in the mountains in this downpour I imagine," Trinidad noted.

The two mourners were sitting side-by-side in the straight-backed, hard-as-nails wooden pews of Estes Park's Woody Canyon Funeral Home.

"Should we slip these guys a couple of bucks?"

"Already taken care of," Trinidad announced.

"Pay you back?" Buster speculated.

"Instead of money, I'll take some of your famous ribs, baked up in that barrel contraption of yours," Trinidad suggested.

"Okay, ribs it is, plus also some cash," Buster insisted. "You ain't been at work for going on a week am I right?"

"Eight days off the clock," Trinidad confirmed.

"That's a chunk of change for being absent," the old man guessed. "I imagine you ain't getting paid for them missed days."

"Luckily, I work nights," his young companion joked. "Seriously, I'll get by."

"Speaking of getting by, how's things working out—you bunking with Bambi I mean?"

"Word spreads fast, I guess," Trinidad blushed.

"Small town, big ears," Buster ventured. "That sweet gal sure looks good in black," he added as Bambi glided past and slid smoothly into the pew just behind the cyclists.

"Ain't that the truth?" Trinidad agreed.

Someone pulled the plug on the funeral home's recorded organ music. In the abrupt silence, the mortician seemed to magically materialize as he made his way toward the lectern where he pivoted awkwardly to survey the essentially empty room.

"Looks like you're on. You up for this?" Trinidad asked.

"Glad our Ma ain't alive for this send-off," Buster sniffed. Clutching his eulogistic remarks—three modest sentences hastily scrawled on a wrinkled index card—the old man tried to stand. "Give us a hand, son," he requested.

Trinidad helped Buster up wondering to himself whether his frail companion could possibly be the same octogenarian who, just days ago, had led a Grand County deputy on a merry chase through the forest. Clinging to Trinidad's stout arm, Buster tottered toward a broad wooden podium where the mortician stood stiff as a proverbial two-by-four. Nodding tautly, the rigid man offered his clammy hand and uttered a clipped mumbled sentence which might have been a symptom of gastric distress or an offer of condolence. Nodding to the mortician, Trinidad deposited Buster at the podium, then took a seat beside the cyclists.

"I'm the oldest," Buster told his sparse but attentive audience. "I should have looked out for Saul better. Should have watched out better for my little brother."

Following the old man's remarks, the ceremony was short and sweet. The clergyman on-call turned out to be a retired soccer referee who was also a talented soloist. His rendition of "The Sun'll Come Out Tomorrow" seemed to touch an emotional nerve with everyone, including the recruited cyclists whose skin-tight togs had inspired Buster to wonder aloud how the athletes could manage the task of urinating. To their credit, the young men did a fine job. There were six of them, all impossibly lean except for one chunky rider —a Frenchman whom the others referred to as "their Clydesdale."

The half-dozen idled riders had truly seemed charmed when Trinidad approached them with the idea of serving as impromptu pallbearers. Though clad in outlandishly colorful outfits, the crew was appropriately reverent throughout the service and incredibly steady while bearing the casket. They moved gracefully, like a well-calibrated machine, despite having to maneuver in their wonky road-cycling shoes. Even the staccato clicking of six pairs of stiff-soled, cleat-slotted, footwear on the funeral home's linoleum seemed fitting as the earnest young men strode down the aisle in unison. The recruits carried Saul's mortal remains steadily onward, their coordinated progress marking a perfect cadence in time with the organist, who—consistent with Buster's wishes—enlivened the processional by performing an upbeat instrumental rendition of Ben E. King's "Stand by Me."

Invited to rise by the taciturn mortician, Buster, Bambi, and Trinidad followed Saul's coffin as the procession passed through the funeral parlor's double-wide entryway and down damp external stairs. Outside, the rain had vanished and, in its place, an incandescent rainbow shimmered in the brightening sky.

"Everything but flowers," Buster sniffed. "Just as well," he added. "Saul's fiercely allergic, you know."

Interment in Estes proved to be the most practical decision—far better than a return trip over Trail Ridge where, a passing motorist assured them, snowflakes were beginning to fall even as Saul's body was transported to the cemetery. The way snaked along Fish Hatchery Road. The dead man's sparse entourage included the hearse bearing Trinidad, the living twin, and the doppelganger corpse; Bambi following in the shared Mustang; and the six cyclists crammed into the funeral home's trailing mini-van.

When the procession reached the cemetery's wrought-iron portico and passed beneath, Trinidad wondered to himself how many casual visitors over the years had followed the signs to Estes Greens expecting to arrive at a golf course rather than a graveyard.

Estes Greens wasn't the only cemetery in the mountain town, but it was the vintage boneyard and the one furthest from Elkhorn Avenue—the town's main drag. Its out-of-the-way location placed it far from the hullabaloo of downtown Estes where wandering crowds of tourists ran the retail gauntlet of taffy-shops, souvenir vendors, and caramel corn hawkers. In contrast to the hustle and bustle of Elkhorn Avenue, Estes Greens was a sedate haven which, true to its name, was inhabited by buffalo grass, sagebrush, ferns, and other flora which exhibited shades of mint, emerald, jade, tea, and avocado green. The place was a veritable Eden surrounded on all sides by the towering branches of conifer, juniper, and ponderosa. Here and there, this riot of vegetation was interrupted by stately marble obelisks, weathered pillars of bronze, and rows of modest granite headstones arrayed in ranks and files like silent sentinels.

When Saul's mortal remains were lowered into his freshly excavated grave, Buster knelt heavily down to palm a handful of dirt which he dropped onto the descended coffin.

"A little help," the old man requested as he reached up to solicit Trinidad's strong arm to regain his feet. Buster stood at rigid attention while, one by one, the pallbearers shook his hand and offered their condolences.

"Let me stay here a while," Buster said.

Trinidad left the old man at the graveside, perched on a folding chair. He watched a moment to make certain Buster was okay, then joined the departing cyclists to walk toward the vehicles. Leaving Buster alone turned out to be a mistake—one that Trinidad nearly regretted for the rest of his life.

Chapter 28

Error
2019/2:05 p.m. on June 8

Thinking back to that near-fatal error, Trinidad halted his story and fell silent.

"The bear strikes again?" Ranger Heckleson guessed.

"Yeah," Trinidad confirmed, "the dad-burned bear strikes again."

Chapter 29

Ghost
2006/Late Morning on October 10

Jackhammer Marsh considered himself a ghost.

Which is to say that, despite his enormous physique, he thought of himself as invisible. The alternative was unthinkable. Which is why he believed he could stand so near the Estes Park grave site without being noticed.

Invisible. Invincible. Invisible. Invincible.

This silent mantra permeated Jackhammer's thoughts as the brightly colored cyclists paraded past his position. If any of the departing personalities noticed the giant man, clad as he was in an unseasonable buffalo robe, they didn't acknowledge the presence of the apparition.

Perhaps Jackhammer's dark outfit blended with the shadowy bark of the sheltering ponderosa pine trees behind which he obscured his hulking torso. The trunks were thick and close, forming a windbreak along Fish Hatchery Road and marking the edge of the remote Estes Park cemetery. Perhaps the departing mourners thought he was a canker or a malformed burl, a bulging growth, a dead thing affixed to the living wood.

Then again, maybe he *was* invisible.

Looking back, even Trinidad passed within shouting distance of the villain, yet failed to notice the man. And the fledging concierge, who was beginning to think of himself as Buster Bishop's protector, categorically failed to comprehend the danger.

Chapter 30

Acorn
2019/2:10 p.m. on June 8

"Missed sensing the danger totally, absolutely, and utterly," Trinidad admitted.

Ranger Heckleson was sympathetic.

"A blind pig can't be blamed if he don't find an acorn every time," the old ranger observed.

"Nice of you to say so," Trinidad said as he favored his host with his patented smile.

"I can be nice," Heckleson assured his guest. "I'm passable nice some of the most of the time. But don't keep me on edge, son. I'm like some cat on a hot tinker's dam to hear what comes next in your story."

"I'm going to continue things from Jackhammer's point-of-view and, to do that, I'll need to turn the calendar back a bit," said Trinidad. "You okay with all that?"

"Full-steam ahead and damn the tomatoes," Heckleson declared.

Chapter 31

Sidecar
2005/Afternoon on December 6

Ten months before his October 2006 trip to Grand Lake to pursue his revenge, Jackhammer Marsh was sufficiently lucid to desire a spin on his Harley-Davidson. It had been years since he'd felt the urge. His misfortunes had scarred him. Two decades in prison had humbled him.

"Ride the wind," his prison shrink had told him during his transition counseling.

"What's your heart's desire?" she'd prompted him.

"Screwing what's-her-name from *Baywatch*," he'd responded.

"Not your fantasy," she chided. "I want to know your fondest wish."

When the soon-to-be-released prisoner didn't respond, she tried another tact.

"What do you most look forward to doing this time next week?"

"I—I want to ride my Hog," he answered.

"Another sexual fantasy?" she grinned.

"I mean my motorcycle—my Harley—I want to ride my Harley. I want to feel the wind."

"Now we're getting somewhere. That's the spirit. Go out, Francis, and ride the wind!"

Jackhammer nodded. There was a time when he would have killed anybody who called him by his odious given name. He couldn't kill Doc Juno, of course. After some casual research in the prison library, he'd discovered that Juno was a goddess. That about summed up his dreamboat of a prison psychiatrist. Doc Juno was the only woman, excepting his mother and sisters, whom he respected. It was not that he completely disrespected women. He simply had no use for them. And, given the stark reality of his ruined face, he imagined the feeling was mutual.

As for his mother and sisters, where his family had gone remained a mystery. They just up and left one day. They were there in the morning at breakfast and then everybody was gone along with their clothes and most of the household appliances which were not nailed down. Everything except the toaster. No note. No nothing. Their unexpected departure had occurred when he still had his looks. Now that his looks were history, they wouldn't recognize him.

Catching himself ruminating about the past, Jackhammer sighed. 2005 was drawing to a close. He was out of prison, but he'd yet to feel anything like freedom. Moping in the confines of his cramped two-room house, he might as well be back in his constricted cell. His desire to ride his Harley represented the first spark in his painfully slow reintegration into society. How had that desire morphed into a weird combination of rehashing his prison counseling sessions and speculation about his missing family? Just goes to show how the troubled mind can wander.

Focus, he told himself as he rummaged through the drawer of his bedside table. He couldn't seem to turn up the key to the shed which served as his garage. Frustrated by his lack of progress, he expanded his search to include every inch of his tiny house.

While he looked high and low for the mislaid key, despite his best efforts to remain in the moment, his addled mind strayed to his time in prison and he cursed.

"Crap-a-rama," he growled. "Double-crap-a-rama."

His restrained language, a remnant of having to suppress his profanity in the presence of Doc Juno, would have entertained his former cellmates. During his twenty-six years, three-hundred-and-forty days as a guest of the State of Texas, he'd shared space with fifteen different convicts. In prison for more than two decades, he'd had plenty of time to study the Texas Code of Criminal Procedure. He knew the relevant citation by heart: 42.1, subsection 3g. Also known, among prisoners, as simply "3G," penitentiary shorthand which translated as "aggravated assault."

Jackhammer remembered the name of his victim even though he'd completely forgotten the man's face. It'd been a dark night and Jackhammer had turned the tables on Imago Cognito, a rival gang member who'd tried to ambush him. He'd acted in self-defense, but the jury didn't see it that way. Red Bishop's testimony about Jackhammer's role as leader of a lawbreaking biker gang had sealed the deal. The assault verdict was a powerful reason to hate his so-called victim and also the inspiration for the big man's grudge against the Grand County sheriff.

When he'd arrived at the penitentiary, Jackhammer had been hot for revenge. His ire was sufficiently vigorous to encompass both Red Bishop and Imago Cognito. As far as the huge convict was concerned, both men were equally to blame. If Imago hadn't shoehorned his way into Jackhammer's life and hadn't filled Jackhammer's head with the notion of riches, there would have been no reason to confront Red Bishop. And if Bishop hadn't stuck his oar in, Jackhammer might have skated by with a more lenient sentence. If those things hadn't happened, Jackhammer would still have his looks and his freedom.

Adding insult to injury, both men had shown up to put the skids on Jackhammer's parole hearing. While the years stretched out, Jackhammer nurtured his thirst for vengeance, dividing his ire between the sheriff and the biker. Then came news which honed Jackhammers wrath to a fine point. Cellmate number seven, serving time for wire fraud, had known Imago—grown up with him in Brooklyn, in fact. Seven's report that a motorcycle crash had reduced Imago to a paralyzed husk—a pathetic statue who'd lost all mobility and all faculties save the ability to hear and speak. Imago's fate may have been tragic and yet it freed Jackhammer to concentrate the whole of his wrath on Red Bishop. As for Imago, he'd undoubtedly see the bastard in hell.

"A bad dude," Seven declared. "He didn't prosper for long after you and him tangled. Got what he deserved, for certain."

"Won't be showing up at my next parole hearing, I guess," Jackhammer speculated.

"Not unless they prop him up and bring him to the hearing strapped to a Milwaukee hand-truck," Seven chuckled.

Number Seven was a peach of a guy.

To pass the time in prison, Jackhammer did three things. He studied Texas statutes in the inmates' law library. He pumped iron and he played BINGO. Number Seven was his BINGO partner. The two shared one card. The prizes were pathetic and nonlethal items which could not be fashioned into weapons. Things like stuffed animals and Nerf Balls—the world's original indoor ball. The grand prize was a Nerf Football—something bored and hostile men behind bars would kill for—literally.

Jackhammer and Number Seven never won the top prize.

The big man's fondest memory of each BINGO game occurred halfway through the process when the emcee had already called most of the letter-number sequences. After hearing "B-3, I-19, N-43, G-56, and O-71," Number Seven would wink at his companion and shout out "3G—for pity sakes—call 3G!"

That was always good for a laugh.

Too bad Number Seven was only serving three-to-five with time off for good behavior. Just like his sisters and mother, Jackhammer's hands-down favorite cellmate was there one day and absolutely gone the next.

Focus, Jackhammer admonished himself as, at last, he found the mislaid key and bundled up. Outside, it was a bitter cold December day as he crunched across the snow-covered path which led to the old shed. Anybody who thinks it doesn't snow in Texas would be in for an unpleasant surprise every winter. Reaching the shed, he found the side door ajar. He didn't recall forgetting to latch it.

"And where's the damn padlock?" he asked.

A wave of apprehension swept over the giant man and he felt a lump forming in his throat as he shouldered his way through the narrow doorway.

It was dark inside the shed. Seconds passed before his eyes adjusted. When he could see, he closed them, willing the apparition before him to disappear or, better yet, turn back into what it used to be. But, when he opened his eyes, his motorcycle was still gone. Somehow, some way, and some time somebody had stolen his sturdy vintage Harley and—like a human pack rat—left in its place an unsubstantial Ural.

Cursing in earnest, he pushed the wonky cycle into the winter sunlight thinking he would keep moving for three blocks until he came to the ravine where he'd fling the abomination over. No way was he going to ride the thing—he hadn't sunk that low.

As he pushed along the snowy pavement, a truck slowed. The driver rolled down his window.

"How much?" he inquired.

"Pardon?"

"How much for that little beauty? I won't dicker. I assume it don't start."

Jackhammer ignored the man, but the truck continued to dog his steps.

"Okay," the man said. "You win. Name your price."

"Buzz off," Jackhammer said as he straightened up to his full height.

If the driver was shocked by Jackhammer's appearance, he didn't show it. Instead, from the safety of his vehicle, he suggested this oversized pedestrian with his ruined face and crippled bike do something which was anatomically impossible. Then he hit the gas, fishtailed his truck on the icy street, and roared away.

As Jackhammer struggled on, two more vehicles pulled up and tried to strike a bargain. By the time he reached the ravine, his low opinion of the Ural had evolved from grudging resignation to full-blown admiration.

"Everybody wants it so bad," he reasoned. "Gotta wonder."

Turning back, he re-deposited the Ural in his shed and went inside to think. What did he know about Urals? He guessed this one was from the mid-1960s, a vintage which placed it in the era of his favorite music. Though exotic, the Russian-made machines were fairly dependable motorcycles. Their main design flaw was their balance. They were built to accommodate a sidecar. More to the point, as a street vehicle they were decidedly unstable without the steadying influence of a sidecar. The Ural could be modified, but taking it any distance without the appendage was a risky venture.

From his days as a Merchant Mariner, Jackhammer seemed to remember the saying "holes is holes" which, as he recalled, meant "any port in a storm." Certainly, a storm had upended his life. He had a Bible. One of his more irritating cellmates had tried to convince him that a troubled soul could turn to the holy book for answers. For his money, the Texas statutes held more answers than any scripture. And yet—

"Holes is holes," he told himself.

Securing the Bible from its neglected perch in a seldom visited cupboard, the huge man sat down heavily at his kitchen table and opened to a random page.

His selection fell in the Old Testament and his eyes landed on 1 Kings, Chapter 19, Verse 11 and he read:

"And, behold, the Lord passed by, and a great and strong wind rent the mountains, and brake in pieces the rocks before the Lord; but the Lord was not in the wind: and after the wind an earthquake; but the Lord was not in the earthquake: and after the earthquake a fire; but the Lord was not in the fire; and after the fire a still small voice."

Jackhammer placed his hand on the passage and closed both eyes—listening, he imagined for a still, small voice. He seemed to hear something—as if detecting a distant radio, he sensed the strains of a song from the 1960s—something about a biker and his girlfriend. He couldn't recall the title or the teenybopper lyrics, but he remembered the tune which was punctuated by the sound of a revving engine. He glanced at the kitchen clock. There was still time to do what needed to be done.

Donning his Prickly Pear colors and a mismatched array of cold-weather gear, he returned to the shed. Balancing on the Ural, he started the unfamiliar machine and made his way downtown. As he rode, he was anticipating trouble. His goal was to visit the Anarchy Choppers Cycle Shop in China Berry and ask for the modification. When he did so, somebody might make a wisecrack and that might trigger aggression and that aggression might land him back in prison.

Chill, he told himself.

Arriving on Triple Play Street, he backed the Ural into a parking chute, found the door, and shouldered his way inside. Like everywhere else in his home state, the cycle shop displayed two flags: the 1893 national emblem of the Republic of Texas and the Confederate Stars and Bars.

Moreover, as if to prove that he was definitely still in Texas, every man in the place, workers and mechanics alike, wore the standard uniform: a denim top with the sleeves shorn off to create a southern muscle shirt and tight-fitting rain pants with heavy-duty zippers on pockets and cuffs. For riding the wind, add a vest, a leather jacket, boots, and a helmet and you have an archetypical motorcycle jockey—recognizable worldwide and on most neighboring planets.

Which is why Jackhammer should have attracted attention, clad as he was in his ubiquitous buffalo robe; his bald head swathed in a chartreuse bandanna tie-dyed in shocking shades of avocado and artichoke; his ruined face as pale and gaunt as a cheap Halloween mask; his knee-high camouflaged duck boots squeaking as he lumbered across the concrete floor. Conversation should have ceased as he advanced through the shop interior. Critical eyes should have marked his progress. Somebody should have turned down the raucous country music. But, as Jackhammer made his way through the windowless building, none of that happened.

He remembered thinking, *invisible—invincible.*

Jackhammer spotted the proprietor, a broad-shouldered mountain of a man from West Texas who went by the handle *Spider.* The guy was nearly as tall as Jackhammer with a shaved head and walrus moustache. Keeping one eye on Jackhammer, Spider moved casually toward the stack of pallets which constituted the shop's reception area. His expression suggested that something about the visitor seemed familiar. Everybody knew that Spider prided himself on never forgetting a face. Jackhammer guessed what Spider was thinking.

Probably, he thought, *the big galoot is positive he's never before seen what's left of this particular stranger's face.*

Slipping behind the makeshift desk, the owner and operator of Anarchy Choppers placed both hands on the greasy top and leaned forward. It was a pose which, Jackhammer suspected, meant the cautious man was pressing his crotch against the softball bat hidden there. Held in place by a pair of open-ended motor-mount clips, the uncompromising weapon was always at the ready for easy access. Spider offered the advancing stranger a tooth-gapped grin and, with a barely perceptible riffle of one shaggy eyebrow, he apparently signaled the others to continue going about their business.

"Help you?" Spider inquired.

"Need an after-market sidecar mounted," Jackhammer intoned, keeping his voice low.

"A sidecar?" Spider whispered, adjusting his volume to accommodate his customer. "What're you ridin'?"

"Ural 749cc."

"Model?"

"M-62."

"Two or single-wheel-drive?"

Jackhammer held up two fingers.

"Open sidecar or torpedo?"

"Torpedo."

"Cash?" Spider asked.

"Cash," Jackhammer assured him.

"Care if the color matches?"

"Don't care."

"When?"

"Now."

"Let's see the money."

Chapter 32

Dishes
2019/2:15 p.m. on June 8

"So, the old villain got himself a side-car," said Heckleson. "My recollection is that a Ural cycle ain't worth a tinker's damnation without a side-car—your balance is all cattywampus without it. So, if I was to take notes—which I ain't—is the side-car somethin' I should make a note of?"

"I'll connect the sidecar up after I help you with the dishes," Trinidad promised.

"Well, I gotta say, you've hit on the main limit of my social calendar," the old ranger laughed. "I ain't got enough plates nor cups nor bowls to serve up breakfast *and* lunch *and* supper without which somebody fills the sink and scrubs up. So, if you're game, there's suds juice in the empty beer bottle and a scrub-brush in the coffee can."

"More than happy to help," the detective said. "I'll wash and you dry."

"That's a plan," said Heckleson.

As the two men dealt with the breakfast and lunch dishes, Heckleson whistled a tune and Trinidad hummed along.

"*Camp Town Races*," the old ranger said. "They don't write songs like that no more. Them old songs is the pizza-resistance of the melody world."

"That's for certain," Trinidad agreed.

Contentment ruled the Heckleson kitchen as the two friends worked for a time without speaking until the dishes were thoroughly washed, dried, and organized in the old ranger's no-frills open-faced cupboard.

"Ready for that sidecar?" Trinidad asked.

"Ready," Heckleson answered.

"Okay. Now that we know a bit more about Jackhammer, let's take our story back to 2006 and Saul Berman's interment in a remote Estes Park cemetery."

Chapter 33

Minutes
2006/Late Morning on October 10

From his position in the trees, Jackhammer stared across the October graveyard in the direction of his Ural. Twenty minutes ago, he'd killed the engine to avoid the noise, stealthily pushed the chopper—sidecar and all—uphill for thirty yards, and hidden the motorcycle behind the screening foliage of a lilac bush, a few feet from Saul's freshly dug grave. The lilac blossoms were dead, well past their prime, but still dense enough to conceal the bike.

Then he waited for the others to arrive.

Now that everyone but the old man had come and gone, Jackhammer was on the move. If he could manage the deed unobserved, he'd knock his victim senseless, truss up the old timer, fold the unconscious man into the sidecar, and secure the bonnet in place. The huge man figured it would take five minutes to make Buster Bishop disappear.

He did it in three.

Chapter 34

French
2006/Late Morning on October 10

Trinidad was bidding goodbye to the big bicycling Frenchman—the one his mates had christened "The Clydesdale." He was shaking hands with the man, the last of the pallbearing cyclists to depart the cemetery, when he heard the unmistakable rumble of a motorcycle springing to life. Both men turned to look in the direction of the sound at the same moment the speeding Ural came barreling along the graveled roadway. Bearing down on the astonished pair, the careening cycle forced the men apart and barely missed striking them as it roared past. Skidding onto the pavement, the Ural took the corner on Fish Hatchery Road at top speed, wobbled precariously, and vanished from sight.

As is often the case in close encounters, the scurrying pedestrians managed no more than a cursory look at the rocketing motorcycle with its daredevil rider bending low over the handlebars. Shaken by the near-collision, Trinidad and the Frenchman sought to regain their composure. Turning to follow the path of the vanishing vehicle, they stared in shocked disbelief while echoes of the Ural's lively motor continued to linger in the mountain air. Though equally stunned by the narrow miss, the Frenchman spoke first.

"Mon Dieu," the Clydesdale exclaimed. "God Almighty but that bagger is in a rush. Hurtling he goes, as if he fears to be left behind like the *Lanterne Rouge.* He speeds *'a bloc* and he's unlikely to survive the next bend, let alone that boulder-garden of baby-heads and tombstones around which our van driver swerved on the way up here. I see a biff-and-bacon in that one's future and the vultures are *absolument certain* to see a yard sale. *Ecoutez-moi bien,* mark my words, there goes a dead man."

Bambi had joined the two men and, as the Frenchman hurried off to catch a ride with the mini-van, she offered to translate.

"Well, my handsome friend, you've just been bitch-slapped by a trainload of cycle racing talk," she explained to a bewildered Trinidad. "I caught most of what that hunky French cyclist said. I used to date a road racer who was also a hill climber—he used to make cute remarks about my breasts—anyway the big dude's jargon sounded familiar, even though his sexy accent and tight pants kept distracting me and breaking my concentration. Flathead bikers and pedal-pushing cyclists don't always get along—for true believers it's either motorcycles or bicycles—hogs or hubs. Anyhow, some of what the big guy said was French, but most of it was cyclist slang. So, let's see—he called the guy on the motorcycle a 'bagger,' which is another way of saying 'loser.' To 'auger' is to crash, especially if the rider plants his face on the pavement. So, 'boulder-garden' and terms like 'baby-head' and 'tombstone' are all different ways of describing rocks in the road. And a 'biff' is also a crash—a cooler version of 'wipeout.' And 'bacon' accurately describes a painful road-rash which lacerates elbows and skins knees during a crash. And 'vultures' are bike racing spectators who haunt dangerous corners on a cross-country ride hoping to see a pile-up. And I think 'yard sale' is a way of describing the debris left over when several bicycles collide in mid-stride and strew riders and parts all over the asphalt."

"Wow," Trinidad exclaimed. "I take them all back."

"Take all what back?" Bambi asked as she gave her new beau a peck on the cheek.

"Every dumb blonde joke I ever heard or told or laughed at."

"That's sweet," she said. "You coming or not?"

"I need to retrieve Buster," he said.

Bambi craned her neck to look beyond Trinidad's broad shoulder. "I see a grave and a chair," she said. "But I don't see Buster."

Chapter 35

Beautiful Trouble
2006/Late Morning on October 10

Trinidad spun around, nearly losing his balance on the graveled roadway, and rushed back to Saul's grave. Bambi followed behind, hampered by her sandals and unable to match her companion's speed.

By the time she reached the grave, Trinidad had already called Buster's name four times before rushing to the promontory which marked the edge of the cemetery grounds. Bambi joined him and the two stood together on the hill.

The vista offered a spectacular view of a vast landscape—a broad expanse of emerald green hills forming the alpine park for which Estes is named. Longs Peak was visible in the distance. The sky, so recently obscured by dense rain clouds, was clear and impossibly blue. A breeze stirred. In the distance, cars and buses could be seen meandering to and from the mountain resort. Overhead, a squadron of ravens circled in a lazy, ascending arc.

"A murder," said Bambi.

"What?"

"That's what you call a flock of crows," she clarified. "Anyway," she added, "the view is gorgeous, but still no Buster."

"Holy shit!" Trinidad exclaimed as he recalled the careening motorcycle. "The bear!"

"Where?" asked Bambi.

"On the motorcycle!" Trinidad shouted as he took her hand. "Let's move! Aw hell—hold on!" Frustrated by Bambi's halting progress, he picked up the dawdling woman, balanced her in his brawny arms, and carried her across the graveyard.

"Jeepers you're strong!" Bambi remarked and then she grew silent as the pace of Trinidad's progress over the grass took her breath away.

"Sorry," he apologized as he rushed toward the Mustang. Maintaining a balanced stride, like a sure-footed stallion, he passed over the uneven ground, moving swiftly and seemingly unhindered by his attractive cargo. "I'll put you down," he offered.

"Not on your life," she laughed. "This is one thrilling sensation! I feel like a new bride being carried over a threshold as wide as a football field. I wouldn't miss this trip for the world! Carry on, my hero!"

When they reached the Mustang, the enthusiastic woman wriggled out of Trinidad's arms, landed expertly on her feet like a dismounting gymnast, and held out her hand for the ignition key.

"I'll drive, cowboy," said Bambi. "You ride shotgun and catch some shut-eye. I have a feeling you've got a long night ahead. Which way did the bear go?"

Skirting the main drag, Bambi guided the Mustang back up Highway 34 to the Rocky Mountain National Park's Fall River entrance station where the ranger on duty flagged her down. Smiling, she pointed to the Grand Lake Lodge employee sticker.

"Never mind the sticker, honey," the ranger gushed. "That smile of yours is enough to get you in," the infatuated man assured her.

"Aren't you sweet, Mister, uh—?" she struggled to read the ranger's name tag.

"My last name's pronounced 'None,' but you can call me Dave," he blushed as the driver of the RV behind honked impatiently. "Well, duty calls," the ranger frowned. "Anyway, you have yourself a nice day."

"Just one question before we go," Trinidad asked.

The ranger leaned down to regard the passenger he hadn't noticed.

"Didn't see you there," he apologized.

"I get that a lot," Trinidad admitted. "I just wanted to ask if you happened to wave a motorcycle through. It would have been a foreign job."

"Driven by a bear," the ranger recalled.

"That's the one," said Trinidad. "Any passengers?"

"The sidecar cover was clamped in place," said the ranger. "So, all I saw was the rider in the buffalo robe."

"Did you get a look at the guy?"

"The guy was big and wearing one of those Nazi helmets and a dust kerchief on his nose and mouth, so not much to see. A friend of yours?"

"Hardly," Trinidad declared and he was about to ask more when the RV honked again.

"One more honk from that character," whispered the ranger—his tone conspiratorial, "and I feel a wheel-well to wheel-well inspection coming on. Better get back to my line of impatient tourists. You both have a nice day," he added as he took one last longing look at Bambi's cleavage, then got eye contact with Trinidad and winked as he addressed the younger man. "And I'm pretty sure you, my friend, will be having a *really* nice day."

"Same to you, sir," Trinidad said.

As the Mustang left the gatehouse behind and traversed the scenic vistas of Trail Ridge Road, Trinidad tried to piece the facts together. He had no doubt that Buster Bishop was a prisoner—forced somehow into the kidnapper's sidecar. But for what reason? Both twins had apparently been snatched by the same individual—a hulking man wearing a buffalo robe—a huge male who could easily be mistaken for a bear. And the man was apparently trying to conceal his identity.

Crap, he thought. *Could it be?*

The motorcyclist was about the same hunky size as Bob Ferryman. But that was absurd—wasn't it?

Focus, he told himself. *Stick to the facts.*

Why either brother had been taken was unclear. Whatever the motive for the abductions, Buster was in trouble and Trinidad had no idea where the mysterious stranger had taken the old man. He was reasoning in circles until his companion pulled him out of his thoughts.

"I get that all the time," Bambi said.

"Pardon?"

"That 'hello, beautiful' treatment from our ranger friend. You must get it too, being the handsome devil that you are," she continued.

"Oh," Trinidad said, her point beginning to dawn on him. "The beautiful-people syndrome? Others are fascinated by your looks and don't take you seriously. We're good looking and therefore we have value. Being attractive is handy when your beauty opens doors, but it gets in the way of people getting to know the real you."

"Let's get married," Bambi joked. "You understand me. I understand you and our kids would be gorgeous."

"Eyes on the road please," Trinidad chided his heartbreakingly stunning companion. "And how about using that beautiful brain of yours to help me think of a way to help Buster."

"Is he in trouble?" she asked, her tone turning deadly serious.

"He's absolutely in trouble," Trinidad said. "And I haven't got a clue how to help."

"Man," Bambi declared, "do we ever need a detective."

Chapter 36

A Terrible Burden
2019/2:30 p.m. on June 8

"So, this Bambi was a looker?" Ranger Heckleson interrupted.

"Big looks and big heart," said Trinidad.

"Must be a terrible burden," said the old ranger as he absently fingered his scruffy beard. "Being beautiful, I mean. What's it like?"

"Ask my Annie," Trinidad smiled.

"I'm asking *you*," the ranger insisted. "What's it like to always be the handsomest guy in the room? They say beauty gets as beauty does. Is it the same with handsome?"

"Beauty is in the eye of the beholder," said Trinidad. "God made us all in his image. I think everybody's beautiful and handsome in their own way."

"The way I heard it, beauty is in the eye of the *beer-holder*," Heckleson laughed. "And an on-looker would have to be pretty drunk to mistake me for somebody who's supposed to resemble the Deity. And, by the way, from how y'all describe this Jackhammer character, it sounds like he was a hard-nosed, unattractive, and generally unpleasant hombre, common as cornbread, can't dance, can't sing, and too wet to plow."

"Would it surprise you to know that Jackhammer had a hard life?" Trinidad asked.

"That's an old story that don't cut the cheese with me," the old ranger scoffed. "I've had a hard life too and y'all don't see me throwin' old timers off of buildings and stuffin' senior citizens into a motor-biker side-car."

"All I'm asking is for you to withhold judgement until you hear his side of the story."

"I'm a fair man," said the old ranger. "I'll hold my peace fer now."

"So, you won't kick if I take a side trip to fill you in on Jackhammer's life story without revealing how I know so much about it?"

"I guess I can sit still fer that," Heckleson assured him. "So long as y'all throw in recollections of Bambi now and then—just to keep up my interest."

"Roger that," said Trinidad.

Trinidad continued his story by assuring Ranger Heckleson that spending the night in Bambi's arms had provided sufficient stimulation to take his mind off the puzzle of the marauding bear and the missing twins.

"Nothing like a loving woman to clear your head," he told the old ranger, who nodded in agreement.

"It's a gift," Heckleson agreed. "And don't y'all never forget it."

The two men were silent for a moment, each lost in thought. After a time, the old ranger spoke.

"So, just how hard was this-here Jackhammer character's life?" he asked.

"It was pretty damn hard," Trinidad said. "Our villain had a tough life—not that his sad upbringing will, in the end, justify all he did. But it's one hell of a backstory."

"Forge ahead," Heckleson encouraged. "And I won't be surprised if this-here desperado turns out to be a couple of sandwiches short of a picnic."

The Life and Times of Jackhammer Marsh

1955—Born Francis Sydney Marsh in Smew, Oregon.

1957—In the wake of tragedy, his family moves to Texas.

1963—Endures swimming lessons at San Antonio YMCA.

1970—Discovers football at China Berry High School.

1971—Without forewarning, his mother and sisters abandon him.

1974—Graduates high school and briefly enters Merchant Mariners.

1975—Joins a biker gang and commits tattoo parlor assault.

1976—Fateful poker game leads to the Trail Ridge incident.

1977—Suffers personal tragedy, emerges from hiding, and returns to Texas.

1978—Sentenced to prison, serves more than two decades.

2005—Re-enters society, briefly seeks clinical help.

2006—Returns to Colorado.

Chapter 37

Jackhammer's Tale: Early Years

According to Trinidad, Jackhammer Marsh was born Francis Sydney Marsh in the tiny Oregon coastal town of Smew—named for an elusive waterfowl. He was just two years old when a five-day rain caused his entire village to tumble into the ocean on the crest of a gigantic mudslide. The slide took not only the Marsh cabin, but also the Smew harbor and the family's fishing trawler. In a flash of thunder, lightning, and sodden soil, the boy was homeless. Two days later, he was fatherless.

Deprived of his livelihood, Jackhammer's old man borrowed a dinghy and rowed until he reached a rocky outcrop where the shattered shell of his ruined trawler was stranded in the midst of a colony of puffins. Ignoring the antics of the comical birds, the forlorn fisherman shipped his oars, filled the pockets of his pea coat with rocks, and lowered himself over the stern.

A week after Nadir Marsh's lifeless body washed ashore, his widow gathered up her children and left the coast. The boy was too young to comprehend his father's death, but his mother and sisters were scarred by the angst of that tragedy. Riding a midnight bus, the family landed in San Antonio, Texas, where Ousel Marsh used her last dollar to rent a motel room and set out looking for work. For a year, she waitressed and sang torch songs in a murky tavern to support the family. When minimum wages and tips weren't enough, she turned to exotic dancing which led inexorably to prostitution. While their mother slaved to feed them, the boy and his two older sisters flitted from school to school, never lingering long enough to make permanent friends. Despite the transitory nature of their schooling, the girls were sociable and outgoing and seemed to get by wherever they ended up. Their younger brother had a rougher time of it.

At age eight, he attended a Catholic Youth Summer Camp where he fell victim to a brutal swimming instructor who was more interested in flirting with female lifeguards than teaching prepubescent boys. Rather than providing lessons, the sadistic man opened each session by throwing his two dozen charges into the deep end—taking credit for those who managed to swim on their own and reporting his failures as "unteachable."

Those who swam, swam. Those who nearly drowned stopped coming to the unhelpful class. Refusing to quit, Jackhammer persisted. In the end, he survived the ordeal even though he never mastered the art of propelling himself through the water. Willing himself not to sink, he floated like a cork. Activating his defiant personality, he mustered an uncommon endurance which allowed him to tread water with a stamina that bordered on the perpetual. Which is how he survived for the duration of his otherwise unproductive swimming sessions—even as the traumatic experience continued to haunt him.

"Canst thou swim?" the CYC instructor had whispered to his trembling charges every morning as, one-by-one, the cruel taskmaster grasped each boy's puny arm and flung him in. It was a voice which continued to trouble Jackhammer's sleep and a mocking interrogation which, in times of stress, he repeated *sotto voce* to himself.

In school, other boys made fun of his feminine-sounding name and he endured a playground fight every day of his young life until reaching puberty. Over a single summer, he grew eight inches and gained twenty-five pounds. In June, he left school a bullied wimp. That September, he returned as a giant among pygmies. Going forward, he was always the biggest and toughest boy in his Texas classrooms. Poor as a sawmill rat, he was often short of cash. But the muscular lad habitually solved his financial problems by appropriating lunch money from his weaker classmates. In short order, the former victim mushroomed into a classic bully.

In 1970, the family relocated to the small Texas town of China Berry where he entered high school. Discovering a knack for football, he channeled his aggression and earned a starting position as a freshman. Proudly sporting his letter jacket, he enjoyed a fleeting period of notoriety and small-town success. His outlook and his grades improved. However, his fortunes fell during his sophomore year when his mother and sisters abruptly pulled up stakes and left town. He never saw them again. Abandoned and confused by their unexpected departure, he brooded for a time, then recovered and poured all his energy into school and football.

By sheer force of will he managed to graduate in 1974. Seeking a vocation, his bulk and bluster inspired him to join and briefly serve in the Merchant Mariners where he reached the brink of manhood. He thrived in maritime service only to encounter yet another cruel twist of fate when rumors began circulating that he'd killed a shipmate.

During what turned out to be his final voyage, a crewman had been found bludgeoned to death. Although he was innocent, the big man's reputation for aggression made him a prime suspect. When his returning ship anchored in the Straits of Florida, he was confined to quarters. On the eve of a floating inquiry, he commandeered a lifeboat and nearly drowned in an attempt to flee.

His time with the Merchant Mariners had been spent as a dockhand, loading and unloading freight. In a pinch, he could operate a motorboat and row like a mindless galley slave. But he knew nothing about sailing or steering and never learned to navigate.

After two weeks adrift on a punishing ocean, the fleeing lad managed to miss the Bahamas entirely before drifting into Cuban territorial waters. Clumsily beaching his unwieldy craft near Moa, he crawled onto a spit of sand where coastal militia seized him. He spent months in a Havana jailhouse until an unexpected intervention freed him. His deliverance was secured by a former neighbor of his mother, a native Texan who happened to be occupying the governor's chair and used his influence to secretly lobby for the young man's release.

With a grudging sense of gratitude, when Jackhammer returned to Texas, his first official act was to vote to re-elect Governor Dolph Briscoe. That vote turned out to be his one and only instance of citizenship in a lifetime spent skirting the law.

That summer, alone and unfocused, Jackhammer reached a crossroads. Enamored since childhood with the mystique of motorcycles and bikers, the young giant was inexorably attracted to the Texas chopper culture. This fascination extended to his taste in music. Ignoring the temptation to embrace country-western, he fell hard for pop tunes of the 1960's, and—consistent with his growing interest in leather and hogs—he embraced the nostalgic song-story of a misunderstood biker. Adopting that one-hit-wonder as his theme song, he never looked back.

Within months of his return to America, he was initiated into the Mid-Texas Prickly Pear Riders, whose gang colors of avocado and artichoke were designed to elicit comment as a pretext for free-for-all fistfights. At the time of his initiation, owing to some mysterious biker culture calculus, his given name morphed from Francis Sydney to "Jack."

His "Hammer" honorific was added in 1975 when his aggressive nature landed him in jail. His official offense had been to press his right hand against the earhole of a local character and repeatedly slam the man's skull into the unyielding casement of a stainless-steel sterilizing machine. Had others not intervened, he would surely and literally have *hammered* the man to death.

This horrific assault was committed to revenge an unfortunate happening—a misunderstanding which some considered a practical joke. The victim whom Jackhammer attacked was a Texas tattoo artist known on the streets of downtown China Berry as *Trash-Polka Ike.*

A transcript of the civil trial reported that Jackhammer, a newly initiated Prickly Pear, had—in keeping with the dictates of his gang—scheduled an appointment with Ike to obtain his obligatory tattoo. Jackhammer arrived, stripped off his shirt and drank lustily from a proffered bottle of spirits. Moments later, the muscular man plopped face-down on the establishment's grimy table and fell fast asleep.

At midnight, Jackhammer awoke lying in an alleyway with a splitting headache and a burning sensation on his back. Struggling to his feet, he stumbled home. Next morning, it took several minutes and a series of awkward poses at his bathroom mirror to read, in reverse, the words which Trash-Polka had etched into his back.

Enraged, the infuriated biker threw on his China Berry letter jacket, danced into his jeans, and angrily plodded fourteen blocks in bare feet to confront the tattoo artist. Jackhammer found the offending individual in the act of sterilizing needles and other paraphernalia. He knocked the instrument tray from the startled man's grip, yanked open the door of the sterilizing mechanism, and shoved Ike's head into a swirling typhoon of steam and high pressure. Then he pulled his victim out and proceeded to hammer the wretched man's head against the metallic surface of the autoclave.

All this to avenge the message permanently scratched onto the broad canvas of Jackhammer's back. It was an episode of violence which led to his first arrest.

At the trial, Ike testified that he'd been roaring drunk the night he tattooed his assailant. Working in a stupor, with Jackhammer laid out on one table and an equally intoxicated woman on the other, the inept tattoo artist managed to mix up his customers.

"It were an honest mistake," he told the court. "So alike them two phrases was and me three or four sheets to the wind. It's a wonder my spelling survived."

In the fog of the moment, Trash-Polka made the mistake of etching the message intended for his female customer on Jackhammer and vice versa.

"The woman was least upset," the lamebrained artist recalled. "When she got home, she called to thank me. Said she'd been wonderin' whether or not to quit her job as a preschool teacher and torpedo her marriage and go on the cross-country road bicycle circuit—whatever in hell that was. Said the words I inked on her back was—and I'm quoting now: 'a message from God Himself.' A sign, she called it, that her mission in life was to 'ride the wind.' Never mind that what I wrote on her was intended for Mr. Marsh. She thought them words I scratched onto her back meant some two-wheeled aluminum jobs—you know—them fancy bicycle machines that people in tights race with.

"Funny how that worked out," said Ike. "Not funny 'ha-ha,' but funny weird-like. Funny how the little lady who was a mother of two bouncin' baby boys got my attacker's tattoo and what she wanted ended up on the giant panda that almost done me in. Well, you see, your honor, and gentle-ladies and gentle-men of the jury, the words she ended up with was: *You can't scare me...I'm a Biker.* That's what she ended up with. Whereas, I guess we all know what my mugger got, which was the other one—which was: *You can't scare me...I'm a Mother.*"

At this juncture, the transcript indicated that the judge had to admonish members of the court and the jury and spectators not to laugh while Jackhammer sat hunched over at the defendant's table, stifling his temper and turning beet-red with embarrassment. The record shows that, on advice of counsel, Jackhammer remained mostly mute throughout the trial. The only words attributed to him were a reply of "Yes, sir" when the judge instructed him to remove his shirt to show the jury the offending tattoo which formed the crux of the proceedings.

In the end, the jury proved sympathetic to Jackhammer whom they felt was the wronged party. Siding with the assailant, the seven male and five female jurors awarded Trash-Polka Ike a meager cash settlement of one dollar. For Jackhammer, who'd been obliged to bare his torso in open court, the jury recommended a minimum sentence, which, allowing for time served, meant the mortified man could go free.

Humiliated by the experience, Jackhammer hired a more dependable tattoo artist to amend the message on his back. Initially, he was unimpressed with the woman's modification plan, which was to truncate the final word and add a stylistic insect. The revised version would, the artist assured him, continue to suggest the wearer wasn't easily frightened, while also adding to his mystique by equating himself with—of all things—a moth.

"So, your plan is to make it say: *You can't scare me, I'm a Moth?*" Jackhammer sounded dubious. "I want something tough," he reminded the new artist. "What's tough about a moth?" he wanted to know.

"Are you kidding?" the craftsman replied as she directed his attention to her display wall. "Take your pick of these beauties: You've got your Polyphemus or cyclops moth with a wing-span of half a foot and weird spots that look like blood-shot eyes. You've got your ghost moth—maybe not your cup of tea, I guess. Ah, here's your huckleberry! As you can see from my drawing, this critter has markings which resemble a skull. They don't call this beauty *the death's head* for nothing. As shown, I'll accentuate the skull and minimize the moth. This will be a one-of-a-kind creation—a masterpiece of intimidation."

"Just so it fixes the screw-up," Jackhammer insisted.

As for the mother who received his biker tattoo, Madeline Carol Ulsh divorced her husband of ten years, left her toddlers behind, cut her hair short, and embraced women's cycling. Winning one of the world's premier long races, the intrepid rider mastered 900 miles of distance, cycling for days as she traversed the entire length of Great Britain. She accomplished this feat while Jackhammer Marsh was on trial. She earned accolades, signed endorsements, and rode merrily on, never knowing his fate.

In September 1975, while Madeline Ulsh was cycling into history, Jackhammer began rising through the Prickly Pear ranks until he became the gang's charismatic honcho. To cement his role of pack leader, he pursued other manly interests. Sporting his new death's head tattoo, he briefly gained illicit notoriety as a bare-knuckle boxer and exhibition wrestler—fighting real opponents and trading mock holds with pathetic actors. For a few months, he competed in squalid backrooms and on the undercard in dingy arenas as "Marsh the Moth." Eventually, he stumbled into a poker game, won an unredeemed lottery ticket, and headed to Colorado.

Chapter 38

Better Half
2019/3 p.m. on June 8

"You might suppose that the lottery ticket was the sole motivation for Jackhammer's 1976 trip to Colorado," Trinidad told the old ranger. "But, having gotten to know the man, I believe his pride and his love of biker culture contributed to his decision to steer his motorcycle to the top of Colorado. That fateful journey along Trail Ridge Road forced him into a legendary confrontation with a posse of deputies and forest rangers. Which is what caused Jackhammer to seek revenge for the sheriff's alleged transgression. Which compelled the disillusioned man to commit a rash act which doomed him to life as a freak who longed to be invisible and drove him to kidnap first one twin and then the other and—"

"Holy Mother!" shouted Ranger Heckleson. "Y'all give me whiplash with that machine-gun blast of plotlines! That's way too much information fer this old noggin to absorb without which I have at least a nibble more of dessert. Could we take a break just now? My sweet tooth is battling with my bladder fer attention. I gotta piss and eat some sugar and I'd rather do the farmer first and the ladder second if it's all the same."

"Let's take five," said Trinidad. "I need to call Annie anyhow."

"Boy oh boy," laughed the old ranger. "Is you is or is you ain't already married?"

Trinidad sat on the Ranger's broad porch and dialed the landline at Lavender Hill Farm. It rang five times.

"Scriptor-Sands residence, lady of the house speaking. Duffy ain't here," Anne answered.

"You know it's me, right?" Trinidad asked.

"That's what caller ID is all about, I reckon," said the bride-to-be.

"Have you thought any more about the hyphen?" asked the prospective groom.

"I'm dropping it," Anne assured him. "Annie Sands is plenty fine for me."

"You might be the perfect woman," Trinidad suggested.

"Not hardly," she laughed. "Although parts of me are *absolutely* perfect."

"Trying to concentrate here," said Trinidad. "You're making it difficult."

"So," Anne's voice took on a tone of mock seriousness, "what's up, Doc?"

"Just checking in," he said. "How's the bridal shower going?"

"Lunch is over. Eventually we're going to get to the gifts and games. As we speak, the ladies are on the front porch cranking the ice cream maker," she announced. "I was out there supervising which is why it took me so long to catch the phone."

"I guess I can't talk you into using the electric one," he wondered.

"Nope," she declared. "Grandma's old hand-cranked machine makes the ice cream taste better every time. You're missing a treat."

"Save me some?" he suggested.

"Not likely," she replied. "How's your bachelor wing-ding shaping up?"

"Uh—" Trinidad began, uncertain if he should divulge the details of the unexpected shoot-out.

"I know about the dust-up," she informed him. "Madge got the call from here and filled us all in when she got back."

"Oh," said Trinidad.

"Glad nobody we know got hurt," Anne said. "But sad about the young man. Somebody's gonna get some bad news, I guess."

"I guess," Trinidad agreed. "Anyway, my party's going okay. Dallas is feeding me well—we just finished a late lunch. We're about to have dessert and more conversation."

"Dallas? Is it okay to call our ranger Dallas now? That's one hell of a whole lot better than calling him *Fingers*, no? So, what are you two talking about, I wonder?" she asked.

"Old times," he said.

"His or yours?"

"Mine."

"Spirits of Grand Lake?" she guessed.

"Yep," he admitted.

"Short or long version?' she wondered aloud.

"You know me," he laughed.

"So, it's the long version," she decided. "That oughta get you home about midnight."

"Probably," he agreed. "I don't think my host will be satisfied with half-measures."

"Well," she sighed, "the bunkhouse is all ready for you. Naturally, I won't be there to tuck you in. I've got a busy day tomorrow in case you've forgotten."

"How could I forget our upcoming Lavender wedding?"

"You'd better not forget," she declared. "I don't have any interest in being left standing at the altar. And by the way, you can stop trying to hide your wedding shoes, because I found them again."

"No boots, I guess," he said. His tone was hopeful.

"No boots," she affirmed. "And you'd better show up wearing that custom cummerbund and bow tie or I'll know the reason why."

"Yes, dear."

"Am I turning into one of those nagging wives already?"

"Not even close," he assured her.

"I love you, Mr. Sands."

"I love you, Mrs. Sands."

"Come and get it!" the old Ranger shouted.

"Second dessert time," Trinidad told his love.

"You boys are gonna spoil your supper," Anne warned. "Anyway, I don't know what you're having, but it won't measure up to our home-made ice cream—not to mention the treat I have in mind for you this time tomorrow."

"Trying to concentrate," Trinidad laughed. "So long, honey."

"Bye-bye, dear-heart."

After another generous helping of Heckleson's legendary cherry cheesecake pie, Trinidad was encouraged to resume his story.

"Where was I?" he asked as his host cleared away the dishes.

"Y'all managed to pull this-here Jackhammer Marsh out of Texas and up to Colorado," the Ranger recalled, "where he had himself a run-in with the law which I'm purdy sure was represented by none-other than our old friend, the Grand County Sheriff Red Bishop—in his younger years."

"You're a fine audience," Trinidad declared. "And a good listener. To continue, the date was July 4, 1976, America's bicentennial and about a month before Colorado's centennial celebration. Which made it about as special a Fourth of July as you can imagine and here was Buster Bishop standing in the middle of Trail Ridge Road, on the hottest day of summer, watching and waiting."

"Let me guess," Heckleson interrupted. "He was way up top—posse and all—watchin' and waitin' fer the arrival of Mid-Texas' own Prickly Pear Riders."

"Bingo," said the detective.

"And what, I wonder, caused the sheriff to set himself up there?"

"The reason was July 1975," Trinidad said.

"I'll hazard another guess," the old ranger said. "Could it be that the Prickly Pears had been up to previous mischief at Grand Lake in '75?"

"Yep," Trinidad confirmed. "So, let's take up the story from Buster's point-of-view."

Chapter 39

Buster's Tale: The Trail Ridge Incident
1976/July 4

Independence Day 1976 marked an anniversary—one which the Grand County Sheriff was unlikely to forget. Exactly one year earlier, over the Fourth of July weekend of 1975, an argument between the Prickly Pears and a rival gang from Wisconsin turned ugly. The two gangs tangled in the parking lot of Grand Lake Lodge. Five shots were fired. One errant slug pierced the canopy above the swimming pool and a second bullet shattered the front window of a commuter bus. Three nodules of lead were unaccounted for and, although no injuries were reported, the incident rattled tourists and alarmed local residents.

Local folks were particularly shocked because gunplay within sight of Grand Lake hit much too close to home. Shots fired in anger had the unwelcome effect of reigniting memories of an earlier Fourth of July incident—a 19th century skirmish known locally as "The Shootin'."

Most participants in the 1883 shoot-out and those who witnessed the calamity had passed away and the few remaining were aging and forgetful. But recollections of that tragic day were passed on to surviving kin and, for some, old resentments continued to fester. The location and timing of the 1975 shoot-out definitely stirred things up. Surviving families from both sides of the 1883 episode were especially upset. Tensions were running high.

So, when word reached Grand County that the Mid-Texas motorcycle gang planned a return visit to the Colorado Rockies, Buster Bishop was having none of it. Because 1976 wasn't on the Wisconsin gang's radar, an exact reenactment of the previous year's battle was impossible. But the Prickly Pears had a knack for stirring up trouble. As a staunch proponent of law and order, the sheriff was determined to avoid a repeat of the prior year's shoot-out and he most certainly wanted to quell anything remotely resembling the lakeside massacre of 1883.

Acting swiftly and decisively, the Grand County lawman rounded up a posse consisting of his regular crew of deputies, three dozen town volunteers whom he duly deputized, and six forest rangers. Appropriating eight out-of-service school buses from the local district, he transported his crew to the Alpine Visitor Center. When the buses were empty, the industrious sheriff ordered the drivers to position the bright yellow vehicles to form a ragged line. Strung out bumper-to-bumper, the buses stretched across the highway and into the Center's broad parking lot forming a semi-circular gauntlet.

The school bus roadblock was solid, yet sufficiently porous to allow for penetration by tourists and local traffic. Buster planned to stop the Prickly Pears, but he had no intention of impeding the flow of commerce on which the town and leadership of Grand Lake so depended. The vast majority of traffic was allowed to ebb and flow along the wild and lofty highway. But there'd be no welcome and no passage granted to fifty-eight trouble-making bikers who sported the garish colors of the Texas gang.

Buster established his barricade. Then he posted lookouts at the steepest stretch of Highway 34 leading to the summit of Trail Ridge Road. The lookouts included two clear-eyed teenagers whose post on the ridge above the Rock Cut Corner formed the lynchpin of his operation. That pair of watchers had one mission and one mission only. When they spotted the Prickly Pear procession, they were under orders to report the sighting using a hand-held two-way radio.

Chapter 40

Present Day Objections
2019/3:30 p.m. on June 8

"And before you ask," said Trinidad as he anticipated the old ranger's objections, "there weren't any practical wireless phones in 1976—unless you consider clunky devices which were unreasonable to lug around. State-of-the-art portable phones weren't all that portable in the mid-1970s and even the best ones only held a serviceable charge for a half-hour at most and required ten hours to recharge. The cell phone technology of the 1970's was wonky at best and—just like today—the devices didn't work well in an alpine wilderness. And, in anticipation of your next protest, the landline phone at the Alpine Visitor Center wasn't working on the day in question. So, two-way radios formed the only lifeline between Buster's intrepid lookouts and his assembled mass of gatekeepers."

"Two-way radio then," the old ranger concluded. "Like World War II all over again."

"Roger that," said Trinidad. "And, to continue that line of thinking, it was an episode of World War *III* which Buster was hoping to avoid."

"So, what about the details of this-here look-out post?" Heckleson asked.

"Well," said Trinidad, pleased to note the ranger's professional interest in a fellow lawman's preparations. "Being 12,190 feet closer to the sun than a New England beachcomber seemed to make July 4, 1976, just that much hotter. The notion that a mountaintop is hotter than a lower elevation is an idea which may not stand up to scientific scrutiny, but it's a concept which might account for the irritable discomfort of the two lookouts assigned to Rock Cut Corner. I spoke to both of them while searching for clues to the whereabouts of my missing old timer and I think I can do a pretty fair job of reproducing their experience. Shall I tell you what I remember about their conversation that day?"

"I'm hangin' up on your every word," said Heckleson.

"I'll take that as a yes," Trinidad decided. "Now, I don't recall their names, so I'll call them lookout number one and two."

"Sounds fair."

"Give me a moment," said Trinidad as he briefly closed his eyes to remind himself of one of several 2006 interviews which he'd conducted to learn more about Buster's disappearance. Among other leads, he'd spoken with the two youngest members of the Trail Ridge posse. He borrowed a tape machine, recorded the meeting, transcribed the cassette, and kept the transcription. Later, as part of his community college program, he tapped into that resource to write up a case study in the form of a screenplay. It was in the process of writing out the dialogue that he decided to disguise his subjects' identities by giving them aliases, which is how he managed to forget their real names.

"My criminal justice professors liked it," Trinidad bragged. "One teacher said the dialogue reminded him of Shakespeare's use of the gravediggers in Hamlet. 'Insightful comic relief,' the teacher called it."

"I picture y'all as a brown-nosin' teacher's pet," said Heckleson.

"You've got that right," said Trinidad. "The faculty loved me."

"Figures," sighed the old ranger. "I wasn't nobody's favorite student. I barely squeaked by in the academy classes, but get me out in the field and there's a different story."

"Yeah-boy," agreed Trinidad. "Remember, I saw you in action today."

"Don't remind me," said Heckleson. "So, any-how, let's hear this-here gravedigger's scene."

"Right now?"

"If it ain't too much trouble," the old ranger pleaded. "I ain't gettin' any older, you know."

Trinidad smiled and paused just long enough to further pique his host's interest. The detective took a deep breath, then returned to the scene of the observation perch situated high above the Rock Cut Corner and did his best to recall the dialogue between the two young lookouts posted there.

Chapter 41

Spotters
1976/July 4

"Damn it's hot," lookout number one complained.

"Hotter than hell," agreed lookout number two. "Your turn," the sweating boy held out a pair of binoculars to his companion, intending to swap them for the radio.

Number one was skeptical. "You sure you remember what to say if we spot them," he prompted.

"Shit," said number two. "I forgot again. Let me see the dang code book."

"Anyone ever tell you that you've got the memory of a gnat?" asked one.

"Are you even spelling *gnat* the right way?" asked two.

"Like you know how to spell anything," one declared.

"Give me the book or shut up and give me the radio," said two.

"Here's your book," said one. "You'd better study while I keep the radio."

According to Trinidad, as last-minute and totally civilian additions to the Trail Ridge posse, the two teenagers had been obliged to study the Grand County law enforcement and volunteer fire department code book. Most of the multi-page pamphlet consisted of scanner frequencies, trunk frequencies, and talk-groups—a dense collection of numeric tables which were unintelligible to the uninitiated. The code book also included an alphabetical list of common first-responder jargon and it was this list that two wanted to re-examine.

"Uh—is this one of them L.K.A. things or something else?" two ventured.

"Well, knot-head, we ain't likely to be running into a 'last known address' situation out here in the middle of nowhere," growled one, his tone impatient.

"So, it's a BOLO?" two guessed.

"Close," said one, as he translated the abbreviation for his slower co-worker. "Be-on-the-look-out is the orders which the posse gave us when they sent us here. BOLO means be on the lookout. That's what we're doing up here at the high point—we're following orders to be on the lookout for them bikers and— Oh crap!"

While the young lookouts argued, the first ranks of an advancing armada of motorcycles suddenly appeared on the ascending curve leading to Rock Cut. This abrupt visual sighting was instantly followed by the thunderous roar of the Mid-Texas Prickly Pear Riders as the group of fifty-eight advanced two-by-two along the narrow pavement, making a beeline for the lofty corner.

Far above the roadway and hidden from view by the advancing bikers, two snatched the radio, completely forgot the signal code and lost all composure as he blurted out his frantic report.

"Hogs over High Point!" he declared. "Hogs over High Point!"

Two's agitated message rocketed across the four-and-one-half miles which separated the lookout point from the visitor center. Arriving there, it received a mixed reception.

"Ack," Sheriff Bishop complained as the impetuous words echoed in the summer mountain air. "Turn that damn speaker down."

"Hey, Red," one of the assembled onlookers quipped. "Which comedians do you got up there on point? Cheech and Chong? George Carlin?"

"Are them lookouts even old enough to drink?" shouted another spectator. "Because they sure sound drunk to me!"

"Who in hell did we put up there at Rock Cut?" Buster Bishop asked his deputy.

"Two high school jocks," said Harlan. "There wasn't nowhere else to put them. You told me they was young and strong climbers and clear-eyed. You figured they couldn't get into trouble manning that post."

"Figured wrong," said Buster. "Can you imagine what would have happened if those boys messed up and failed to report that our unwelcome guests are practically already on our doorstep?"

The sheriff fumed for a moment more, then sprang into action.

"Get the hell ready, you bunch!" he shouted to the milling posse members. "Look alive and, for got-sake, try to look tough. These ain't some tweakers or platoon of homeless deadbeats coming our way. These are gen-u-wine, died-in-the-wool, Texas skull-splitters. Remember what they did to our town last year! Remember how your womenfolk couldn't walk the street! Do you want bullets flying where your kids play? Remember—"

"Remember the Alamo!" shouted a wag from the surrounding crowd.

"Harlan!" fumed the sheriff.

"Yeah, boss?"

"Take whoever's got a badge and move this crowd the hell back behind the barricade where they're out of earshot! The last thing we need is some town yokel hurling insults at these motorcycle gorillas! And Harlan—!"

"Yeah, boss?" Deputy Harlan asked.

"If you see any open containers, confiscate the booze! And if anybody objects, slap the asshole in cuffs!"

"You got it, boss!" said Harlan as he pulled his night stick and recruited six uniformed men to help push back the onlookers.

Spectators had started arriving early, before first light, assembling by osmosis in response to rumors circulating in Grand Lake that something big was happening at the Trail Ridge visitor center. By noon, the group had grown to more than a hundred, many of whom had leaked past a porous line of snow fence which had been called into service to form an improvised attempt at crowd control.

Now Buster had two problems: rolling thunder advancing along Trail Ridge Road and a growing chorus of smart-alecky bystanders crowding his roadblock. Not only that, but it was beginning to rain.

As he watched Harlan go, the sheriff slipped on his China Berry letter jacket. It wasn't regulation, but it was warmer than the cloth coats the county provided. Besides, he loved that old jacket. It was unique and he was just sentimental enough to cherish the memories of his high school days in Texas, growing up in the shadow of San Antonio, playing football, flirting with cheerleaders, circling a suburban 'dizzy block' in his vintage Chevy. Wearing the jacket made him feel safe and strong and, right then, he needed to feel that way.

Buttoning up, Buster heard paper rustle and abruptly realized he'd forgotten to remove the memento. His inside jacket pocket was a poor place for his mother's message, especially on a rainy day. He'd pocketed it months ago with the intention of taking it to Hot Sulphur Springs to have the VW repairman translate the writing and then he promptly neglected to run the errand. Hans was not only the nearest German the sheriff knew; the old timer was the only German speaker he trusted. He vowed to deal with the paper as soon as he got back home. Why was he procrastinating about getting the thing translated? On one level, he longed to know the contents. On the other hand, the prospect frightened him. The writing might contain news of his long-lost brother—maybe not. Maybe he should just leave the thing as it was—an indecipherable message from the past.

Put it in a proper plastic sleeve, he told himself. *Take it down to the bank and stick it in the deposit box. Salt it away. Bury it somewhere besides your damn pocket.*

Thoughts of his late mother and his vagabond brother made Buster sniff. The untranslated message had been delivered by the daughter of his mother's friend. The woman had expressed condolences for his loss and hinted that his brother was alive and living in Arizona. He hadn't known his mother at all and, so far as he knew, she'd only held him for an instant before he and his brother were snatched away. Even though he'd put on a brave front and shown little emotion in the presence of the messenger, news of his mother's death hit him hard—almost as hard as news of his brother.

His natural mother was gone. His brother might be alive and may or may not show up. As for his adoptive family, only memories remained and those were fading. The now-defunct plumbing business which once displayed the Bishop name was shuttered and the old commercial panel truck put out to pasture. Just this morning, the sheriff had driven by the salvage yard and the old van was still there, rusting in the mountain air. The truck, like his deceased step-parents, had served its purpose. Now the machine and the people had ceased to function.

Elmer and Esther Bishop had given him a stable home and treated him well, but the stoic, and hitherto childless, couple had kept the boy at arms' length. Growing up, he'd worked for Elmer every summer, snaking drains, plugging leaks, and maintaining the vintage pipes at Grand Lake's historic lodge.

To make ends meet, the family had been obliged to serve as live-in custodians at Grand Lake Lodge—giving the aging couple and the impulsive youngster the run of the place. Elmer and Esther Bishop were dependable caretakers and, in exchange for their labors, the lodge allowed them to maintain their plumbing enterprise on the premises, even installing a phone in the family cabin with a designated business line.

Ultimately, the business closed, but Elmer and Esther were allowed to stay. Years after the couple passed away, Buster returned to reside in the old family cabin—which amounted to one-half of an antique duplex. A lifelong bachelor with simple tastes, the county's newest deputy sheriff was content to dwell in the cramped, yet familiar, surroundings. Unpacking his bags, he was charmed to find the family's old rotary telephone still clinging to the kitchen wall. Grasping the receiver, he dialed the operator.

"That you, Maude?" he asked.

"Who's speaking please?"

"This is Buster Bishop," he explained.

"Red," Maude's tone was dubious. "When did you grow up? And when did you get home?"

"Yesterday," he declared, answering the last question first. "And never," he added.

"Heard you were hired to keep the peace," Maude continued.

"Yes, ma'am."

"Don't they know your history?"

"I've changed," he suggested.

"We'll see, I reckon," Maude said, unable to disguise her skepticism. "What name shall I put down for your exchange? Surely you don't want to be listed as *Bishop Plumbing.*"

"Don't I?"

"Hmm," the operator hummed, but Buster could hear her pen scratching and he pictured her making a note of his decision.

"Serving Grand Lake since 1922?" she asked.

"Just like it says on the van," he affirmed.

"Like it *used* to say," she corrected. "Apparently you haven't seen the old Plymouth lately. Your pop's paint job hasn't stood the test of time."

"Does she still run, I wonder?" asked Buster, his tone wistful.

"Needs an engine to run," said Maude. "And rubber tires. Not but a shell these days," she added. "Next I suppose you'll be asking where you can go to view the body."

"You read my mind," said Buster.

"Not likely and wouldn't care to, thank you. Last I looked, the Plymouth was occupying a choice spot in Benson's scrapyard. But we've blabbed long enough. Let's free up. Somebody with a real job might need to use the line."

"10-4," Buster laughed.

"Don't try to dazzle me with your law lingo, young man," Maude scolded. "You know as well as I do police and sheriff don't talk like those television actors."

"No, ma'am."

"Out," said Maude. "That's goodbye to you, tenderfoot."

"Out," Buster agreed.

Two decades had passed since he sat at the old kitchen table, teasing Maude. Now the old lady was gone too, her neglected grave—last time he looked—overgrown with nettles, the headstone nearly invisible in a tangle of bindweed. But that was all water over the dam. Everybody was gone. For the record, he had no family, but that didn't stop him wanting to make them proud. He'd stand tall and do his duty and hope somebody, somewhere would celebrate his fortitude.

Feeling sentimental, the sheriff turned his head, hoping nobody noticed, and took out his handkerchief. Blowing his nose, he daubed his eyes, adjusted his cap, and struck a disinterested pose as he watched grumbling spectators being herded away from the front lines of his barricade. Eying the mob, he made a mental note. Next time, if there ever was a next time, he'd expend the same effort erecting a barrier to keep spectators at bay as he spent building a barricade to keep the fast-approaching bikers out.

His preparations made, his jacket in place, a misty rain beginning to fall on Independence Day, Buster "Red" Bishop, duly-elected sheriff of Grand County, turned to face the day's on-rushing menace.

Chapter 42

Picture
2019/4 p.m. on June 8

"Let me ask y'all somethin'," the old ranger interrupted.

"Go ahead."

"This-here story of yours—mind you I ain't complainin'."

"What about it?"

"Well—" Heckleson began, then hesitated. "It's like this: suppose you and me was both workin' a jig-saw puzzle together—one piece at a time. Suppose I'm doin' my part, but y'all are way ahead on account—"

"On account?" Trinidad prompted.

"On account of you've already seen the big picture," the old ranger noted. "On account of y'all seen the picture on the puzzle box, where-as I'm just fumblin' along, tryin' to pick up a piece now and then. In this-here tale of yours, y'all know the whole story, where-as I'm just hearin' it a little piece at a time. See what I'm drivin' at?"

"You need a bigger picture to understand where the pieces fit," Trinidad suggested.

"That's the truth of it," the old ranger admitted.

"That's fair," the detective agreed. "How about I conjure up a picture for you to hang your hat on—a summary, if you like?"

"Now you're talkin'," said Heckleson. "I'll pull up the sofa and get summarized." Crossing to the living room, the enthusiastic ranger pushed old magazines, a photo album, and other debris to one side, clearing off his broad sofa to make room for himself and his guest.

"How do you want this?" Trinidad asked.

"Can y'all take it slow?"

"I can give it a try," the detective said. "Too bad Annie isn't here. This summing-up is her specialty, but I'll do my best."

"That's all a fella can ask," Heckleson said as he took a seat.

Settling into the old ranger's well-worn sofa, Trinidad began his summation.

"Let's visualize a garden gate which pivots on a sturdy hinge. If the gate swings one way, a person finds himself in the past. If it swings the other way, time moves forward. Let's say that the hinge is a pivotal point in time when circumstances bring people together who ordinarily don't interact. So, there's your puzzle picture: a garden, a gate, and a hinge. With me so far?"

"Clear as mud in May," Heckleson responded and, perhaps sensing that his guest might not catch the drift of his comment, he added, "I can see it all just fine, Slick. The picture on the puzzle box shows a garden, a gate, and a hinge."

"Great," Trinidad said. "Now, class, see if you can tell me what—in my story so far—constitutes the hinge."

The old ranger was silent for several ticks of the clock before his face lit up in a wide grin.

"The Trail Ridge dust-up," he said with confidence.

"Bingo," said Trinidad. "Everything that happened before Jackhammer and Buster Bishop squared off high in the Rockies in 1976 led the two men inextricably to that hinge-point. And everything that happened afterward motivated Jackhammer's thirst for vengeance, placed Buster in jeopardy, and doomed his brother."

"And sucked y'all into the story," Heckleson surmised.

"There's your summary and your picture," Trinidad confirmed. "So, I'm guessing that keeping that hinge in mind as we go forward will help you follow the rest of my story. Ready to move on?"

"Happy as a clam at high tide," the old ranger assured his guest.

"Great," said Trinidad. "So, let's return to 1976 and the Trail Ridge showdown."

Chapter 43

Jackhammer's Tale: The Trail Ridge Incident
1976/July 4

On his first-ever trip to Colorado, Jackhammer was leading the pack as he and his gang rolled along Trail Ridge Road. His original Harley-Davidson Shovelhead was thumping and rumbling like a well-oiled John Deere Tractor. He'd outfitted the durable motorcycle especially for this demanding road trip. Replacing the machine's factory chrome with stainless steel, upgrading to an electric starter, reconfiguring the tailbone-bruising rigid frame with after-market shocks, and accumulating countless additional modifications might have been a mechanic's nightmare, but the result was worth it to prepare for his end-game. As a result of targeted alterations, his Harley was not only rigged for a daring cross-country run, it was also a beauty—a sweet ride.

"Sweet!" he shouted as he tossed his head and twisted the throttle.

Spurning a helmet, he let the mountain wind whip his velvety locks into a golden frenzy. The chicks loved his hair—couldn't leave it alone when he bedded them—said they got lost in its sensuous tangles, said it ignited their desires.

He tolerated their commentaries.

As long as they gratified his needs, he didn't mind what they said during intercourse. They could recite the Gettysburg Address for all he cared. Let them fondle his hair and prattle about the experience if that made them happy —and apparently it did.

He glanced at his image in his rearview mirror. He had to admit that his hair was something special—a perfect complement to his handsome, square-jawed face—a flawless visage that featured his sky-blue eyes, aquiline nose, and perfect teeth. Every part of him, from head to toe, was perfect, and every part was classified "extra-large."

Which is why I am, he reminded himself, *a dynamic love machine and unquestioned leader of my Texas pack.*

That thought triggered the elusive song which had been pulsating through his subconscious for more than a decade. The lyrics were lost to him, the title a mystery, but the tune was always there.

It was there even now when Jackhammer's attention should have been on the geology lecture vibrating through the compact headphones which pressed against his perfectly formed, shell-like ears. The audio cord which emerged from each earpiece snaked languidly downward to intersect just above the huge biker's manly breastbone. At that intersection, two gossamer threads intertwined into a single strand which flowed farther down to merge with a portable cassette tape player. To keep the instrument safe, he'd tucked the whirling player securely into a specially-designed leather pouch and secured it in place with a custom strap which encircled the fork of his well-appointed Harley. The state-of-the-art player was a one-of-a-kind device—a prototype purchased by Jackhammer in Houston for the outrageous price of $150.

It'd been an impulse buy and he might have been insane to invest so much in an experimental device. Given the unpredictable state of the 1976 audio cassette industry, critics might say the battery-operated player was a luxury with zero reliability and even less practical utility. Still, he wanted it, even though he himself possessed only one functional cassette.

He'd purchased the recording by mistake. Buying the tape in a dingy Texas curio shop had been an impetuous act, a chance acquisition concluded when Jackhammer mistook the scientific title printed on the plastic cassette case for a musical genre. How was he to know that Precambrian Rock didn't refer to a sub-classification of rhythm and blues? Expecting music, he ended up with a talking-book cassette, an audio version of a scholarly work of nonfiction which extolled the virtues of Colorado geology.

He might have pitched the talking cassette. The science bored him, but the soothing voice of the narrator held his interest. So, he listened and—knowing his trip from Texas to Colorado would take him through a buttload of geology—he brought the tape along. As it happened on that July day, the tape proved to be mildly interesting and amazingly prescient. Because, as he rolled up Trail Ridge Road, the contents of his geology cassette seemed to coincide with the passing topography.

"In the Lava Cliffs," the lecturer declared, "we see faulting and the clear indication of Precambrian Rock—all dramatic features which are the direct result of distinct geological activity."

"Blah-blah-blah," Jackhammer mocked the recording. "It's rocks, people. Just rocks. It ain't rock and roll and it ain't rock-it science. It's—uh—"

He couldn't think of another witticism, so he switched off the player and concentrated on keeping his track, just to the right of the double-yellow line. Celebrating his virility and feeling fine and frisky on such a warm summer's day, the huge biker glanced at the upcoming milepost.

"24.6," he read the number aloud as another mysterious pop song coursed through his head. Even though the titles and words eluded him, the tunes stuck and that was enough. The notes permeated his subconscious and he hummed along, transporting himself to the sort of high which lesser mortals took drugs to achieve.

It's all about the notes, he reminded himself.

Back in the real world, Jackhammer noticed that the roadside numbers were getting smaller. A clear indication, to a seasoned highway traveler like himself, that the numbering of the asphalt on which he traveled didn't originate at Estes Park. That mountain town was behind them, to the east, whereas the pack's final stop lay ahead, to the west. The fact was that Trail Ridge Road—also known as Highway 34—began on the other side of the Rockies. Milepost 1 was over there somewhere and, depending on how one looked at it, you might say they were figuratively traveling backwards to reach the gang's destination.

Or, more correctly, my destination, he thought.

The pack hadn't wanted to return to Colorado, had no interest in revisiting the scene of last year's gunplay.

"They'll be waiting for us," Bogy Fountain, the pack's immediate past-capo, had warned him.

Jackhammer had missed last year's confrontation with the Wisconsin gang while Bogy had been there and in the thick of the fracas. Bogy may or may not have fired the first shots. But, unknown to all involved in the 1975 shoot-out—including the Wisconsin combatants, the Grand Lake pigs, and the Prickly Pears—the diminutive man had taken a bullet in the chest. The uncomplaining biker had ridden all the way from Colorado to his home crib in Texas, with a pencil point of lead lodged inches from his heart, only to collapse on his mother's front porch.

Bogy healed quickly and Jackhammer had only to glance to his right to see the small man keeping pace. Getting eye contact, Bogy raised a fist, then pointed to his mouth and one ear. Clearly, he had something to say.

Jackhammer removed the spindly earphones and slowed his bike. Maneuvering closer to his neighbor and cocking his head, he shouted.

"What?"

"They'll be waiting for us," Bogy repeated his earlier warning, his voice sounding hollow in the cavern of his over-sized helmet.

"Let them wait," said Jackhammer. "Ease over."

At a hand-signal from their leader, the entire line of riders eased off the pavement, angling toward the narrow shoulder. Wriggling in sequence from front to back, undulating as an entity, like a huge snake, each pair down-shifted in turn and glided to a stop.

When the gang relinquished possession of the pavement, a sizeable accumulation of motorists—all of whom had become stuck behind the closely-packed bikers—began to pass. While the traffic steadily cleared, Jackhammer unplugged and stored his earphones. With his audio equipment properly stowed, the big man dismounted and strode toward a rock wall which bordered the drop-edge of the roadway and served as a guard rail. The huge man placed two hands on the waist-high obstacle and paused a moment to take in the view. Then, ignoring signs forbidding the practice, he pivoted and swung onto the crest of the wall. He achieved this agile feat with a single unhurried motion—like a gymnast mounting a pummel horse.

Standing erect atop the wall, Jackhammer had an unobstructed view of the winding road which lay ahead. Holiday traffic was heavy and vehicles flowed in both directions. Looking uphill, he used his perfect eyes to follow the movements of two high-profile vehicles: a bus traveling toward his position and a delivery truck going the opposite way. He watched both conveyances until the former drew abreast of him and the latter was out of sight. Both vehicles were making progress, but each was navigating through decidedly different traffic.

After the backlog of vehicles spawned by his biker group had passed on, upward bound traffic had begun to flow normally—a vehicle or two at a time and spaced apart. In contrast, cars, trucks, and buses coming down were clustered in knots of a dozen or so. Someone up above was controlling the downhill flow by letting a set number of vehicles pass at regular intervals.

For Jackhammer, these observations confirmed Bogy's suspicion that someone was indeed waiting. Someone in authority must have established a roadblock. The barrier lay ahead, probably on the far side of the summit. And the summit, his geology tape had informed him, was close—a few curves away at the most.

Bogy had been waiting patiently at the base of the wall, either willing to trust his successor's judgment or unwilling to risk the climb. Jackhammer folded his large frame and sat cross-legged on the rocks looking not unlike a mystic deity in contemplative repose.

"Your thoughts?" he asked his audience of one.

"Turn around or—" Bogy began.

"Or?" Jackhammer prompted.

"Ride into the shit," Bogy suggested.

"And, we ride in, no?" Jackhammer laughed as he eased to the ground. "Now, Bogy. Before we risk the ride, let's have a poem!"

In a firm voice which belied his diminutive stature, Bogy turned toward the road and roared for attention. When the gang had gathered in an obedient semi-circle, the small man held forth:

"The fiery gates swing wide and we, my friends;
every mother's son, from front to end;
each gnome and troll and elf;
will face down Hell itself.
So, bone-up firm, my bonnie boys, and ride;
ride hard, ride swift to feed the beast inside."

"Mount up!" Jackhammer commanded. As the others reacquired their bikes, Jackhammer straddled his Harley and swiveled round to survey his gang.

What would these slow-witted minions think, he wondered, if they knew the true reason for our mission here at the top of Colorado? What would their comeback be if they knew they'd been dragged a thousand miles to make one man— namely me—comfortably rich? They joined this trip to prove that nobody says "no" to a Prickly Pear. What if they knew the truth?

"On me, boys!" he shouted as he engaged the clutch and reclaimed the alpine pavement. Leading his pack into the next corner, he roared up the inclined straightaway and involuntarily patted the breast pocket of his China Berry letter jacket. It was a motion designed to assure himself that his ticket to the sweet life remained safely concealed there. The ticket was secure and it wasn't going anywhere—not until he made it whole and redeemed it. It was safe in his jacket and wearing the jacket meant everything was going to be okay. Even if a roadblock lay ahead, no way would such a minor inconvenience thwart his master plan. He'd cut through the blockade like a hot knife through butter. He and his jacket were not to be denied.

For the rest of his gang, jackets trimmed in the gaudy Prickly Pear colors were the uniform of the day. For Jackhammer, the good old orange and black was all he needed to feel like a winner. Years ago, he'd earned the China Berry jacket fair and square as a fierce and universally feared linebacker for his state championship high school football team. It was his uncompromising symbol of pride and accomplishment. He rode in the jacket. Made love in the jacket. Slept in the jacket. He took it off to shower of course, but, the rest of the time, on his feet in the daylight, rain or shine, hot or cold, whatever the weather, he wore the jacket—removing it rarely and then only to fight. If he had his way, he'd be buried in the jacket, assuming he ever died, which was far from a foregone conclusion.

Invincible, that was his motto. He might, he imagined, live forever. What was to stop him? He Bishopwas a mean dude with a brutal reputation and a made-in-the-USA tattoo to prove it. Just let some road-blocking pecker-woods try to stop him. Just let them try.

Twenty-five minutes later, the Prickly Pears reached the Grand County roadblock. As a misty rain abruptly ended and the bright July sun broke through vanishing clouds, words were exchanged and Jackhammer challenged the local sheriff to a personal duel. The two men locked eyes for a full minute. Only when the sheriff blinked did the huge biker allow his gaze to stray to the man's name badge.

"Bishop," Jackhammer scoffed at the name which struck him as comically pious. "You'd better say your prayers. When I knock you on your bony ass, you'll stand aside," he told the lawman as he removed his jacket, gently folded the keepsake, and carefully draped it over the nearest wooden barricade.

"You need a hand, Red?" a spectator shouted.

Red Bishop, Jackhammer thought. *When Bogy writes up an account of this fight, he'll have a field day with that moniker. Here's one Red who'll wish he'd stayed in bed,* he smiled.

Rolling up his shirt sleeves, Jackhammer turned his back on his opponent and addressed his closing remarks to his assembled men. "This pig will stand aside," he repeated, "and we'll be on our way."

"If that happens," said Sheriff Bishop as he removed his own jacket, "I'll be the most surprised man in the county."

"Get ready to be sur—" Jackhammer began as he spun around to face the sheriff. But the big man never got to finish his sentence because his agile opponent rushed forward to deliver a single crashing blow which sent the larger man reeling. With a look of profound disbelief on his face, Jackhammer shuddered like an autumn aspen, collapsed to both knees, and slumped backward—as limp and flaccid as a stunned tuna flopping on the deck of a trawler.

Thunderstruck by the unexpected punch, the astonished giant stared up at the Colorado sky. Unable to stand, he listened helplessly to the sound of a battalion of motorcycles receding into the distance and knew in his heart that his gang was retreating.

Then, the world went black.

Hours later, when Jackhammer came to his senses, he found himself bent-double over the seat of his Harley, his body cradled in an embryonic fetal position, like an unborn chick. Someone had covered his prostrate body with the letter jacket. A forlorn symbol of his downfall, the crumpled jacket seemed to amplify his defeat, like a friendless flag draped over an abandoned coffin.

Though the muscular man was in spectacular shape and the best of health, it took several agonizing minutes to get his bearings. Checking his surroundings, he discovered he was miles from the site of his ignoble defeat. Somehow, he'd been dumped on an Estes Park side street with no idea and no memory of how he got there.

When at last he regained his equilibrium, the day was far advanced. Donning the jacket, he patted the pocket to reassure himself that its contents remained undisturbed.

Steering the Harley through a busy intersection, Jackhammer parked, slipped into a convenience store, shoplifted a map, and set off at a frantic pace. His new plan was to reach Grand Lake by an alternative route. But roadwork frustrated his progress and, despite a valiant attempt, he reached the town much too late.

Chapter 44

Heat
2019/Late Afternoon on June 8

The kitchen wall vibrated with a buzzing tone as an unexpected phone call interrupted Trinidad's narrative.

"I thought that historical instrument was merely for decoration," Trinidad joked as he helped the old ranger extricate himself from the low-slung sofa.

"Not hardly," his host said.

The old ranger ambled across the living room carpet to reach the kitchen. The vintage wall phone rang persistently until the lumbering man arrived and extracted the receiver.

"Heckleson," he informed the caller. "Yep. Yep. Nope. Yep. Nope. Yep. Going there now."

"Trouble?" asked Trinidad as he joined his host.

"Is there any other kind?"

"Where we headed?" Trinidad inquired.

"Meth camp," said Heckleson as he grabbed his rifle. "Gotta rescue some dogs," he announced while opening a drawer to locate another weapon. "Take this."

Trinidad took the proffered holster and pistol. Cinching the belt, the detective followed the ranger down the porch steps and out across the dirt-packed yard in the direction of the old timer's dusty Land Rover.

The meth camp was eleven miles into the 'Dobies over a crooked dirt road lined with litter of every description. Most of the roadside trash was coated with a thick brown layer of 'Dobie dust and unrecognizable, except for several yellow metal boxes which appeared to be recent additions.

"How many do y'all make it now?" the old ranger asked as his Land Rover passed yet another yellow box.

"So far, I count eleven stolen newspaper boxes," Trinidad said. "Illegally harvested, not for their reading material, but their hidden treasure. Glass doors smashed and coin reservoirs pried open to steal the quarters. No wonder I can never find a newspaper when I want one."

"Down south," Heckleson declared, "we call them self-service news dispensers honor-boxes—meanin' the customer drops his quarters in and, on his honor, takes only the papers he pays for."

"Honor-boxes? That's a decent name for the way the transaction is supposed to work," said Trinidad. "If only," the detective added with a frown.

"Twelve now and here's number thirteen," the old ranger noted as they came upon two more purloined dispensers. "And still counting."

Following a serpentine array of crap, the Land Rover rolled through a mass of roadside clutter. It was an unholy mess which was only exceeded by the pile of junk which they found at the end of the road. An isolated niche, the squalid place consisted of a pair of trailer houses squatting in a tangled nest of discarded appliances—old washing machines and dryers, three stoves, and a cluster of refrigerators and freezers. The cannibalized sailboat was there, of course, though how it had been transported from its initial resting place was a mystery. Someone had spray-painted the hull a garish mixture of highway orange and forest green. The mast sported a homemade jolly roger—a tattered black canvas decorated with stark white splotches meant to represent skull and crossbones. A rough wall composed of several dozen rubber tires filled the space between the trailers, one of which was nothing more than a burned-out shell. A rusty chiminea and four shabby folding chairs formed a ragged circle in front of the assembled tires. A lopsided wind-chime mounted on the drooping cord of an insubstantial clothesline twirled in the late afternoon breeze. The same breeze caused flocks of discarded plastic bags to float and dance among the debris.

"Visible from outer space," Trinidad commented on the sprawling mound of junk and trash.

"No doubt," the ranger agreed. "From the look of this disaster, I'm guessin' the occupants couldn't organize a bun fight in a bakery. But, just in case, let's make sure the premises are deserted."

A by-the-book search-and-seizure sweep found the trailers empty. The two men returned to the Rover and Heckleson wheeled past the mess, aiming for a nearby hillock.

"There's our next target," the old ranger announced.

Tucked in a declivity at the base of a low hill was a black Bentley, its side and back windows heavily tinted, its front windshield obscured by a silvery frost shield secured in place with bungy cords tightly wrapped around the automobile's driver- and passenger-side mirrors. No way to see out, no way to see in.

"Duck blind," said Heckleson as he parked and left the engine running. "Here's where we separate the cream from the crap," he added as he activated the Land Rover's p.a. system. "Vehicle," he commanded, "windows down, step out slowly, back to me." He waited two heartbeats, then killed the engine, pulled his rifle from the Rover's driving scabbard, and stepped out onto the dusty ground. "Tits up," he advised Trinidad and when the detective didn't immediately follow his lead he added, "Pull your pistol, son."

Heckleson motioned for Trinidad to move to the rear of the Bentley while he approached from the front. "Put your hands on that-there trunk lid," he whispered. "Feel fer movement." Then, louder, the ranger repeated his earlier demand. "Vehicle there!" he shouted and his booming voice echoed against the hillside. This second command elicited motion and a whimper from the Bentley followed by a half-dozen strident barks, the muffled sounds alternating between plaintive yips and a full-throated snarl.

"Two refugees," Heckleson decided. "Just like our telephone lady said."

Trinidad moved away from the trunk and side-stepped in the ranger's direction. "Fill me in," he suggested.

"Madge on the phone said their meth-head in custody was cryin' about his pets left in a hot car," said the ranger as he set the safety and handed the unfired rifle to his young companion. "Hold this piece while

I see whether or not our two tweakers was dumb enough to leave their luxury automobile out here in the middle of somewheres with the doors unlocked."

Apparently, the Bentley owners were suitably careless because the driver's side door yielded to the ranger's firm hand. Opening the door freed two frantic dogs—a petite brown Chihuahua and its larger silver-gray companion. As both creatures burst into the sunshine, the big animal made a beeline for one of the trailers while the smaller dog stumbled a few steps and collapsed.

"Might think the big one would be most parched by the heat," said Heckleson as he leaned down to scoop up the tiny animal. "But I reckon this little fella's miniature system took it harder. There's two military cans of water strapped to my back bumper. Y'all see to the big guy and I'll douse this midget."

The large animal was waiting patiently on a strip of AstroTurf nailed at the base of the narrow metal steps leading to the unburned trailer—someone's idea of a lawn, no doubt.

"You want a shower or just a drink?" asked Trinidad when he arrived with his camo-colored water can.

The creature cocked its head as it stood up. It was then that the detective realized his patient was missing a front leg and he could also see that he wasn't dealing with a domestic dog.

"El lobo," he began, then corrected his observation. "Pardon me, miss, I meant to say *matalobos*. May I offer you some refreshment?"

The female wolf sat back on her haunches and eased down onto the threadbare carpet, extending her good leg at an angle, her truncated stump also angling in. If both legs had been whole, she'd be crossing her paws in the universal canine pose of alert obedience.

Searching the cluttered ground, Trinidad found a half-moon hubcap which he centered in front of the creature and filled with water. Eyeing the detective, the wolf sniffed at the makeshift container and dipped her nose in. Seconds later, she engaged her tongue and began to lap noisily.

"More, yes?" Trinidad asked as he refilled the hubcap. He knelt to fill it a third time, then stood up to regard the drinking animal. "You'd be a stranger in these parts, I reckon. Were you shot or caught in a trap?" he wondered aloud. "Your stump is well-healed. So, I'm guessing you were young when the trauma struck you. And you would be how old now?" he tried to catch a glimpse of her teeth, knowing even a clear view wouldn't tell much.

What was it Annie said about clues to animal age?

The cementum at the base of a tooth offers some guidance, but good luck having a non-sedated wolf hold still while you conduct your oral exam. A critter's head can reveal much, his bride-to-be once told him. Cementum annuli methodology holds that you can read the calcified circles surrounding the roots of teeth as though they were tree rings. Or you can check to see if the cranial bones have or have not sutured together.

"Handy methodology for guessing the age of a long-dead prehistoric critter," Anne had told him when he was helping her cram for her graduate program orals. "But not so useful for evaluating living, breathing beasties. You'd practically have to slay and skin your subject to do a proper analysis."

Trinidad regarded the prone animal before him. *What,* he wondered, *will be the fate of this semi-feral creature if we turn her over to animal control? On the other hand, one glance at this beauty and my Annie will be all for adoption. We've already got a pet and I have a feeling our intrepid K-9 will be unwilling to share her kennel. But anything will be better than putting this girl down.*

As if reading his thoughts, the wolf regained her feet and glanced at the trailer, then at the detective. She held her gaze for a few seconds before pushing off with strong back legs and rushing headlong, at an astonishing pace, through the jumbled yard. She paused at the edge of the camp, looked back one last time, and vanished into the 'Dobies.

"Something y'all said?" asked the old ranger as he arrived with the smaller dog cradled in the crook of one brawny arm.

"The lady opted for freedom," Trinidad guessed.

"Smartest critter in the room," Heckleson decided. "As fer this little guy, it looks like I've got a friend for life. I think we're done here unless you and me want to string bob-wire around this mess and set fire to the God-forsaken place."

"Tempting," Trinidad suggested and his off-hand comment was greeted by a rolling clap of thunder.

While they ministered to the animals, the changeable weather had spawned an ominous expanse of menacing clouds. In the distance, the dark outline of Grand Mesa seemed to meld into an inky sky, steadily transforming the once-clear horizon into a pulsating expanse of deep and roiling violet. An elongated flash of fork lightning united the darkening sky with a distant patch of earth, delivering a growl of proximate thunder and hastening their departure.

"Better move out," the old ranger decided, "before this-here junkyard gets itself electrified, or turns into the mud-pit from hell, or both."

"Roger that," said Trinidad. "And it's getting late. Not sure I'll have time to finish my story."

"Y'all just try leavin' lest you tie up your tale," said Heckleson. "Better give me the full version, other-wise I'll be tossin' and turnin' all night while I try to puzzle out the final chapters."

"We're making progress," Trinidad assured him. "And, if your invitation still holds, I figure I'm about a pitcher of lemonade and modest supper away from my coda."

"As I recollect my limited study of music, which I learned about in school back when Saint Peter was a boy," Heckleson said as they reached the Land Rover, "I'm guessin' this-here coda of yours refers to the eventual end of a long stretch of melody. So, never fear, when we get back home, I'll rustle up some lemonade and, as promised, your invite includes supper grub—cooked just-right even as we speak in that new-fangled slow cooker of mine. Meantime, I have to ask do y'all plan to serenade my kitchen-work with that harmonica that's always in your pocket?"

"I'll entertain you with a tune while you get the lemonade going," said Trinidad as he removed the gun belt and stowed the rifle and pistol. "And I might even have a lullaby for our little friend."

"No need," Heckleson whispered as he carefully fastened his seatbelt to gently encompass the little nodding Chihuahua. "This-here little tyke is already in la-la land. Plum tuckered out, I reckon."

"A friend for life," Trinidad noted while his host made a U-turn and guided the Rover back into the 'Dobies.

Chapter 45

Detour
2019/Sunset on June 8

Arriving back at Heckleson's hilltop home, Trinidad sat on the side porch playing his harmonica as the old ranger checked his slow cooker and mixed lemonade. When his host excused himself to empty out a shoebox and find an old sweater to prepare a bed for the little rescued dog, the detective concluded his concert and took the opportunity to collect his thoughts. The threatened rain had rocketed northward, leaving the 'Dobies high and dry, but rewarding the region with a spectacular sunset. Sitting alone on the side porch in the waning afternoon, the detective mulled over his options.

The next chapter of his story had to do with his former shortcomings. It was one thing to recount his drinking behavior among fellow recovering alcoholics at an AA meeting. It was quite another to admit his past indiscretions to an acquaintance, even the old ranger whom he'd come to consider a close friend. But there was no denying that, thirteen years ago, his drinking had been a factor. His alcohol problem hadn't begun that autumn at Grand Lake, but it certainly inhibited, and nearly scuttled, his quest to locate Buster Bishop. The past was past and maybe it would do some good to take Heckleson into his confidence. Lord knows, confessing everything to Anne had been a blessing.

Confessing—a blessing, Trinidad told himself. "I'm a poet and don't know it," he announced aloud to his host who emerged from the house cradling the Chihuahua and signaling for quiet.

"Asleep?" the detective asked.

"Off and on," Heckleson confirmed. "His bed's all fixed up, but he don't seem willin' to hit the sandman trail just yet. Torn between stayin' up and dozin' off."

Balancing the nodding dog, the old ranger eased into his seat and settled with the determination of a man who had no intention of rising. In the growing darkness, a lone cricket chirped. Then stillness reigned until a distant howl drifted across the darkening landscape of the 'Dobies. The sound caressed the adobe hills, rolled against the Mesa, and met its rebounding echo somewhere in the margins of the dying sunset.

"Your wolf maybe?" Heckleson whispered.

"Maybe," Trinidad speculated. "She probably didn't run far."

"Thinkin' of her little amigo maybe," the old ranger guessed.

"No doubt."

"One more chorus and we'll know for certain," Heckleson said.

A few beats later, the canine anthem sounded again—louder this time and closer. On cue, two strident yips emerged from the Chihuahua. Then, as the day ended, the detective, the ranger, and the small dog were enveloped in silence.

"Well, looks like our critters has settled for the night. So, pick up your tale," he told Trinidad. "But keep your voice down. Taco's had a rough day. He needs his beauty sleep."

"Leave it to you to name your new pet dog after a Mexican entrée," said Trinidad.

"It suits him," Heckleson whispered, then beamed like a proud parent. "Look how the little fella's all scrunched-up, cozy as a rug-bug, lookin' fer all the world like a folded tortilla. So, let's not wake him."

"How's this for volume?" Trinidad inquired.

"Just right," said the old ranger. "I'll sit on this side so's y'all can blab in my good ear."

"Roger that," said Trinidad. "So, let's leave Jackhammer to wend his way through a Grand Lake detour in the summer of 1976 while I return my storyline to October 2006."

Chapter 46

Mists
2006/October 13

Buster Bishop had been missing for three days and Trinidad seemed to be getting nowhere. He was feeling useless, sleepwalking through the hours, moping around the lodge, when he decided to walk downhill to the nearest payphone and call home.

The phone rang four times before his mother answered.

"Been worried," she told him.

"Sorry," Trinidad said. "Busy with school," he lied.

"I checked and found out you left," she said. "But never mind. What's done is done. Where are you now?"

"Grand Lake," Trinidad admitted. "Does Dad know?"

"Waiting for the right time to tell him. When can we expect you home?"

"Can't leave right now," he said and the catch in his voice surprised him. "My friend is missing and I'm trying to help."

"Helping is good," she said. "You always were good to your friends and I know you know best what to do. You just come when you can. And, son—"

"Yes, Ma'am."

"Don't forget to call more often."

"I won't. Love you. Gotta go."

"So, well, we love you too and miss you heaps. You take care of yourself and be careful. And I hope you find your friend."

"Thanks."

Trinidad always felt better after talking to his mother. She had a way of reminding him that he could handle things. Walking away from the vintage phonebooth, he took out his harmonica, played a tune, and wondered if there would ever come a time when he didn't turn to his mother for comfort and advice. He had school friends in Boulder who hadn't spoken to their parents in years. The parents weren't dead, just placed forever on the sidelines.

How is such a thing even possible? he wondered.

By the time the refocused young man reached his apartment, he'd worked out what he needed to do. It took some persuading and a cash bribe, but Trinidad managed to convince Casey to take his night shift. Negotiating with his odious co-worker was a mortifying experience. But it would have been even more awkward to ask Bambi for a favor, so he held his nose and made a deal with Casey.

Trinidad waited for twilight, then he shouldered his pack, picked up his sleeping bag, and set out. Hiking to the far edge of Grand Lake, he was bound for a spot not far from the East Inlet. The location was hard to explain to visitors since the area is also known as the West Portal, owing to the fact that the *western end* of the Alva B. Adams Tunnel resides there.

As he walked toward his destination, Trinidad still found it hard to comprehend that the controversial tunnel existed. But the gigantic portal was hard to miss. So, like it or not, the tunnel was definitely real and there was no denying that it was doing its job. Both a feat of engineering and a point of contention, the structure more than accomplished its single-minded purpose, which was to force millions of gallons of Western Slope water to defy Nature and flow east to serve the burgeoning populations of Colorado's Front Range. Constructed to serve a virtually unquenchable thirst, the conduit transported water to Denver and other urban communities on the eastern side of the Rocky Mountains. The provocative tunnel had, in its day, spawned protests and conjured up its own set of specters and legends.

"But that," Trinidad said aloud as he walked, "is another story. For now, I'll take one legend at a time."

The autumn nights had grown crisp. With each step, his breath shaped visible puffs and silence reigned, fusing lake and sky and shore into a single expectant entity.

A few short weeks spent at the lodge had exposed the impressionable young man to a variety of legends concerning Grand Lake. Some informants renamed the water Spirit Lake. Some pronounced the lake cursed. Others christened it sacred. And every tale seemed to rely on hearsay. Frustrated by his inability to locate Buster Bishop and confused by conflicting versions of the Grand Lake story, the unrequited searcher decided to take matters into his own hands.

If the lake held secrets, he was determined to unlock those riddles. If the lake harbored spirits, he'd seek them out and solicit their help.

Reaching the boat launch, Trinidad placed his burdens on the damp wooden planks and watched the autumn sunset trickle rivulets of molten gold onto the mirrored surface of Grand Lake. A chorus of crickets and frogs held forth in a nearly deafening throng then, abruptly, the rustic concert ceased as an inescapable, saturating tranquility overwhelmed the scene. In the quiet and gradually, like a slowly spreading frost, a dusky haze materialized to inhabit the space between fading daylight and darkening water.

By diminishing stages, as the day ended, the haze melted to form vertical pinches of wispy mist which stretched skyward like the final smoky updrafts of a dying campfire. Forming columns of radiant fog, the meandering mist advanced eastward until it encircled the waiting man. Surrounded by haze, Trinidad watched fleeting shapes writhe and warp, resolving and dissolving into ephemeral images which are the stuff of legends.

He'd come to the water's edge to immerse himself in the rising vapors. For better or worse, he'd tap into the water's most mystic legend, in hopes of summoning whatever spirits dwelt in its depths. Unrolling his sleeping bag, he crawled inside and prepared to spend the night, lying awake, if he could manage it, to watch and listen from dusk to dawn. He'd stay there all night and alone, hoping to learn for himself if the old stories were true.

There are many versions of the so-called Ute Legend, including a surplus of tales repeated around countless Anglo campfires. Not to mention innumerable fictions told to visitors. This oral tradition has been amplified in written form, including tortured verse penned by non-Native poets and synopses reprised, ad infinitum, in regional promotional literature.

If such ubiquitous and unauthorized stories are to be believed, something profound and tragic happened here in early times. Whatever transpired, it took place before hardy trappers and questing miners arrived on the shores of Grand Lake and before resident Utes were evicted from their ancestral lands. The thing happened beyond the memory of living eyewitnesses. It happened without a newspaper reporter on the scene. There was no aspiring novelist to record the incident. No painter or sketchbook artist to capture the scene. No hieroglyphic etcher to memorialize the event. No petroglyphic artisan to incise a rock and no pictographic interpreter to splash pigment on stone. No telegraph or telephone or television on hand. Not a single hovering drone nor ubiquitous cellphone camera.

Some say the stories are wrong. Some say the stories are correct.

Over the years, the Ute Legend has been distilled down to a persistent yarn—a ghost story kept alive by those who got it secondhand while sitting cross-legged around the dying embers of distant fires. Folded into a repertoire of sleep-over fiction, the Ute tale has been introduced as a true story. Though told alongside such classics as "The Golden Arm" and the ever-popular "Headless Hitchhiker," the Ute story is consistently singled out as a factual account. Yes, there had been an attack. Yes, people had drowned. Therefore, their sad spirits linger at Grand Lake. Though embroidered and warped by repeated telling, the account was nevertheless passed along as gospel. Trinidad had first heard it from Bambi who heard the story from her roommate, who learned it from their housemother whose brother absorbed it at scout camp. And so on.

But whether anything happened at all is a matter of conjecture.

Chapter 47

Visions
2019/Dusk on June 8

"What can I say?" Trinidad asked the old ranger. "When it came time to understand the Grand Lake legend, all I had to go on were hand-me-down reports. I needed something more visceral, more immediate, more personal. I thought I might find it that night on the water."

Silence occupied the space between the two men.

"Well," his audience of one prompted.

"How do you feel about visions?" Trinidad asked.

"Was y'all drunk?"

"I may have needed a drink, but I was sober as a judge," Trinidad assured his friend.

"But asleep?" Heckleson clarified.

"Asleep in *this* world," the detective said.

"Mercy," said the old ranger. "Well, let's have the whole hog of the enchilada."

"Okay," Trinidad said and he got eye contact with his host. "This is the truth, okay?"

"Never doubted it," Heckleson assured the detective. "So, let's have it and don't spare the horseradish. But hold on a bit until I put this little pup to bed."

Fifteen minutes later, the old ranger returned.

"Warms the cocktails of my heart to have that little tyke here," Heckleson said as he resumed his seat. "Miss havin' a dependent underfoot. I guess you never miss the water 'til the well runs dry."

Trinidad grinned, then cleared his throat and continued his tale.

"As 2006 drew closer to winter," the detective recalled, "the October days were growing shorter. Nevertheless, daylight still lasted a few ticks beyond eleven hours. True dusk arrived on Grand Lake about 6:15, although surrounding peaks swallowed the daylight much earlier. The rising sun—officially scheduled to appear around 7:15 in the morning—was unlikely to reach the lake until closer to eight. The temporal math was tyrannical. No matter how I parsed the time, it looked like my plan to sleep on one of the lake's open docks meant I was in for a long and chilly night. With each passing minute, the temperature plummeted. The cold kept me mostly awake, but I drifted in and out of sleep. Muddled thoughts coursed through my mind, clouding my semi-lucid moments, while my deeper slumber was populated with technicolor images."

"Y'all had visions," the old ranger guessed. "Sober visions," he added.

"I had 'em," Trinidad confirmed. "I had 'em full-on, thick on the ground, twice on Sunday, and up to my elbows in spades."

"By the bucketful?" Heckleson asked.

"By the ever-loving brimming bucketful," Trinidad assured his host.

"Total recall?" Heckleson asked.

"Total," Trinidad declared.

"Understood," the old ranger noted. "So, let's hear what y'all got."

Chapter 48

Guide
2006/Late on October 13

While Trinidad held his restless vigil on the margins of Grand Lake, unending waves caused the floating dock to undulate gently like the soothing, steady motion of a rocking cradle. As thoughts ebbed and flowed, mirroring the rhythm of the waves, his existence dissolved, by relentless degrees, into the realm of deeper slumber. External time traced its inexorable journey from dusk to dawn while the sleeper's internal clock became stuck in a perpetual cycle. Like expanding ripples drifting outward when a stone penetrates water, his dreaming mind drifted beyond the present. Rather than progressing or standing still, time turned on its heel and retreated to the distant past.

Trinidad's guide was an old woman—or seemed to be one. It's difficult to say. Let us say, for the sake of clarity, that it was an old woman who spoke to him—gruff yet patient—amazed at the youth's ignorance, but also charmed by his thirst for knowledge.

What do you want, child? the woman asked.
Who are you?
I am called Sweetgrass, child. Survivor of the fatal ambush. Tree-dweller. Shore-runner. You would call me Truth. Some call me Ylem. I am what I am. What do you want, child? she asked again.

Where are you?

We are here, child. What do you want? she asked a third time.

I seek a man who is lost.

All men are lost, child.

This man has been taken against his will.

The will is illusion. There is no will of the individual. Only the all.

This man will be harmed if I do not find him.

You make yourself too important. Your thoughts deceive you.

What must I do to understand?

To ask is to begin to understand. To seek is to understand.

What should I ask? How shall I seek?

Ask for understanding. Seek understanding.

Help me understand.

Open your mind. Open your heart. What do you see?

I see a house. A house on a lake.

Follow the track and find your answer.

But where—where?

Trinidad recalled that he seemed to awaken, but knew he was dreaming. The surface of Grand Lake seemed awash in candles—thousands, perhaps millions of candles seemed to float on the waves. It was as if every star in the night sky had descended to populate the dark water. He heard accumulating voices, troubled cries which were instantly swallowed by a rising wind. A gale blew, roiling the water and extinguishing all except a single candle which seemed to hover, like a lantern, and skim above the churning waves. Flying northward, the moving candle collided with and ignited the far shore. The flash was brief, like a single burst of a strobe light, but the pulse lingered long enough to illuminate the silhouette of a wooden boathouse.

When Trinidad opened his eyes, the wind had indeed risen and he was greeted by an icy spray of waves cascading over the wooden dock. Stumbling out of his damp sleeping bag, he was about to abandon his quest when he noticed a flicker of light on the northern shore. Someone was carrying a lantern. He only caught a momentary glimpse, but it was enough.

Chapter 49

Boathouse
2019/Dark on June 8

"And you're tellin' me that this-here vision is gonna lead y'all to check out the Grand Lake boathouses?"

"That's about the size of it," Trinidad confirmed.

"So, did y'all finally find what y'all expected in them boathouses?"

"Not exactly," Trinidad admitted.

Chapter 50

Track
2006/Morning on October 14

Dawn was breaking as Trinidad collected his belongings, left the dock behind, and made his way to the graveled road which ran along Grand Lake's northern shore. Acting on his vision, he was planning to conduct a systematic search of several boathouses when he stumbled onto a freshly plowed track. The clearly unsanctioned pathway had been etched into a damp expanse of scrub grass which separated the unpaved roadway from the shoreline. A pair of narrow cuts formed a tandem trail which gave the impression that two giant snakes had slithered from road to shore. Such irregular scars could only have been made by the passage of a sidecar tethered to a motorcycle. Some random rider might have careened off the access road and headed cross-country toward Grand Lake, but he doubted if any law-abiding motorcycle jockey would take such a route. Only a desperate rider would carve this hasty path and he was certain the kidnapper was desperate.

Trinidad had abandoned his legal studies, but even a first-year pre-law student would recognize the point at which a kidnapping morphed into homicide. The demise of Buster's twin might turn out to be accidental, but harming a kidnap victim amounted to an aggravated offense, which meant the death penalty would be on the table when the perpetrator was apprehended.

"Good luck with that," he said aloud as he wondered what method of restraint and how many posse members it was going to take to bring the giant kidnapper to heel. He himself had barely glimpsed the man, but everyone seemed to equate his size with that of a bear. It was a comparison which suggested the mysterious fugitive was a formidable foe.

Following the trail, Trinidad discovered that the track faded when he reached harder-packed ground, but its trajectory was clear. Where the kidnapper had stashed the motorcycle was uncertain, but there was only one boathouse nearby. For a moment, he hesitated, wondering if he should proceed or go for help. Chances were the villain and his prisoner were long-gone. By now, the trail would've grown cold, but the boathouse might yet hold clues. Before seeking help, he'd take a quick look inside.

Placing his pack and rolled sleeping bag against the building's exterior wall, Trinidad moved cautiously as he traversed the wooden slats of the wharf which lay alongside. Reaching an entryway, he tested the dilapidated door and eased through.

In the dim interior, he caught sight of Buster, the old man's gagged face peeking through one end of a canvas shroud. Only the head was visible. The rest of him was encased like a mummy. Trinidad took a tentative step toward his imprisoned friend. A rustling noise caused him to turn as the looming figure of a fur-bound creature emerged from the shadows. The figure rushed forward and the young man's inquisitive exploration ended instantly with a sharp blow to his forehead.

Trinidad awoke to the sound of dripping water. A torrent of October rain hammered on the roof above. At least he guessed he was under a roof. It was pouring. His head hurt and he was freezing, but he wasn't wet. Therefore, logic suggested he was under a roof.

"Logic," he said aloud and the word hung in the humid air, sounding flat and stifled. "Logic," he repeated, imbibing the word with venom as he verbally chastised himself for his idiocy.

Lying on his side, Trinidad flexed his fingers to test the restraints which pinned his hands behind his back. The knots were tight and rough fibers cut into his wrists. A web of strands encircled his torso, forming a constricting cocoon which held his chest, imprisoned his stomach and crotch, and snaked down to confine his legs. As a sailor, his primary thought was someone would be missing a halyard line. As a would-be detective, his considered opinion was he was royally screwed.

His encounter with the bear had been brief.

The kidnapper must have heard Trinidad's footsteps on the boarded wharf; heard the young fool pause outside the entrance; listened as he tried the knob; heard him struggle with the door—so crooked that it had to be pried open; heard the vintage hinges creak like a constipated church organ; and heard the damn thing slam unaccountably shut after he'd passed through.

Sighing with abject misery, Trinidad recalled the immense shape of his assailant and revisited his thoughts about what it would take to corral the big man. But such speculation was fleeting. For the time being, that pursuit and capture would have to be someone else's problem. Because his own aborted attempt had allowed the villain to escape and left him, Buster's would-be rescuer, trussed up like a Thanksgiving turkey.

Meanwhile, his ears were still ringing from the blow which had knocked him senseless. Scrunching his eyes against the pain, he could feel a layer of encrusted blood plastered on his left temple. What had the man, if it was a man, used to knock Trinidad senseless?

Whatever had been used to strike the bumbling concierge, it had done a thorough job because the muted light slanting into the boathouse through slits in porous walls suggested the day was ending. He'd blundered inside in the early morning. Now it was nearly dusk.

Wriggling like a seal, Trinidad tucked his chin to stare past his restrained feet. If a boat had once been tied to the now empty slip, that craft was long-gone. A combination of unwise noises had alerted the villain and the huge assailant had made quick work of his inept pursuer. He'd subdued Trinidad with a single blow, hamstrung his unconscious visitor, and made good his escape.

Trinidad had envisioned himself the dashing hero, arriving in the nick of time to save Buster. Instead, he'd played the buffoon, stumbling into an ambush, unable to help the old man, unable to help himself.

"No help," he said aloud and then he repeated the thought. *Nobody's coming,* he reminded himself. He hadn't told anyone where he was going—not even Bambi. He'd made his own bed, now he'd have to lie in it.

How long?'

Someone might notice the track he'd followed. But, if no one was curious, it might be hours before anybody wandered by and made their way along the wharf to try the door. It might be days. Probably, this late in the season, it would be weeks, presuming anyone came at all.

Awkwardly raising his head, he sought to examine his surroundings. Recognizing the place as Ferryman's boathouse, he groaned. It would be a long time before his former guide, who'd been so generous with his time and information, returned to this spot. When they last spoke, Ferryman revealed that he'd be departing for a six-month obligation of National Guard duty. The trusting man asked Trinidad to keep an eye on the place.

So much for Trinidad's tour of guard duty.

How many boathouses had the bear burglarized in search of an operational vessel until he stumbled upon *Osprey*? The search had delayed him long enough so that Trinidad, even with his late start, had managed to intercept kidnapper and prey, only to fall victim to the former and fail the latter.

Trinidad had blundered into Ferryman's boathouse in search of clues, but he had little to show for his botched examination. The stolen vessel was a motorboat which might mean the kidnapper was no sailor. That passing notion was merely a deduction, but it seemed important to the fledgling investigator. It was the first of many presumptions he was destined to make on that fateful day.

"Never presume," he said aloud. "It makes an ass out of you and me," he added, feeling uncertain that he was correctly repeating one of Casey's sarcastic sayings. "Damn, I could use a drink."

Following the echo of his spoken words, Trinidad rolled onto his back and winced as his bound knuckles scraped across rough wooden planks. He stared up at the ceiling and found the view above festooned with a dense array of spider webs. As the rain continued, and without hope of escape or rescue, he sought to take his mind off his troubles by studying the gossamer webs.

Hadn't Ferryman commented on them—apologized for neglecting his housekeeping? Said it was the maid's day off? What did he—?

Suddenly Trinidad's mind was infused with a penetrating thought.

Suppose Ferryman wasn't pulling guard duty. Suppose this boathouse hadn't been burglarized. What if—what if Ferryman and the bear were one and the same. Like the bear, Ferryman was a stout individual with broad shoulders and a linebacker's torso. Trinidad had been looking for an exotic villain. What if the desperado was a local? Ferryman would be a logical choice. Otherwise—out of the myriad of boathouses lining the shore—why choose this one? What was wrong with Ferryman as a suspect?

Everything, Trinidad decided.

On the morning the roof caved in and Saul disappeared, Bambi Taylor had reported that a big visitor, a man overdressed for the weather, had come to the concierge desk the day before to ask about Buster. If Ferryman had been that visitor, she'd have recognized the local character and used his name. But what if the mystery visitor had no connection with the kidnapper? That still left Ferryman on the suspect list. Meanwhile, what about this Scott guy? Trinidad had yet to meet the man who shared the clandestine Shadow Mountain dock and at least two boats with Ferryman? And yet—

Crap, Trinidad told himself. *You're thinking in circles within circles—a good way to disappear down a drain. Forget this idle speculation. Think about something else.*

Looking up again to study the ceiling, he decided he was seeing old constructions. Fresh work by contemporary spiders would, he guessed, be invisible against the dim ceiling. On the other hand, old webs, which had been abandoned, would have unraveled and tangled into elongated wisps of willowy whiteness. Gazing aloft, he could see dozens of anemic strands which stood out starkly against the background of dark, moist wood. Everywhere he looked, spent webs dangled haphazardly and, propelled by some unfelt breeze, the inelegant display of insubstantial forms rotated languidly.

Like cotton candy in a slaughterhouse, his mind told him.

It was an odd thought and one which made him wonder if the kidnapper's villainous blow had caused him to suffer a concussion. His brains had been scrambled by a cranial shock and recovering his senses might prove to be a memorable convalescence—presuming he lived.

Presuming I live, he thought. Once again, he found himself presuming and he realized he was still caught in a vortex of circular thinking, a clear indication, he presumed, of concussive behavior.

"Never presume," the unhappy youth said aloud as he closed his eyes to prepare himself for what looked to be a long wait.

"It makes a 'pre' out of you and me," came the unexpected reply as an enthusiastic Bambi and a frowning Casey knelt at their co-worker's side and began the arduous task of undoing a cavalcade of tightly constructed knots.

Chapter 51

Drunk
2006/Late Afternoon on October 14

After freeing Trinidad, his liberators pulled him outside where they propped him on the wharf with his back against the boathouse. He'd been saved, but the rescue proved bittersweet. While Bambi knelt at his side, Casey gleefully took charge of the situation by deciding to summon the authorities. In search of a cellphone signal, Casey moved away to pace the shore.

"We're back together again," Bambi confessed when Trinidad's nemesis was out of earshot. "Sorry," she added, "couldn't seem to help myself."

"How?" Trinidad asked.

"It just happened," Bambi began to explain, then halted. "Oh, you mean how did we find you? Well, it wasn't easy. The messenger you sent wasn't all that helpful. No offense, but next time you might try to choose somebody under the age of a hundred."

"I—" Trinidad began, but found he couldn't finish his thought.

"Anyway," said Bambi, "the old lady finally had to write out her message—most of which was unclear except I certainly recognized the word 'boathouse.' There were plenty of possibilities and we searched in vain until we saw that cut in the grass, then spotted your pack and bedroll, which is what led us here. Are you sure you're all right—I mean not hurt of course—but also are you good with me and Casey?"

"Understood," Trinidad croaked, his throat parched from his boathouse ordeal. "Understood," he repeated, although he didn't really understand at all. He had no recollection of telling anyone what he was up to, let alone sending a messenger. Nevertheless, for a third time he said, "Understood." Then he closed both eyes in an effort to make sense of things. He needed to concentrate which proved to be a challenge as Bambi took a deep breath and launched into one of her marathon commentaries.

"You're a peach," she said. "But you're also a mess...I've asked you twice how you ended up here...and all I got out of you was something about chasing down that old Ute Legend...my mom says that old legend is a sum-say—you know sum-say this and sum-say that...until you don't know what to believe... everybody has an opinion...just like the debate over where the Colorado River begins...sum-say the river starts in Grand Lake, sum-say the headwaters start at Poudre Pond...sum-say Lark City's the source...I say not worth fighting over...but anyway, what I started to say is I think you'd better call your folks...remember you said you might, so I think you should do that soon...as for right now, you just rest and sit tight...I'll be right back."

When she left—presumably to see what progress Casey was making—Trinidad opened his eyes and languidly turned his head to keep an eye on his rescuers. When Bambi reached Casey, words were exchanged and the pair wandered far from the shore, apparently arguing.

Seeing the couple distracted, Trinidad struggled to his feet and slipped away. In the regular world—in a world not shifting in and out of time—he'd have gathered up his pack and sleeping bag. As it was, he left them behind. As for his rescuers, let them make their calls. The last thing he wanted was to face scrutiny and answer questions posed by law enforcement. If the law arrived, what would they do? Probably chew him out. Possibly arrest him for trespassing. It was a bleak prospect. Suppose he wasn't arrested and an ambulance came to whisk him away. How could he help Buster if he was hospitalized? Whatever the authorities had in mind, Trinidad didn't relish their intervention.

Better, he decided, *to disappear.*

Shunning contact with his co-workers or anybody else, he walked back to the lodge, locked himself in his tiny room, and slept the remainder of the day away, refusing to answer the door.

When the knocking ceased, he pulled himself out of bed, stumbled to the bathroom, and switched on the light.

"You look like crap," he told his bedraggled reflection.

Using masking tape and strips torn from an old t-shirt, he managed to bandage his aching head and lacerated knuckles. To hide his head wound, he left his Stetson at home and emerged from his self-imposed exile wearing his uncle's close-fitting watch cap.

Walking downtown in the dark, he used a rear entrance and planted himself on a bar stool at the Rope-a-Dope Saloon.

Hours later, the unhappy concierge was still there, balancing on the stool as he nursed a broken heart. Sitting alone, he realized his heart actually hurt—almost as much as his bruised head and fingers. Deep in the smoky recesses of the empty tavern, he swallowed his third margarita, thought of Bambi, and told himself it was probably impossible to get drunk on three southwestern martinis. Which would have been a reasonable conclusion had he not preceded that trio of relatively pedestrian drinks by downing six vodka gimlets and prefacing those half-dozen cocktails with four stout beers.

"Don't never misk your lubricants," he slurred when the bartender arrived to announce he was cutting him off.

Sliding to the floor, Trinidad found his feet, made his way unsteadily to the back door, and stumbled into the night. He started toward the lodge, but the uphill pathway discouraged him and, like a true river, he changed course and headed downstream in the direction of the shore. Which is how the intoxicated youth found himself approaching the vehicle bridge which spans the narrow channel connecting the natural waters of Grand Lake with the impounded waters of Shadow Mountain Reservoir.

His journey took him in the wrong direction. He was heading downhill into the woods, not uphill toward his room, and traveling south instead of north. And yet—given that he could have stumbled bodily into and drown in either the lake or the reservoir or the channel, taking the bridge was a passable idea.

Seasonally speaking, it was a relatively warm night—about 40 degrees—a veritable heat wave in October. Expunged of tourists, the town was quiet. Stars abounded; their sheen made all the more brilliant by the waning glow of a gibbous moon in its last quarter. In the final analysis, walking south might not have been a dangerous decision or even a foolish one had Trinidad not fixed his gaze on the dim moon and made himself dizzy. With an audible sigh, the dazed pedestrian sat wearily down, folded his inebriated torso into a fetal position and fell fast asleep, beneath the overarching support beams of the highway bridge and smack-dab in the middle of the pavement.

He slept until dawn when a blaring horn broke into his dream. The warning sounded again and Trinidad managed to open one eye. Having struggled in his sleep to find a satisfactory position, he'd eventually adopted a face-up posture. Lying on his back, he opened both eyes. Staring upward, he studied the latticework of girders which crisscrossed the bridge's superstructure. So similar to interlaced spider webs were the interlocking beams that he thought for a moment he was still stuck inside Ferryman's boathouse.

A third toot from an impatient horn and a diesel truck wheeled around, then hit its brakes to drone ominously with its front tire vibrating inches from the young man's skull. A window whirled down and the driver cursed at the prostrate drunk before roaring away.

"That was an unkind comment," Trinidad assured the departed motorist who was instantly out of earshot.

Another honking vehicle rocketed past and Trinidad took the increasing traffic as a sign that he'd better remove himself from the road. He stumbled to the edge of the bridge and was peering over to consider the narrow waterway below when the strident airhorn of a passing boat brought him firmly to his senses.

"Okay. Okay," he insisted. "I get the picture. I don't belong here. I'll go home."

Searching the horizon and presuming it was morning rather than sundown, he estimated where east should be, turned 90 degrees, convinced himself he was heading north, and stepped in that direction.

He found the going level and he made good progress. Wending his way along narrow byways, he walked through a neighborhood of closely packed houses and cabins. Some were historic buildings, some modern, and all doing their best to reflect the town's unique knotty pine exteriors. Coming abreast of one historic structure, he waved languidly at a woman in period costume who was sweeping the front walk. She smiled a maternal smile, shook her head, and returned to her task. He passed by dwelling after dwelling, admiring each unique exterior formed by geometric clusters of small, rough-hewn logs running vertically, horizontally, and at 45-degree angles, depending on the whims of the builder.

As Trinidad trudged along, the variegated exteriors reminded the dazed pedestrian of the crazy-quilt patterns constructed by his mother, grandmother, and maiden aunt. Growing up, he looked forward to helping those much-loved women as they congregated in his grandmother's farmhouse to blend the ritual of autumnal sewing with the timeless joy of gossip. His job, as a skinny runt of a kid, was to crawl beneath the quilting frame to retrieve errant threads and dropped needles.

Steeped in that warm memory, he glanced back for another look at the sweeping woman who must have completed her chore because she was nowhere to be seen. Continuing on, he found himself wishing he could reverse the clock and return to that simpler time when the world made sense. In those carefree days he was a happy and helpful kid.

Look at me now, he chided himself. *What would Grandma make of me—a wretched jilted lover, haunted by spirits, shambling through deserted streets, nursing a hangover, and praying my bladder will hold?*

Reaching Grand Avenue, he sought to locate coffee and a bathroom, not necessarily in that order. But town businesses were shuttered and the streets were deserted.

"Of course," he decided, reminding himself that nothing was amiss. After all, it was early in the morning during mid-week in the retail doldrums which fell between the rush of summer tourists and advent of the Christmas-shopping crowd.

Although Trinidad understood the reasons for the slumbering town, his sphincter was tightening and his complaining bladder about to burst. Seeking relief, the questing concierge decided to retrace his steps in hopes of converting a discretely unoccupied alleyway into an emergency latrine.

To this end, he stumbled back along Vine Street and discovered, to his relief, that some kind soul had plopped a portable latrine in the alleyway adjacent to the old Cottage Camp building. An historic site which used to accommodate early 20th century tourists, the building served as a monument to hardy motoring pioneers who'd once endured a daunting automobile journey over alpine roads to reach the Grand Lake community.

"Any port in a storm," he told himself as he trundled inside the latrine, slid the "occupied" bolt home, and took a seat. Still hungover and with nothing to read, he closed his eyes, let his weary head loll forward, and was soon fast asleep.

How long he lingered there, cradled in the dark confines of that state-of-the-art outhouse, he was uncertain. What he did remember was awakening with a start, fumbling for the flush level until he realized there was none, and using the last of the toilet paper. Standing awkwardly to re-buckle his trousers, he stumbled outside into the blinding sunlight and barely missed being rundown by a passing horse and buggy.

"Mind yourself, pilgrim," called the driver.

Trinidad watched the vintage conveyance rumble past, marveling at the driver's period costume and wondering whether he'd missed a memo regarding some sort of pioneer celebration. He was still pondering that idea when another buggy heading north and a horse-drawn wagon heading south converged on his position.

"Give way!" the wagoner shouted.

"Get out of the damn street, tenderfoot!" yelled a man across the road.

Trinidad took several steps backward and nearly lost his footing as his heels collided with a raised wooden sidewalk. Jostled by passersby, he sought refuge in an open doorway and gazed in amazement at a passing cavalcade of horses, wagons, and pedestrians crowding the narrow thoroughfare and filling rough-planked sidewalks on either side.

The walkers, mostly men, were burdened by packs of every description. Many carried shovels and picks slung over broad shoulders. The entire scene resembled a vintage photograph with everything rendered in sepia tones. The people, the animals, and the landscape seemed to glow with honey-colored light.

"Dreaming," Trinidad told himself aloud. "Hungover, screwed-up, spiritually saturated, and trapped in a crazy dream."

"Ain't we all, brother," quipped a voice at his elbow. "Buy us a drink?"

"Where's everybody headed?" Trinidad asked.

"Silver strike—or a rumor of one. How about that drink?"

"I think I've had enough," Trinidad decided.

"This ain't about you, sailor. I'm the one what needs a drink."

Trinidad ignored the thirsty man, joined the throng, and soon found himself miles from Grand Lake, standing in a field of snow and freezing. Several forms approached him, but drifted by, each passage gracing him with a momentary warmth which quickly vanished as the specter dissolved. A final apparition paused beside him and she—for it was clearly a woman—spoke.

"May it serve you well," the specter declared. Then the lingering spirit fell silent for a heartbeat only to continue in a cadence which conveyed a sense of urgency

"Turn back," she said.

"He needs you now."

"Nothing here."

"Turn around."

"Go! I'll be all right."

The spirit vanished and, though his feet remained still, Trinidad seemed to glide, like an ice skater, involuntarily over the snow in the direction of a cluster of wretched buildings. Swirling wind stirred the snow and, on the crest of that breeze, he heard the melancholy warble of a bugling elk. He drifted onward until he reached and passed a hand-lettered sign.

"Lark City," he read aloud.

"Go! I'll be all right," a voice seemed to answer.

He attempted to turn, but his body would not obey and he continued forward—conveyed headlong by an unseen force. In the distance, he sensed movement. The sensation was indistinct, as if a cloud had descended and assumed a corporeal shape which rose on two legs and rushed in his direction. As the shape drew nearer, it resolved, like a film coming into focus, until he saw, too late, that it was a bear—a huge dark bear on a collision course.

"No!" he shouted as he threw up his arms to protect himself from the impact.

Chapter 52

Sober
2019/Darker Still on June 8

Trinidad paused, realizing he'd been so caught up in his memories that he'd actually raised his arms in a protective stance. Embarrassed by his fervor, he dropped his guard and looked to his host for comment.

"So," the old ranger offered an evaluation of Trinidad's latest narrative, "here's a cautionary tale fer all youngsters what thinks drinkin' to excess is a picnic. I've been buzz-brained my share of times, but never so drunk as to be transported into a past with such life-like characters and places."

"Count yourself lucky," said Trinidad. "I'm not proud of my drunken exploits even if they did offer me a glimpse of Grand Lake in its mining hey-day. I can't explain that porta-potty portal to the past. The whole point of my relating this particular incident is to testify that the town, the lake, and the whole atmosphere of the place are overflowing with nostalgic energy. The past is ever-present in those mountains and it just takes a little nudge—whether alcohol-induced or the result of an active imagination—to take a modern-day visitor down a wistful rabbit hole. Jackhammer felt and experienced it. I did too and I doubt there's a single insightful visitor who doesn't feel some unknown force pulling them, for better or worse, into the place's bygone history.

"The years orbiting Grand Lake are all jumbled together, like the exteriors of their crazy-quilt buildings, and the centuries are separated from one another by a thin veneer which, every now and then, dissolves when past and present collide."

"A vortex," Heckleson suggested. "I heard-tell of them two-way portals which tempt us here present to journey into the past and beyond. Like a whirlpool that might suck a feller into distant memories or future fantasies. A feller might be tempted to jump ahead or back when he ought to focus on the here-and-now. When he ought to face what comes up today—not wallow in the past or speculate, all dreamy-eyed, about some unknowable up-comin' time."

"Why, Dallas," Trinidad observed, his eyebrows arching to their maximum height, "I believe you've taken on the role of official sage and resident philosopher of the 'Dobies."

"Fling your load of manure a bit wider," said the old ranger. "It's gettin' way too deep in here fer us common folks. What I'm sayin' is we done sold our cow, so we don't still need your bull."

"Point taken," said Trinidad as his host's hall clock struck the hour. "And I'd better speed up my story or else I'll never make it home at a decent hour."

"The decent hours has come and gone," said Heckleson. "Meantime, I've got a notion I myself can guess what's comin' next."

"What's your best guess on what the next chapter will bring?" Trinidad asked, his interest truly piqued by the old ranger's prediction.

"I'm thinkin'," said his host. "That it's just about time fer the long arm of the law to enter the picture."

"And you'd be one-hundred-percent correct," said Trinidad.

Chapter 53

Law
2006/Late Afternoon on October 14

Years ago, trying to shake off a hangover, a younger—but unfortunately not-wiser Trinidad was struggling to emerge from a vivid daydream. He placed both hands over his eyes, rocked to-and-fro on the seat of the portable toilet, and shouted "no" over and over again.

"Yo!" a rhyming echo punctured Trinidad's dream.

"No!" he shouted.

"Yo!" the echo repeated. "Yo! Police! Open up!"

Trinidad's vision faded as a strident voice reached his ears. The sound pulled the dreamer back to the real world. It was dark inside the latrine and despite the unlovely accommodations, he felt safe there. Given a choice, he'd stay where he was. But the voice of authority was ordering him into the light.

"Sorry," he attempted to apologize through the door. "Must've dozed off."

"Open up! Do it now!"

Sheepishly, Trinidad unlatched the door.

"Cap off and let's see those hands!"

Trinidad removed his watch cap, clutched the covering in one hand, and raised both arms.

"I know this guy," the deputy said. "You can put your hands down. Are you injured?"

Trinidad involuntarily fingered his head and answered, "Just a scratch."

"Some scratch," said the lawman as he eyed Trinidad's array of bandages.

Gathering his wits, Trinidad stared at the portly man's name badge and read it aloud.

"Woodward," he said as he recollected meeting the deputy on the day Saul was killed.

"That's me," came the reply. "Grand County Deputy Sheriff Woody Woodward and that would make you Trinidad Sands. We met at Shadow Mountain."

"I remember," Trinidad said.

"A sad business," said Woodward. "And you and the old guy gave me a run for my money as I recall."

"Sorry about that," Trinidad apologized.

"No worries," Woodward assured him. "Most folks would say I needed the exercise. So, anyway, your girlfriend's been calling us every hour-on-the-hour asking can we do a welfare check on you. Went to your place last night, but found it unlocked and empty. Checked around town and left my card at all the bars. This morning the Rope-a-Dope calls and says someone of your general description left around midnight, but wearing a cap instead of a Stetson. Then, this morning, a couple of drivers called us to report a body on the bridge and while I was up there about to call dispatch and call for boats to drag the canal, I get a call that somebody answering your description went into this-here latrine, but didn't come out again. So, I put two-and-two together and took a chance and banged on the door and here you are."

"Here I am," Trinidad confirmed.

"And here we go," said Woodward. "Follow me please."

"Am I under arrest?"

"Not hardly," Woodward assured him. "But the sheriff wants to talk to you and what the sheriff wants, I want."

"That sounds like a good policy," Trinidad guessed.

"Yeah-boy," said Woodward as he directed Trinidad to the front passenger seat. "You ride along with me. The back seat is for perps which you ain't—not yet anyway."

"Much obliged," said Trinidad.

"Protect and serve," said Woodward as he climbed into his patrol car.

Sheriff Al Crosswind sat at his desk reviewing the contents of a folder while Trinidad waited nervously in an adjacent office chair.

"Hmm," Crosswind said as he closed the folder. "Son, do you have any idea what a pain in the ass you are?"

Trinidad was tempted to answer that he was well aware of that fact, but he held his peace.

"So, seems your girlfriend has a theory about why no one's seen hide-nor-hair of Red Bishop since his brother's Estes Park funeral," the Sheriff said. "What's your story?"

"Pretty sure Buster's been kidnapped," Trinidad responded.

"By a—" the sheriff opened the folder to re-read the contents. "*By a bear,* it says here. Or somebody dressed like a bear—is that your story?"

"Yes, sir."

"Hmm," Crosswind sighed. "And driving a motorcycle?"

"Appears like."

"Funny that no one else has seen this particular bear," the sheriff noted.

"Just me and Bambi, I guess," Trinidad agreed.

"Hmm," Crosswind said. "And this Bambi is a deer?"

"The girlfriend," whispered Woodward who stood nearby.

"Ex-girlfriend," Trinidad corrected.

"So," said Crosswind, "you and your—ex-girlfriend—saw this bear at the cemetery."

"Not sure if Bambi saw him or not," Trinidad clarified. "But I'm pretty sure the Clydesdale will remember seeing him."

"The Clydesdale—?" Crosswind wondered aloud.

"The Frenchman," Woodward explained. "One of six cyclists who served as pallbearers at the Estes funeral."

"So," the sheriff ventured with a withering look at his know-it-all deputy. "Let me see if I have this straight. You and your—ex-girlfriend—and Red Bishop and the Clydesdale and five other bike riders all went to Saul's funeral in Estes Park. Everybody left except you and the horse—the Clydesdale that is—and then what happened?"

"Red was kidnapped—I think," Trinidad said.

"You think?"

"Well—" Trinidad hesitated.

"Says here, this Bambi didn't actually see anybody kidnap Red," the sheriff noted. "Did you see this alleged kidnapping?"

"No, but—"

"No," Crosswind agreed, his unfriendly face distorted in a caustic smirk. "What Bambi says you saw was somebody dressed like a bear, riding a motorcycle."

"None saw the motorcycle too and the rider," Trinidad added as he suddenly remembered the ranger who'd flirted with Bambi at the Rocky Mountain National Park entryway.

"None saw the motorcycle?" Crosswind snarled. "What the heck does that even mean?"

"Ranger None," whispered Woodward.

"Oh, None," said Crosswind as he re-opened the file and shuffled through the papers. "And Dave None says here that he saw the motorcycle and someone dressed in a long coat, etcetera, but what he don't say is anything about seeing Red."

"Sidecar," Trinidad suggested.

"What do you mean 'sidebar?' Are you invoking your rights to talk to a lawyer?"

"Not sidebar, chief," Woodward whispered. "He means the motorcycle had a sidecar."

"Don't you have some work to do, Woody?"

"Not at the moment," Woodward frowned.

"Well, go do something somewhere else," the sheriff fumed. "You're beginning to get on my nerves with all your uninvited comments."

"Okay, boss," said Woodward.

The sheriff watched to make certain his kibitzing deputy was out of earshot, then he addressed Trinidad. "Look, junior," he said, "you seem to think

I've got nothing to do but chase after you and waste time looking into Red's situation. You're more trouble than you're worth and those two brothers have a reputation for playing hide-and-seek. It's my considered opinion that Red's still upset about Saul's accident and the old troublemaker has wandered off to be alone for a while—just like he did at the reservoir when we recovered his brother's body. And what the hell Saul was doing up in our lookout tower messing around with matches and a kerosene lamp is anybody's guess and just another indication that he and his elderly brother were never playing with a full deck—"

Trinidad started to comment, but the sheriff cut him off.

"Let me finish," Crosswind demanded, his voice exhibiting unmistakable signs of a fraying temper. "We're short on manpower here and we don't have time to be chasing our tails. We've got Ranger None's statement—*no Red*. And we've wasted time trying to track down this Frenchman and even if we find the elusive cyclist what will he tell us—again, *no Red*. Your ex-girlfriend's already given her statement which says *no Red*. I'll stretch a point and grant that some guy in a weird outfit may be riding around on a motorcycle, but there ain't one scrap of actual concrete evidence that—bear or no bear— there's any foul play involved in Red Bishop's supposed disappearance. I've got Estes P.D. looking for him down the mountain and my guess is he'll turn up when he wants to be found—"

Again, Trinidad started to say something and, again, the sheriff shut him down.

"I'm talking. Did I ask you to say anything?"

"No, sir."

"So, keep your mouth shut and I'll talk for you," the sheriff growled. "Because, junior, I know what you're gonna say. You're gonna protest and ask who tied you up? Who bruised your head and hurt your hands?"

"Well, who did?"

"Hell," said the exasperated sheriff, "I have no idea. But I do have a theory. You drink a bit, I'm told."

Trinidad remained silent as Crosswind thumbed through his file folder.

"I have a statement here from one Jackson Casey which suggests that you have a habit of falling down drunk on a regular basis and—"

Trinidad made a sputtering sound.

"And," the sheriff continued, "Mr. Casey surmises that you conspired with parties unknown to have yourself tied up so as to elicit sympathy from Miss Taylor, whom he says, and I quote, 'dumped you like yesterday's newspaper.' He also says you're a worthless employee with a string of unexcused absences who's about to be fired from his lodge job and a troublemaker and a cry-baby. What do you say to that?"

Trinidad's wounded feelings overwhelmed his anger so that—although he'd intended to respond with unbridled rage—he was so hungover and his emotions were so raw that the hurt was evident in his voice.

"He can't say that about me," Trinidad whined.

"Are you gonna cry?" the sheriff mocked.

"No," Trinidad said, his voice small and unsteady.

"You are!" the sheriff taunted. "You're damn-well crying! Nobody cries in my office! Get the hell out of my sight!"

Chapter 54

Advice
2019/Early Evening on June 8

"So," Heckleson decided. "Seems like the local law wasn't much help. No call fer this-here well-named character to treat yourself like that. Appears like y'all was already rode hard and put away wet and here this Crosswind goes and kicks a fella while he's down."

"I was down that much is certain," the detective admitted. "About as low as I can ever recall."

"Which meant y'all was on your own," his host observed.

"Looks like," Trinidad agreed.

"Well," the old ranger said, "I just got two words of advice for your younger self—and them words is: watch yer back."

The old ranger's two-word observation was actually three, but the detective absolutely comprehended the message.

"Words to live by," he told Heckleson as he picked up the thread of his story.

Chapter 55

What Happens When You Don't Watch Your Back
2006/Morning on October 15

A day after losing his composure in the sheriff's office, Trinidad pledged to sober up and fly right. Having humiliated himself in the face of authority by shedding tears of frustration, and having survived one near concussion, the questing concierge should have been sufficiently gun-shy about continuing his search for Buster Bishop. But, as a young man, Trinidad was nothing if not hard-headed. Alone in his room, he sat on his cot and spent hours re-thinking his actions, from the east-side dock to the boathouse to the channel bridge, trying to sort out real events from hallucination—trying to make sense of it all.

He concluded that three things were certain: he'd seen his friend held captive, he'd been struck and hog-tied by the kidnapper, and the law wasn't going to do a damn thing about it. Which meant it was up to him.

The visions he experienced wouldn't be admissible in a court of law, but they were nevertheless instructive. The candles had pointed the way to the boathouse, that much was clear. But what was the lesson of his imagined journey back to Grand Lake's mining days? The answer, he decided, must have something to do with the ruins of Lark City. For days on end, no one had reported seeing the illusive bear. What better place to escape notice than an abandoned ghost town?

Inspired, Trinidad rose up and, like some western hero riding to the rescue, he traded his watch cap for his Stetson. Yearning for answers, he rushed outside, hurried to the Kauffman House, and pounded on the museum door until one of the volunteers opened up. He probably sounded like a madman as he earnestly pleaded for directions to Lark City. As luck would have it, the volunteer was a long-time resident—the same pleasant woman he'd passed on his contemplative walk from the bridge. Learning of his interest in the ghost town, she offered to draw him a detailed map of the route.

Standing in the museum, Trinidad tried to bridle his impatience while the woman took pains to sketch her map. She wore a vintage outfit—no doubt a requirement for an emulator playing the role of a pioneer woman. As she completed her task, the volunteer seemed to sense the young man's agitation and asked if he was in a hurry.

"An all-fired hurry," Trinidad confirmed.

"I think I can be of assistance," said the resourceful woman. "The hike to Lark City covers more than seven miles—much of it uphill. If you truly wish to travel rapidly, I'm happy to help. I have no further obligations here. If you can obtain your own transportation, I'll meet you at the trailhead and I'll bring my horses so we can ride together. You do know how to ride don't you?" asked the volunteer as she glanced at Trinidad's Stetson.

"Since I was a baby," Trinidad assured her.

"Alrighty then," said the volunteer whose enthusiasm suggested she relished the adventure.

The turn-off to the trailhead, according to the well-informed volunteer, was about ten miles up the new road. By which, Trinidad supposed, she meant Highway 34.

"Keep a sharp lookout," she advised, "or else you'll miss the trailhead. Your first landmark along the new road will be the Harbison homestead. Keep Green Mountain on your right shoulder. You'll pass Onahu where, if you had more time, you could visit our old cabin. Eventually, you'll come near Joe Fleshut's place, but I doubt you can see it from the road. Listen to me prattle. It's not as if you won't have my map in hand. In any event, you might come to a sign for Beaver Creek, but that's not your turn, you keep going. If you cross Squeak Creek, you've gone too far. And, another thing, as I understand it, you'll need to go into the National Park. Are you familiar with what they call Trail Ridge Road?"

"Yes, ma'am."

"Land sakes, don't be so formal. We've met before, but you probably don't recall, so let's get reacquainted. I'm Miss Josephine Leander Wescott. It's a mouthful, I know, so you may call me Jo," she said as she concluded her introduction and offered her hand.

"Trinidad Sands," he replied. A moment of awkward silence followed as Jo raised her eyebrows and cleared her throat. "Oh, sorry," her visitor said as he recollected his manners, removed his hat, and gripped her delicate fingers.

"Such a reassuring hand," she blushed. "A warm handshake is the mark of a true friend," she added.

"Nice to know," said Trinidad and, charmed by her generous praise, it was his turn to blush.

"Now, young man, I've detained you long enough. We must speed you on your way, so down to our business," said Jo. "From what I know of the park, you must pay to enter. Do you have any money?" Miss Wescott's inquiry was genuine and the sincerity of her concern puzzled Trinidad until he realized that, unshaven and bandaged like a prize fighter, he must look like a tramp.

"I have money," he assured her. "In any event, the vehicle I have in mind to use has a sticker that'll get me in free."

"A sticker you say? Such wonders one encounters in this modern world!" Jo exclaimed.

"The sticker is handy for sure," Trinidad agreed. "Meanwhile, I can't go wrong with your fine map."

"May it serve you well," she said.

"So," Trinidad decided, "I'd better go. What vehicle should I look for at the trailhead?"

"Oh, that won't be a worry," she assured him. "I'll be the one holding the horses."

Trinidad rushed from the Kauffman House, sprinted uphill to the lodge, and stopped by his room to remove his wonky bandages. Gathering some necessities, he hurried outside and reached the employee lot in record time. It wasn't his turn to use the shared car, but that didn't stop him from hot-wiring the Mustang. In minutes, he was on his way.

When he reached the modest log structure which served as the park's west entrance station, he was only mildly surprised to find Ranger None manning the post.

"I recognize this vintage Ford," said the ranger. "And haven't we done this before?"

"A few days ago, you waved us in at the other end," said Trinidad.

"*Now* I remember," None said and Trinidad thought he could guess the reason for the dreamy expression on the ranger's face.

I know that look, Trinidad told himself. *A clear case of one more male launched into the vapors by fond memories of the many charms of Bambi Taylor.*

"Your friend's not with you I see," the ranger stated the obvious.

"Not today," Trinidad said. *And not tomorrow either,* he told himself. *Or anytime, ever.*

Trinidad's pained expression must have betrayed his melancholy thoughts because, when Ranger None next spoke, his voice conveyed a genuine sense of empathy.

"Not today," the ranger repeated. "That's tough. But I'm sure it'll all work out for the best."

"You didn't happen to see a horse trailer go through ahead of me by any chance?" Trinidad asked.

"Nope," the ranger laughed. "And, before you ask, I also ain't seen a bear on a motorcycle. You have yourself a nice day."

Trinidad put the Mustang in gear and entered the park. Almost immediately, he was obliged to steer past a double-parked tourist who was crowding the highway shoulder to take photos of a roadside moose. Continuing on, he guided the Mustang through an endless colonnade of stately pines which lined the highway like posted sentinels—tall and straight and eerily silent.

He used a bent paperclip to tack Jo's map to the Mustang's dashboard, believing he'd have to consult it often as he drove. But oddly, he found he had total recall of each detailed landmark so that, after positioning the diagram in easy reach, he found no need to consult it.

As he journeyed farther into the park, a single drop of rain splashed onto his windshield. He reached for the wiper knob, but stayed his hand when no additional droplets followed. Just one drop, nothing more. He glanced up at the passing sky, but saw only unblemished blue.

"Weird," he told himself as he returned his gaze to the road just in time to stomp on the brakes—a sudden move which halted the Mustang and killed the engine.

The moose which blocked the highway was in no hurry. Appearing out of nowhere, the ambling animal might be on the way to somewhere, but wherever it was headed, the journey seemed to require no urgency. Four more steps—one for each of its sizeable feet—and the beast halted just shy of crossing the centerline. With a languid oozing motion which would have made a special effects technician proud—the unhurried animal turned its huge head and regarded the Mustang and its startled passenger.

For five seconds—no more, no less—the gangly beast held Trinidad in its untamed gaze. Then, having mastered the feral equivalent of a staring contest, its eyes strayed as the massive head swayed back to its original position, the burly chest engaged, and the body followed.

Trinidad watched the animal until it reached the shoulder and seemed to melt into a dense stand of roadside willows.

Double weird, he told himself as he fumbled with wiring and restarted the Mustang.

He traveled on, cautiously scanning both sides of the highway, slowing at each curve, taking precautions in case another moose appeared. None did. He saw no other wildlife, or anything else for that matter. In fact, he suddenly realized that, after passing the double-parked photographer just beyond the park entrance, he hadn't encountered a single motorist—no traffic at all, in either direction, and no vehicles in the roadside pullouts or parking areas. No signs of intelligent life whatsoever—not counting the moose.

It was October, of course. But it was also Saturday and the highway should have been buzzing with activity. Yet there was no one to be seen.

"Crap!" he chided himself as he passed a sign for Squeak Creek and made an irksome U-turn. *Missed my turn!* he told himself.

Rapidly retracing his route, he made a hard right to reach the service road leading to the Colorado River Trailhead. The entryway paralleled the highway and led to a looped parking area. There was no sign of a vehicle and trailer, but Jo was there, dressed for a ride and—as promised—holding two horses.

"Where's—?" Trinidad started to ask.

"No time," she declared as she tossed him the reins. "Storm's coming! Let's mount!"

As Jo cantered away, Trinidad swung into the saddle, glanced briefly at the clear blue sky, spurred his horse, and galloped after his guide. At first, the trail was wide enough to ride abreast.

"You sit well," Jo said.

"Back at you," Trinidad concurred.

"Mind your knees," she advised as trailside trees began to pinch the narrowing track. After a mile, the two riders encountered a steep grade where they decided to walk the horses. Both mounts were sure-footed Rocky Mountain horses, bred for trail riding, but Jo's decision not to chance the grade made sense.

"Buck and Rev can take this hill just fine," she said. "But mounted hill-climbing requires confidence and Buck needs to trust you—you understand."

"Absolutely," Trinidad agreed.

"There's plenty steeper coming," Jo said as the two riders reached the crest and remounted. "Believe it or not, this was intended to be a wagon road—the main supply route for Lark City. It's a wonder those wagons, not to mention regular stagecoaches, made passage—but they did."

Clearly, Jo knew the trail and its history well.

"You live in these parts?" Trinidad asked.

"After a fashion, yes," said Jo and her tone suggested she'd prefer to change the subject. "Hopefully the downed trees have been cleared. We'll encounter water in the meadows, but fording should be easy this time of year. We'll cross the bridge at Lark Creek. I declare that girl's father has a passion for naming things after his daughter. Hmm—that's odd."

Jo reined in her horse and dismounted to examine a trailside declivity.

"Track of something—not a wagon. What do you make of it?" she asked her companion.

Trinidad remained in the saddle, abruptly alert.

"Jo, I—"

Somewhere in the trees behind them, the sudden growl of an engine made both horses shy. Rev snatched the reins from Jo's grip and bolted. Buck circled while Trinidad kept his seat. The reverberating echo faded as the unseen source moved away, its trajectory clearly receding toward the trailhead. As the sound diminished, Rev halted nearby and, checking on his companion, Trinidad could see that Jo had wrapped a bandanna around her rein hand.

"You're hurt," he said and started to dismount.

"Turn back," she said.

"He needs you now."

"Nothing here."

"Turn around."

Jo stared at her companion who seemed frozen in the saddle.

"Go!" she urged. "I'll be all right."

As if awakening from a stupor, Trinidad wheeled Buck and raced off in pursuit of the ebbing sound.

"I'll come back for you!" he shouted over his shoulder.

"Nothing here," her voice reached him—the words swallowed by the forest as he galloped around a tight corner. Buck's nostrils flared and the scent of freshly expelled exhaust reached Trinidad's senses in the same instance.

"Bastard!" Trinidad swore as he veered off the trail and urged Buck across a broad meadow. Crashing through the clearing, the thundering horse scattered a herd of grazing deer then startled a covey of grouse. Racing cross-country, Trinidad sought to cut the switchbacks in an effort to gain ground on his adversary.

Looking ahead, he saw a cloud of grosbeaks burst from distant treetops, then another flock filling the sky just beyond the first group. Then a third flock flew up, then a fourth—a series of startled birds, agitated by the passing motorcycle and marking the villain's escape route. Clearly, the fleeing scoundrel would reach the end of the trail and the highway before Trinidad could overtake him. The kidnapper's unwilling victim may still be with him, or Buster may be held captive somewhere else—either way the huge fugitive was a menace who needed to be stopped.

Moments later, Trinidad reached the trailhead. Reining in, he leapt from the saddle, intending to hobble Buck and leave the horse to Jo's care. Rev, her temporarily startled mount, hadn't strayed far and he was certain she'd soon be following. Meanwhile, he needed to hurry. He'd reconnect with the woman later.

She said Buster needs me now. She urged me to go. She knows these mountains, he decided. *She'll be okay. See to the horse,* he told himself.

There was a lasso tied to saddle strings. He freed the rope and hurriedly knotted a crude, double-looped hobble. By rights, he should dig a hole and set a picket rope or, at the very least, unravel the coarse fibers to make for a softer hobble restrain, but there wasn't time.

"Sorry, boy," he told Buck. "I'll make this up to you one day."

As if to say Trinidad was forgiven, the obedient horse allowed the young man to thread the makeshift hobble onto a pair of sturdy legs. Then the animal lowered its majestic head and began to graze a clump of trailside sweetgrass. Convinced that Buck would only be temporarily abandoned, his rider rushed away to restart the Mustang.

"Damn," Trinidad cursed.

The fleeing criminal had probably intended to flatten all four Mustang tires, but—with Trinidad giving chase—the perpetrator only managed to deflate one. Hearing the ever-nearing percussion of Buck's hot pursuit, the harried man must have curtailed his sabotage and roared away, leaving the damage unfinished.

"Gotta chance it," Trinidad decided. He took a quick look at the spot where he'd hobbled the horse and felt his heart jump when he didn't immediately spot the animal. Much to his relief, a second glance resolved the mystery. The apparent disappearance had been an optical illusion manifested by the dappled grey of Buck's mane so matching the trunks of a stand of aspens that the grazing horse was practically invisible.

Coaxing yet another start from the over-worked Mustang, Trinidad rammed the car into gear and raced along the access road. It was a jarring journey with one deflated tire wobbling noisily while the metal rim plowed into the asphalt. As he gathered momentum, steering became a challenge, but he was determined to push the limping Ford to its maximum speed. And yet he had to come to a full stop when he reached Highway 34.

"Which way?" he asked himself. "Which direction?" he posed the question to the Universe in general, just as a panel truck reached the intersection and roared by.

Bishop Plumbing, the side panel declared. *Serving Grand Lake since 1922,* said the subscript.

Following in the wake of the truck, Trinidad wheeled right and headed back toward town. Against all odds, he managed enough speed to pass the truck. Glancing in the rearview mirror, he caught a momentary image of the receding vehicle, briefly contemplated the irony of the truck's commercial message, then lost sight of it as he rounded a tight curve. What the overtaken driver made of the weaving Mustang, with its exposed rim clanking and ruined tire smoking, was anybody's guess. All Trinidad knew was there'd be no more stopping until he returned to Grand Lake.

Chapter 56

Other Things Which Happen
When You Don't Watch Your Back
2006/Afternoon on October 15

Reaching the park exit, Trinidad roared past an astonished Ranger None in a hail of mechanical clatter and burning rubber. The careening car shuddered as it entered the sweeping highway curve which led back to Grand Lake. Pressing the accelerator, the questing concierge glanced in the Mustang's rearview mirror. He could just make out the ranger's receding silhouette—a human pinwheel with one hand gesticulating wildly while the other pressed a phone to his ear.

So, he told himself, *the authorities have been alerted. I wonder if our efficient ranger also called in today's sighting of a marauding bear.*

"Aw hell!" he yelled as he fought with the Mustang's vibrating steering wheel to complete yet another U-turn. Speeding back toward the entry point, he cursed himself for his inattention, bypassed the ranger again, and retraced his route. Moments ago, he'd glimpsed a roadside scar, but its import hadn't immediately registered. Pushing the Ford back up Highway 34, he relocated the spot. Hurriedly downshifting, he hit the brakes and pivoted right to align his front wheels with the cross-country track left by a long-gone motorcycle.

"Hold on," he said to no one in particular, as he gunned the Mustang and dived onto the track. It broke his heart to savage the landscape, spewing mud, rocks, and tundra as he left the pavement and careened through the roadside meadow, but it couldn't be helped.

Here we go, he thought as he steered around a downed tree and a cluster of boulders. *Ranger None won't be reporting a bear-sighting after all. My quarry had enough sense to leave the pavement before reaching the park exit. To avoid scrutiny, he must have come overland in the first place. Now he's cutting corners again, so I can't count on the cavalry and I'm still on my own. Hope this bucket of bolts holds together, because there's no way I'm losing the scent this time!*

Glancing at Jo's map as the Mustang bounced over rough terrain, Trinidad instantly visualized the kidnapper's intended destination. What the huge man had been up to in Lark City was unclear. On the other hand, what the fleeing criminal had immediately in mind was abundantly evident.

"He's heading for the falls," the well-informed concierge assured himself.

In the past few weeks, Trinidad had directed plenty of lodge visitors to the picturesque spot. It was an easy hike to Adams Falls and also a modest cross-country drive, if someone was reckless enough to gouge an improvised road through the wilderness. Tourists loved the falls. What motivated the kidnapper to make a beeline for the place was uncertain.

All Trinidad knew was the prowling bear was on the run and up to no good. Meanwhile, he was the only one pursuing the criminal and it must rankle the man that the same young fool kept popping up to dog his trail. Still, whatever anxiety the kidnapper felt, it would be nothing compared to the angst he was inflicting on Buster Bishop.

Why drag the old man all over the county? What could possibly be motivating the villain's marathon of unfocused wanderlust? Why bounce from Estes to Grand Lake, from bike to boat and then bike again? Why go from Grand Lake to Lark City only to retrace the route?

Trinidad would be asking those questions, and many more, when he brought the zig-zagging bastard to heel.

Topping a rise, he spotted the motorcycle. The machine was cantilevered at a weird angle, the bike on its side, seemingly buried in the ground, with the sidecar stranded skyward. Stopping just short of the wreck, he hesitated, not wanting to stumble into another ambush. But he thought of Buster's peril and decided to risk it.

Pocketing Jo's map, Trinidad gathered up his tools and eased out of the Mustang. Moving as close as he dared, he picked up a stone, hurled it at the sidecar, and listened intently—hoping to hear sounds of stirring. No such noise reached his ears—only the gentle purr of an autumn breeze and the distant rasp of a raven.

A knoll overlooked the crash site. Scrambling up, Trinidad looked down on the scene. From his elevated position, he could see that the cover of the torpedo-shaped sidecar had been jettisoned. The cavity where Buster had been imprisoned was empty. Once again, kidnapper and victim had disappeared. The only difference was, this time, the pursuit was timely and the pursuer had a pretty good idea where the prey was headed.

Earlier that day, as Jo crafted her detailed map of the region, Trinidad had wondered why she'd chosen to expand her Lark City diagram to include details of sites far from the ghost town, particularly places adjacent to Grand Lake. Looking back, her work seemed prophetic, although—as he gazed ahead to orient himself to the terrain—he dismissed that assumption. Jo's extraneous additions were merely coincidental. She mentioned that they'd met before and he decided that prior encounter must have been in connection with his concierge duties. Aware that the young man was well-acquainted with the Grand Lake area, her motivation for including sites near the lake must have been to provide him with the context of familiar landmarks. Whatever her reasons, the map was a godsend and he kept it close.

The disabled motorcycle had met its fate at a point which marked the end of passable ground. Abandoning the Mustang, Trinidad gathered up his cargo and proceeded on foot. After hiking a mile, he happened upon a scout troop doing trail maintenance and learned from their leader that his crew had spotted what appeared to be a huge bear, carrying a burden and walking upright on two legs.

"A bit too much imagination," the leader suggested as he warily eyed Trinidad, who'd arrived at the trail-work site armed with a baseball bat and hammer.

Confirming that the unknown entity seemed to be heading toward the falls, Trinidad left the bewildered scouts behind and broke into a dead run. Locating the upper reaches of the trail, he rushed down. His steady progress was soon rewarded by the sound of the falls ahead.

Chapter 57

Adams Falls
2019/Nearly Suppertime on June 8

"You know the place, I think," Trinidad told his host.

"I was there as a cub," the old ranger confirmed.

"Then you'll recall that, not far from the ledge overlooking Adams Falls is a cul-de-sac with steep sides and a solid bottom. It's a deep cauldron which resembles an amphitheater. The sizeable indentation was carved into the porous rock eons ago. It's hard to imagine that the small stream which trickles over the present-day falls was the source of such dramatic erosion, but all indications are the watershed once hosted a far more vigorous current. As for why Jackhammer ended up there, I learned much later that he'd been drawn to the place by his spirit guide—a consultation with this trusted counselor being the reason, he says, for his unusual detour to Lark City. But I didn't have the advantage of such revelations when I arrived that day and looked down into the cauldron. I was working in real time and had absolutely no clue why the huge man had carried Buster Bishop to Lark City only to turn around and return to the present spot. Turns out, the delusional kidnapper imagined he was subjecting his prisoner to some sort of cosmic trial. In his mind, the natural amphitheater served as a courtroom."

"Calculatin' buzzard," Heckleson suggested.

"Calculating as they come," Trinidad confirmed. "But, at that particular moment, also extremely irrational."

Chapter 58

Cauldron
2006/Near Dark on October 15

The autumn day was waning, but—even in the gathering darkness—Trinidad recalled that his eyesight was strangely unhampered. Approaching the cauldron, he peered over the ledge and had the sensation of perceiving an artificially enhanced scene. He seemed to be viewing a theatrical stage illuminated by brilliant floodlights and, like the setting, the players below were also starkly visible.

He saw Buster Bishop—a gag stifling his mouth and stout rope restraining the old man's arms and legs. The prisoner sat stiffly on a coarse rock bench which formed one edge of the cauldron. While Buster remained motionless, his captor paced back and forth, gesticulating emphatically, in a bizarre pantomime of bluster and anger.

Moreover, he was, indeed, wearing what appeared to be an ankle-length fur coat which gave him the appearance of a bulky animal walking upright on stout hind legs.

Here's our bear, Trinidad thought.

The huge man was too far away to discern his face or hear exactly what the restless giant was shouting. But the implications apparent in the rise and fall of his caustic tone were all too obvious. The kidnapper was annoyed and laboring diligently to work himself into an increased state of agitated indignation.

Trinidad feared the unstable villain might snap at any moment and, to make matters worse, it was beginning to rain. The sooner Buster Bishop was removed from the line of fire, the better. Crawling back from the ledge, he unfolded Jo's map, used familiar landmarks to confirm his position, and quickly formulated a plan of attack. To have any chance of success, he'd have to stage a flanking movement. His only option was to out-maneuver the huge man and take him from behind.

Jo's map described a narrow tunnel, an old exploratory mine shaft, which ran at a roughly 45-degree angle from an exterior entrance in the upper edge of the cauldron to an opening in the interior wall. Her sketch was merely a crude outline, but now that he was on the scene, he could fill in the details. In fact, some sixth sense seemed to compel him to tap into newly inquired insights. Closing his eyes, Trinidad visualized himself traversing the tunnel, surprising Buster's captor, and rescuing his friend.

The opening at the terminal end of the tunnel was ideally positioned since it occupied the wall above and behind the kidnapper. Given the kidnapper's size, Trinidad's chief allies were stealth, cunning, and surprise. He'd rely on those things and enhance his chances by employing certain tools he'd stashed in the Mustang before stealing it. Namely, the baseball bat in his right hand and the eight-ounce ball peen hammer tucked firmly under his belt.

A momentary search revealed the tunnel entrance—nearly invisible to the casual passerby, but apparent enough to a meticulous seeker. Taking a deep breath, Trinidad hung his Stetson on a protruding branch, parted a screening layer of brush, removed a pair of loosely-nailed boards, and ducked beneath a rough archway.

Against his better judgment, and in opposition to his tendency toward claustrophobia, he got down on all-fours and crawled into the constricted opening. As he left the fading daylight behind and inched forward in the growing dark, he heard a clap of thunder as, outside, rain arrived with a vengeance. Sheltered by the rocky channel, he remained dry. What the pouring rain was doing to his exposed Stetson, he didn't like to think. No time to retrieve the abandoned hat. For now, pressing forward was his only option. His chief solace lay in assuring himself he was safely concealed and unlikely, in such a confined spot, to encounter his giant adversary.

He was certain the kidnapper wouldn't be watching the tunnel exit and confident that the huge man couldn't access this confined corridor. Besides, he detected sounds ahead and these echoes, amplified by the narrow passageway, confirmed that the fuming man was continuing to lecture his prisoner. Which convinced Trinidad he'd have the element of surprise on his side. If his calculations were correct, he should emerge behind the distracted man and sufficiently low to manage a modest jump to the floor of the amphitheater. If he moved quickly and remained quiet, he should be all right. If nothing else, reaching the terminus of the tunnel would provide a nearer vantage point from which he could calmly assess the situation and plan his next move.

The kidnapper didn't appear to be armed, but suppose the man had a pistol. Shots fired would prove fatal to someone attempting a frontal attack. Coming from behind, Trinidad would be close enough to spot a firearm and sufficiently hidden to avoid having his head blown off.

Though the outside temperature was dropping as the rain continued, it was stifling inside the cramped tunnel. Crouched over and unable to stand erect, Trinidad progressed slowly and the walls seemed much too near in the cloying darkness. The channel was curved so he couldn't see the far end. As he shuffled forward, his chest began to tighten and his breath grew labored. Just when he thought he was running out of oxygen, he detected a subdued glimmer of light ahead. Moving with a purpose, he picked up his pace and was on the verge of reaching the exit when the floor and walls of the tunnel began to vibrate.

He heard it then—a gurgling movement of air and water pushing from behind. Dropping his bat and fumbling to discard his hammer, he freed his hands and endeavored to scramble forward. But he started much too late to escape the onrushing torrent as a flash flood swamped the tunnel. Like water surging through a fire hose, the unbridled current scoured the walls and overwhelmed the unlucky youth.

Caught in the relentless flow, Trinidad was swept off his feet and propelled helplessly forward. His tumbling body rocketed toward the narrow exit. Seconds later—with the force of a helpless cork expelled from the neck of an effervescing bottle—he shot out of the tunnel in a hail of water, mud, and rocks. Plunging down the wall, he landed face-first on the sodden floor of the amphitheater. Bruised and sputtering, he attempted to stand until a crushing blow delivered by the enraged kidnapper sent him crashing to the ground.

Chapter 59

Shadow Mountain
2006/Evening of October 15

Waylaid at the Adams Falls amphitheater, Trinidad slipped in and out of consciousness as he endured the shock of being knocked cold, trussed up, manhandled, and hauled down a rocky trail. Had he been more aware, he might have marveled that his assailant was able to manage two captives—using one muscular arm to sling the younger man over his shoulder while herding Buster along with a pistol gripped in the other hand. He'd eventually learn the details from other sources, but, at the time, he could neither fully understand, nor clearly see what was happening.

Trinidad's blurred vision was further inhibited by the jarring pace set by his captor and by the limits of his imperfect field of vision—he was, after all, facing backwards. In short, his eyes provided little information. His ears and other senses proved more reliable. As the trail descended, he could hear shore waves and feel the lake breeze.

Feeling less jostled as his captor reached level ground, Trinidad momentarily relished the fresh air, only to be flung, like a sack of potatoes, down the companionway steps of a waiting boat. Below decks, he felt the vibration as the craft's auxiliary inboard engine sprang to life and sensed himself fading as the vessel moved over dark water.

After a time, Trinidad was vaguely aware of frenetic movements on deck, then silence ruled as he lost consciousness.

Eventually, the boat seemed to reach its destination because he was dragged from below and propped up to have his leg ropes untied and removed. Barely able to stand, he was soon forced to walk uphill in the dark. Apparently unburdened of restraining ropes, Buster walked alongside, helping his young would-be rescuer maintain his balance. Walking was a neat trick for Trinidad whose upper torso was still restrained by a cocoon of rope. The upward trek was arduous and, whenever the old man and the young concierge paused, they were pushed relentlessly onward by their bellowing captor.

Trinidad put one foot in front of the other, walking in a daze until he swooned and fell heavily. Unable to rise, Trinidad felt himself being lifted skyward again as the angry, muscular kidnapper was once more obliged to bodily carry his younger captive while pushing the old man forward.

So, Trinidad's awakening consciousness told him, *this patchwork of memories has to mean I'm no longer in the amphitheater, therefore I'm somewhere in another set of woods—possibly on the shore of Shadow Mountain Reservoir.* This thought represented his final lucid recollection before blackness once again descended.

Sometime later—how long, he couldn't be certain—Trinidad regained his senses and sat up. He awoke to a world of pitch darkness. With his captor and Buster nowhere in sight, he scrambled to his feet, pressed his back against the nearest tree, and busied himself with trying to loosen the knots which bound both hands behind his back. The ropes were woven lines— some type of polyplastic. They seemed tight, but he continued to worry the knots, scraping the ropes and his knuckles against the rough bark of the pine trunk as he labored to be free.

As he worked with grim determination to escape his present situation, his recovering mind took an unplanned detour.

Involuntarily, his thoughts were transported back to a childhood memory as he recalled seeing his grandmother in the hospital. The old woman was stiffly bound like a horizontal statue, her frail body immobilized by restraining blankets laid crosswise and tucked tightly underneath the mattress.

He was ten years old and terrified as his mother furiously chastised the nurses and orderlies.

"To posey a person in this day and age! You ought to be ashamed! Look and see how swollen her hands and arms are!" Trinidad's mother shouted. He'd never heard the soft-spoken, polite woman raise her voice, let alone yell at another person in anger.

Hiding in a corner of the hospital room, his younger self slipped behind window curtains and watched the drama play out.

"I ought to have you arrested," his mother continued. "For shame! No! Don't touch her! I'll do this myself!"

Then, in a tone more familiar to the frightened boy, his mother addressed Grandma Sands.

"Here, Mother," she cooed as she untucked the restrictive blankets. "I'll help you up. We've got to get you moving to get the swelling down in those arms and legs. Shorty," his mother used his family nickname, "come out from there. I know you're scared, but come and take Grandma's arm."

The two of them got the old lady out into the brightly lit hospital corridor and walked her up and down until a harried looking doctor showed up to try and calm the situation. Years later, Trinidad recounted this childhood trauma to a high school friend whose goal was to study medicine. The brainiac recoiled in horror. Then she told him, in no uncertain terms, that his mother had been absolutely right to read the riot act to the hospital staff.

"Bedridden patients accumulate all kinds of risks," his adolescent classmate declared. "Hands and hips swelling for starters. And this business of restraining someone with blankets—Middle Ages stuff! We did that as children in camp—did you never posey a fellow camper—pinning their arms and legs so they couldn't get out of bed? Oh no, not you, Mr. Goody Two-Shoes! But it happened, believe me! Just never thought I'd hear about it happening in the American healthcare system anytime since the 1700s!"

Why this particular memory had popped into Trinidad's spinning head, a decade later and 300 miles away from the limits of his southern Colorado hometown, he couldn't fathom—at first.

Then it dawned on him.

Hands and hips, Trinidad thought to himself as he ceased to struggle with the restraining ropes. *Chances are every part of me is swollen from being stowed below decks and tied-up like a rodeo calf. Time to get some circulation going.*

Moving away from the tree trunk, he stomped his feet, shrugged shoulders, and shook his head—anything to get his blood flowing. Then—in the wake of a feverish spate of frenetic activity—he pulled both hands free and the remaining rope fell away.

"Like shucking a crayfish," he crowed aloud. Then he instantly fell silent, listening for movement, uncertain if his captor was out of earshot. As both eyes fully adjusted to the darkness, he blinked, then scanned his surroundings.

A small campfire was burning in the center of what he now recognized as a forest clearing surrounded on all sides by dense trees and thick undergrowth. Moving cautiously in the dim light of the anemic flames, Trinidad paused beside the firepit and knelt down to pick up a good-sized limb. For an instant, as he tested the limb for balance, he wondered what had become of his baseball bat. It was an idle thought because, seconds later, a meaty hand on his shoulder derailed whatever plan was forming in his still addled brain.

"Drop it," an angry voice commanded.

Trinidad spun from the unexpected grip and did his best to strike his assailant, but the man blocked his blow and the limb tumbled, unused, to the ground. Unwilling to surrender, Trinidad grabbed the huge man and the two fell into the fire, wrestling and cursing. Fearing sparks, Trinidad grappled with eyes closed as smoke tinged his nostrils and lodged in his throat. In the brief struggle, Trinidad's attacker pivoted behind, pulled his opponent up, and locked the young concierge's head and neck in a chokehold—calculated moves which suggested more than a passing familiarity with wrestling prowess. Caught in an uncompromising grasp, Trinidad opened both eyes and caught a glimpse of Buster, standing just beyond the firelight. The old man was seemingly frozen in place until—apparently resolved to help—he took a step forward.

"Run!" Trinidad managed to croak, and he was temporarily elated to see Buster scramble into the darkness. Gasping for air, the choking youth felt his knees buckle as his defeated body slumped downward in an awkward heap.

Chapter 60

Under Sail
2006/Midnight on October 15

Trinidad lay sprawled on the ground, his breathing labored as he listened to someone's rambling diatribe. The villain sat a few paces away, bathed in moonlight as he balanced straddle-legged on a downed log. The huge man was apparently talking to himself, his face downturned and obscured in darkness, while he loaded cartridges into his revolver.

"Shit," the villain sneered. "Needed a got-damn break, didn't get a got-damn break of no damn kind. Just my luck to draw a pair of old farts—two slippery peas in a pod—twin assholes who was old as the hills but quick on their feet—*canst thou swim?* First the dang look-alike brother kicks over my kerosene lamp, sets the cussed tower blazing, sprints away, and makes a two-story jump for it. Not my fault the dumb ox dies, but no turning back once that sneaky old bastard hits the ground. Johnny Law's bound to go ahead and stretch that tower-spill to murder and throw in arson to boot. So, I figure I got nothing to lose—*canst thou swim?*

"So, I wait and watch and make a plan to corral the other twin. So, then what happens? His friend just now wiggles out of the ropes, kicks up a ruckus, and the other old buzzard breaks free—makes tracks and disappears—gone whole-away in the dark. A wild and crazy cuss, just like his brother. Probably the old devil won't make it, running like that, double-timing through the woods, at his age. Maybe he'll bash his head on a tree in the dark and save me the trouble. Should've shot the old varmint. Should'a shot him where he stood 'stead of wrestling with the other bastard. Tried to plug the old fart when he ran, but couldn't wing him in the dark. Wasted bullets. Won't get no second chance—*canst thou swim?*"

As the big galoot droned on, covering the same ground over and over again, Trinidad tried to grasp his situation. The man was apparently thinking out loud, but repeating himself and making about as much sense as a congressman.

Lying on his side, unbound, but still unable to rise, Trinidad turned his head, willed his eyes to focus, and found himself face-to-face with the smoking end of a discarded stick of firewood. Stifling a cough, he extended his hand to flick the hazard away.

The smoking wood triggered a cascade of memories.

Ah, he remembered, *the firepit wrestling match—not one of my finer moments. So, I'm here on the ground and Buster is—*

Trinidad labored to recall those fleeting seconds before the huge man's powerful headlock ushered his opponent into a state of temporary oblivion.

Did I hear shots? I definitely heard shots! But Buster must have gotten away. Didn't the shooter say so—?

Before Trinidad could convince himself that Buster was okay, the jabbering abruptly ceased. In the stillness which followed, Trinidad looked across the clearing to watch the huge man raise his head. Though the darkness and distance made it impossible to see his face, the man's posture projected an unmistakable impression of intense scrutiny. Motionless and silent, the man stared hard at his prostrate prisoner for several seconds before lowering his head and speaking aloud again, but this time in a barely audible stage whisper.

"Only thing for it now is," the kidnapper intoned, "I gotta erase our witness—*canst thou swim?*"

Chambering a round, the big man stood rigidly up and crossed the clearing to tower over Trinidad. Seeing the pistol, the captive stirred and tried to rise, but couldn't find his balance.

"Don't try anything," the man warned. "I'm not called Jackhammer for fun and I'm plenty pissed-off enough to pull this damn trigger. And don't think I won't drop you in your tracks if you run."

"Run?" Trinidad asked as his head continued to buzz. "You choked me hard enough. What makes you think I can stand up, let alone run? And where the hell are we anyway?"

"Never mind where we are. That's for me to know. And this 9-millimeter says you'd better get on your feet and be quick about it! Let's go! Up, I said!"

Trinidad got as far as all-fours.

"Give me a minute," Trinidad requested. He was stalling—hoping his mind would clear. He'd overheard his captor's murderous threats, heard his nonsensical questions about swimming, and seen him loading his weapon. The huge man was towering over him. His prisoner was helpless.

Why am I still alive? Trinidad asked himself. *Think!*

He'd been ordered to stand up. Once he was on his feet, would his captor fire the fatal shot? Time seemed to suspend as Trinidad struggled to gather his thoughts.

Four things seem certain, he thought. *First, fantastic as it seems, my abductor is named Jackhammer. Second, Buster has escaped, apparently unharmed. Third, like a broken record, this Jackhammer character keeps asking himself the same stupid question. What the hell is with this, 'Canst thou swim?' And finally, wherever we are, we're no longer anywhere near the amphitheater. Somehow, while semi-conscious, I've been transported, by water if snatches of my returning memory are to be believed, to the shore of either Grand Lake or Shadow Mountain Reservoir or Granby—not that it matters which—*

"I'll give you 'til the count of three," Jackhammer snarled. "One, two—"

"Save your breath," Trinidad suggested. "I'm up."

The burly man kept his pistol trained on his prisoner. For three heartbeats the two stood motionless in the dark. Then Jackhammer spoke.

"Here's what I need," he said. "You're gonna sail me back across to the first lake and I'll leave you on the far shore for somebody to find at daylight. Play ball and you'll live to see the sunrise."

He's lying, Trinidad thought and his face must have betrayed his inner thoughts because Jackhammer's next words renewed his threat.

"Try anything and you're dead. You'll walk ahead where I can keep an eye on you. So, move," he ordered as he pushed Trinidad toward a break in the trees.

As the prisoner's toe encountered an unseen root on the primitive trail, he lurched forward.

"Watch it!" Jackhammer shouted. "I already got one pigeon loose in these woods."

Ah, Trinidad thought as he regained his balance. *So, I didn't imagine Buster's escape.* With that firm realization, Trinidad felt a surge of relief and a returning sense of resolve. *Buster's long-gone and probably unhurt,* he told himself. *He's somewhere in the woods and, whatever happens now, he's safely hidden and I'm on my own—which is probably best for both of us.*

Walking in the pale moonlight was tricky on uneven ground, but Trinidad kept his balance, his confidence steadily increasing as he and his captor trekked through the crisp night air. Each step into the cold and each cycle of frosty breath rejuvenated his senses. By the time captor and prisoner had traveled several paces, the younger man's head had cleared.

Awakening perhaps an hour ago, Trinidad had managed to free himself. But Jackhammer had discovered his captive upright and bested the younger man in a brief wrestling match. While still conscious, Trinidad had pleaded with Buster to run and, just before collapsing, he now remembered catching an unambiguous glimpse of the old man hightailing it into the dark woods. Two, maybe three shots had followed and Trinidad remembered hearing Jackhammer curse—a sure sign that the villain had missed his fleeing target. Trinidad had lost consciousness then, knowing that he himself was in deep crap, but convinced Buster had made it.

Struggling to ground himself in the present, Trinidad concentrated on the trail which stretched before him. Several moments passed as the two men moved silently and steadily downhill. The way seemed familiar and Trinidad soon decided he'd trod this same route on the day he and Buster came to claim Saul's body.

Jackhammer was dogging his steps, in easy reach, but Trinidad recognized his chances of overpowering the huge man were slim. Pivoting, however rapidly, to grapple with his armed abductor would be suicide. He'd wait until they re-boarded *The Dawn Ambler*—the handsome sailboat which his returning memory convinced him lay dead ahead. The boat had been stolen, of course. He remembered her well, remembered sailing with Ferryman and being allowed to take her out twice on his own.

As for tonight's trip onboard *Ambler,* although imprisoned below-decks, he recalled hearing the unmistakable sounds of someone—probably Buster —striking the mast. It would have been a necessary maneuver to allow the boat to pass beneath the bridges spanning the narrow channel connecting Grand Lake and the larger reservoir. Assuming the mast was still down, the sails would be temporarily neutralized.

That'll be a good thing, he told himself.

Eventually, the two men reached more level ground and Jackhammer insisted they pick up the pace. Moving more swiftly in the darkness, Trinidad heard distant waves lapping against an unseen obstacle and the percussive sound of *Ambler's* vinyl fenders bumping against weathered planks—noises which absolutely convinced him they were headed for Ferryman's floating dock. A month had passed since his first encounter with the illicit anchorage—exactly thirty days since he and Ferryman had cruised to the Osprey islands. That idyllic September trip seemed a distant memory. As for the more immediate past, those recollections were steadily returning to him.

Thinking back to tonight's earlier passage, Trinidad remembered *Ambler* rolling lustily on the heaving surface of Grand Lake and pitching vigorously among the equally treacherous waves of Shadow Mountain Reservoir. He had a vivid recollection, viewed from below and through the frame of the open companionway, of the big man crouching in the stern, a cringing pose which suggested Jackhammer was no sailor.

Trinidad remembered arriving at the hidden dock. Jackhammer had removed the ropes entwining Trinidad's legs, then forced both prisoners to disembark—pushing them up the trail.

Reasoning it out as the dock drew ever nearer, Trinidad guessed that *Ambler's* inboard engine must have been rendered useless, undoubtedly sabotaged by Buster while Jackhammer was removing Trinidad's leg restraints. Moreover, Trinidad would bet anything that the irascible old man had also managed to shift the oars overboard. *Ambler's* oars must be missing, her mast must be down, and something must be wrong with her engine—all reasons why this Jackhammer character wanted his prisoner to *sail* him back to a friendlier shore.

With each step toward the unseen reservoir, Trinidad grew more certain his captor was keeping him alive for one purpose only. The disillusioned and desperate man needed his prisoner's help to return to the civilized shore beyond. It was too far to walk in the dark. Jackhammer's only hope for escape required a functioning sailboat and an experienced sailor.

"Finally," Jackhammer snarled as they emerged from the forest and advanced toward the dock.

When they reached the wooden walkway, Trinidad was discouraged to see that *Ambler's* mast remained in place. Apparently, this Jackhammer character had forced Buster to reseat her mast without an opportunity for further sabotage. Whatever the case, the mast was up again.

That's inconvenient, Trinidad told himself. *But a mast without sails is merely a wooden spar and work will still be required to trim the sheets—work for which Jackhammer, I suspect, is wholly unqualified.*

As the two men climbed onboard, Trinidad made his decision.

He'd get the boat underway and watch for his chance. *Ambler* was a ready craft and—under less dire circumstances—sailing her would be a joy. A joy, but by no means unchallenging. Trinidad could feel the wind and smell rain. A storm was brewing and the sailboat was yawing handsomely in her temporary slip, as she rocked from side-to-side on the rising breeze. *Ambler* was already dancing. When the sails were hoisted her deck would be lively.

"You'll need to give me a hand," Trinidad suggested. Hoping to force the wary man into an awkward movement, the captive gripped the stern line and offered the loop to his wary shipmate.

"Figure it out," Jackhammer growled as he brandished his pistol and sought to keep his balance on the undulating deck.

"Okay," Trinidad shrugged. "Have it your way. I can manage alone. Just depends how big your hurry is."

"Don't worry about it," the desperado scoffed. "One of us is living on borrowed time and it ain't me. So, get your ass to work!"

"Love to," said Trinidad. "But I need you to mind your feet. Not much chance of me hoisting sail with you standing on the halyard."

"Don't tell me what to do, smartass," the armed man declared, although he momentarily glanced down and repositioned his feet so he was no longer standing on the lines which crisscrossed the deck. "Just shut your mouth or I'll put a bullet in your leg."

Trinidad remained silent as he did all one man can do to ready a sailboat.

No sense trying the man's patience, he thought. *Better to be running with the breeze, surging through the waves, where a savvy sailor can turn the wind and water to his advantage.*

Hours ago, when Buster had docked the *Ambler,* the efficient man must have re-seated the mast but left the sails—so majestic when filled with an enabling breeze—limp and unfurled. The sails hung languidly—looking like and about as useful as spent banana peels.

Yet, even with its canvas corralled, *Ambler's* bow and stern lines remained taut. The fore and aft tethers which affixed the boat to the dock were rigid as violin strings and buzzing with unsettled tension. Even with her sails furled, *Ambler* was literally straining at her leash. A little canvas and the sleek tender would literally jump onto the waiting waves. That sudden surge would be enough to unbalance anyone unprepared for the shock.

"Somebody needs to cast off," Trinidad suggested.

"Think I was born yesterday?" Jackhammer asked. "Get up there where I can see you and unhook the front rope," he demanded using his pistol as a pointer, then keeping the weapon trained on his prisoner as Trinidad made his way forward. "When that damn front rope is off, I'll cut the back rope," Jackhammer added as he took a seat in the stern.

Only an unschooled landlubber, Trinidad thought, *would say "rope" when the correct term is "line."*

Under Jackhammer's watchful gaze, the scheming captive knelt down, loosed the bowline, and fought to keep his balance as the partially un-tethered Ambler slammed into the dock, then swung toward the heaving reservoir. Crouching low, Trinidad moved nimbly along the port-side life-line, placing one foot in front of the other and holding on with the fingers of one hand. Thinking to himself, *one hand for the job, one hand for the boat,* he made his way aft until he reached a point where he could duck under the boom and lower himself into the cockpit.

Standing on the stern deck and keeping his distance, Trinidad turned to face Jackhammer and braced himself at the crest of the companionway. His head was completely clear now and his memory was surging back.

It occurred to Trinidad that his aborted attempt to pull off an ambush at the amphitheater had saddled Jackhammer with two captives. Leaving Adams Falls behind, the huge man must have forced Buster to walk to the Grand Lake shore, keeping the old man covered while also, somehow, managing to carry Trinidad's limp form. Calling upon superhuman strength, Jackhammer must have lugged one man and pushed the other down a rocky trail to reach the lake.

Buster had been obliged to climb on board. Trinidad recalled being manhandled by the muscular kidnapper like an oversized parcel of carry-on luggage. Groggy and disoriented, he'd been roughly pushed down the companionway. In the darkness below decks, he'd only had an instant to reacquaint himself with the contents of the sailboat's cabin before he lost consciousness.

Fully recovered now, Trinidad made a rapid mental inventory of objects below—striving to remember what was down there.

Could anything there be enlisted as an improvised weapon? he wondered.

Ambler was a handy vessel—a rugged example of the Catalina class. Trinidad recalled her to be about 22 feet from bow to stern—a bit out-sized for the mountains, but more than equal to the sometimes-turbulent waves of Shadow Mountain Reservoir. Not to mention the unpredictable surface of Grand Lake, Colorado's biggest and deepest natural body of water. Below decks, she boasted sleeping space for three with a tiny galley, small dining table with molded benches, and an array of cubbyholes. Recalling what he could of the cubbies, Trinidad drew a blank.

No help below, he thought as he took a preliminary step forward.

"Stay back," Jackhammer ordered.

Keeping a close eye on his prisoner, the big man reached behind to cut the stern line. The tether was wet and thick, so it took several diligent strokes to saw through the fibers with his ordinary pocketknife. Trinidad could feel *Ambler's* deck shuddering with anticipation. Even without her sails, the untethered boat would be a handful.

When the stubborn line parted at last, the boat leapt northward, then swung through the compass like a storm-tossed cork. Even in the protected bay, a growing breeze caused *Ambler* to catch a line of waves amidships and crab-walk over the next swell. As the boat continued to whirl, Trinidad decided to take charge.

"You're in my way," he told the armed thug.

"What?" Jackhammer mumbled.

"Surrender the helm unless you plan on steering," Trinidad shouted to be heard above the freshening breeze. "Give way or we'll spin our way to the bottom!"

Seeming to acknowledge the danger, Jackhammer struggled to his feet. Warily maintaining his balance, he grappled blindly for a handhold while eyeing his prisoner. With effort, the huge man remained standing, his free fingers clinging to the starboard stanchion while his left hand grasped the pistol. His stance was awkward but solid enough to keep the weapon squarely aimed at Trinidad. At this close range, if forced to fire, the big man was unlikely to miss.

Trinidad kept his balance and pointed toward the helm, seeking permission to approach the stern. Jackhammer waggled his pistol, urging his prisoner to take up his post.

"For shit-sakes," the kidnapper growled, "corral this tub before I chuck my guts!"

Trinidad suppressed a smile as he took a seat, grasped the helm to control the rudder, and pushed *Ambler's* nose into the wind. Instantly, the boat ceased its aimless rocking and began to rise and fall with the onrushing current.

"I can't get going unless we get canvas up," Trinidad announced. "The water will be choppy once we're beyond this harbor. We can coast out on the off-shore breeze, but to make headway on the reservoir, we'll have to tack against the wind. Come man her helm and keep us in irons while I set sails or we'll find ourselves back on the dock."

"Shit," said Jackhammer as he changed places with his prisoner. "Get on with it and drop the play-by-play. Just do what you have to do to get this bucket moving back to the far shore."

"Like I said..." Trinidad began the thought, but left it unfinished as he deftly scampered forward to hoist the mainsail and set the jib. While he worked, and trusting that his captor would be unable to interpret his movements, he covertly reached around the mainmast and unhooked the fiddle blocks which held in check the forward end of the boom. As wind filled the spread canvas, he moved quickly, running one hand along the freed spar, exerting subtle pressure to keep the boom roughly horizontal as he made his way aft.

This time he didn't have to tell Jackhammer to move. Anticipating his prisoner's desire to regain the helm, the huge man moved aside. Trinidad slid one hand along the boom, keeping it steady as he took his captor's place. Having gained control of both helm and boom, Trinidad was reviewing the odds that his calculated risk would work when he noticed his target, rather than standing on the deck in harm's way, had planted his sizeable derriere on the wooden rails of one of the stern's elevated seats. Perching in *Ambler's* aft-most corner, the thug seemed intent on placing himself out of range.

Has he guessed my plan? Trinidad asked himself. *Only one way to find out.*

Emerging from the protected confines of the harbor, *Ambler* caught the night wind and leaped onto the more challenging surface of Shadow Mountain Reservoir. Seconds later, the sailboat seemed to stall, then the craft surged again. After sunset, mountain breezes are generally mild, but tonight's storm had increased the wind to a sporadic squall which alternately caressed and assaulted the sails. The gusts were sharp and irregular, but the seemingly random flurries signaled their intentions to the informed observer.

Seated at the helm with both feet planted firmly on the deck, Trinidad was ideally positioned to interpret the wind. The calculating captive felt the rhythm of the pulsating reservoir as the sailboat's hull sliced through sporadic waves. To influence the sailboat's course and force his captor to abandon the elevated stern seat, Trinidad had merely to flick the helm, then nudge the mainsheet. Responding to these delicate maneuvers, *Ambler* heeled crisply to starboard. It was a subtle, yet decisive tactic which drenched the unprepared gunman with a healthy spray of icy water.

"Crap!" Jackhammer sputtered as he leapt from his exposed position, landed heavily on the pitching deck, and pivoted like a punch-drunk heavyweight to face his seated captive. The large man swayed awkwardly—his entire body invested in maintaining a menacing stance. Gaining his balance, the villain solidified into a looming mass. Seemingly magnified by the darkness, the man became a solid, hulking statue, a bulwark of colossal muscle and apparently rooted to the wooden planking until he raised his arm and Trinidad heard the pistol cock.

Jackhammer was staring directly at his prisoner as he aimed his weapon.

"Say your prayers, mister crafty bastard—" the villain began, but abruptly truncated his threat as the wind dropped and lightning flashed. The unexpected discharge illuminated the scene and gave Trinidad—who'd only seen the man in shadows—his first clear view of Jackhammer's ruined face. A second flash painted the suddenly calm water a translucent shade of gold, causing Jackhammer to shield his eyes against the glare. When the huge man dropped his arm, the muzzle of the pistol drifted downward until the weapon hung languidly down—as limp as a laundered sock and about as useful. Staring intently beyond the stern, Jackhammer's gaze drifted beyond Trinidad.

Fixing his eyes on the water, the huge man stood amazed as ghostly vapors encircled the sailboat.

"What? What?" Jackhammer repeated. "What?" he asked again. His attention was riveted on the milling vapors as the dormant wind returned to fill the sails.

Now or never, thought Trinidad.

"Canst thou swim?" Trinidad surprised himself by asking the question out loud.

"What the fuc..." the gunman began, but his response was lost when the sailor seated before him threw the helm to lee, let go the mainsheet, and sent the free-swinging boom careening from port to starboard. The unexpected blow struck Jackhammer shoulder-high, dislodging the unfired pistol and sweeping the yowling man into the dark water.

Chapter 61

False Summit
2019/Suppertime on June 8

"Seems to me," said Heckleson, "that your tale has reached its climax. Or is this business of dunkin' your villain merely one of them false summits which might maybe bamboozle a mountain climber?"

"I'm afraid you're right," Trinidad admitted. "Like a mountaineer mistaking an intervening ridge for his ultimate destination, knocking Jackhammer overboard marked the end to a portion of my recollections. But that act also launched the beginning of my journey to understand what the hell was going on."

"There does seem to be a few holes in the Swiss cheese of your story, if you don't mind my sayin' so."

"Let's take on those holes one at a time," said Trinidad. "You serve supper and I'll entertain your questions."

When the two men were settled around the kitchen table, the old ranger said grace, then picked up his fork and—using the utensil as a pointer—commenced his inquiry.

"First off," Heckleson began, "I understand that this-here Jackhammer character was convinced he had to get to Grand Lake under a certain time period and believed he'd been cheated by Red Bishop which is what eventually steered him to a kidnappin' binge. Plus, I understand that somethin' happened to ruin his pretty-boy looks and that he blamed Bishop fer the disfigured result. And I also caught the idea that Jackhammer was someway convinced that Bishop had a treasure which, if the crazy fool could only get his hands on it, would go a long way, in his addled mind, toward satisfyin' his need fer revenge. Do I got that straight so far?"

"Yep," said Trinidad.

"So, here's what I don't get," said Heckleson. "Why was it so dang important for Jackhammer to get up to Grand Lake that July of 1976? And how did his looks come to be all mangled-up? And what was it made Jackhammer so all-fired certain-sure that the Bishop clan had a treasure and where was this so-called treasure and what was it?"

"Let me help you out," Trinidad offered. "You recall that the biker and the sheriff had similar letter jackets?"

"That's as clear as a bell-weather," said Heckleson. "I reckon that, despite the odds of such a thing bein' true, they each went to the same Texas high school. Am I got that right?"

"Yep," said Trinidad.

"So am I also right if I guess that, during that-there Trail Ridge dust-up, somebody someway got somebody else's wrong jacket—and don't just say 'yep' consarn it!"

"You are absolutely, positively, 100-percent, died in the wool and twice on Sunday, correct," the detective laughed.

"Hell-fire," growled the old ranger. "Don't make me sorry I stopped y'all sayin' *yep.*"

"I'll behave," said Trinidad. "So, a key question becomes, as you succinctly put it, why was Jackhammer in such an all-fired hurry to get to Grand Lake? Which leads to other inquiries, such as, what happened when he arrived late? And what was it about the misappropriated jackets, that so altered the course of disparate lives?"

"Jiminy!" exclaimed the old ranger. "Here we are at the dang garden gate again and the wind is about to hit the woodpile and I never thought to ask even half them questions."

"Well, allow me to enlighten you," said Trinidad. "And please pass the potatoes."

When the detective's plate was filled to overflowing, he re-commenced his tale.

"Let's begin with the reasons Jackhammer wanted to reach Grand Lake on a certain timetable. For starters, I should explain that, long after Jackhammer was fished out of the reservoir, duly tried, and sentenced, I had the opportunity to interview the convict in some depth. So, at this juncture, I'm prepared to share what I learned from the man's own lips, supplemented with what I gleaned from interviews with others. Will that approach work for you?"

"Do I got a choice?"

"Of course," said Trinidad. "I can go home now and send a special messenger over with my written account of my post-dunking interviews with Jackhammer and Buster and other primary personalities in the Grand Lake saga. Or I can just keep doling out the story in bite-sized chunks. Your choice."

"No sense to rob Peter to pay the piper," said the old ranger. "I'll take the bites."

"Wise decision," Trinidad agreed.

Chapter 62

The Jailhouse Interviews
Recalling the Events of June and July 1976

In Trinidad's initial post-incarceration interview with Jackhammer, the huge prisoner claimed that half of a winning New York lottery ticket had come into his possession. Furthermore, he maintained that this particular particle of pasteboard was in the pocket of his letter jacket on the day of his Trail Ridge dust-up with Sheriff Red Bishop. The prize, he said, was no less than $200,000. He also claimed that the missing portion of the ticket was in Grand Lake, in an envelope, in a waterproof plastic sleeve, taped to the underside of a gas can in a lakeside boathouse. As Jackhammer saw it, the two halves needed to be reunited and transported to a New York claim center no later than midnight on July 6, 1976—one year from the date of purchase. How the thing got torn in the first place is a bizarre story. But suffice it to say that Jackhammer was anxious to motor up to Grand Lake in order to reunify the winning ticket and still have time to claim the money.

On July 1, just prior to Independence Day 1976, Jackhammer had been at home in China Berry, Texas, and embroiled in a marathon poker game, sitting across the table from a transplanted New York State biker named Imago Cognito. The game was Texas Hold 'em and he and Cognito were both riding winning streaks. By midnight, six other players had folded, leaving Jackhammer and Imago to battle for a $6,000 pot. Jackhammer held a solid full house and Imago's hand fell short. So did his marker. From Jackhammer's recollections and the testimony of other bikers present at the game—including a mentally alert, though physically challenged, Imago Cognito—Trinidad learned the details of that decisive poker contest as well as events which preceded and followed that fateful night.

The notion that Imago intended to evade his poker debt, led to tense negotiations which amounted to Jackhammer's powerful fingers closing around his opponent's windpipe. Fearing extinction, Imago convinced Jackhammer to accept his portion of a lottery ticket in lieu of cash owed. Pleading for his life, the visiting New Yorker intimated his belief that the severed ticket —which displayed three correct numbers—was a potential winner. He and Apia Bota, his former girlfriend, had bought the ticket together the previous year, on July 6, 1975. A few months later, autumn arrived, the relationship cooled, and Imago dumped her. Feeling betrayed and ornery, the departing woman tore off the right-hand edge of the lottery stub, dividing the original six-digit number in half, and fled with her portion as insurance that the often-volatile Imago wouldn't pursue her.

Once Apia was safely away, in an effort to placate Imago and discourage pursuit, she sent a terse letter to her ex- letting him know where he could find the remainder of the ticket. It was her idea to squirrel it away in a Grand Lake boathouse—an obscure location which was apparently on her escape route north to Canada.

Momentarily annoyed by his ex-lover's subterfuge, Imago had fretted for two days, then he grew angry until he hooked up with a new flame, whereupon the fickle biker's anger faded to indifference. Eventually he disregarded Apia's letter and entirely forgot the severed ticket and might never have given it a second thought had his memory not been jogged nearly a year later by a tidbit of unanticipated news.

On a sweltering day at the end of June 1976, word reached Imago that Apia had been shot dead during an aborted drug bust in rural Saskatchewan. Though a native New Yorker, Imago was living in mid-Texas when he got the news. Transmitted through the biker underground, the message from Canada was unexpected, but it failed to prompt grief or even mild regret. Instead, it ignited a more primitive, more visceral emotion.

In Imago's withered heart, the news of Apia's death spawned nothing short of an overwhelming episode of unvarnished greed—a compelling greed which sent the otherwise impassive biker scrambling.

Excavating every inch of his squalid China Berry apartment, Imago searched in vain for a trio of casually discarded mementos. The targets of his desperate quest were Apia's final kiss-off letter, his half of their mutual lottery ticket, and the New York State Lottery brochure outlining contest rules. He had a vague memory of fingering Apia's letter, crumpling the envelope, briefly unfolding it to place the torn lottery ticket inside, then shoving the envelope and brochure into—

Into, what?

Imago had rifled through every nick and cranny of his disorganized Texas dwelling without uncovering the forgotten relics. Defeated, he sat in the middle of his kitchen floor, cursing and sputtering.

Where? Where? Where?

He quizzed himself relentlessly until at last he struggled to his feet and fiercely yanked open his refrigerator. So violent was this movement that it dislodged the contents, a single beer bottle, which tumbled out and burst like a pinata on the kitchen tile. It was then that recognition dawned on Imago's troubled brain as he remembered the collection of bottles, cans, and boxes of paper scraps and junk mail which he'd recently lugged to China Berry's Waste Center.

Two days ago, on an unseasonably warm Friday morning, he'd been sitting in front of a fan in his underwear when he heard a radio announcement that the city was offering a promotional cash-for-trash incentive to encourage local residents to recycle. Possessing an abundance of trash and perennially short of cash, Imago borrowed a truck and loaded seven large cardboard boxes brimming with paper, empty beer bottles, and soda cans. Tossing in a few scraps of roadside trash, he started the old truck, and transported the load across town.

He'd arrived at the isolated collection building just as the center was closing for the weekend. Standing on the threshold of the broad entry door that
afternoon, he heard an unholy racket as distant laborers wrestled with mountains of cardboard. Imago rang the bell. One worker halted his fork-lift, left
the machine running, and shuffled toward his waiting customer. After eying
Imago's load, the taciturn man grunted, offered him a wrinkled two-dollar
bill, and directed him to a row of bins.

Each bin was clearly marked for aluminum, tin, glass, plastic, electron-
ics, and paper. Apparently, recycling patrons were expected to sort their own
loads. With the paltry payment in his pocket and the attendants busily obliv-
ious in the far corner of the cavernous building, Imago had no intention of
parsing his offerings. Unsupervised and disinterested, the impatient biker
had dumped everything into the paper bin.

Happy Friday, suckers, he'd told himself.

The papers he sought had to have been among the crap he tossed into
the distant bin. His memory jogged, Imago grabbed his .22 pistol, bolted
through his front door, and rushed down the swaying metal steps of his
building's wobbly fire escape. Hitting the ground at a dead run, he pocketed
the gun, fired up his Indian Scout, and roared down the complex's graveled
driveway. The careening motorcycle spewed pebbles and dust as Imago took
the corner. Barreling along a side street, he scattered a group of neighbor kids
playing stickball and headed for the highway.

The waste center would be closed on Sunday, of course. But since when
had a locked door stopped him? Although the center occupied a sprawling
warehouse, the building's contents amounted to glorified trash, so he imagined security would be minimal.

When Imago reached the center forty minutes later, it took no time at
all to pick the ordinary padlock on a side door. After a cursory look around
to make sure he was entering unobserved, he sidled inside to be greeted by
a snarling obstacle. He hadn't counted on the guard dog. His small caliber
pistol was virtually silent and, as the animal crouched menacingly in his path,

a well-placed bullet solved his problem. When the big Rottweiler was down, just to make certain, he strode forward, pressed his boot on the animal's neck, and put a second bullet in its twitching head. For a fleeting second, he wondered if he'd be able to have the business cited for failing to post a "Beware of Dog" sign.

Despite the dim light inside the unlit warehouse, Imago rapidly located the bin where he'd recently deposited the contents of his unsorted boxes. He was gratified to find the thing as he remembered it and apparently not yet emptied. Without hesitation, he pulled himself over the rim and tumbled inside.

Trying to recall the order of his dumping, he pushed bottles and cans aside. He was certain he'd thrown the paper in first, before adding the unauthorized junk on top. It was dark in the building and darker still in the bin. Pawing through layers of trash, he'd been knee-deep in discards and down to his final match when he found them. The envelope was neatly nested in a cocoon of junk mail as if it had been waiting to be recovered. He couldn't find the brochure, but decided its contents weren't critical.

Discarding the match, he climbed out of the bin, walked unhurriedly past the murdered dog, and let himself out. Tucking the envelope into his jacket, he started the Indian and roared away. Halfway home, a fire engine passed him on the two-lane road leading to and from the Paper Tiger Refuse and Recycling Center. Moments later, a second engine sped past, followed by a third one and a fourth. If he felt any guilt about what may or may not have transpired after he left the center, it was trumped by a stronger feeling of exhilaration. When he reached the highway and glanced back to see billows of dark smoke churning into the sky, the possibility of being arrested for arson was the furthest thing from his mind. As he guided the Indian onto the wider pavement, he was already thinking of ways to spend his potential winnings.

Back in his apartment, he used his vintage computer to search for the latest New York lottery results. It took some time. The computer wasn't his thing. He'd won it in a card game, but had yet to master it. Nevertheless, he eventually found what he was seeking.

The numbers in Imago's possession matched the first half of the winning sequence. He couldn't recall the three missing numbers, but he figured the odds were in his favor. Delighted by the possibility of claiming the jackpot, he re-read Apia's letter and made plans to depart for Grand Lake to pick up the missing half of what he hoped would be the winning lottery ticket.

But first, he needed money for gas and other trip expenses. It was a long way from the plains of Texas to the Colorado Rockies and he, as usual, was dead-broke. Racking his brain for fundraising ideas, Imago recalled the weekly poker game held in the backroom of China Grove's Anarchy Chopper Shop. Waiting for game night would be cutting the redemption time close, but he needed ready cash. So, he waited two days and unwisely got involved in a Texas poker contest.

Imago was winning and should have walked away, but his streak seemed solid, so he decided on one last hand. When Jackhammer Marsh's huge paw closed around Imago's throat, the New Yorker wasn't absolutely certain he held a winning number, but half a ticket along with information leading to the remaining portion were all he had to bargain with.

After Imago limped away from the poker game, Jackhammer discovered that the three digits on the severed ticket formed the tantalizing beginning of a number which led to the lottery jackpot. Placing his portion of the ticket in the inside pocket of his letter jacket, he had his mechanic work overtime to prepare his Harley for a hard ride.

With his motorcycle duly prepped, Jackhammer quickly gathered his gang and embarked for the Colorado Rockies, intent on retrieving the missing slice and claiming the prize. Once he rejoined the ticket, the optimistic biker figured the drive from Colorado to New York would take just over a day of hard riding. It would be a near thing, but entirely possible for a determined road warrior like himself.

The sheriff's 1976 Fourth of July roadblock thwarted Jackhammer's plan and, seeing their leader humiliated, his gang abandoned him. Left alone, their fallen leader was faced with an unwelcome 143-mile detour to reach Grand Lake via U.S. Highway 40. As luck would have it, construction crews were working on the road, which added six hours to the detour.

As the fuming biker passed the final construction barricade, he realized it was much too late to achieve his goal of reassembling the lottery ticket and making a cross-country dash to New York. Nevertheless, Jackhammer was determined to press on. Robbed of the opportunity to collect his winnings, he'd invent a way to enact his revenge on the lawman who'd frustrated his plans and that bastard lawman's town.

Jackhammer had journeyed to Colorado and started up Trail Ridge Road with the idea of redeeming a windfall lottery ticket for two-hundred grand. He could have used the money of course. But being denied the opportunity and the thrill of racing cross-country to claim his prize became less about the money and more a point of pride. He'd wanted a chance, that's all. He'd wanted a break.

Red Bishop had spoiled things. Red Bishop and his damned roadblock had caused the delay which forced Jackhammer to miss the July 6 redemption deadline. Red Bishop's lucky punch had embarrassed the huge biker. That humiliation had conjured unwelcome memories of schoolyard taunts and the mortifying tattoo incident—traumas which continued to haunt him—painful recollections which inflamed his ire. The interfering sheriff was going to pay for this blow to Jackhammer's ego. Grand County was going to pay. Grand Lake was going to pay.

By the time Jackhammer reached the outskirts of the village of Grand Lake, the long summer's day was dissolving into dusk. Attracted by the glow of an isolated payphone booth, he pulled over and laid hands on a weathered directory dangling there.

"Bishop...Bishop...Bishop..." the questing man muttered aloud. He thumbed through the directory with only a faint hope of finding the offending lawman's address listed there.

"What the fu—?" His astonished inquiry was lost as a droning dump truck roared by—the speeding vehicle passing so near that the impact of its trailing wind vibrated the insubstantial glass and aluminum door of the phone booth and nearly uprooted the Harley's kickstand. Unfazed by the careening truck, Jackhammer ripped the directory page from its paperback mooring. There was only one listing bearing that hated name and he'd have to presume that the sheriff resided somewhere in the neighborhood of Grand Lake Lodge.

Armed with this tenuous clue, the disillusioned biker opened up his Harley and flirted with the idea of roaring full throttle into the heart of the settlement. He was tired and sweaty and angry as he rounded a curve where, abruptly, he slowed down and veered left. If the sign commanding the intersection was to be believed, a right turn led to the main drag. The left fork directed him to the lodge which the now-vandalized phone directory had listed as the site of Bishop Plumbing.

Reaching the roadway leading to the lodge, he pulled to the shoulder and was about to dismount to take a piss when a bull moose appeared on the pavement. For a moment, in the gathering darkness, the two powerful beings stared at one another—Jackhammer unfazed by the looming creature and the moose apparently curious about the man who straddled the idling machine. The animal cocked its head and seemed to listen intently as Jackhammer repeated the same puzzling question over and over again.

"Canst thou swim? Canst thou swim?" his question just audible above the burbling rhythm of the Harley's well-tuned engine. Jackhammer popped his bike into gear, drove a few feet closer, stopped, and revved his motor. Then he moved closer still and repeated the same sequence.

The moose didn't move its feet and each time the biker advanced, it got eye contact, clicked its teeth, lowered its head, and squared its massive shoulders—defiant posing which might be interpreted as a precursor to charging.

"Fish or cut bait," Jackhammer warned the moose.

Perhaps the animal comprehended the ultimatum, or maybe it was bored with standing in the road. Whatever its motivation, the moose slowly turned around and began to amble with a deliberate, unhurried pace, along the middle of the pavement leading to a broad archway.

For a time, the man watched the moose. As it neared the arch, an owl screeched high in the surrounding forest. Following the sound, Jackhammer glanced skyward. It would be another week before the July moon would be full. Now it was a pregnant waxing crescent, its semi-circle visible through the evergreens, bright with potential. But there was light enough and, even without the benefit of a full moon, Jackhammer could see that the keystone of the arch exhibited the rack of a long-dead elk.

Mounted high above the road, the impressive antlers were vivid in the moonlight. Spanning the arch and pinned in place like a frozen butterfly, the relic glistened with a pallid shade of ghostly white. The rack was perfect—if the remnants of a decapitated animal may be called perfect. It was a sportsman's dream: symmetrical and majestic. But its mute grandeur was lost on the moose which passed indifferently beneath the archway.

The departing animal gave no sign of comprehending the irony of having sauntered through an opening decorated with its dead cousin. The moose's pace was slow, its demeanor apathetic. Just as it had dismissed the man on the motorcycle, it seemed to take no notice of the skull and antlers. Reaching the far side, the moose faded from view as its dusky bulk steadily melded into the darkness of the surrounding forest.

In contrast to the indifference of the live moose, Jackhammer was enamored with the deathly rack. Staring upward as the night gathered around him, the biker was imagining the delicious vision of Sheriff Red Bishop's head on a pike. He was about to pull his gaze from the archway when he saw the vivid spark of a shooting star as it streaked across the dark sky.

"Fire," he told himself as the kernel of an idea lodged in his brain and began, like a growing ember, to smolder there.

Chapter 63

Colorado's Best Kept Secret
2019/8 p.m. on June 8

"There's a difference of opinion about the inception date of Grand Lake Lodge," Trinidad told his host. "Some historians put the date at 1920. The sign on the archway spanning the lodge's entrance road says 'established 1925.' Suffice it to say the lodge is old."

"About as old as Buster Bishop, I reckon," said Heckleson. "Mind if I have a bit of the hard cider?"

"Be my guest," said the detective.

"Won't make y'all feel like you're missin' out?" Heckleson asked.

"Not in the least," the younger man assured the old ranger. "And I appreciate your concern."

"Won't be a swingin' bachelor party without which at least one of us gets a bit buzzed—beggin' your pardon."

The pair, whose professed purpose was marking the demise of Trinidad's bachelorhood, had moved from the kitchen to the side porch—as much to avoid the bloodstained back porch as to be in position to observe the lingering sunset. Heckleson left his guest alone while he returned to the icebox. Trinidad took advantage of the intermission to text his bride-to-be.

"What up?" he wrote and he was momentarily crestfallen when he didn't get an instant reply.

"OMG," came the reply several seconds later. "You can't text the bride b4 the weeding it is bad luck."

"Using voice to text?" His typed inquiry rocketed into outer space and back down again to reach Anne at Lavender Hill Farm.

"Wedding is bad luck." She attempted to edit her earlier message.

"Love you. Gotta go," he typed.

"Lug you 2. C U tomorrows," came the ungrammatical reply.

"Never understood what you young folks see in them magical phone machines," Heckleson observed as he returned to the porch with an oversized mug.

As the old ranger settled back into his chair, Trinidad could hear liquid sloshing—a booming sound not unlike the pounding of ocean surf. Presumably the mug was filled to the brim with his host's home-brewed hard cider. Aware of his guest's interest in the giant container, Heckleson offered an explanation.

"Got this somewheres back east," he said.

"A souvenir," Trinidad guessed.

"You gull-darn super detective," Heckleson grinned. "What give y'all the first clue that this-here is a souvenir? Did y'all notice it's decorated with a bunch of little-bitty checkered flags or maybe y'all spotted the giant red-white-and-blue NASCAR logo here on the side?"

"Or maybe my Xray vision allows me to read the 'made in China' label on the bottom," Trinidad joked.

"You're over-cookin' my grits," Heckleson sputtered in mock indignation. "If your done flirtin' long distance with that filly of yours, let's get back to your tale. So, which is the date of the lodge bein' made? Or is it seven of one and a baker's dozen of the other?"

"To hear Buster Bishop tell it, 1920 has to be right since his mother was working at the lodge in '21—the year of the old sheriff's birth."

"That's good enough fer me," said Heckleson.

"And yet, the sign hanging from the archway where Jackhammer plotted his revenge says 1925. But more importantly," Trinidad added with a conspiratorial tone, "what do you think it says on the backside of the sign? What do tourists leaving Grand Lake Lodge get to see as they pass back under the archway?"

"So long?" the old ranger guessed.

"Close," said Trinidad. "It says, *'Thank you—tell your friends about Colorado's best kept secret.'*"

"And you're about to tell me that Red Bishop's treasure is Colorado's best kept secret," Heckleson surmised.

"Good guess," said Trinidad. "But there's more than one secret—"

"Which is—"

"Sip your cider," Trinidad laughed. "And I'll pick up the thread of my story which will transport Jackhammer from his brief encounter with a wandering moose to the Grand Lake Lodge and the secret of the unlucky biker's rendezvous with destiny."

Chapter 64

The Jailhouse Interviews
Recalling What Happened Late at Night on July 4, 1976

Following on the heels of his encounter with the indifferent moose, Jackhammer remembered concealing his Harley in a clump of aspens. Standing among the shadowy trees, the huge man removed his letter jacket and donned a dark sweater. Then he walked the last two miles of Grand Lake Lodge Road until he reached a broad parking area.

Adjacent to the main building, the paved lot was filled with sedans, trucks, jeeps, station wagons, and even a few motorcycles. It was an impressive array of visitor vehicles sporting license plates from every corner of the nation and—if you count Mexico and Canada—a few machines from beyond America's national borders. It was an ample display which suggested that the Independence Day crowd had fully occupied the lodge. Given the variety, a license plate collector might consider himself to have arrived in Heaven. An automobile enthusiast might feel the same.

Ignoring most of the nighttime display, Jackhammer focused on the cycles. One in particular had caught his eye. He couldn't be sure in the dim light, but with each step toward the parked machine, he grew more certain. He wasn't imagining it. There was no mistaking the distinctive red Indian Scout of Imago Cognito with its classic lines, 745cc engine, and pretentious blue wheels—an affectation which Imago loved and Jackhammer despised.

"What the—?" Jackhammer asked aloud, but didn't finish the question as he sensed movement to his right.

A torque wrench and a crankcase splitter look about the same, in the dark, in motion. Whatever the ambusher was wielding that July night in the Colorado mountains, the sound of it whizzed past as Jackhammer leaned left, sidestepped, and pivoted to clamp the would-be assailant in an uncompromising headlock. Like a pro-wrestler—a role he'd briefly mastered—Jackhammer applied steady pressure until the smaller man in his grip began to puddle into the unforgiving pavement. First Imago's knees buckled, then his upper body seemed to telescope downward in a series of impossible bends. Something crunched and it was over.

Jackhammer never learned that night, nor did he care at the time, whether the New Yorker lived or died. He simply rolled the unconscious man over and rifled through his pockets until he found what he was certain he'd find there. Extracting the thing, he noticed it was wrapped in a protective plastic sleeve. Examining it in place, he didn't open the plastic. The sliver of pasteboard encased inside seemed a perfect match to the half-ticket he'd left behind with his Harley. The portion the huge biker held in his hand—Imago's portion—was printed in muted umber ink on a pasteboard background of yellow-gold. Like Jackhammer's half, this fragment was watermarked with an official state seal. The main difference between the two halves was the signature. The corner of Imago's half was signed in an illegible scrawl by someone purporting to be Chairman of the New York State Racing and Wagering Board.

Tricky to counterfeit, Jackhammer told himself. But not impossible, he completed the thought.

And yet, what did it matter now? What did it matter if the thing matched? He'd begun his quest for the remnant he liberated from Imago's pocket with high hopes. Now that his plans had been crushed, he didn't even bother to check the numbers. They were as irrelevant as the blue tires on the New Yorker's motorcycle. Jackhammer looked at the lump of a man lying on the pavement. Then he glanced at the mass of vehicles clustered around the crime scene.

Did someone see? Probably not.

A typical spectator would have cried out, but—except for the subtle sound of displaced air as the metallic weapon glided past his skull—the entire episode had been conducted in absolute silence. He'd leave the lump to be discovered—dead or alive—by an amorous couple strolling in the pale moonlight, or an early-rising dog walker, or some guy coming to pick up the trash. It was no concern to him.

The ambush perpetrated by Imago had diverted Jackhammer from his mission—but only temporarily. Grasping the ticket—sleeve and all—in his powerful fingers, he turned away from the prostrate man as though his being there, sprawled awkwardly on the cold pavement, was entirely commonplace. Moving on, Jackhammer left Imago there. He had other fish to fry—figuratively speaking. He was looking for the kitchen.

Statistics identify the room which houses the cookstove as the most likely ignition source for a fire which consumes a wooden structure. There were sufficient lights in the parking lot and on walkways leading to the main building for the searching biker to confirm that the lodge was absolutely flammable. Its stairs were wooden, its decks were wooden, its columns and joists and supporting beams and roof and walls were all made of timber.

Jackhammer left the parking lot and mounted the lodge's main stairs. As he neared the crest of the solid stairway, he met a uniformed youth—apparently a waiter—coming down.

"Evening," the boy said as he rushed by, corkscrewing down a series of landings and exterior stairs until he passed beneath a yard light and vanished in the darkness.

It was a brief encounter. Jackhammer had turned his head, taking pains to obscure his face and he hadn't replied to the boy's comment. The shadows on the stairway were deep. The boy might be able to identify him in a pinch, but he wouldn't have gotten a good look in the dark and, besides, by the time anyone got around to questioning the staff, the huge biker planned to be long-gone. Reaching the top step, Jackhammer advanced along the wide entryway, colliding briefly with a hanging porch-swing which he set careening into an exterior wall.

"Shit," he grumbled as he reached out to steady the undulating swing.

He stood still for a moment, listening. Hearing no movement, he tried the double doors and was unsurprised to find them locked.

Good, he told himself. *A locked door means everybody's gone. So, chances are nobody's inside. No witnesses and nobody to interfere.*

To enact his revenge on Sheriff Bishop, Jackhammer craved a spectacular fire. People might be hurt, might even perish. The vengeful biker put aside thoughts of collateral damage. Whatever the cost, he'd trigger a blaze. If he managed a large fire, the flames may or may not reach the sheriff. It would have to be enough to harm the man indirectly by igniting the sprawling lodge which housed the Bishop plumbing enterprise. It was an intangible hope, but it would have to be enough.

A few minutes spent probing for prospective entrances yielded an unlocked window. He worked his fingers beneath the casement of the lower sash, eased it up, and climbed inside. Another five minutes of searching led him to the kitchen where he located the gas stove. Still gripping the partial ticket in one hand, he used the other to grab wads of paper napkins which he stuffed beneath the burner grates. He shoved empty cardboard boxes to the front of the stove, then piled them as high as possible, leaving just enough room for him to pass a hand through the wall of fuel to reach the burner knobs.

Then he went looking for matches.

His plan was simple. Matchbook in hand, he'd open a kitchen window to make sure the blaze he was contemplating had plenty of oxygen to work with. Next, he'd ease one of the front burner knobs on and allow a trickle of gas to escape. Finally, he'd put a match to the plastic sleeve containing the worthless half-ticket, toss the burning thing in, make sure the initial blaze ignited, and run like hell.

The rest he'd leave to chemistry.

And his scheme might have worked had it not been for one small wrinkle of which he was tragically unaware. The night cook, an older man with little practical experience as a chef, had sprayed commercial cleaner in the stove's oversized oven and left for the night, not realizing the entire kitchen device was designed to activate a self-cleaning cycle.

The instant Jackhammer struck the match, the unlucky arsonist was doomed. By fateful coincidence, the lighting of the pasteboard symbol of the huge biker's repressed anger coincided with the automated onset of the cleaning cycle. The resulting tower of flame flashed up like a roiling bomb blast, singeing Jackhammer's exposed face and arms, scorching his clothing, igniting the pyre of fuel the huge biker had assembled, and roaring skyward to engulf the ceiling.

Reeling with spasms of searing pain and choking from heat and smoke, Jackhammer rushed toward the open window. Whirling in frantic, fiery rotations like a gyrating dervish, he reached the opening where he dived headfirst into the casement. Crashing through in a hail of shattering glass and wood, he tumbled into the night, forced himself erect, and hurtled pell-mell in the direction of the lake. Whether caught in the grip of shock or by the exertion of some superhuman strength of will, he ran noiselessly without uttering a sound—a silent human torch—careening over the sloping ground.

As he advanced, the commands *stop, drop, and roll* penetrated his consciousness and he obeyed. Extinguishing flames, he regained his feet as his desire to escape overrode his thoughts of seeking help. Reacting on instinct, he'd raised his hands to protect his eyes from the kitchen flare-up, but his arms and much of his face had been scorched. How badly he was injured, he didn't care to know. He had to reach the lake. The lake's cooling waters would absorb his pain. The lake would save him.

Finding he had a substantial distance to cover, he mastered his agony and pumped his powerful legs—miraculously dodging trees, then careening through streets and skirting contact with a few wandering pedestrians—until at last he reached the shoreline, scrambled across a wooden dock, and fell smoking into the dark embrace of Grand Lake.

How he mustered the instinct to tread water, how he managed the strength to keep afloat, why his heart didn't stop, why his breath didn't still—Jackhammer would never know the answers to such fundamental questions. He was also incapable of remembering how long he was immersed in the icy waters. He did recall hearing thunder and being vaguely aware of spasms of sheet lightning illuminating the dark sky somewhere above his throbbing head. The scene seemed, oddly, to be bathed in a peculiar patina of golden light. He remembered the storm, but his memory failed when he attempted to recall how he managed to grasp a piling and pull his shaking and aching body up onto the slippery surface of a rain-soaked wharf.

Hearing thunder and distant sirens, he fled from the shore, colliding with trees, falling and rising and falling again as he struggled through the dark forest. Hours passed as he bumbled along. Somehow, by first light, he stumbled into a ribbon of water and splashed upstream until he reached a handful of dilapidated structures. Lurching into a low opening, he struck his head and fell hard onto the unforgiving surface of a rough dirt floor.

He lay, senseless, for a cycle of one and perhaps two days, until he felt an unknown hand gripping his left foot. Rising awkwardly on one elbow, Jackhammer looked down along his supine body to find a chubby raccoon scrounging at his feet, the curious animal's deft fingers plucking at the biker's bootlaces. Chattering as it worked, the raccoon seemed unaware that the laces were attached to a boot which was attached to a man who—given a rock and the opportunity—could crush the creature's skull.

Semi-conscious and fixated, Jackhammer continued to stare at the busy animal until, almost apologetically, the huge man cleared his throat.

"Chit," the raccoon uttered a single syllable and established momentary eye contact before taking one last tug at the bootlaces and pirouetting to duck outside.

Jackhammer waited to make certain he was alone, then he laid back and wept. The macho biker hadn't cried since—he couldn't recall the last time. But, isolated there on the rigid dirt floor, his face a mask of pain, his arms aching, his head buzzing, he cried until the pain of salt tears coursing across his raw cheeks forced him to stop. Willing his tears to cease, he whimpered until exhaustion carried him blissfully away.

Sleep was sporadic and troubled by vivid hallucinations. When the suffering giant awoke, he presumed he was still submerged in the icy embrace of Grand Lake. His eyes were open, but his vision was stifled by an interlaced layer of translucent green. A damp aroma—a combination of pine boughs, moss, and freshly-harvested leaves—permeated his nostrils. He reached to clear away the obstruction, but a firm hand arrested his movement.

"Old Father," a voice sounded in the dark. "As you sent the waterfowl, as you sent the duck, as you sent the turtle, grant me the healing power of your emerging Earth. Bring forth the waters. Bring the spirits of the Dead. Bring the buffalo again. Bring all things and press their healing mercy upon this unfortunate man. Bind his wounds."

After a pause, the voice continued, each word resonating with an honest cadence which suggested the speaker was in prayer.

"Progenitor, sky-dweller, we call you holy. Your future reign is ruled by all you desire here below an also above. Provide us today with all we need. And absolve us according to our absolution of others. And tempt us not, but be our protection against dark forces which seek to ensnare us. Because you stand as our dominion, you are our strength, our radiance, and our ever-lasting triumph beyond the end of time. This I believe. So be it, now, and ever-more."

Recalling this invocation, Jackhammer paused and earnestly addressed his interviewer.

"That last part sounded familiar to me," he told Trinidad. "Do you see what I mean?"

"Familiar, yes," Trinidad agreed. "I'd have to say your recollection of that recitation seems to paraphrase *The Lord's Prayer*."

"Funny, huh?" Jackhammer observed. "Not funny 'ha-ha,' but funny strange. I can't recollect the title nor lyrics to any of the old-days songs that repeat in my head, but I can remember Ylem's prayer without a hitch. Weird, huh?"

"That's one word for it," said Trinidad.

Sitting at a stark prison table, in a sterile visitation room, Jackhammer continued his remembrance by declaring that he had learned much from dis-embodied voices and shadowy figures who drifted across his field of vision and seemed to speak to him. Voices declared that his search for an improvised shelter had landed him in the ruins of an abandoned cabin. The apparitions who invaded his thoughts informed him that his dreaming mind had been transported back through time to 1879. The voices insisted that the surrounding area had once been home to as many as 500 souls—a mushrooming population of questing miners whose lust for riches had lured them to the Colorado mountains.

"This-here town be Lark City," one wraith intoned. "An icy hell-hole where dreams of riches go to die. Where miners toil beneath the snowy sky," a pair of phantoms harmonized.

Obviously in the throes of delirium, Jackhammer's troubled mind managed to meld imagined scenes of the past with his own nostalgic musical memories. His addled brain conjured up visions of hard-luck pioneers who lived and nearly froze to death in Lark City—a late 1800s mining camp situated north of Grand Lake. But his troubled mind also combined historical mirages with snippets of modern-day tunes. Recalling the notes, but unable to remember exact lyrics, he invented his own. He'd heard the music, of course, and possibly he'd read about the miners prior to his Colorado trip, probably in a Grand County travel brochure. Either that, or he'd been visited by actual spirits. As for the latter possibility, the hard-headed biker told himself this wasn't so—unless it was.

"I may have seen and heard them things or just dreamed some of it," Jackhammer said during his marathon jailhouse interviews with Trinidad. "But I'll tell you one damn thing. Those pioneer miners might have been pulling my leg, but Ylem was real—and she was right in front of me—as close and real as you and me. That much I'll swear by! That much I'll swear!"

While reminiscing, the huge convict had become so agitated in his recollections that, notwithstanding the lengthy restraining chain which pinned him to the visitors' desk, he was on his feet and leaning in Trinidad's direction. It was an outburst which obliged the shepherding detention deputy to take two steps forward and admonish the prisoner to settle down.

"Sorry about that," Jackhammer apologized to Trinidad as he resumed his seat. "I'm okay," he told the guard.

"Nearly time," the deputy reminded both men.

"Shit," Jackhammer whispered.

"Volume," the deputy demanded.

"Didn't mean to waste everybody's time," Jackhammer said in a voice which was contrite but also, consistent with the deputy's wishes, audible. "I'll control myself in future and things'll go better. See you soon?" he sounded hopeful.

"I'll be back in twelve days," said Trinidad and, seeing the huge man visibly deflated, he clarified his schedule. "Look, I've got finals to study for and then it's home for the holidays. You wouldn't want me to miss the family dinner, or flunk out and end my project, would you?"

"Nope," Jackhammer agreed. "You keep at it, college boy. I still got a shi—boatload to tell over."

A buzzer sounded and two correctional officers arrived to escort the prisoner back to his cell. Trinidad gathered up his recorder and notes, stood, and walked toward the exit where he encountered the deputy who was busy typing on a small handheld device. He waited patiently for the deputy to finish.

"Sorry," the deputy apologized. "I just got this new Telstra—it's an amazing piece of machinery. I looked up that word the prisoner used. Simply amazing."

"See you in January," Trinidad told the deputy. "So, I'll wish you a happy 2007 now."

"I won't be here," the deputy replied with a hint of regret in his voice.

"Quite a story so far," Trinidad suggested, knowing this particular lawman had been present during his original session with Jackhammer and throughout all the subsequent meetings stretching over several months.

"It'll make one hell of a term paper," the deputy said.

"I'll fill you in when you're back on duty," Trinidad promised.

"That'll be peachy," the deputy decided. "Do you want to know what it means?"

"What means?" Trinidad asked, genuinely perplexed.

"That new word the prisoner used," the deputy explained. "I typed it in like I thought I heard him say it—phonetically, you know? But my Telstra corrected the spelling and you'll never guess what it means."

"It sounded familiar," Trinidad admitted. "And I figured I'd look up the spelling when I transcribed my recording. What did you find out?"

"*Ylem*—it's spelled capital *Y* then *l-e-m*. Pronounced *I-lum*—not quite island and not quite *I'll-um*."

"And it means—" Trinidad prompted.

"My bad," the deputy apologized. "My Telstra says *Ylem* is something the Greeks used to describe the prime substance. Also, the word in Hebrew means something like the space between Heaven and Earth. Basically, the word means how everything began—it's the start of everything. Well, anyway, Merry Christmas."

"Same to you," said Trinidad as he offered his hand.

"And, since it'll be awhile, Happy New Year too," the deputy added.

"Ditto," said Trinidad.

Chapter 65

Legends
2019/Growing Late on June 8

"So," the old ranger interrupted, "seems like both y'all and this-here deputy was all gaga over every word of a convicted felon—especially his connection with some super-natural *I-am* character, am I right?"

"That's the case, I guess," Trinidad admitted. "Jackhammer's story was compelling and not just his personal exploits, but also what he says he experienced in the aftermath of his aborted attempt to burn down Grand Lake Lodge. Not only that, but his use of Ylem seemed to resonate with me. It seemed like I should know the name. Turns out, I did."

"Y'all believe all that?"

"Well," Trinidad said, "I have to admit I was skeptical of the testimony of a giant fugitive, sheltering in an isolated cabin, suffering alone with deep second-degree and full-thickness third-degree burns. Who knows what to make of episodes which ran the sensory gamut from bizarre hallucinations to undocumented spiritual visitations? Throughout our talks, Jackhammer continued to insist that, though some of his memories of that time may be attributed to his injuries, a physical someone or something—a presence he called it—actually came to him in the abandoned cabin. Not only came and went, but stayed with him and nursed him back to health. He also claims that this same ministering angel located his motorcycle, brought the machine to Lark City, and concealed it against the day when her patient was fit to ride away. She also retrieved his precious letter jacket and presented it to him as a token of her affection. Was the presence he remembers as Ylem a man, or a woman, or even a real person? Apparently, it was a tangible and resourceful being. Otherwise, how did Jackhammer survive and how did he recover his jacket? Who moved his motorcycle? Someone must have nursed him. Someone must have helped him. Who's to say it didn't happen?"

"I'm still waitin' to hear if y'all believe it," Heckleson reminded the detective.

"All I can tell you is I tried to verify Jackhammer's account of one particular Grand Lake legend—an ancient story he heard from Ylem. My research uncovered several conflicting accounts as I constantly ran into the same problem which was, only the oral tradition of the Utes could confirm or dispute the facts of the legend and the Utes aren't talking."

"Fuzzy stories by unreliable witnesses," Heckleson observed. "That has to mean that y'all ended up with nothin' but half-truths which added together still don't make a single fact which a body can take to the river bank. Leaves a fella up a creek, I reckon, without a leg to stand on."

"Couldn't have said it better," Trinidad decided.

"How's about keepin' that Chesterfield Cat grin off your smart-alecky face?" the old ranger scoffed. "And how's about y'all tell me what it is y'all *do know* about this-here so-called legend? Even if y'all don't know much, go ahead and tell me what y'all sorted out and let me jump to my own conclusions."

"Here goes," said Trinidad as he took a deep breath and reported his findings regarding one of Grand Lake's most enduring legends. "According to unsubstantiated sources, an ancestral band of Utes—numbering somewhere between a dozen souls to as many as three hundred—were camped on either the northern, southern, eastern, or western shore of Grand Lake at either high noon or early morning or dusk on a clear or overcast or middling day in August or March or October. The group consisted of both sexes and at least three generations ranging from the elderly to babes in arms. Either as a precaution or out of habit or without forethought, the band had either posted sentries or not posted them and the sentries, if there were any, had either fallen asleep or been looking the wrong way when a rival band of forty or several hundred or sixteen Arapahoe or Cheyenne braves or some from each tribe inched forward or fell pell-mell in a revenging or unprovoked attack. During the resulting skirmish or pitched battle, the Utes loaded old people, children, and/or women onto one or a half dozen or several wooden rafts which were poled or rowed or sailed to the middle of the deep lake for safety. The Ute braves either lost or won the battle or they survived to a stalemate. Whatever the result, before the rafts could be retrieved, a sudden wind of unimagined fury or an unaccountable wave of incalculable height or both or neither arose and capsized the rafts dooming all aboard to a watery grave. Some accounts say there was a lone survivor—a baby suspended in a tree by her mother—a distraught woman who later drowned.

Other accounts say this baby survived the tragic storm only to be slain by retreating enemy warriors. Still others dismiss the tree-baby tale as a myth within a myth. Cobbling together multiple versions of the story and adding new wrinkles, Joseph L. Wescott, a Grand Lake pioneer, sought to capture the legend in more than 300 rhyming couplets. Allegedly inspired by a lakeside conversation with a Ute elder, Wolcott's 1882 poem represents yet another interpretation of the attack and subsequent drowning.

"And," Trinidad paused to catch his breath, "assuming any of those things actually happened, those who hear one tale or the other, are told that the bodies of the lost never resurfaced. If storytellers are to be believed, mists rising from the surface of Grand Lake at dawn and twilight can be interpreted to resemble the outlines of the drowned. Moreover, narrators describe eerie echoes which saturate the post-sundown and predawn darkness and swear that these unexplained sounds constitute cries of the missing. To this day, Utes, we are told by everyone except the Utes themselves, avoid the lake as a place of sorrow and ill luck. Without citing sources, chroniclers of these tales have maintained that, since the time of the alleged tragedy, Grand Lake has, among the Tribes, been called *Spirit Lake.* In conclusion, does the surface of Colorado's deepest natural lake occasionally roil like an undulating ocean? Do sudden storms erupt in the mountains and rocket over the churning lake with the power to capsize watercraft? Do microbursts, abrupt downdrafts, and wind shears sometimes strike with-out warning? Yes," Trinidad answered his own inquiries. "Do the spirits of the departed writhe at dawn and dusk? Does the darkness evoke the voices of the dead?"

"Yes, or no?" the old ranger posed the unspoken question.

"Jackhammer certainly thought yes," Trinidad ventured. "Scientists can postulate reasons for mist. No body of water, be it haunted or not, is immune from the effects of air and moisture reacting to temperature differences. And a mysterious sound, heard in the absence of visual con-text, can be disorienting. But who am I to discount the things which Jack-hammer saw and heard and felt?"

"He kept firm to his story about his time in that-there tumble-down cabin?" Heckleson wondered aloud.

"He consistently repeated his recollections," Trinidad confirmed. "This uniformity of content seemed to add credence to his story even though I've heard the idea of consistency compared to hobgoblins—"

"I know that hobgoblin guy," Heckleson interjected. "It's an idea of that-there Ralph Waldo Emerson, the past-time poet. Ahem," the old ranger stood erect holding one finger aloft and placing his other hand on his breast in the classic stance of one who was about to recite.

"Go ahead," Trinidad encouraged his old friend.

"I give you 'The Concord Hymn' by Ralph Waldo Emerson," Heckle-son prefaced his piece, then paused to ensure that his audience of one was paying strict attention. Trinidad nodded and the old ranger began.

> By the rude bridge that arched the flood,
> Their flag to April's breeze unfurled,
> Here once the embattled farmers stood,
> And fired the shot heard round the world.

"Well, it was a fair start, but that's all I can recall of that poem I had to put to memory and speak out in grade school. I recollect how proud my parents was that day I stood up bold as brass and said that poem out-loud without missin' so much as one syllable," he sniffed. "Now, what in Hell's Green Acres was we talkin' about before this old fool drifted all misty-eyed into my boy-hood days?"

"Ghosts," Trinidad reminded his host. "Or rather, *spirits,* as I gather the Utes prefer to think of the departed. Grand Lake, for better or worse, is home to a legion of spirits and it's no surprise that three overlapping echoes of the past converged at Lark City and drifted into the conscious- ness of Jackhammer who was, by all accounts, near death himself."

"Three past echoes, y'all say? Well let's see now, there was all them unfortunate kin who perished on the rafts," said Heckleson as he recalled the Ute Legend. "Then there was the miners which worked their diggin's and some of which died in the old ghost town. That's two crowds of spir- its—but y'all say three. What am I leavin' out, I wonder?"

"1883," Trinidad offered the date as a clue, then added an additional hint. "July 4th of that distant year."

"Ah," the old ranger surmised. "Not quite the shot heard 'round the world. More like the shots heard 'round the lake."

"Exactly," Trinidad confirmed.

"So, is it your idea to include *The Grand Lake Shootin'* as the third set of ghosts?" the old ranger asked. "I know that tale, as who among lawmen don't. A sad business when them that wore badges stepped over the line. But, here now, do y'all mean to say that spirits from that long- ago shoreline gunplay visited old Jackhammer? Was there a visit from those parties what fought over which village was first in line to become the local county seat?"

"Something like that," said the detective. "However, Jackhammer didn't report a visitation from the 1883 crowd. His brush with *The Shootin'* was more contemporary and less direct than a genuine haunting."

"Which means what?" Heckleson raised an eyebrow.

"Can I interest you in a history lesson?" the detective asked.

"My most favorite subject in school," the old ranger declared. "The past is like the future, only later. I'd love history even more if it weren't fer all them dad-burned dates."

"I'll keep the numbers to a minimum," the detective promised. "I'll continue my story by reminding you that old wounds heal slowly. I'm talking not only about Jackhammer's physical wounds and his deeper injuries—his feelings of enmity toward Red Bishop and his desire for revenge. I'm also talking about the legacy left in the wake of the 1883 incident."

Chapter 66

The Jailhouse Interviews
Recalling August 1976, as well as January 2006

Jackhammer told Trinidad that, weeks after surviving the fire at Grand Lake Lodge, he awoke in his Lark City hideaway to discover his angel was gone. Contemplating that disappearance as a sign, he was trying to choose whether to stay or go. Guided by Ylem's counsel, he decided that—despite his troubles, despite his damaged face and scarred arms and hands—he was content. Responding to Ylem's ministrations, his pain had ceased. As for his poor skin, it was what it was. His once proud face was a ruin which, he knew, would never be restored.

Sitting in the dark, Jackhammer concluded that—though he was hungry and vulnerable—he would stay and endure whatever happened. The fugitive would abandon his desire to injure Buster Bishop. He would surrender his longing to return to the world. He'd spurn his motorcycle as a symbol of his misspent past, leave the machine hidden, consign it to the elements, and subsist in the husk of Lark City, even if it meant dying there. Having decided to remain, he was celebrating his decision, stroking his beloved letter jacket, and humming contentedly to himself when a pair of hikers arrived to stand in his tumble-down doorway.

Seeing a huge figure crouching and droning inside the barely recognizable remains of an ancient log cabin, the two were momentarily frozen in place. Jackhammer had his back to the door, his attention focused on the grimy letter jacket in his lap while he sang snatches of nostalgic songs. When he fell silent, the frightened woman emitted a startled gasp. Curious, the ghostly being turned to regard his visitors and revealed the mangled aspect of his ravaged face, causing the man and woman to flee in mortal terror.

By the time authorities returned to the cabin, whatever the couple had seen was nowhere to be found. The hikers swore that they'd stumbled across Big Foot himself. The rangers had their own theory of the alleged encounter.

"Meth," they wrote in their official report. It was a terse conclusion which drew a veil over Jackhammer's bungled crime and his months-long sojourn in one of Colorado's vanishing ghost towns. The steadily eroding site lies just inside the boundaries of what is now Rocky Mountain National Park. Only a few juxtaposed logs mark the place and nothing remains of the cabin where Jackhammer spent his uneasy convalescence in 1976.

Years later, Trinidad read the rangers' report and tracked down the hikers who still lived in the county. Which is when he discovered the connection between the couple who stumbled on Jackhammer and the 1883 shooting.

If the decades-old legacy of the shooting had endured, the couple would never have been in the forest that day. In fact, if the anguish of past generations had prevailed, they would never have become a couple.

A few generations ago, the hikers who encountered the injured biker would have been considered a star-crossed couple. They would have been declared an unlucky pair, burdened by a checkered past no less daunting than the heritage which strove to thwart the love of Romeo and Juliet. The bride-to-be, a woman on the cusp of her 30th birthday, hailed from Hot Sulphur Springs. Her ancestor was accused of planning the 1883 ambush. The prospective groom was a native of Grand Lake—a local man who turned out to be a direct descendant of one of the county commissioners who was gunned down nearly a century before. Had the feud continued through the years, Alice Miller and George Webb wouldn't have been on speaking terms, let alone walking in the woods on that July day and contemplating marriage.

And yet, their role in Jackhammer's story had been decisive. Without their intervention, the unhappy giant may have remained in Lark City, a declining and forgotten hermit. Likely, he would have perished in isolation. As he listened to Jackhammer reminiscing, it seemed to Trinidad that the wounded biker had been teetering on the edge of oblivion that summer in 1976, only to be discovered and consequently inspired to move on. It was a course correction which altered not only Jackhammer's life but also the lives of Buster and Saul, not to mention Trinidad himself.

Four generations had passed since Alice Miller's great-great uncle hatched his plot to throw a scare into his archrival. The entire incident revolved around the question of where the Grand County seat was to be located. In 1874, two years before Colorado statehood, the territorial government established Grand County and chose Sulphur Springs as county seat. The town of Grand Lake sprang up five years later on the crest of a mining boom and, in 1881, the county seat was theoretically relocated there. Alice's ancestor was a Hot Sulphur Springs resident and booster who insisted that the county seat be returned to his town. Adding fuel to a simmering cauldron of competition between the two emerging towns, that ancestral booster allegedly conspired with others to perpetually delay the transfer of written records, thus obliging Grand County residents to continue conducting county business in Sulphur Springs.

The booster's competitor for political influence was a progenitor of George Webb. The two pioneer men had once been partners, but a spate of double-dealing and high-handed maneuvering had left them embittered enemies. To the chagrin of the Sulphur Springs booster, the former partner managed to get himself appointed to the board of county commissioners. In this capacity, he and his supporters were adamant that the county seat remain in Grand Lake.

The increasingly hostile encounters between the one-time partners came to a head on the Fourth of July 1883 when Alice's ancestor met with his followers, including the county sheriff and undersheriff. The outcome of that ill-fated meeting was a plot to throw a scare into county commissioners and officials. The idea was to don masks, lie in wait, and accost the commissioner party as they made their way along the shore of Grand Lake. Drawing pistols and issuing threats, the Sulphur Springs booster hoped his armed gang would convince opposition politicians to leave Grand County.

But the scheme backfired. It literally backfired.

On that Independence Day long ago, Grand Lake residents were enjoying fireworks, beer, and holiday refreshments when someone—either the intended victims or assailants—pulled a trigger and an eruption of gunshots shattered the celebration. At first, the sounds were presumed to be merely the reports of exploding fireworks. But soon celebrants lounging on the porch of the nearby Fairview Hotel flocked to the scene to discover two men dead and two mortally wounded. The body of one commissioner was found floating in Grand Lake, a bullet through his heart. The scheming Sulphur Springs booster, still wearing a mask, was dead where he lay. Carried from the scene of the carnage, his one-time partner eventually bled to death in the parlor of the Fairview, leaving a blood stain which persisted for years until the building was demolished. The commission clerk also survived that fateful day only to die two weeks later.

To those four deaths were later added one confirmed suicide and one undocumented demise of a pair of Grand County lawmen. Following the shooting, the conspiratorial sheriff and undersheriff—to differing degrees—came to terms with their roles in the ambush. After claiming innocence, the sheriff ultimately shot himself. As for the undersheriff, that missing man's possessions, including his blood-stained saddle, were discovered miles away in Utah. The undersheriff's body was never found and some believed he staged his death to escape capture and punishment.

The shocking "wild-west" incident was written up in newspapers from California to Rhode Island and everywhere in between. Even the tamest headlines trumpeted "The Colorado Crime" and "The Colorado Tragedy." *The Tennessean Newspaper* of Nashville spoke of "A County Quarrel." Other journalists were less gentle. *The Gazette* of Cedar Rapids, Iowa, led with a page-one story under the banner "Ways of the Wicked." And *The County Democrat* of Mineral Point, Wisconsin, typeset a double headline declaring: "Shot Down in Cold Blood: Assassination of Three Officials of Grand County, Colorado!"

The incident had far-reaching repercussions. Nearly two years after the tragedy, a disheartened citizen was quoted in the Fort Collins, Colorado, *Express* as having "a discouraging outlook" on the future of Grand Lake. In November 1885, the informant lamented that the town's population had slipped from 150 souls to no more than 40 with only 28 adults voting in the current election. He put the precipitous decline down to a variety of factors: the high cost of living, the stagnation of mining activity, hard winters, lack of railroad facilities, and "the unfortunate feud two years ago which ended in the killing of several of the county's prominent men."

Adding insult to injury, in the wake of the shooting incident, the Grand County seat was ultimately returned to Sulphur Springs, where it remains today. Decades later, in an act which smacked of irony, the vintage stone building which had spawned the controversy was torn down to make way for a more modern structure. The entire matter was a sorry business and, for some, a grim legacy.

Four generations are a long time to hold a grudge. The wound was still fresh with the brother of one fatality who alarmed his children with talk of revenge. Seeking to escape the burden of vengeance, the eldest boy, Alice's great-grandfather, officially petitioned the county to alter his surname. Coincidently, county records show that the great-grandfather of one of the alleged ambushers took the same route a few months later. Consequently, by the time the couple's grandfathers were born, two notorious names associated with the tragedy had morphed into Miller and Webb.

Years passed and recollections faded.

The feud was a distant memory when Alice Miller and George Webb met in Kremmling at the Middle Park Fair and Rodeo where George was riding bucking steers and Alice was superintendent of swine operations. Their romance blossomed and their future was decided in August 1976 when the pair entered Rocky Mountain National Park to hike the Colorado River Trail. Deep in the woods they both revered, George produced a ring and proposed and Alice agreed to be his wife. Acting on their mutual affection, the pair was either willfully bucking history, or blissfully unaware of the ancient feud. Whatever their motives, the loving couple shaped a cosmic reconciliation between distant remnants of two families who had every reason to be quarreling. Moments after they had sealed their engagement, the jubilant couple hiked to the abandoned site of Lark City where they stumbled upon Jackhammer.

Years later, to complement Jackhammer's jailhouse interviews, Trinidad made contact with the couple. He met the Webb's at their Kremmling ranch, which—viewed through the lens of the 1883 Grand Lake shooting—might be thought of as neutral territory. By then a junior college student majoring in criminal justice, Trinidad concentrated his questioning on the events of 1976 while purposely avoiding any mention of the 1883 incident. Perhaps neither knew their history, or maybe they were honoring family tradition to never speak of that day. For whatever reason, the subject never came up in the course of their two-hour interview. The old days weren't on their mind, but 1976 was definitely on their radar. Responding to Trinidad's questions, the couple maintained that they'd always remember their 1976 hike.

"How could we forget?" Alice asked. "And how could we know the creature we encountered was human?"

"A terrible shock," George recalled.

Back in 1976, unaware of his effect on the hiking couple, Jackhammer had altered his plans. Hypersensitive to signs and portends, he was convinced that the pair represented yet another spiritual visitation. Their message, conveyed by occupying then disappearing from his doorway, was abundantly clear. They were beckoning him to follow. Thus, he donned his letter jacket and walked away from the ruins of Lark City. Recovering his hidden Harley, a determined Jackhammer managed, by sheer force of will, to make his way back to Texas.

Fearful of arrest, the injured man rejected the idea of seeking medical care for his wounds which healed imperfectly, leaving parts of his body cruelly scarred and his face forever ruined. He hid his infirmities as best he could, donning disguises in daylight, venturing out mainly at night. Having worn his letter jacket on his taxing journey from Colorado to Texas, Jackhammer resented the once-revered garment as a symbol of his failures. Curbing thoughts of the thing's sentimental value, he stuffed the unwashed jacket into the Harley's saddlebag, crammed the bag into an unused cubbyhole, and— distracted by other troubles—completely forgot the leather pouch existed. As for the motorcycle, he parked it in the shed and abandoned it. The discarded items remained there for years until January 2006 when their owner grew nostalgic and fancied a ride, only to discover the unexpected truth that someone had helped themselves to his Harley and left the Ural in its place.

Chapter 67

Demons
2019/After 10 p.m. June 8

"And we know the rest," interrupted Heckleson. "Instead of tossin' the Ural over a cliff, he kept it and went lookin' for a side-car."

"Exactly," Trinidad agreed.

"And since the only thing which a macho Harley-Davidson has got in common with an ordinary Ural is both machines have handlebars, what I wonder would be the motive fer this-here sudden urge on the part of a died-in-the-wool biker to move from manly motorcycle jockey to a side-car freak show?"

"What indeed?" Trinidad asked.

"There y'all go again," complained Heckleson. "Answerin' a question with a question. Don't you youngsters never get tired of smart-alecky behavior?"

"Never," Trinidad said. "Especially when we know the answer."

"Which is—" Heckleson prompted.

"Jackhammer's Harley was history, but not the motorcycle's saddle-bag which remained hidden in the tumbledown Texas shed he used as a garage. Over the years, he'd completely disregarded this particular link to the past until an icy winter's day three decades after the fire. Alone in his tiny bungalow and cursing his fate, the distraught man began down-ing liquor at dusk and was miserably drunk by midnight."

Recalling his own alcoholic demons, Trinidad paused.

"Take a break?" Heckleson suggested.

"I could do with a coffee," Trinidad suggested.

"Comin' up," said the old ranger.

While coffee brewed, the detective gathered his thoughts. Much of what Jackhammer had revealed during his prison interviews had been highly personal—the sort of things which might have come out in a sharing circle at Alcoholics Anonymous. As the old ranger bustled about the kitchen, Trinidad remembered the challenge of his first AA meeting.

He'd entered the church basement reluctantly, convinced that he was different from the other addicts who assembled there. *I've got this,* he told himself. *I'm not like these other losers. I can handle myself. I can stop anytime. I can take just one.*

Then came the stories and, as each person spoke in turn, Trinidad recognized himself. Every tale of struggle and denial touched a nerve. He remembered feeling scared, but that fear was moderated by the realization that he was not alone. As for what he and others shared that night, he reminded himself of the expectation of confidentiality as well as the oft-repeated mantra of AA: *"What you see here, what you hear here, when you leave here, let it stay here."*

Surely Heckleson, who'd dealt with his share of intoxicated individuals, would understand if Trinidad called a halt short of revealing all which Jackhammer had shared. Surely the old ranger would sympathize if his guest changed the subject. Intent on weaving his tale, the talkative detective had painted himself into an ethical corner.

"Y'all okay with all this drinkin' talk?" Heckleson asked as he handed Trinidad a steaming coffee.

"It shows, I guess."

"One day at a time," Heckleson said.

"Yeah-boy," Trinidad agreed.

"Here's the deal: share what you can," Heckleson told his guest. "Leave out what suits you. I'm certain-sure I can fill in the blanks."

Chapter 68

The Jailhouse Interviews
Recalling January 2006

Continuing his story, Trinidad moved the context back in time to January 2006 and his informant's struggle with his past. Having been saddled with a Ural motorcycle, Jackhammer felt compelled to add a sidecar. He couldn't have articulated his reasons for keeping the machine, let alone accessorizing it. He was acting on instinct—pursuing, without knowing exactly why, an urge to prepare for a journey.

He had no idea where he was meant to go or why the Ural might be needed. Having survived a fire which would have killed an ordinary man and endured a lengthy prison term, the ex-convict decided that—in the end—he'd simply lost his marbles.

"Would I know if I was insane?" he asked himself. "If I was, would I know enough to ask if I was? Where did my life go?"

At two in the morning, on the cusp of a new year, an unrelenting wave of nostalgia washed over Jackhammer. Heedless of the weather, the big man stumbled out of bed and ventured into a freezing Texas downpour to retrieve his stored saddlebag. Extracting his abandoned letter jacket, he wrapped the prized possession in a garbage bag to protect it from the rain. Then he lurched back outside and hurried through the storm.

Returning to his bungalow, he removed his wet clothing, toweled off his soaked scalp, and donned the jacket. Wrapped in the embrace of the familiar garment, he pulled his old high school annual from a neglected shelf, sat half-naked at his teetering kitchen table, and thumbed through the book. Surrendering to a marathon of morbid melancholy, he slowly turned each page, pitifully indulging the past like a lonely suitor caressing a sentimental token. Treating each black and white image with a wistful reverence more suitably reserved for a lock of an absent lover's hair, he lingered over images of school dances, club activities, dramatic productions, music, and sports.

He himself had excelled in sports to the exclusion of other adolescent activities. And yet, these photographs of earnest young people reminded him—too late—that China Berry High School had been a perfect society. In many ways, it had been a slice of Heaven-on-Earth—a place where, as a blossoming teen, he'd felt safe and loved and admired. Pausing at the page containing the senior photo of his unsullied self, he fingered the image and bawled like a baby until his sadness turned to rage. Whereupon, he crumpled the offending page in his powerful fingers and ripped the book to shreds.

It was then, surrounded by the debris of his past and absorbed in the throes of anger and pain, that he remembered the severed lottery ticket. Years ago, as he struggled to navigate the Grand Lake detour, dealt with his treacherous ambusher, triggered the fateful fire, and vanished into the night, the ticket had been entirely forgotten. And why not? The thing was incomplete—he'd burned the missing half. Moreover, the thing had expired. Of what possible use was the utterly unredeemable scrap of that wretched ticket?

Sitting alone, compelled by a mixture of curiosity and wistfulness, Jackhammer put his hand to his breast and fingered the smooth outline of his high school letter. Pressing the contours of the emblem, he heard, rather than felt, the distinct rustle of the memento which still resided in the jacket pocket. He reached inside and probed until his fingers encountered the paper which seemed larger than he expected, and more whole.

Gripping that forgotten relic, he pulled it forth and examined it in the glare of the overhead kitchen light. His mouth gaping, he passed the thing back and forth before his disbelieving eyes, trying to comprehend its meaning. He'd reached into his jacket pocket expecting to find a scrap of pasteboard. Instead, he'd discovered something entirely different.

Somehow his partial lottery ticket had evolved. As if by magic, the severed ticket had transformed into something else. How to explain the object he held to the light? How to explain it?

Chapter 69

From Germany with Love
2019/Nearly 11 p.m. on June 8

"I have it here," Trinidad patted his breast pocket, "if you'd care to examine the evidence."

"Y'all don't mean it," the old ranger suggested.

"Cross my heart and hope to—" the detective began.

"Don't finish that-there old chestnut sayin'," Heckleson warned. "My dear sainted mother—God rest her blessed soul—always thought sayin' that whole sentence was bad luck."

"I'll just cross my heart then," Trinidad assured him.

"Good lad. So, let's have a gander," said the older man as he held out the fingers of his giant suntanned hand, the missing digits wriggling in anticipation.

"It's a little worn," Trinidad apologized as he extracted a dog-eared postcard.

"Yacht Race on Grand Lake, Never Summer Range in Distance, Rocky Mountain National Park, Colorado," Heckleson read the captioning on the front of the vintage postcard. Then he took a moment to examine the tinted rotogravure which showed a line of boats sailing on a faded blue lake with a muted mountain in the background. Turning it over, he continued his forensic examination. "Addressed to Buster Bishop, but no number nor town. Different ink and different hand, so looks like whoever wrote that name didn't also do the rest. Hmm. Written not in English, except Buster's name, I guess. Now then," he said as he tilted his head to examine the top and bottom left-hand corners, "here we have *Made in Germany. Number 3-5-3-6.* No barcode. And the pasteboard is thicker than your modern printed-in-China crap. Somebody wrote a big message, in longhand, with a fountain pen and used practically every lovin' inch of the back. No stamp in the postage square, no post-mark, and no return address and no date neither. No room left fer to shoehorn them things in anyhow. And it's German for certain—though all but Greek to me. Can't make head nor tails of it. What does it say—I wonder—in old-fashioned English, that is?"

"The translation? Would you be surprised to hear that I know it by heart?" Trinidad asked.

"Not a thing surprises me about your dependable photo-graphic memory," Heckleson responded. "So, say it out in English while I work to follow along—maybe I'll catch a word every now and again."

"Meine Lieben," Trinidad began, then paused while the old ranger squinted and impatiently cleared his throat. Smiling mischievously, the detective commenced his translation:

My loved ones,

I write to you secretly and earnestly in the hope that it will reach you. Not a day goes by that I don't think of you. Not an hour goes by that I don't dream of seeing you. My family is harsh and they punish me for my sins. Maybe it should be so. I hope you are cared for. This card is so small, but I have to use this means to compose my writing. A friend promised me to send it. I pray that you find a means to preserve our family treasure. They urge me to reveal it, but we have been hiding it in the Osprey Hills, albeit far from being discovered. As of now, it seems, you'll need the boat. You'll recognize the place by the bird calls and my skunk rocks. The stripes mark the way. Count five. It's not deep, because we had to work quickly to get it into the earth. Guard it and keep it safe until one day, God willing, we are together again.

With all my love,
Mother.

"Eureka!" the old ranger exclaimed. "No wonder old Jackhammer knew about this-here treasure! Since the school jackets was switched, Red Bishop must'a put his mother's letter there. I'm guessin' our vengeful biker got the thing translated on his own somewhere. If your memory's good—and I don't not doubt it is—then the clues in that-there translation likely meant trouble for our villain. Jackhammer understood part of the puzzle with enough pieces missin' to turn him into a believer in the family treasure."

"You have it exactly," Trinidad agreed. "Which meant our partially informed villain needed to button-hole Buster Bishop to fill in the blanks. And Jackhammer was anxious to return to Colorado so he used the bike he had at hand—"

"And needed the side-car to make the Ural steady enough for the trip north for a showdown with our elderly sheriff," the old ranger guessed.

"Yep," Trinidad agreed. "And, although he may not have considered it at first, the sidecar proved handy when it came time to imprison and transport his intended victim."

"Hold on a dad-burned minute! What about the delay?" asked the old ranger. "Didn't I hear y'all say he inherited the Ural in December '05? And, consarn-it, didn't y'all just now tell me he found the postcard in January 2006? If he was so all-fired het-up to rain revenge on Red Bishop, what took him so damn long?"

"Well," Trinidad reminded his host, "it was winter of course, so that accounts for part of the delay. And recall that he was questioning his sanity and also drinking to excess."

"Rehab!" Heckleson decided.

"Yep," confirmed Trinidad. "Under the mistaken impression that nostalgic longing equated to insanity, the agitated man voluntarily placed himself in a Texas rehabilitation program which put him out of pocket from January to autumn 2006."

"Guess that didn't take."

"Nope," said Trinidad. "He went through the motions, but he emerged from rehab more determined than ever to confront Buster Bishop—not only to avenge the tragedy of his fiery mistake, but to pay the lawman back for his damning testimony and steal the sheriff's family treasure."

"Now, about this-here postcard. I'm guessin' there were two cards—one for each—and I wonder did both brothers understand the mother's message?" Heckleson asked.

"When Buster and I had our long talk, after Jackhammer was safely locked away, the old man said that both boys had figured out what their mother tried to communicate," the detective assured the old ranger. "Over the years, the brothers sailed to the far corner of Shadow Mountain Reservoir where, accompanied by a chorus of osprey calls, they searched every inch of every island until they found her buried treasure."

"On an island?" Heckleson asked. "Well, I reckon that makes a bit of sense, since the reservoir come about long after their mother buried it and I suppose, if the treasure was on a hill, the Shadow Mountain water stranded the spot. But don't I recollect that Buster Bishop pointed you in the direction of some secret spot out there in the forest? This would be when y'all and him and that chubby deputy was hikin' around the shoreline and after the lookout tower burned down and—" the old ranger paused as a broad grin of recognition spread across his weather-beaten face. "Buster's little act—pointin' at a woodpile and shoutin' to the trees—that was all fer the benefit of the bear."

"Exactly," Trinidad confirmed. "Buster knew we were being followed, so he intentionally put Jackhammer on a false trail by making a fuss over an old pile of lumber which was indirectly connected to the treasure but only circumstantially."

"And no ways near the actual treasure," Heckleson decided.

"Not even close," Trinidad agreed.

"So, the treasure was on some hill which got flooded out to be one of the Shadow Mountain islands. And it was sittin' out there fer years, so many paces away from a dark-shaded rock which—I'm guessin'—had some imbedded strips of white quartz to mark the way. Was there all along."

"Yep," said Trinidad. "Only you've got the wrong tense."

"Y'all lost me, son," Heckleson admitted.

"You said 'the treasure *was* on one of the islands," Trinidad pointed out.

"Yeah," the old ranger agreed. "Well, it was, wasn't it?"

"Not past-tense was on the island," Trinidad said as he favored his host with his patented catbird smile. "It still is. What I mean to say is, present-tense, the treasure's still there."

"Y'all mean to say the brothers didn't dig it up?"

"Oh, they dug it up all right and took a couple of sentimental souvenirs, then they left the rest in the ground and covered it up again."

"So, it wasn't no treasure after-all," Heckleson speculated.

"Depends," Trinidad answered.

"On—?" the old ranger prompted.

"On your definition of treasure," said Trinidad. "Put yourself, for a minute, in the shoes of Buster's mother. The year was 1921. A young girl seeking adventure hires on as a waitress at Grand Lake Lodge. At the close of summer, Brunhilda Schmitz finds herself far from home, unwed and pregnant, painfully aware that her condition will cause her to lose forever a loving legacy which, after much pleading and promises of faithful care, her parents had entrusted to her. Though of little value outside the family, even as antiques, a modest collection of ancestral dishes and cutlery had been placed in a vintage chest. And Brunhilda had been allowed to add that chest to her luggage when she set sail for America with the firm, absolute, and unbending understanding that she was to keep it always near her. Notwithstanding family tradition and in opposition to custom, the young maiden had been granted this unique privilege. The exception had been made in anticipation of the day when she was destined to marry, in America, the well-to-do offspring of a German merchant. It was an arranged marriage. The future groom was the up-and-coming son of a family acquaintance. That family friend was an ambitious immigrant who'd arrived years earlier to make his fortune in New England shipping—a fortune vast enough to send his boy to Harvard. Brunhilda's unwealthy parents were unable to sail to America to attend their daughter's wedding. But the understanding was that riches would flow to the bride's family once the marriage was solemnized and consummated. Everything depended upon their daughter's chastity and her sincere promise to keep her treasure safe until her wedding day."

"By golly, you're talkin' about a buried chest the which amounted to Brunhilda's ever-lovin' dowry," said Heckleson as the realization animated his features, the rising emotion causing the old ranger's already ruddy complexion to glow like the fiery expanse of a West Texas sunset.

"Yes," Trinidad confirmed as he prepared to relay the rest of the story which Buster Bishop had confided in him. "So, now that we understand Brunhilda's actions, let's fast-forward to mid-October 2006 when I ended up as Jackhammer's prisoner. Seeing the huge man subdue me a second time, Buster ducked into the woods intending to stay hidden and hope for a chance to help me. Then, hearing several shots as he ran, he figured I was a goner. Otherwise, he told me later, there's no way he'd have abandoned me that night. Thinking me dead, the old man saw his chance and bolted into the dense shoreline trees with the villain's shots ringing in his ears. Fortunately, Jackhammer missed and, far from perishing in the woods, the escaped prisoner circled back to disable *Dawn Ambler's* engines and jettison her oars. There hadn't been time to sabotage the mast and sails, but Buster was convinced he'd done sufficient damage to strand Jackhammer. His mischief complete, the old sheriff confidently hiked to safety, navigating well-remembered trails, until he reached a roadway at first light where he thumbed a ride and called the authorities. One day after Jackhammer had been fished from the reservoir and placed in custody, Buster and I were reunited and he told me the details of his mother's story."

"Hold on, now," interrupted the old ranger. "Answer me this: exactly how could this-here orphan son, who I'm guessin' did never know his mother who died, find out so much about her past story?"

"It's a fair question," Trinidad admitted. "But perhaps you've failed to consider that Buster and his brother Saul had access to another informant. Someone who knew about the box. Someone with contemporary knowledge about their mother."

An interval of silence followed this revelation as Heckleson pondered his guest's remarks. At last, the old ranger spoke.

"How's this for a preposition?" Heckleson asked. "The postcard said *we hid the treasure—we had to work quickly.* Which means somebody helped her bury the box," he guessed. "And that somebody is the somebody what filled in the son about the mother."

"You'd make a great detective," Trinidad noted. "So, I'll pick up the story as related to Buster by that certain someone."

Chapter 70

Spunk
1921 and Beyond

When the informant related the events of 1921, Buster embraced the tale of his mother's exploits as the stuff of yet another Grand Lake legend.

Faced with having compromised the possibility of her impending arranged marriage and contemplating the prospect of having her dowry chest and its precious contents confiscated by her enraged parents, Buster's distraught but resourceful mother took decisive action. The spunky adolescent girl confided in a friend and the pair hatched a plan. Using guile and charm, they secured a boat and talked someone into lending them a horse and cart. Then, in the predawn darkness, the two girls lugged the wooden chest to the shore and placed it onboard the boat. As the sun was rising, one co-conspirator rowed the chest across while the other mounted the borrowed horse and pulled a wooden cart around Grand Lake.

Meeting on the far side, the pair somehow—using the cart and horse—managed to transport the chest westward into the forest. To avoid scarring the chest's ornately painted sides and top, they'd wrapped the thing in blankets—which was a prudent precaution given the uneven ground and the wayward motion of two commandeered shovels which slipped from side-to-side in the cart's bed as the horse advanced.

Lavishly decorated with flourishes of floral and geometric patterns which framed a detailed cameo of a young woman, the chest itself was a work of art. The girls treated the container with reverence. They considered it a magnificent reliquary which safeguarded the precious family treasures ensconced inside—a revered vessel no less sacred than the Biblical Ark of the Covenant. When the insubstantial cart struck a boulder and gave way, the determined pair abandoned the conveyance, threaded a rope through hand-forged iron handles on each side, and fashioned a crude harness. Securing their cargo in a tightly wrapped cocoon of blankets, they compelled the horse to drag the chest over dew-slicked stretches of cheat grass. The girls walked alongside, each one carrying a shovel. They continued on, leaving behind the pile of wooden rubble which Buster and Trinidad had come upon on the day Saul died.

There were no islands in 1921 and the reality of Shadow Mountain Reservoir was more than two decades away. Dragging the chest behind their animal required a circuitous route to avoid rocks and trees which took time. Hours passed while the two determined youngsters journeyed farther until, at last, they decided on a hiding place. They climbed a hill and, using distinctive rocks as landmarks, marched off five paces and commenced the arduous task of digging a hole. The day was waning and, not wishing to chance the forest in the dark, they dug in haste. Eventually, they managed to carve a shallow depression—not a profound or even a proper hole, but deep enough to obscure their burden. Keeping the chest in its protective blankets, they manipulated the rope to lower it in.

Nearing exhaustion, the two girls rained shovelfuls of dirt and stones upon the chest trusting that its heavy lid—held in place by stout hinges and secured by a sturdy hasp and staple—would hold. By the time they finished their desperate work and cajoled their exhausted horse to allow them to ride double, their hands were bleeding and marred by blisters.

Throwing decorum to the wind, the pair rode bareback through the darkening forest. Passing the ruined cart, they wondered aloud what lie they'd tell the owner to account for its disappearance. Eventually, by some miracle, they managed to return to the spot where they'd moored the rowboat. Arriving there, Brunhilda secured from her friend a promise to keep the chest's hiding place secret until she herself could somehow manage to return to reclaim the treasure. The two friends parted company then, the pregnant Brunhilda rowing away to return the boat and her companion galloping away to reunite the horse with its owner.

Her partner in crime, Clarise Gonzales, her dearest and closest friend, fulfilled her promise until failing health compelled her to pass the secret on to her daughter, Louella. With her dying breath, Clarise entreated Louella to remember the story and do all she could to contact Brunhilda and, if possible, reunite her with her lost children and buried treasure. The faithful daughter committed the story to memory and, eager to fulfill her mother's dying wish, Louella used her traveling schedule and overseas contacts as an international airline stewardess to fashion a plan to get a message to an aging Brunhilda.

Finally, in 1963, Louella was able to honor her mother's wishes by locating Brunhilda. In a detailed letter, the faithful daughter informed Brunhilda that Clarise had died. She also communicated news of Brunhilda's children. Working with Grand County officials and newspaper archives, Louella had learned that one twin son had been adopted by a Grand Lake family—longtime residents who owned a local plumbing service. The other boy—after living with a couple a mere twenty miles away in Hot Sulphur Springs—had resettled somewhere in Arizona, possibly in a town called Prescott.

As for the buried dowry, a field trip to Colorado allowed the daughter to confirm that the treasure remained safely hidden—albeit stranded high and dry on an island created by the subsequent formation of Shadow Mountain Reservoir. The spot Brunhilda and Clarise had once reached by horseback was now only accessible by boat. The island, Louella informed her correspondent, was occupied by flocks of osprey raptors whose lofty nests ringed the hiding place.

Louella's informative letter reached Brunhilda on her sixty-first birthday. A spinster, estranged from her family and living in the totalitarian regime of East Germany, she'd given up hope of retrieving her treasure, let alone learning the fate of her long-lost sons. Upon receiving word of her late friend, her dowry, and her children, she sat down at her kitchen table, took up a pen, gazed out her apartment window at the smoking factory towers of Dresden, and composed two postcards. Her English was rusty so she relied on German to convey her heartfelt messages. Placing both cards in an envelope purloined from the shop where she worked as a seamstress, she added, in passable English, a note to Louella Gonzales imploring the daughter of her faithful friend to deliver the cards to her boys, if humanly possible. Then she addressed the envelope, affixed as much postage as she could lay her hands on, and trusted to God and the Communist postal system that her letter would be delivered.

Chapter 71

First-Hand Account
2019/11:30 p.m. June 8

"Believe it or not, in 1975, a full twelve years after that missive was posted," Trinidad said, "the faithful daughter received Brunhilda's battered and heavily hand-cancelled envelope. Louella Gonzales had retired and moved to Steamboat Springs where she ran a bed-and-breakfast. She immediately attempted to make contact with Brunhilda only to learn that the old woman had died the previous summer. Buster asked Louella to come to Grand Lake so I could hear her firsthand account. Miss Gonzales turned out to be a fine-looking middle-aged woman. She reported that, upon receiving the unexpected letter and learning that the writer had passed away, she embraced the steps necessary to complete her mission. Within a year, utilizing methods which would make a detective proud, the resourceful daughter managed to get a line on both brothers. With a profound sense of purpose, she ultimately tracked them down, and delivered Brunhilda's long-delayed postcards into the hands of her long-lost sons."

"A miracle," Heckleson decided.

"Roger that," Trinidad agreed.

Chapter 72

Finding Buster
Recalling Events of 1975

Speaking with Trinidad, Louella recalled that she had minimal trouble locating Buster who was, after all, a public figure—albeit retired. Feeling Brunhilda's message too personal, she did not feel it proper to have either postcard translated. She contacted Buster Bishop, gently broke the news of his mother's death, and arranged to meet him on the broad porch of Grand Mesa Lodge—on the very porch where, more than five decades earlier, her mother and Brunhilda had hatched their girlhood plans.

With a tender motion, she placed Brunhilda's postcard in Buster's hands. He thanked her rather stiffly and, with an unexpected air of indifference, merely glanced at the card and placed it in his jacket pocket. Louella recalled being mildly disappointed at the time. However, upon further reflection, she decided she understood Buster's lukewarm reaction. After all, he had never known his mother and might be harboring a child's resentment at having been abandoned.

When it came to the subject of his brother, Buster was more animated. Louella reported being truly surprised to learn that Buster had no knowledge of Saul or his whereabouts. Conceding to his fervent request, she promised to seek Saul out and do all she could to aid in a brotherly reconciliation.

Chapter 73

Finding Saul
Recalling Events of 1975

According to Louella, Saul turned out to be a rodeo cowboy, living and working in the western town of Prescott, Arizona. Saul's adopted last name proved to be Berman. His adoptive father was a sixth-generation entrepreneur of German extraction. His adopting mother was a recent immigrant from Israel, hence his Old Testament first name. When Saul was in his teens, both parents were killed in an auto accident during a whiteout blizzard. The couple's natural-born children garnered the lions' share of the Berman estate and the twice-orphaned lad was left to fend for himself.

Which suited the young man fine.

Self-sufficient, willful, headstrong, and naturally ornery, Saul was busting broncs and breaking hearts in Prescott until advancing age and one too many paternity suits caught up with him. Which was about the time that Louella Gonzales blew into town, stayed long enough to stir Saul's nearly dormant loins, and left behind a decidedly horny and thoroughly perplexed fifty-four-year-old ex-rodeo rider.

Unlike his taciturn brother, Saul wept openly at the news that his mother was dead. His upbringing in a German household allowed him to translate the postcard and the translation made him even more emotional. News of Buster hit him like a thunderbolt.

318 Donald Paul Benjamin

Learning that he had a twin brother only a day's automobile ride away, Saul stole a Mustang (the car, not the horse—he was merely impulsive, not completely crazy.) Keeping one step ahead of the authorities, the felonious desperado headed north—more-or-less learning to drive on the way. Passing through the Navajo Reservation, he nearly collided with a stray yellow dog that darted onto the narrow pavement. Rolling on, he stopped to admire the Four-Corners Monument, then crossed the San Juan River and wheeled through spectacular alpine vistas. He was making good time until he totaled the speeding Mustang above the Colorado town of Ridgway, near the intersection of Colorado Highway 145 and an isolated dirt pathway called Last Dollar Road.

"Figures," he reportedly said as he studied the road sign. Wallowing in the irony, he extracted himself from the wreck, reached into his hip pocket, and examined his nearly empty wallet.

"Last damn dollar for damn sure," he confirmed.

Lacking resources or a logical plan, he hitchhiked toward Ridgway and asked to be dropped off at the edge of the modest settlement. Standing on the outskirts, he paused to examine the "welcome" sign and took a moment to contemplate the hidden meaning of the missing "e" in the town's name.

"Politics," he decided.

Saul Berman knew all about politics and he figured he was about to step into a shitstorm of that most misunderstood aspect of the social sciences. He'd learned from the heartbreakingly sexy Louella Gonzales that his twin brother, Buster, had once been and might still be the sheriff of the sprawling county which encompassed Grand Lake—both the town and the lake— as well as Saul's hometown of Hot Sulphur Springs. As he started walking toward Ridgway, he considered the politics of Grand County.

The tantalizing Ms. Gonzales had reminded him that the towns of Grand Lake and Hot Sulphur Springs were rivals with a history of bad blood dating back to the late 1800s—at which time an armed gang shot the crap out of some other bunch over which village would become the county seat. As a native of Prescott, Arizona, Saul knew all about the competition for governmental honors.

Prescott had once been the territorial capitol, until it wasn't, until it was again, until an upstart settlement to the south—a desert stronghold named after a mythical bird—took the capitol honors for good. Saul had grown up in Prescott and he'd been to the asphalt jungle known as Phoenix and he'd seen the state legislature in session and, as far as he was concerned, Phoenix could keep the capitol and welcome.

"Politicians," Saul was known to say, "is why the Good Lord invented duct tape and the 50-caliber machine gun."

It wasn't a particularly coherent saying, but everyone who heard it seemed to comprehend the sentiment and nod in agreement.

Be that as it may, Saul left the welcome sign behind and trailed on into Ridgway. As he walked, he reached into his front pocket, nursed his final dollar, and whistled a passable version of the repetitious Jeopardy melody designed to prompt contestants to stop dithering and come up with a plausible answer phrased as a question.

"What are the chances," he speculated aloud, "of a long-lost brother finding happiness, contentment, and a steady girlfriend in Grand County?" Don't answer that one, he told himself. *Don't you damn-well even think about answering that one.*

Chapter 74

Loose Ends
2019/Nearly Midnight on June 8

Trinidad paused and examined the old ranger's face in an attempt to determine if his audience of one was still following the thread of his narrative.

"Are you with me?" the detective prompted.

"Just about," said Heckleson. "Y'all done a good job of tyin' up loose ends which was rattlin' around in my brain-pan. Such as, what the treasure was, how the boys found out about its whereabouts, and how Saul happened to come up from Arizona to Colorado. I even know how this-here Jackhammer character come to know and believe what he did about the treasure."

"All on account of the fist fight," Trinidad said.

"Which caused that old garden gate to swing on its gull-darn hinges at Trail Ridge Road as fur flew between Red and Jackhammer," the ranger recalled. "Then, after the dust-up, the two coats got mixed up. Jackhammer got the sheriff's jacket and vice versa."

"And in the pocket of the sheriff's jacket—" Trinidad began.

"Jackhammer found the postcard," Heckleson completed the thought.

"Bingo," said Trinidad.

"Which has got to mean that our sheriff found just what we'd expect in the biker's jacket—" the old ranger guessed.

Trinidad grinned as he and Heckleson shared a knowing look.

"You want me to say it?" Trinidad asked.

"Yep," said the ranger.

"Had to be," the detective said, "the one-and-only missing half of one pesky and potentially valuable, date-sensitive lottery ticket."

"Don't suppose I'm liable to see y'all pull that-there ticket out of your pocket," Heckleson suggested.

"Nope," said the detective. "The ticket, if it ever existed, is long-gone. Buster doesn't recall finding the thing. He guesses it got sorted out at the dry cleaners who automatically tossed it as a bit of worthless trash. As for the postcard, when it didn't turn up in what he assumed was his letter jacket, he figured he'd mislaid it. Eventually, when brother Saul showed up with an identical postcard in his possession and the ability to translate the thing—thanks to the German heritage of his adoptive family—the two brothers took turns reading and re-reading the translation."

"So, up until his brother arrived," Heckleson suggested, "Red Bishop had no clue what the card said."

"That's true," Trinidad confirmed. "And, when he learned the contents, the twins set sail to search for the treasure."

"The treasure which got one killed and nearly killed the other brother plus your-own self."

"Plus earned Jackhammer Marsh a life sentence," Trinidad added.

"All on account of a ticket, a postcard, and a fist-fight," the old ranger decided.

Trinidad recalled a poem from his childhood.

> *Little drops of water.*
> *Little grains of sand.*
> *Make the mighty ocean.*
> *And the pleasant land.*

"The *Little Things Poem*," Heckleson beamed. "Julia Carney, 1845." With that introduction, the old ranger continued the poem from memory.

> *So, the little moments.*
> *Humble though they be.*
> *Make the mighty ages.*
> *Of eternity.*

So, our little errors.
Lead the soul away.
From the path of virtue.
Far in sin to stray.

Little deeds of kindness.
Little words of love.
Make our earth happy.
Like the Heaven above.

"And you claim you didn't pay attention in school!" Trinidad prodded his host.

"Poems stick with me," the old ranger said.

"I noticed," Trinidad concurred.

"Seems like that-there lottery ticket turned out unlucky," Heckleson observed.

"Seems like," Trinidad agreed. "Were you ever tempted to play the lottery?"

"Well," said the old ranger, "I've been lucky at times and when things are goin' my way, somebody always suggests I should buy a ticket. But I figure it would be a stupid thing to do since I'd be bound to lose and losin' would just make me feel stupid all over again. Meantime, I reckon the floor is open for one last helpin' of information about old Jackhammer."

"There's a bit more to say," the detective confided.

"It's a tall wonder the hombre even survived," the ranger observed.

"You've got that right," Trinidad agreed.

Chapter 75

Revenge
2019/Midnight on June 8

As Heckleson settled in, Trinidad reported the closing installments of his story.

"Years ago, when I interviewed Jackhammer in prison, he revealed he still had nightmares about his fiery ordeal at Grand Lake Lodge. His ruined face tells it all. Overlapping scars give his entire head the appearance of a bust which a sculptor commenced, but left unfinished. Resembling arbitrary bits of rough clay, nodules of veined flesh are haphazardly encrusted on a field of translucent skin. It's a pallid background, a pale membrane stretched tight over his massive skull. Frozen in place, his sad face is incapable of achieving anything beyond a permanent grimace. His is a mottled visage—marbled throughout with strands of pink and white and blue like the exposed flesh of a skinned rabbit. His hands and arms are similarly scarred. His eyes alone are left to convey his emotions—his eyes and his voice."

"Burned," the old ranger said.

"Burned," the detective agreed.

"Burned bad and needed somebody to blame."

"In spades," Trinidad confirmed. "And, as if the fire wasn't enough, he also had it in for Buster Bishop because of the sheriff's role in investigating and prosecuting the assault of Imago Cognito. His testimony that

Jackhammer was spoiling for a fight on the night he mugged a rival biker went a long way toward sending him to prison for aggravated assault."

"If you're after revenge, dig two graves—" Heckleson began.

"—one for your victim and one for yourself," Trinidad completed the well-remembered maxim.

"Two graves," Heckleson repeated. "Remember the first time you heard that old chestnut?" he asked.

"Criminology 101," Trinidad recalled. "Learned it back in college."

"I myself learnt it at the School of Hard Knocks," Heckleson declared. "That and when to duck," he added.

"Even Jackhammer learned it eventually," Trinidad said. "I remember the last thing I said to him, just before I wrapped up my case study and headed back to school. After several weeks of interviews, I found him to be troubled, but intelligent, and I made the mistake of suggesting that he was too smart to be in prison."

"'I ain't smart,' Jackhammer told me. 'Ain't a single smart person in this lock-up. All we got inside here—all we'll ever have inside here—is dumb people.'"

"So, it was your long-time talks with the prisoner what give y'all the private dope on his inside thinkin' and secrets," Heckleson suggested.

"That's about the size of it," Trinidad confirmed. "It was instructive— a deep dive into the criminal mind. The Jackhammer interviews have guided my thinking throughout my chosen career. Glad I had a chance to hear his side of things. Glad he didn't drown."

"The first one y'all didn't kill," Heckleson suggested.

"The first one for sure and definitely the biggest one," Trinidad added.

"Speakin' of revenge," the old ranger speculated, "what are the chances that-there big galoot is due fer a parole?"

"Last I heard," said the detective, "he's become a reliable trustee and he's consistently rejected all efforts on the part of lawyers and other advocates to advance his release."

"Found a home, I reckon," Heckleson surmised.

"A safe place where he isn't afraid to show his face," Trinidad said.

"So," said the old ranger as he stretched and yawned, "I reckon that pretty much wraps up your tale—unless you're willin' to satisfy my curiosity about how your other cast of characters has fared."

"You'll be wanting to know what became of Bambi," the detective guessed.

"That crossed my mind," the old ranger admitted. "Plus, of course, where old Red ended up—presumin' he's still kickin' and alive."

"Buster Bishop passed away years ago," said Trinidad. "And no one was more surprised than me when I learned his last will and testament directed that the deed to Lavender Hill Farm be passed on to me. Which turned out to be the unexpected wrinkle which brought me here to Western Colorado to plant and harvest—"

"And detect," added Heckleson.

"That too," Trinidad laughed. "Meanwhile, Sheriff Bishop's legend lives on. In his later years, he became a local celebrity. You ought to have heard the venerated old-timer holding forth on weekend nights in the summer on Grand Lake Lodge's broad viewing porch. And, just this year, I learned that Grand Lake's own Rocky Mountain Repertory Theatre is set to complement their memorable catalog of outstanding Broadway productions by staging a rollicking musical based on Buster's exploits. Thanks to local enthusiasts, the premier production of a limited run of 'Hogs Over Highpoint' will debut this September with an all-star cast which includes a cameo by the ever-popular and still spectacular Bambi Taylor playing herself."

"Count me in fer that shin-dig," Heckleson declared. "I'll be too late to shake old Red Bishop's hand, but I reckon I wouldn't be sorry to catch a glimpse of that-there Bambi. So, how about we plan a field trip, y'all and me and your new missus. I'm all-in fer a front row seat at that Grand Lake clam-bake. The smell of the crowd and the roar of the grease-paint will be what I'll be cravin' fer damn sure!"

"Never took you for a patron of the arts," Trinidad observed.

"I may not know much about art," said Heckleson, "but I know what I think I'm goin' to like, so sign me up fer a dose of high-up-in-the-Rockies culture."

"You're on my list," said Trinidad as he stood, retrieved his Stetson from the hall-hook, and fished out his car keys. "Any other loose ends I can tie up before I head back to the farm?"

"Hold your horses and don't hat-up just yet," Heckleson protested. "Occurs to me that you ain't mentioned how that little lady what guided y'all to Lark City fared."

"You're right," said Trinidad as he resumed his seat. "Must have slipped my mind since that particular piece of the puzzle isn't quite ready to be set in place."

"An open case, do you mean?"

"You might say so," Trinidad agreed. "A missing piece to be sure. However, I'll share a bit more. This won't take long because I don't know much."

Chapter 76

Treading Water
2006/Early Hours on October 16

Back in 2006, Trinidad was determined to keep his defeated foe from drowning. On the heels of the storm, the once-roiling surface of Shadow Mountain Reservoir grew calmer while the breeze, though tamed, remained sufficient to maneuver the sailboat.

While Jackhammer bobbed in the frigid water, Trinidad tacked *Ambler* and reefed his canvas. Positioned a safe distance from the floating man, he flung a life buoy. Trailing a serpentine ribbon of white line, the flotation device landed with a splash within easy reach of the defeated culprit.

"Catch hold!" Trinidad shouted and, when his adversary didn't react, he pulled in the line and cast the highway-orange, donut-shaped life saver a second time—then a third. "I can do this all night," he informed the reticent man.

"So can I," Jackhammer replied, his voice sounding clear across the water.

Trinidad fingered the flotation device before securing it onto its rail hook. Maybe he should leave the villain to drown, sail back to the dock, and launch a search for Buster.

"I'll leave!" Trinidad shouted. "I mean it!"

"Who's stopping you?" Jackhammer retorted.

Diluting the huge villain in the reservoir had been the only way to control him. By rights he should sink, but he continued to bob on the surface, like a giant, obstinate cork. Flummoxed by the big man's refusal to be rescued, Trinidad examined the reservoir, trying to gauge whether this ludicrous combination of a free-floating boat and stubborn man was likely to remain together until dawn. If so, where on the broad shore would they be likely to land? The current might carry them back to the marina, where—days ago— he and Buster had conducted their fruitless search for Saul. Hoping to spot shoreline lights, Trinidad looked in that direction.

The lights were there, surprisingly bright, and on the move.

With a growing sense of relief, Trinidad watched in wonder as the lights expanded to form an advancing line. Soon he could see a flotilla of vessels headed his direction. Lights flashing and air horns blaring, the hard-charging boats surged forward. Drawing steadily nearer, each lively hull carved a silvery path upon the dark reservoir, churning up ribbons of foam which swirled and sparkled in the dim moonlight. It was a spectacular site and a welcome one.

"Cavalry," Trinidad said aloud.

"Shit," Jackhammer complained, the resignation apparent in his voice.

The boats arrived. A platoon of uniformed occupants fished Jackhammer out, dried him off, and arrested the somber man. As Jackhammer was carried away to face charges, the crew of the lead patrol boat helped Trinidad aboard and took *Ambler* in tow.

Waiting at the marina—along with a gaggle of emergency medical technicians—were Buster Bishop and Deputy Woodward. Conspicuous by his absence was the Grand County sheriff. As Woodward remained apart, conferring with the EMTs, Trinidad and Buster stood on the marina dock and shook hands.

"Ain't we a pair?" the old man asked as he used his bandaged hand to point out his companion's injuries.

"Should have seen the other guy," Trinidad said. "Looks like almost everyone is here to get a piece of the action. Almost."

"Sheriff got himself put on administrative leave," Buster whispered as he guessed the meaning of the young concierge's headcount. "Kept telling the dang fool to watch out for the county's new-fangled surveillance cameras. He forgot once too often that the new edition includes sound recording. Oh, don't look so stricken," he assured Trinidad. "I've seen his dress-down of you and believe me that was one of his milder outbursts. He's been on the bubble for months. Now the bubble burst. So, say hello to Acting-Sheriff Woodward and mum's the word."

Trinidad looked up to see Woodward looking chipper as he ambled their way.

"I'll need a statement," said Woodward.

"I'm all yours," said Trinidad.

An hour later, having hitched a ride in the deputy's squad car, Trinidad said goodbye to Buster and asked to be dropped off at the Kauffman House where he made inquiries regarding Jo. The response was unexpected.

"No one here by that name," said the bespectacled curator.

"Josephine Leander Wescott?"

"The last name rings a bell, but she ain't on our staff and she ain't no volunteer. You must have got the name wrong."

"She was here yesterday afternoon," Trinidad insisted.

"Yesterday?" the man said. "Impossible. For one thing, we were closed all day for training—a long-delayed field trip to experience the site of *The Shootin'*. Do you know about our little incident?"

"I know of it," said Trinidad. "And I also know that yesterday she and I—" Trinidad halted his statement and fixed his eyes on the wall behind the curator. A photograph hung there and, as silence stretched between the two men, he stared hard at the image. Following his visitor's gaze, the curator seized the teachable moment.

"Quite a story there," the man said as he cleared a space on the counter. Beaming at Trinidad, he exhibited the fervor of an avid historian who was about to dazzle his audience of one with a healthy dose of local history. "Let me show you," the delighted man announced as he pirouetted to face the wall and reached for the photograph. Using both hands to firmly grasp the frame, he expertly disengaged the braided wire, and turned back to place the picture in front of Trinidad.

"This is a personal favorite," he grinned. "Taken in Lark City about 1881. Sadly, no name attached to this hardy pioneer woman. She's posing on the trail, standing straight and strong as the pine tree beside her, and leaning ever so slightly on a shovel or it might be a straw broom. The log buildings behind her look a bit run-down, but you can tell she's a survivor. Do you see the bandage on her hand? They certainly made them tough in those days."

"Can I get a copy?" Trinidad asked

"For a price, of course."

Chapter 77

Photograph
2019/Past Midnight on June 9

"I have the copy," said Trinidad. "It's hanging in the farmhouse living room as we speak. Annie asked about it—not jealous, just curious—and I mentioned it was an old friend. Looking closer, she said she liked the woman's spirit. I told her I agreed."

"So, y'all believe this-here photo-picture looks like your 2006 horse-woman?" Heckleson asked.

"That piece of the puzzle remains unsolved," Trinidad answered. "That day, more than a decade ago, I returned to the trailhead, thinking to rescue Buck and hoping to find a trace of Jo."

"Nothin' there," the old ranger guessed.

"No trace whatsoever," Trinidad said with a decisive glance at his wristwatch. "Well, I really do have to get going this time."

"Before y'all leave, just tell me once more where and when this-here lavender weddin' of yours is set for," Heckleson requested. "I swear I ain't able to keep it straight."

"Two-o'clock," Trinidad reminded his host. "In the afternoon," he added helpfully while he watched the old ranger pull out a dog-eared pocket notepad and a wretched stub of a pencil.

"Two-o'clock," Heckleson repeated the time as he etched a reminder onto a tiny page of his minuscule datebook. "And the place one more time?"

"Chapel of the Cross," Trinidad said. "You want me to spell it?"

"Don't be a smart-ass," Heckleson chided. "Y'all think I don't know how to spell that little white church?"

"I'm sure you can spell," said Trinidad as he moved closer to peer over the old ranger's broad shoulder. "Just wondering if the abbreviation 'C of C' will mean anything to you tomorrow afternoon."

"You're about as funny as a rubber bedpan," Heckleson scoffed. "I'll be there—no worries. As long as I don't remember to forget."

"Great," Trinidad said. Then he laughed and added, "And, one last thing, Annie said to be sure to remind you to bring your fiddle."

"Wouldn't feel dressed without it," said Heckleson as his grandfather clock chimed the quarter-hour. "That makes midnight and beyond," he noted. "Better hit the road, Slick, before one of us—and it ain't gonna be me—turns into pumpkin pie."

"Goodnight," said Trinidad. "And thanks for hosting the best and only bachelor party I ever had."

"So long," said the old ranger as he escorted his guest toward the back door. "Enjoy your final last hours as a free man. From now on, old son, you're in fer a bumpy ride."

"Looking forward to it," Trinidad announced as he started down the back stairs. "See you tomorrow. I'll be the one wearing a cummerbund and a cat-that-ate-the-canary grin."

"And I'll be the old fart with the fiddle," Heckleson shouted after him.

Epilogue

2019/4 a.m. on June 10

Trinidad's cell phone rang six times before the sleepy detective could locate the warbling device. If their honeymoon hadn't been postponed, he and his new bride would have muted the intrusive instrument. But a process server had crashed their June 9th ceremony to deliver an untimely summons. The trial requiring their appearance was on the court docket for June 14 and there was much to do. The unwelcome intrusion had forced the newlyweds to compromise the magic of their wedding night by staying awake to review an enormous pile of case files. It couldn't be helped if Trinidad and Anne had any hope of being ready to give coherent depositions. After a busy evening spent reading and re-reading documents and leaving and retrieving phone messages, the fatigued couple had just dozed off when the predawn call shattered their belated slumber.

"Better get this," the detective sighed.

"Hell!" Dallas Heckleson cursed on his side of the call. "Hell's bells! If that don't make the cow jump up over the damn moon! My rainy-day! Gone—oh gone fer good and gone!"

On the heels of this wild introduction, the frantic caller launched into an agitated narrative, only about a third of which made sense to the sleepy detective on the other end of the line.

"Breathe," Trinidad reminded the old ranger. "Let's go over that again. Are you absolutely positive? Are you certain-sure the Eisenhower dollar I buried is the high-class '72-D? Like you said, you've got a coffee-can full of coins."

"Oh," the old ranger gasped. "It ain't here. Don't y'all think I looked? Just after the wedding, I got home and was puttin' the fiddle away and makin' sure Taco was tucked in fer the night when I thought to take a look at my rainy-day dollar. And I looked and looked, the whole blessed night! I even got out the magnifyin' glass and looked long and hard. It ain't here, I tell you! It ain't here!"

"Okay," said the detective. "Suppose it's out there in the 'Dobies. Over yonder in the ground. No reason to panic. We know where it is—don't we?"

Heckleson may have nodded, but the response was much too subtle to be detected miles away with the distraught caller on speaker phone as Trinidad endeavored to help the old ranger calm down.

"Dallas," Trinidad repeated. "We know where the dollar is, right?"

"I reckon it's still in the ground," Heckleson admitted. "So far as I know—" his voice trailed off.

"Well then," Trinidad assured his anxious friend, "there's nothing to be done until first light. Get some sleep. I'll have Luis come by with the farm's metal detectors. I'm betting you and him can sweep the ground and turn up the coin, no doubt."

"Luis will be here at sun-up?" the old ranger sounded doubtful.

"First thing," Trinidad guaranteed.

"Okay then," said Heckleson. "Nothin' we can do 'til sun-up."

"That's about the size of it," Trinidad agreed.

"Thirty-eight and a half millimeters," the old ranger mumbled.

"Pardon?" Trinidad responded.

"Twenty-two grams," Heckleson added. "That's about the size of it. The Eisenhower's about as heavy as a pair of underwear. Weighs about as much as all the raisins in your cereal box. A bit less heavy as two Oreo cookies. A little more than—"

"I'm not sure we're accomplishing as much as we might here—" Trinidad began.

"Give me that phone," Anne demanded. She'd been standing a few feet away while the men jabbered and her tone suggested she'd lost patience with their wrangling.

"Dallas," she said. "Can you hear me?"

"Loud and clear, Miss—I mean Ma'am," Heckleson responded.

"You got lights on those buggies of yours?" she asked.

"On my ATVs? Yeah," the old ranger answered.

"Well," said Anne, "fire up those puppies. I'll send Luis right over."

"If y'all say so," said Heckleson, his tone noticeably brighter.

"I do," said Anne. "So, get your big-boy pants on and get ready for a night patrol."

"Yes, ma'am."

"And one last thing," Anne said. "Be sure and call Jack or Marge or who's ever on dispatch duty so the sheriff's office knows what you and Luis are up to. Wouldn't do to have the law think those meth-heads were acting up again."

"You're a pistol!" Heckleson said.

"You can take that to the bank, cowboy," said Anne. "I'd come there myself if me and my darling husband weren't on the D.A.'s list to testify."

"Give my regards to the big-wigs in Grand Junction," Heckleson said. "I'd better get dressed fer action."

"Good hunting," said Anne.

"Same back at you, darlin'."

Spirits of Grand Lake
Chronology of Events: Past and Present

Date unknown—The Ute tragedy at Grand Lake.

1874— Grand County, Colorado, established and Sulphur Springs named county seat.

1879— Population of Lark City mining community reaches 500.

1881— Town of Grand Lake makes a claim for county seat.

1883— *The Shootin'* incident on the shores of Grand Lake.

1920s—Grand River renamed Colorado River.

Grand Lake Lodge established.

Unwed mother Brunhilda Schmitz gives birth.

1963— From East Germany, Brunhilda writes hopeful postcards.

1975— The tattoo incident.

Prickly Pears motorcycle gang involved in a modern-day Grand Lake shoot-out.

Cognito Imago purchases a New York Lottery ticket.

Brunhilda's long-delayed postcards arrive in America.

1976— The Trail Ridge incident.

2006— Brunhilda's postcard falls into the wrong hands.

Trinidad Sands drops out of college, begins work at Grand Lake Lodge, and tries his hand at detective work when a participant in the 1976 Trail Ridge incident returns to terrorize Grand Lake.

2019— Trinidad's bachelor party during which he recounts all of the above.

About the Author

Donald Paul Benjamin is an American novelist who specializes in cozy mysteries and high fantasy. His writing includes elements of romance and humor. He also writes about Western Colorado history. He is the author of the *The Four Corners Mystery Series, The Great Land Fantasy Series and the Surface Creek Life Series.*

In addition to his writing career, he also works as a freelance journalist, cartoonist, and photographer. A U.S. Army veteran, he served three years as a military journalist and illustrator, including a tour in Korea. Trained as a teacher of reading, he has worked with a wide variety of learners from those attending kindergarten to college students. He also holds an advanced degree in college administration. He lived in Arizona and worked in higher education for more than three decades before retiring in 2014.

He now lives in Cedaredge, a small town on the Western Slope of Colorado, where he hikes and fishes in the surrounding wilderness. He and his wife, Donna Marie, operate **Elevation Press**, a service which helps independent authors self-publish their works (see info on the following page).

Email: elevationpressbooks@gmail.com
Studio Phone: 970-856-9891
Mail: D.P. Benjamin, P.O. Box 603, Cedaredge, CO 81413
Website: https://benjaminauthor.com/
Visit the Author's Facebook Page under: D.P. Benjamin Author
Instagram: https://www.instagram.com/benjaminnovelist/

The Four Corners Mystery Series

- **Book 1:** *The Road to Lavender*
- **Book 2:** *A Lavender Wedding*
- **Book 3:** *Spirits of Grand Lake*
- **Book 4:** *The War Nickel*
- **Book 5:** *Rare Earth*
- **Book 6:** *Walking Horse Ranch*
- **Book 7:** *Lavender Farewell*

The Great Land Fantasy Series

- **Book 1:** *Stone Bride*
- **Book 2:** *Iron Angel*
- **Book 3:** *Redhackle*
- **Book 4:** *Bindbuilder*
- **Book 5:** *Nachtfalke*
- **Book 6:** *Isochronuous*
- **Book 7:** *Ruth and Esau*

Surface Creek Life Series

- **Book 1:** *A Surface Creek Christmas: Winter Tales 1904–1910*

In paperback or Kindle on **amazon.com** and **barnesandnoble.com**.